PROMPT EXCURSION

LEWIS S. KINGSTON

ISBN-13: 978-1-7394831-0-4 (eBook edition)

ISBN-13: 978-1-7394831-1-1 (Paperback edition)

ISBN-13: 978-1-7394831-2-8 (Hardback edition)

First published in 2023.

A *Positive Wave Print* book.

www.positivewaveprint.com

contact@positivewaveprint.com

PROLOGUE

A feeble alarm continued to sound as the temperature on the bridge of the incapacitated spaceship dropped below minus forty degrees. Celsius and Fahrenheit collided and fleetingly agreed that, yes, it was particularly cold; the kind of cold that would cut clean through your skin and straight into your bones, Jack Frost clawing at your every fibre, in an agonising and antagonising fashion.

The audible alert faltered for a moment, stuttering and wavering disconcertingly, and then resumed, its power source stabilising, as it continued to try and wake the sole person within earshot. It droned on, persistently, the last in a long line of automated systems and alerts, all now discharged, damaged, or cast into space, in a last-ditch effort to prevent the death of the crew and the loss of the ship.

The alarm's repeated *Pan-Pan-Pan-Pan!* slowly and soberly ground to a halt, its batteries finally dying, as a person floated toward the now-silent panel, unconscious and blueing. They sailed by, slowly, and bumped into the corner of a control console; a small puff of ice emanated from their suit, followed by an alarming and brilliant shower of sparks, casting staccato light into the dark void of the cabin.

Involuntarily, the person twitched. Lights slowly crept across a small display panel on their wrist, followed by a single plain text message: *Suit operations resumed.* A small animation popped up on the display, showing a harness clipping together, and indicated that power was available. Clicks and whirrs followed as heaters energised, fluids began circulating, and injections were administered. Sensing a little stimulation was required, the suit applied a mild electric jolt to its occupant.

A scream ripped through the bridge, tearing the silence apart. The suit couldn't be gentle; its inhabitant needed to be quickly extricated from the arms of hypothermia-induced death into blindingly painful life. Their heart pounded, lungs heaved, mind exploded, and muscles convulsed. More stimulants, stabilisers and slowly increasing heat flowed forth from the suit, while monitored readouts swung wildly from someone being very much alive to borderline dead, and then back to somewhere in between. The suit was intently aware that the process was damaging, but the survival of its occupant was the sole motivation it could remember and act upon.

The wrist-mounted display pinged noisily, its updated readouts showing that attempted communication with the ship, or anyone else that was supposed to be on the ship, had failed. Nothing was broadcasting, nothing was receiving, and the panel displayed a sad-looking emoticon in response. The screen flickered for a moment, briefly displaying lines of corrupted text and blank sectors, and then the emoticon reappeared.

A moan echoed through the desolate space as chemicals coursed through the suit's occupant, revitalising them, while the suit busied itself with assessing its own status. Its report effectively read *Not good*, and the section on its power sources *Really not good*, but its occupant was alive, so it took a little consolation in the fact that it hadn't failed miserably, yet.

The suit took a moment to scan its surroundings, its unwatched display showing brief analyses of various visible and non-visible light spectrums, acoustic patterns, thermal and emission readings, and defunct data streams. There was little to detail; the bridge appeared structurally sound, but some of its componentry and metals were becoming brittle. All six key stations were also present and correct: navigation, pilot, and engineering, up front, and the captain's position, flanked by countermeasures and offensive systems, behind.

The displays and control panels around every seat were all abnormally dark, and a thin haze of frozen moisture was creeping inexorably over every surface and switch, marbling the tops of the flat titanium and glass surfaces. And, more pressingly, every station was unoccupied. The suit's files were incomplete, and some damaged, but it knew the manifest had eighteen names on it. And, according to its archived instructions, at least three people had to be present up front in the ship's last reported state.

In the distance, something rumbled. The deck plates vibrated slightly and a hollow grating noise gradually worked its way through the ship, followed by an erratic harsh pattering. A small exclamation mark appeared on the suit's panel, its intensity growing for a moment, and then it disappeared uncertainly into nothing.

Absolute silence resumed its place in the cabin, followed by a hint of a sharp odour, as the temperature continued to creep ever downwards. The suit sounded a loud alert, hoping to prompt a useful response, but nothing changed. In some respects, it realised, this was acceptable; the ship had not rapidly disassembled itself and space remained safely outside, easing its concern and allowing its delicate medical operations to continue at a safer pace.

The suit's cameras continued to scan for signs of life or activity as it rotated with its cargo slowly, floating freely a foot or so off the floor. Only a solitary small panel, marked Last Line, at the rear of the bridge, showed any evidence of power: a single flashing underscore, small and green, had made a home for itself in the top-left corner of the computer screen.

An animation of signals marching outwards from the suit's position, as it powered up its communications relay again, played on its display. The markers went back and forth, up and down the length of the ship, cycling, seeking meaningful contact. The animation suddenly stopped and was replaced by a progress bar as a brief flurry of new data packages sprung into the suit's communications buffers, and then the sources disappeared.

Four, tallied the wrist display, alongside small pictograms of other crew members, before showing an illustrated overview of the ship. The signals were coming from almost the rearmost point, just over half a mile away. Another small exclamation mark popped up, between two expanding arrows that faded in and out, indicating the sources were weak.

The suit continued to attentively dole out medical care from its limited resources, titivating its inhabitant, but nothing changed. In something resembling annoyance, it sounded another prompt, attempting to coerce a human consciousness back into play. Unanswered, it dropped into a low-power mode, trying to conserve every amp in its deteriorating batteries. The lights on its panels dimmed, shutters slid quietly over its cameras, and its surroundings drifted by unchecked.

The minutes trickled past until one of the suit's remaining internal processes lapsed and reset. Its sole surviving management system sluggishly pondered if the required routine checks were essential but, given the uncertainty of its situation, it eventually relented and made power available. Both its microphone and speaker circuits sprang back to life, permitting a self-test to ensure that it was producing alerts that could be heard. As it expected, its notification rang true and clear, at a precisely defined and audible level, filling the cabin briefly and jarringly with artificial noise.

But, still, nothing changed. The suit idled for a moment, its remaining efficiency cores fervently occupied with managing its power, and then, as an aftercode, it ramped up the gain on its microphones, seeking anything of interest or comfort. It longed to hear the reassuring thud of cushioned airlock ring on cushioned airlock ring: a ship docking. It knew the sound well, but still played its stored acoustic signature back for itself a few times, making sure it would recognise the task-fulfilling pattern.

The suit picked up some noise, in the far distance, but nothing discernible or useful. It flashed an assessment to itself and concluded that the ship was still pitch, frigid and seemingly, from the inside at least, not in a state of powered flight. It could be adrift but, given the lack of input, the suit declined to settle on one or the other. It did not matter; all that mattered was that its occupant survived.

A horrific hammering suddenly tore through the ship, its backbone screaming and shrieking in protest. The suit could hear composites cracking and splintering, metal tearing, a distant cacophony of some unseen eruption doling out devastation. *Not good!*

The suit sensed that immediate action was required and shocked its occupant again, vainly trying to nudge them more into the land of the living than that of the dead. They groaned and attempted to curl into a ball, a move that the suit countered as gently as it could, a reminder of its frail state flashing through its processes. It did not want to face another inadvertent power outage and lie idle while death engulfed its cargo.

But the chaos subsided as quickly as it had arrived, the momentary cataclysm leaving the bridge seemingly untouched. The suit knew that explosions did not generally interact in a positive fashion with heavily armed vessels, however, and that the ship, like itself, could only take so much before it would give out entirely.

Its microphones picked up something new, amid the subsiding din of destruction, interrupting the suit. It hurriedly looped the recording back and boosted it; *Unidentified audio contact* flashed its display, along with a pictogram of a speaker emitting noise. A dull commotion, closer, and unlike those other known and eminently disagreeable noises.

Audio codes were pulled back up, compiled, and run. Acoustics, aberrations, background noise, and multiple passes of waveform-cleaning techniques, all were factored in. The software paused, shifted its simulations, and processed the brief recording again. A dull *thud*, reminiscent of a door being closed several rooms over. And then again, a similar intensity, and again, as if being repeated intentionally.

The display flashed urgently again: *Audio contact.*

An animated marker appeared, indicating further processing was taking place.

Audio contact: Not internal.

The little overview reappeared, showing a flashing dot lingering near the rear of the ship, as the suit began to charge its defibrillator's capacitors again.

The new noise was coming from outside.

CHAPTER ONE

'Oh, fuck,' wailed Johansson, as her brain stuttered back into life, every nerve ending in her body seemingly relaying a crippling blend of torrid numbness and tormenting pinpricks. Her gloved hands instinctively rose to her head, protectively, and came away bloody.

She shuddered, the slickness making her wretch a little, and impulsively drove her fingers through her hair, seeking comfort, her mind screaming ceaselessly into the void. Her head pounded and nausea surged through her, stomach doing little loops as its contents realised they were not bound by gravitational forces.

WherethefuckamIandwhatisgoingonandamIdying? she thought, distraught.

Opening her eyes felt like a concept that would lead to the rest of her day continuing its evidently downwards trajectory, and the pain was doing a sterling job of keeping them scrunched shut. Her chest rose and fell, short breaths, erratic; she pushed a hand outwards and felt nothing in front of her except a relentless cold, and an odd electrical crackling noise shredded the silence. Her wrist felt hot for a moment and then the heat was gone, the cold sweeping violently and unremorsefully back in.

Observe, orient, decide, act rang through her mind briefly, engrained training attempting to kick-start the survival process, before it was rudely cut short by the more urgent and insuppressible thought of *WherethefuckamIandwhatisgoingonandamIdying?* again. She flailed in the dark briefly, panicked, before the training elbowed its way back in, her sky-high pulse and breathing slowing a little.

Start small. Hands out, open and closed; those and my arms seem okay, apart from being freezing. She patted herself down, hands tracing from her shoulders to her knees; *Got the rest of my limbs. Nothing sticking out of me. Suit's damaged. T2 to T3 interconnect, maybe more. And I'm floating.* She touched her forehead again and cursed, in the unlit space, as her fingers revealed a pronounced laceration and an unpleasantly soft-feeling lump. *And I'm not wearing a helmet.*

'Hello?' ventured Johansson, eyes still closed and protecting her from the nightmare beyond.

Maybe it's okay. Maybe someone is here and they will help me.

She rolled slightly, casting her ears this way and that, in a vain effort to hear anyone, anything, something that bode well in the deathly ambience. No such solace came forth and the silence continued, inexorable, and she sensed the cabin becoming colder and darker as her despair ebbed upwards. Johansson shook her head firmly and rubbed her upper arms in an effort to instil a little more warmth and get her circulation going.

The modicum of heat offered some respite and she felt her mind relax for a moment.

What happened?! We were on our way to a station, a ...

A blank.

Something about weaponry.

A slight stabbing pain.

I was supposed to do something, but ... and then?

Her brow crinkled. Jolts of pain shot through her temples,

derailing her irregular and destinationless trains of thought. The cold stabbed at her again, closely followed by a gut punch in the form of oppressive quiet. The usual shipboard hubbub of babbling radio networks, the odd jab from the supporting vessels, and the gentle electronic chatter of all the monitors, relays, readouts and controls, all were absent.

Johansson touched her finger to her neck, pressing down on buttons atop a throat microphone, but the compact personal communications unit, and its bone-conducting headphone, cast nothing but a desolate *ping!* into her ear.

She cocked her head, listening, but there was nothing at all. Even the reassuring whine of the air circulation system and the dull pulsing of the coolant pumps were nowhere to be heard, and the glacial atmosphere told her all she needed to know about the heating situation.

My hearing is probably fucked up, among other things, she thought, grimacing, touching the side of her head tenderly.

'Suit?' said Johansson, hopefully, holding her hands to her chest. It produced a single flat tone, a speaker test, and then went quiet again, offering no support. Its wrist-mounted display was dead, a few wires pulled out of a damaged socket, and the smell of burning insulation tainted the air, but its internal heating elements were working, and the occasional flush of chemicals she perceived mixing with her bloodstream suggested that it was, on some basic level, and for now at least, still functioning. Perhaps it simply couldn't speak.

That last update did make it a bit erratic, thought Johansson, raising an eyebrow at the memory. *But it's doing its job.*

She patted the suit's chest plate thankfully and exhaled slowly and steadily.

Observe, orient, decide, act! danced through her mind again.

She opened her eyes. Nothing. Jet-black nothingness. Nothing from any panels, gauges, switches, instrumentation, cabin lighting, or even any emergency illumination. Johansson's mind raced; *Is our ship completely fucked or am I blind? Fucking brilliant. How do I tell?*

Her hands flashed over switchgear on the suit hurriedly, revealing nothing to her touch but non-functional hardware and more damage, but a glimmer appeared as she swept her hands in front of her; carefully and closely positioning one hand over the main power panel on the suit revealed, to her relief, the dim glow of at least one or two status-related light-emitting diodes. *Alright*, she thought, relief flooding her mind. *Give it a moment: observe.*

Johansson squinted, unconsciously pressing her head forwards into the gloom, digging and sorting through the dark with her eyes. *An all-black quadrant, no good. Another all-black quadrant, no good*; a methodical, professional search, conviction and confidence returning, carried out by mentally drawn box by mentally drawn box. Inch by inch until, in the bottom-right corner of her view, a reward for her efforts: a dulled but glowing illustration, painted in fluorescent tritium, showing a depiction of a person standing on the deck and the orientation of the ship around them. Beneath it, Johansson could just about make out some heavily worn text: BRIDGE / PRI.

Orient. She pushed her arms and legs out, seeking a hard surface, and her left hand came into contact with the corner of a command console. She gripped it as hard as she could and manoeuvred herself into a stance matching that shown on the picture, bringing her feet softly into contact with the floor.

I'm on the bridge. Facing forward, nothing to see. No lights, panels, no indicators, no controls, nothing.

Johansson spun 180 degrees, cautiously, so as not to stress her damaged suit. As far as her eyes were concerned, nothing changed. But the illustration indicated, and something deep in her mind concurred, that the exit from the bridge should be in front of her. Beyond it would be a short passageway that led to an emergency secondary bridge but, as her eyes bored into the gloom, the doorway's presence wasn't obvious.

No lights on the door control panel.

The gears in her head sped up, flashing her images of busted electronics, failed hydraulics, unresponsive secondaries, structural damage, stripped gears, an inoperable manual override ...

I could be trapped in here.

She tipped her head a fraction, an almost imperceptible half-completed shake, blinked, and stared into the nothingness again. Black, black, black, black, not black, black, not black, black, not black; an unperceivable distance away was something small, something flickering, a single winking electronic marker in the dark, its weak pulse uplifting Johansson's own.

Or maybe not.

A prod of the console with a finger provided enough impetus to allow her to drift in the direction of the light and, after what felt like a few metres, Johansson found herself pressing up against the grab bars surrounding the accessway. She wrapped an arm around one, relishing the momentary sense of security, and swung over to the feeble flicker.

A single underscore on a small computer panel greeted her, blinking incessantly and erratically, indicating the associated system was obviously in some form of distress. She wedged her aching fingers under the emergency access panel and yanked it from the underside of the display, and stabbed a button embossed with a dash, a dot, and a dash: interrupt. The display cycled to a blank, and then back to the wavering underscore, and then it shut off entirely. *You bastard*, she thought, poking a button to the right marked with two concentric rings: reset.

The display remained unhelpfully blank, and the darkness of the cabin resumed its assault on her senses, followed by sucker-punches of fatigue, stress, and pain. She rubbed her unbruised temple softly, trying to clear her head, and floated, in the frigid gloom, as the lifeless ship hung around her.

Decide, she thought, the word sounding very distant, coasting through her mind in a quiet, subdued fashion. *Keep moving: decide.*

Johansson pressed her palms against her forehead, as if trying to squeeze some action out of herself, the pain from the swelling sending lightning bolts into the deepest reaches of her brain. Her eyes slammed shut, overwhelmed, and she found herself standing on one of the East Anglia islands, near what used to be Peterborough. Peaceful, restful, safe; the soft *swoosh* of water on the shore, the taste of salt in the air, the intense summer heat, tangible and tranquil. Her toes flexed impulsively, her mind revelling in the vivid sensation of sand compressing beneath her feet.

We could just stay here. You like it here.

Her battered and frozen body concurred. Doing nothing would lead to the inevitable, but doing nothing also required no effort, and it was seemingly more content with that option than any other. Johansson folded her arms across her chest, and exhaled slowly, cautiously, trying to avoid any jarring pains.

You need to establish control, get out, and help others that might be here! shouted her mind, as decades of service and discipline tried to fight back against the rising tide. *Decide!*

She nodded, sluggishly, in the blackness. *There were thirty-six of us, I think, on this ship, in standard conditions.*

But the cold drove forth, like a stallion surging through the mist, pulling the all-encompassing dark along behind it, an impenetrable murk closing around her like a zipper being drawn through the final union of life's frail circle. Her heart rate fluttered, slowed, and her gloved fingers lightly traced the familiar and reassuring outlines of the suit's protective panels, the pair floating quiescently as they and the encompassing leviathan idled towards their end, her feet slowly sinking and softly dragging along the floor as she dwindled.

Just let it go, whispered a quiet voice. *Stay in the sand.*

Decide! screamed her mind in response. *You don't want to be lost, erased and forgotten, like the others!*

She did not understand so her mind screamed again, this time with more anger and a hint of desperation: *DECIDE!*

The ship lurched and a tremor passed underfoot, drawing Johansson back from the precipice. She eyed the curtain of dust that had been shaken from the floor, its particulates slowly rising towards her, enveloping her, as a sudden jabbing sensation struck at her wrist and neck; 'Fuck,' yelped Johansson, as the suit automatically delivered a dose of painkillers, chemical warmers and psychoactive enhancers. Her heart rate jumped, her pupils dilated, and her mind was flushed of that which conspired against her survival.

Andyouneedtodoitforheraswelldontforgether! howled a fresh, clear memory.

'Fuck you, I'm not dying in here,' she shouted into the dark, her body and mind jittering as the suit's synthesised shot went to work.

Act!

Her hands started automatically pulling her along the conduit which ran away from the panel, searching for something more significant and useful, textured gloves readily gripping the hard, smooth cabling.

A cable always goes somewhere useful.

What felt like endless metres spooled by, in the dark, until the thick loom disappeared into a hard edge. Johansson patted outwards, in front of her, and realised that the cable had terminated in a large box.

Maybe I'm up against the ceiling, she realised.

Her fingers probed around its perimeter, revealing six latches. She popped them free, one by one, and then let the cover drift away. Something on the back of the panel clipped her elbow as it sailed away, jarring her slightly, but inside the box was a welcoming sight: an array of bright and multicoloured lights alongside stacks of

13

substantial electronics that looked hardened against external inter-ference, and bulky cable arrays that disappeared through the bulk-head, towards the rear of the ship. *A hardened redundant computer*, she realised, an erratic grin spreading across her face. *This could be just the ticket.*

The matrix of lights did not paint a pretty picture. There was no explanation as to what they meant but a substantial portion were locked solid red, others were flashing red, a handful were amber, a small cluster were green, and a not-insignificant quantity were not illuminated at all. And, upon closer inspection, the cabling that led from inside the module to the display panel, with Last Line stamped on its outside edge, ran into a hefty processing board and battery system that showed few signs of life. Johansson poked around, quickly lifting cables and inspecting the componentry; everything looked physically intact, but a faint smell of long-dispersed acrid smoke suggested that something, somewhere, was deeply unhappy.

Johansson tugged at the Last Line board, freeing it from its enclosure. Underneath, a criss-crossed harness, of hundreds of wires, ran from the rest of the electronics into a breaker block, then on into the board. And, under a little of the light reflected from the lights, blackened and bubbled insulation tracked up and down the cabling on the incoming side of the breaker.

I need a patch kit. Which, in mainline RSF ships, are always ...

She shrieked in annoyance.

Always on the back of the panels, for ease of access.

'Idiot,' she cursed out loud, as the recently dispatched panel banged against something solid in the distance. Johansson pushed off from the wall, following the sound of the panel colliding with unseen elements of the cabin, until she bumped into it herself; her hands fumbled over the panel in the dark, revealing two complete spare sections of cabling on its reverse, raised text on their connec-tors stating EMR FUSIBLE. Johansson pulled one free from its retainer, worked her way back to the enclosure, ejected the spent harness from the mire of electronics, inserted the new one, clamped it down, reinserted the board, and cycled the breaker. A column of standalone lights on the side of the board sprang to life, climbing up and down like an elevator, before each switching from red, to amber, to green.

Over her shoulder, the dormant display sprung to life, casting a bright green glow across the nearest consoles. She hurried over to it, natural endorphins pumping through her nervous system, and pressed her face up against it, pupils wide and searching.

Bold text, a ship identifier: *00046.XP / RSF PROMPT EXCURSION.*

A military ship, yes, thought Johansson, memory flaring for a moment. *And I am a Weapons System Officer.*

She pressed her hand against the bulkhead for a moment, sensing nothing but a reassuring and still solidity.

We were in transit to a station, yes.

The bulkhead remained reassuringly inert.

The ship must have been armed, yes. Did a magazine detonate?

Johansson's eyes narrowed as the display cleared and text began to flow. Error message after error message trawled past: main power, secondary power, tertiary power, emergency power, all gone or inoperative. Communication gone, navigation gone, defence and countermeasures gone, weapons gone, and myriad confusing and conflicting messages about shielding, drive and manoeuvring systems, along with a batch of failures that the system simply couldn't identify.

'I get the idea,' she said to the display, tapping it to skip the remaining messages. It idled again for a moment and then presented an option: *Recommend emer. breaker reset - Y/N. Three charges remain.*

She smiled, her shoulders lifting. She instinctively pushed her right thumb against her ring finger, matching the motion with her left thumb; a loud *click* rang out from the protective strips in the gloves as she snapped the thumb and finger on the right, and then on the left, and then again as she repeated the motion with her thumbs against her middle fingers, one after the other. A hollow *Pop!* followed as she clapped her left open palm against her now-clenched right hand. She did it again, revelling in the musical cascade and satisfaction of progress.

Clickclickclickclick POP.

'And that's why these things still have crews,' she remarked. 'A hand to throw the breakers when the computers clock out.'

She grinned, and pressed Y on the display.

Behind the bulkhead, trigger signals made their way to a batch of explosive-actuated emergency electrical breakers for the ship's main backup systems. A large emergency power relay would couple a distribution board directly to the bridge's battery grid, and smaller relays could tag in air, heat, lighting, in- and near-ship communications, door mechanical power, local base processing, emergency manoeuvring, and the local power section.

A loud *clang*, followed by silence, indicated that the power relay was closed and locked. *Thudcracklethudcracklethudthud-cracklethud*, a noise like that of a fireworks display being carried out within a locked wardrobe underwater, followed it. Johansson played the sound back in her head: five cycled breakers, three still-popped ones. Corrective work would be required before those circuits would stay energised, or something would fail unpleasantly and permanently.

The Last Line display suddenly dimmed, then brightened, plain text being replaced by a more involved and graphical user interface. *Local Base Processing*, thought Johansson, as she watched the display refresh; these ships had scores of computer systems, numbering in the thousands, but Local Base Processing was one of the two underpinning networks of them all.

'At least that should give me something to work with,' said

Johansson, breaking the silence again for her own sanity. 'And at least it should stop me having to fumble around in the poxy dark.'

In the background, the distant hiss of the emergency chemical oxygen generators was slowly overridden by the more prominent, but still quiet by human standards, hum of machinery: air. The shutters on the ducts in the corners of the bridge lifted a little, their flow indicators springing to life as oxygen-containing air began to be cycled around the interior. It was cold air, though; *No heat, so that must be one of the stuck breakers. That needs fixing, or the cold might get me.*

Johansson watched the pressure gauges on the display start to climb, up to the correct one atmosphere and 20 per cent oxygen. 'At least I won't suffocate,' she murmured, as the panel by the door, and the door status indicators, sprang to life. *Door mechanical power*, she thought, mentally crossing another breaker off the list. 'And at least I can get out of here easily,' she said, natural enthusiasm creeping into her voice a little, although the frost creeping through the seals on the door told her little was different on the other side.

The Last Line screen was still updating, windows coming and going as systems reported in, or didn't. Johansson selected an overhead view of the ship, which was overlaid with a series of markers and readouts for its key systems, and studied it. There was little uplifting green on the display; red and amber warnings were everywhere and, more concerningly, some indicators simply weren't reading anything. These failures, instead of solid red, were demarcated by striped black-and-white boxes. There were a lot of them, concentrated around the rear of the ship.

Johansson chewed on her bottom lip.

A Sark-class ship, yes, that's right. I'd recognise it anywhere.

She nodded, snorting a little, as her memory stirred sluggishly.

Spent too much time on these beasts. Far too much.

An uncomfortable feeling flickered through her mind, like an arrow flitting past its target, just as illumination began to creep back into the gloom of the bridge. First, the electric illumination of the tritium-coated glowing markers ramped into life, bringing the warning signs, emergency routing and panel access pointers into clear view. Then, for a moment, full-power illumination flooded the cabin, from floor and ceiling, transforming the bridge from pitch black to an almost ghoulish crisp white, distinctly at odds with its dull grey titanium panelling, dead screens, unlit panels and absence of activity. Johansson shielded her eyes with her hand and squinted through the gaps in her fingers, waiting for some indication of life.

No one is here, that's for sure, and everything else looks deader than a dead thing.

And then, jarringly, the main lights went out and dull blue alternate lights took their place. *Combat lighting*, realised Johansson, *but it should be brighter. And why combat lighting?*

A high-pitched rising and falling warning noise emanated from the Last Line panel. An animated marker rose from one section of the bridge battery compartment display, flared red and yellow, and two circular readouts materialised. One was missing a substantial portion but didn't appear to be dropping at a significant rate. The other, however, was erratic, its percentage waving up and down, struggling.

'Shit,' said Johansson, seeing her chances shrink live on the viewscreen. She floated, watching the display for a moment, before reaching down under the panel to free the emergency operations guide. Printed media had long been dead in most domains, but it was hard to beat the dependability and legibility of some carbon black and varnish soaked into reams of synthetic resins in certain applications.

Speed is of the essence, she realised. *Everything else is future me's problem.*

The output of the lights rose for a moment, then fell away, and smoke drifted from one of the overhead panels. Johansson rifled through the binder hurriedly, looking for anything relating to the bridge electronics. Another *pop!* from overhead, followed by more smoke. She stopped thumbing through the pages, paused, contemplated, rolled, and pushed herself off the floor and towards what was designated the ceiling of the bridge.

She quickly set about freeing panels, stamped MAIN B-A and MAIN B-B, and determinedly dug through the trunking and cabling underneath. Myriad bundles and sections, like those in the Last Line system itself, were scorched, previously bright and clear colours darkened and charred, with many looms appearing ominously jet black in the dim blue light of the cabin.

Johansson forced the harnesses aside and used the suit's built-in driver and flexi-socket to rattle the fixings that retained the shielding on the battery modules themselves. Nuts sailed away from her, like seeds spiralling down from a maple tree, followed by the heavily shielded protective panel itself. The damage was obvious; the insulation on a thick cable had burned away completely on one side, and shorted out on the inside of the battery box, so she tugged it out of the way and into a safe position. The surge had otherwise damaged power control modules, their fused tops blown open like blossomed flowers. Only two, though, and the panel had spares attached to it to account for that. *Click, click!*

'That should do it,' Johansson said, pushing herself away from the ceiling and heading for the door. The warning noise stopped entirely and a happier beep sounded from the Last Line panel; on its display, the previously wavering readout had now settled. Its overall percentage was reduced but the remaining emergency power, although limited and unable to support much, now appeared stable.

That's some time bought. Now what?

The still-blank screens and unmoving gauges offered no suggestions, no clues, no answers. Johansson pressed some buttons on the Last Line display but it was slow to respond, as if dealing with some unseen problem in the background, and then a menu with a dazzling array of options appeared, surging down the screen. She shook her head, hand hovering uncertainly near the display, wary of triggering another failure.

What are we doing again?

She drew a blank and her gaze drifted towards the door.

Going to the beach? To see her, perhaps?

Johansson scratched her wrist and then pinched herself, trying to focus.

Oh, right. Trapped. Let's get out, while we can. Let's be help, or find help.

Her eyes flicked down to the blank display on her wrist for a moment.

'A little assistance would have been great, you git,' muttered Johansson.

The suit remained mute.

CHAPTER TWO

Johansson steadied herself by the door, cleared her throat of the acrid electrical smoke, and grabbed the door control handle. She firmly rotated it clockwise to the first detent, awakening the door, and then rolled it gently counter-clockwise ninety degrees to unlock it. The status indicator was red with a white cross on it; it refreshed to display a solid red, and then settled into a pulsing amber mode. Johansson pulled the actuator firmly towards her, using the brace alongside the door to provide leverage, and amber became green, and then green with a white cross over it.

Open and locked. Just in case.

Mechanisms whirred around the door as bolts retracted, levers disconnected, and motors ran up, and the large diagonally split sections began to retract unevenly into the bulkhead, pausing every few inches.

Those bridge batteries really don't have much left to give, thought Johansson, watching the staccato motion with wary eyes. *Another problem for future me.*

Behind the primary doors were secondary safety doors, although there was a small section of dark passage between the two. The flat panels that formed the walls were occasionally interrupted by stamped sections with faded red stripes on them, and heavily reinforced maintenance covers, the edges and warning text of which had been abraded by years of crew bounding and bouncing through the corridor. But not all was old; freshly painted yellow marks hinted at areas that could be cut, suggesting a more extreme shortcut around the blast-, shock- and space-proof doors, at the cost of uncontrollably releasing whatever was on one side of the door to the other, and vice versa.

Johansson looked at the markings uncertainly and then entered the walkway, her eyes scanning the next door. She knew that behind it was a small secondary bridge, designed for supporting the main or being used in emergencies, and then another door that led to a mess hall, crew quarters, medical station, library, and other lived-in areas of the ship. From that point, access portals provided entry to the network of compact trains and gantries that allowed the crew to make their way to the engineering spaces of the ship. If all was well, there was often little need to venture that way.

The droids handle the hot and heavy stuff, after all, and the repairs.

Johansson squinted as a disconcerting twinge rippled across her chest, and steadied herself against the wall with an outstretched arm.

They should be handling the repairs.

She looked back into the depths of the still-lifeless bridge and grimaced, the ripple shifting into a dull throb.

Should be. I've been out ... for a while? I don't know.

Johansson unconsciously touched her communicator again and a fresh wave of desolate silence was broadcast directly into her ear.

Nothing is out there.

'Keep moving,' she muttered, clenching her fists, trying to instil some calm. 'They'll be on it, or I'll soon get them on it.'

Johansson sluggishly touched her gloved hand to the door and felt a slight drop in temperature, as the cold of the metal syphoned heat away from the suit.

Out of the fridge, into the fridge.

The only consolation was that the existence of the door access panel, functioning normally, indicated that there was an atmosphere of sorts on the other side. Johansson paused and leant back against the outer wall; her head was pounding, heartbeat up and down, joints aching, and sweat kept pooling in her eyes. Her suit seemed to still be providing basic life support, in terms of keeping the pain in check, but she had no real gauge as to the severity of her injuries.

She breathed in, pacing herself. *I've been through worse. Not. But, still*, she thought, smiling a little. The water at the edge of the beach rolled enchantingly between her toes again, and she felt herself falter. She tapped her foot firmly against the wall, forcing the sensation from her mind, and looked dead ahead, focusing intently on the door.

'Alright, next roll of the dice,' she said, resolutely, nodding to herself. 'The bridge is out, maybe the secondary on this Sark has some answers.'

She'd probably know what to do better than I. Well, just keep winging it, as usual.

Johansson smirked, and then gripped the handhold by the door to the secondary bridge and slowly cycled its controls. Its sections responded listlessly and joltingly, like its predecessor, and an alert rang out from the Last Line panel as the bridge's backup batteries faltered.

A hiss of air indicated a slight pressure differential between the bridge and the redundant bridge but, otherwise, the doors continued their respective ascent and descent, revealing nothing but a yawning chasm of black.

Johansson pushed herself away from the door, disoriented and disconcerted by the gloom. The secondary bridge was pitch, even more so than the main. There was nary a glow or source of electric illumination evident anywhere within, and if someone told her the ship ended there then she would have believed them. She hovered in space, eyes focused and watching intently, half expecting something to erupt from the depths. *This isn't one of those films*, she thought, in a vague attempt at self-comfort. *You're 53, not 17.*

She moved back up against the entryway and, subconsciously shielding herself with the wall, peered around the corner. As her eyes adjusted, the dim blue glow of the main bridge revealed nothing but a foot of the secondary bridge, just decking, stretching away. It looked like whatever had taken place had exacted more of a toll on the secondary bridge than it had on the main.

'Maybe this took the brunt of it and that's why the main is still in any way functional,' she said, the sound of her voice settling her. 'Doesn't bode well for elsewhere, though.'

Been a while since I've seen a Sark in a state like this.

Johansson unconsciously touched her head again and winced. The swelling on her forehead extended towards her ear, and the pulpy feel of the flesh made her wretch. Even the softest of touches sent sparks across her eyes. The only consolation came in the form of a few flakes of dried blood on her gloved fingertips; the bleeding had stopped.

Concussed, I bet. Probably why my memory's so patchy.

'A torch would be nice,' she uttered to the blackness.

Bing! it responded.

Johansson froze.

'A torch would be nice.'

Bing!

She cautiously swung herself into the gloom.

'Torch.'

Bing!

Above her, somewhere. Eyes closed, listening intently for the audible alert.

'Torch!'

Bing!

Johansson ran her hands up and onto the nearest panels. She pressed her fingers against one which felt like it had a defined edge with a recessed contact patch. It sank slightly with a little pressure.

'Torch!'

Bing!

The panel vibrated slightly on cue with the noise. Arm extended, Johansson pushed off from the deck more forcefully and pressed firmly on the recessed square of the overhead panel. It clicked, sprung open, and she sensed something moving down past her face.

'Torch!'

Bing!

And a flash!

Johansson reached into the pile of objects, each held in place with elasticated nets, and grabbed the vocal and flashing one. She ran her gloved fingers over its coarse anti-slip coating until a prominent toggle switch made itself known. *Click.*

Light flooded from the front and perimeter of the torch, finally freeing Johansson from the absolute darkness of the secondary bridge. A quick flash around the interior revealed nothing that was about to attach itself to her face, so her attention turned back to the torch's source. It had been resting in a large frame, attached on pressurised struts that had dropped the frame down from the ceiling when the front hatch was pressed. She cast the torch's beam into the aperture from which it had come and realised it was heavily shielded. Johansson turned and ran the torch over the bulkhead, and briefly back into the main cabin, revealing that there were emergency torches in places. However, all were evidently damaged, or simply unresponsive. Someone, apparently, had thought ahead a little and accounted for this degree of potential disruption.

'Thank you,' she murmured, scratching the side of her head slowly.

I wonder what else I'm forgetting.

The torch had a magnetic base, so Johansson stuck it to the corner of a control panel and set about going through the contents of the container, marked EMER2 on the underside: clean water, albeit frozen, a few self-heating drinks, a little food, a medical kit, a selection of additional electrical spares, an in-ship radio, a tool kit, a spare wind-up torch, six flares and a mobile generator. The latter, about the size of a shoebox, used a fuel cell to generate a substantial amount of power for a short period.

Christmas. Praise be.

She pried open the medical kit, extracted a green cylinder, lifted the cuff of her suit on her left arm, pressed the end of the cylinder with hash marks on it to her exposed wrist, and squeezed the button on the top. A fresh but light cocktail of painkillers, enhancers and stabilisers flooded her tired body, offering chemically induced respite and keeping some of the cold at mental bay. The kit had three more green cylinders left, along with three more serious-looking red ones, and two less aggressive blue ones.

'Nothing in these bins for you, I'm afraid,' she said, tapping her suit's blank display screen. 'It looks like someone didn't load these up properly.'

She looked at the suit's blank display again, thinking for a moment.

If the suit's batteries give up, heat's going to become a problem even more quickly. And the rest. And then my ongoing existence will become a problem, too.

Johansson grabbed one of the self-heating drinks, her desire for warmth and her thirst suddenly overwhelming, and twisted the base. It warmed quickly as she fiddled with the in-ship radio, rotating through all the available frequencies, broadcasting along the way. There was nothing coming back, aside from the silence, echoing what she had already experienced.

'So you're probably working,' she said softly, tapping her personal communicator, its composite housing clicking quietly, 'but there's just nothing to listen to.'

Her mind replaced the silence with the sound of waves.

It's been, what, twelve years since I last set foot on Earth? The place is a mess, sure, but I'd like to see it again. And I'd like to see her again.

She continued to float freely as the medicines and boosters roamed through her system, and sucked merrily on sweet yet sickly warm blackcurrant juice from the self-heating container, all while munching on a battery of crumbly, orange-flavoured energy tablets.

Air, a warm drink, some light. Could be worse, she reflected, touching her foot to the deck, waiting for any sign of vibration, but none arose. *And the ship doesn't appear to be degrading any more, at least.*

Her head was still cloudy and she found her eyes narrowing in response to the odd stabbing pain, but the refreshment helped clear her mind enough to focus on the secondary bridge. Johansson moved slowly through it, torch tracing over the panels and monitors, revealing little of use. Every panel was blown, and every light was out. The dull grey inner panels had blackened and partially melted, and any illumination had been incinerated; it appeared that a large electrical fire had occurred, explaining the ominously dark and endless initial appearance of the room. Only the shielded door controls and the neatly protected EMER2 unit had avoided damage. Strange dark swirl marks around some of the larger ducts at the edges of the room caught Johansson's eye and she nodded to herself, an unpleasant look falling across her face.

Mechanical-to-vacuum fire suppression. Things must have been dire.

'It got hot enough in here to pop the emergencies and dump the atmosphere,' she said quietly. 'Looks like they did their job and starved the fire in the sixty seconds they were open for.'

Better to lose the crew in a section than the entire ship, I suppose.

'Been there, done that,' she said, voice louder, as she poked a finger at a charred piece of plastic that was wafting slowly around the cabin. 'And that was on an older one of these, too. Munitions fires are no joke.'

But maybe the system's designer wouldn't feel that way if they were in it.

Johansson tried again to recall what had happened, and what had been going on, but the merest thought of it caused her aching head to explode with pain, or simply not answer at all. Her suit was damaged in places, that was for sure, so the ship had seemingly gone through a distinctly sub-optimal manoeuvre at some point, throwing everything not bolted down into everything else, the everything else usually tending to be bolted down or welded into place, easily winning that particular pissing contest.

She pointed her torch at the ruined panels again, its beam slowly picking out a singed protective cover. Johansson rubbed the top of the transparent box, revealing a large knurled red aluminium knob, with a recessed grip in its centre that could just about accommodate a clenched fist, on a striped yellow background. The indicators and text around the enclosure had been destroyed but the cover did not budge and was locked firmly in place; no one had opened it and activated the control. She looked over her shoulder, at the panels in the other bridge, and saw the same control, untouched. Beneath it, stark red letters: CRASH STOP.

'Well, we're still here, so someone got something right,' she said, pulling her arms close and inhaling deeply, feeling her chest rise. She held the breath for a moment and then released it, the brief pause lending her a fraction of equilibrium. 'And we're still here, so all is not lost.'

Her mind began to drift, snagging on odd details. She unconsciously started tapping her fingers sequentially against her thumbs, trying to sharpen her attention and think more logically. A muddled pool of memories, old and more recent, some jarringly clear and others hazy and obfuscated, mixed torridly with unpleasant blank chasms. She weaved her way through them, eyes closed and tipping her head as she ducked mental voids, but found herself reflexively falling back on the one thing that still rang comparatively clear and true: her training.

'The secondary's in worse shape than the main,' she said, disgruntled, rolling her head slowly and tapping an index finger against the suit's chest plate. 'I can either slog it to engineering and access the emergency bridge, if that's even possible, or I can try and eke some life out of the computers up front, with some work.'

But that's not my forte; I work to punch holes in ships, not patch them up.

Johansson huffed, her arms crossed. The stillness of the ship seemed to amplify with every passing second, and the murk of the secondary bridge grew darker, more intense. The thought of sleep quietly embedded itself in her mind, like a seed planted in a border, and began to grow. She mentally kicked herself, an effort to steer away from the ease of inaction and the outcomes that would likely follow; *You've not been through worse, but you've been through simi-lar. You are trained, you have the experience, and you are capable!*

A fractional grin arose on her face as survival skills bustled their way to the front of her mind. She grabbed some tape from the tool kit in the emergency chest and first set about wrapping and securing the damaged wires and harness on her suit, reconnecting a few plugs that she could identify along the way, and then layered heavy-duty tape patches over the cabling and damaged areas. A few of the lights on the suit's status panel shifted from red to amber in response, making certain death feel a little less imminent. Johansson then carefully flexed her arms and legs experimentally, testing her range of motion and relishing the sense of freedom, and the suit didn't protest. She beamed, her shoulders lifting as some concern sloughed from her mind, and stood to attention.

We're in business, so let's make the best of this time awake, alert and active.

Johansson clipped the tools and tape back onto their retaining pad, and picked up the torch. She held it up to her face for a moment, studying its chunky orange casing and the silver label on its side.

'A Clulite Shipbrite,' she said, surprised. 'I haven't seen one of these for twenty years. I'm going to have to give the loadout team some stick when we get back, that's for sure.'

Observe, orient, decide, act rang like a bell in her mind again, as she fastened the torch to her suit. *Observe? No crew, bridges are effectively out, but some systems are still up. Orient? In the secondary bridge, facing aft.*

Decide? She paused and sucked more warm juice out of its cask, and felt a little more content as the heated fluid coursed to her core. *A Sark, Transit Station T1, unloading, then nothing*, she thought, neurons flickering intermittently. *Departure, destination, task, none of the above?*

Her mind, albeit struggling, politely reminded her that this did not constitute a decision. And, in the background, something new was needling her, taunting her. She scratched the top of her gloved hand, annoyed, trying to isolate the provocative thought.

Sub-optimal.

The phrase repeated itself, over and over, like a child learning a new expression.

'Yeah, tell me about it,' she murmured, the cold stabbing at her again.

I need heat. Act!

Johansson made her way back to the Last Line display at the rear of the main bridge and brought up the emergency breaker display. Air, lighting, door mechanical power, Local Base

30

Processing, and the local power section: those were the breakers that had closed and held, and it was the last that had brought her back to the screen. A directional pad below it allowed her to cycle through some limited options for the systems associated with the now-live circuits, so she dipped into the local power section menu. It presented a short list composed of unhelpful acronyms and abbreviations, all of which sounded imposing.

Best not inadvertently flood the ship with radioactive gases, she smirked, *or dump all of the sodium coolant into space.*

She reached under the screen again and grabbed the emergency manual, flipping through it for power operations, the cold and state of the rapidly decaying batteries playing on her mind. She peered at the pages, trying to resolve the small words through tired eyes, and thumbed further through it until she reached a section marked MAIN POWER LOSS. Johansson started reading out loud, trying to get to grips with the instructions as quickly as possible, playing out the actions in her head.

'1146.2I: Main power loss: In the unlikely instance of main power loss, or a failure of the main fore-to-aft umbilicals or distribution grid, standby reactor 2A of the local power section may be used to provide emergency power to the main crew areas of the ship. Generator output may not be adequate to operate all desired systems, particularly if simultaneous operation is required, but will prove sufficient to enable safe control, stabilisation and repair efforts.'

Okay, she thought, as she drifted around the room. *Need all of that.*

'1146.2S: Main power loss operation: Please consult the Last Line system. To enable generator 2A, select EPU2A. The operation of the standby generator, located aft of the living quarters, is automated. Activation will restore electromechanical main breaker operation and open the emergency breaker. Additional breaker and distribution operations will then be managed by Last Line and

Local Base Processing, once power rises to a level capable of supporting the latter, and charging of the main batteries will commence. Some systems are isolated and not readily accessible; should failure occur, please consult your engineering team.'

That's promising, she thought. *Maybe this juggernaut will come back to life with a kick, and at least I won't die from exposure.*

Johansson left her orbit with the manual and returned to the screen. *Down, down, right, power section, select* went her inputs. *Down, down, down, down, down, down, Jesus Christ, down, EPU2A.* She pressed the button, to confirm her selection and another confirmation menu popped up. *Yes, I am fucking sure,* she snapped, mentally, at the screen. She stabbed it again, and a new window popped up on the display. Another cross-section, this time of a small reactor, with myriad bar graphs alongside; impeller speed, coolant flow, coolant reserve, output, temperature, the list was almost endless, and paging down just revealed more and more readouts.

All were pegged at zero or their ambient neutral state but, as graphical elements of the reactor assembly moved towards other graphical elements of the reactor, the numbers and bars began to climb. But nothing changed. The display behind the reactor read-outs remained unflinchingly similar, and nothing in the bridge showed increased activity. *Just wait.* Uncoloured bars became red, became amber, became green. As the minutes passed, all settled into a level, even green, with each bar graph peaking at approximately the same level. But, still, nothing happened.

Johansson let out a long, agonised sigh. *Should failure occur, please consult your engineering team* chimed like a bell in her head, echoing from the quickly scanned manual. She spun in place, waiting. But, still, nothing happened. *Should failure occur, please consult your engineering team!* The reactor readouts disappeared from the screen and shrank down to a small tab at the bottom. But, still, nothing happened. *Should failure occur, please consult your engineering team!* Johansson gently pounded the titanium surround of the panel, pushing herself away from it, dragging herself back and hitting it again. But, still, nothing happened. *Should failure occur, please consult your engineering team!*

Something went *Bang!* behind the panelling and a loud *crack* erupted from below her. Suddenly, the heavy smell of ionisation flooded the bridges; damaged relays and components began to shower both bridges with sparks, making her unconsciously reach for the fire extinguisher by the door, but, as Local Base Processing began to spool up and take charge, and as systems came online and reported in, automated breakers, switches and switchboards began to calm the chaos. The showers of sparks subsided, the dim blue lights became bright, and, piece by piece, the forward section of the ship came to life.

Johansson grinned wildly, still spinning in place. 'That's more like it!' she cheered, as the main bridge started pulling off a passable impression of being that of a functional ship.

ClickclickclickclickPOP!

'Time for a treat,' she said, cycling the breaker for the heating system. Local Base Processing flared into life, detecting damaged circuits and shunting power around them, the computers assessing, guiding and actuating the ship's functional hardware; there was no *pop!* like before and, seconds later, heat started flowing from the vents around the cabin, wrapping Johansson in a lightly moisturised blanket of warm air as the climate control worked to quickly bring the cabin up to 22 degrees Celsius.

'At least I won't freeze to death now,' she declared happily.

Sub-optimal, said the voice again.

'It really isn't,' beamed Johansson. 'We're getting somewhere!'

Sub-optimal manoeuvre, it stated flatly, its tone hard and aggressive.

Johansson's face scrunched up as she grappled with erratic memories.

Something about weaponry. Unloading, yes?

'That's right. That's why I was here. To manage unloading a ship.'

But not this ship. Another. Another Sark at Transit Station T1.

She squeezed the tips of her index fingers against her thumbs, and closed her eyes, trying to clear the mental fog enough to allow her to snag the next essential thread.

We were set to unload weaponry from a Sark at Transit Station T1.

Her memory abruptly served up a sensation similar to that of being in a slowing lift.

'We were already there,' she mumbled. 'We had arrived, braked, and taken up position, alongside the station and the other ship.'

Sub-optimal manoeuvre, repeated the voice.

'Sub-optimal manoeuvre,' she said, echoing the flat tone of her inner monologue, fingers pinching together more tightly, a realisation dawning.

We had stopped moving and we were safe. But now?!

'Oh,' she shouted, eyes springing open and ablaze. 'Oh, fuck!'

CHAPTER THREE

'Fly ... fly the ship first,' babbled Johansson, as she cast herself into the bridge, lurching along the walkway between the stations. 'Fly the ship first, that's what Taylor always used to say. The pilot's mantra.'

How could I be so stupid? Aviate, navigate, communicate. Stupid fucking concu–

Johansson's outstretched hand guided and braked her erratically to a stop alongside the pilot's position. She pushed herself into the seat, its rough high-grip lining snagging on her suit as she reclined. Her eyes closed for a moment, the bolstering and wraparound displays inducing a snug, secure feel, one long absent from her mind. She bit her lip hard, snapping herself to attention, pushing back against surges of fatigue and nausea.

The displays on the bridge were cycling through solid red, green, and blue, as Local struggled to find its footing, and then suddenly snapped off. A dull whine penetrated the deck, followed by a second, and then a third, building in intensity, pulsing, steadying, and vivid amber text began to pour down the screens. Gauges and indicators flicked to their maximums, jamming against their stops, then tumbled back down to zero, awaiting fresh, live signals.

A solitary beep was followed by another, then a *chirrup*, repeating and multiplying as the stations reawakened from their slumber.

What the fuck do you know about piloting a ship? blurted her mind.

'Enough to know that *Big Ship* A interacting with *Solid Object* B is generally going to result in a pretty shitty day for everyone involved,' she retorted, snappily. 'Including me.'

It's not really the weapons that are the problem. Or the reactors. Or oxidiser. Or the fuels. It's its vector, its acceleration, its mass. This thing's a giant.

Johansson shook her head, feeling her brain vibrate inside her skull unpleasantly, and focused on the main screen.

'I can pirouette a missile around a pinhead, so I'm sure I can at least check if this beast is static or on a safe vector,' she said, reassuringly, rubbing her hands together. Johansson took a deep breath, exhaled, and then let her fingers settle on the controls.

Let's work from the top down.

'Are we closing on the other ship, or that station?'

The acquisition, ranging and identification section of the display was blank.

'Where are we, then?'

The navigation, position and orientation section of the display was blank.

'Okay, what's outside.'

The external camera views were all blank.

'Are we actually moving?'

Her eyes flicked back to the navigation display for a moment, but there was no indication of any speed. Johansson scanned the propulsion section but, again, nothing was registering. She pressed her feet against the footrest, muscles flexing in frustration.

If this station's like mine, or those on the other Sarks, the main reset is to my left, emergency circuits to the right.

Johansson slipped her hand down past her thigh, into the gap between the frame of the seat and the surrounding console, and her fingers roamed up and down, brushing along the top of recessed switches. Two were shielded, with a sprung steel cover preventing any accidental engagement.

Got you.

She lifted the protective cover with her ring finger and firmly pressed inwards on the switches with her index and middle finger. Everything in the pilot's station turned off, and then the displays started the red-blue-green cycle again. Johansson watched intently as the test patterns were replaced with text; checks, tests and readouts flashed past, their speed increasing as the station warmed up.

But then, a jarring line, repeated three times, followed by nothing: *ZANZANZAN.*

Johansson frowned, and glanced around at the other stations. All of the other screens were still showing no data, no readouts, and no imagery.

That's an old code: We are receiving absolutely nothing.

'Of course,' she barked, following it with an exasperated sigh that hissed angrily around the bridge. Johansson closed her eyes again and shook her head slowly, only opening one eye lazily when the console audibly announced it was running again.

She cycled through the options on the display and found a page displaying a raw overview of the ship's flight data. It listed engine activity, thruster activity, reactor statuses, fuel flows, oxygenator levels, assumed, calculated and verified positional data, orientation, commanded inputs, delivered outputs, and streams of data from sensors throughout the ship, but every readout bore one thing in common: three blanking and grim hyphens.

We are receiving absolutely nothing.

She reached down the right-hand side of the seat and flipped up the cover on another large toggle switch. She pushed it forward, the switch thunking loudly as it settled home, and the readouts began to change, the hyphens being replaced by *OOR / SOC.*

Just like that duff Spear Nineteen I fired over the Marius Hills. Sensor Out of Range or Short/Open Circuit. Dead. Like everything on this ship, except me. So far.

She dumped her arms on the seat's rests and pulled herself into the padding, a few changing values ticking by quietly on the screen. Johansson tried to swallow and could not; her throat was dry, cracking, A dull pounding crept upwards from her chest to her head, and her vision blackened for a moment as the suit's chemicals ebbed, weakened and dissipated throughout her bloodstream.

Dead. I'm—

Her half-open eye watched the number of a few readouts ambling up and down, raw sensor data being passed directly to them through backup conduits that stretched the length of the ship.

Only a handful are left. Must have been one hell of a bang.

The numbers were unbiased, flickering back and forth inconsistently. Johansson lifted her head and peered at the screen; one readout showed a one, then a two, then a one, then a three, then a one again. It flicked back to a two momentarily, then a three, and settled there. The number rang in her mind like the tolling of a church tower from miles away, distant but identifiable.

'There were three ships,' she said, shakily. 'There were three ships at the station, including us.'

And that station was where, exactly?

Johansson pressed her finger against her temple. The pain made her vision flare, a brilliant red flash blinding her momentarily.

Red! proclaimed her memory. *Orbiting Mars? Or close to Helios?! Could be!*

'There were three ships at the station,' she stammered, then hesitated, her mind trying to pool what little resources it had and collate some vague kind of picture, like someone picking up pieces of a puzzle that had been scattered on the floor.

The numbers on the screen are about as erratic as my mind.

She made balls with her fists, digging her fingertips into her hands, her teeth grinding, blackness creeping in around the edges of her vision. But the suit didn't seem to be metering anything helpful out.

Maybe it's too dangerous. Maybe I'm–

Johansson jammed the edge of the console into the webbing of the glove between her index and middle finger on her right hand, sending a fresh spasm of pain into her tattered brain. Blood trickled from a tear, tiny globules spattering across the display.

'We were set to unload weaponry from a Sark at Transit Station T1, yes, but there was another ship there as well,' she said, definitively. 'Three ships in total.'

And those numbers are still rolling. Are we moving?

Johansson pushed herself free from the seat and focused on a glowing orientation marker in front of her. She steadied herself, aligning her position and view with its sharp target-like lines. She floated, closed her eyes, waited thirty seconds, resisting the overwhelming urge to sleep, and then opened them again.

I think it has rotated. Fractionally. Has it? Can I tell? Is the ship accelerating, rolling? Maybe?!

The numbers continued to change, their incessant shifting teasing her, taunting her.

Magazine explosion. Tank failure. Collision. Uncorrected, we'd be pushed off station.

'We could be drifting,' she said, the situation slowly solidifying in her mind. 'And we could drift into something else.'

Maybe we already have.

One of the numbers spiked, and then settled back to its previous value.

'And maybe the others are busy dealing with their own problems,' muttered Johansson. 'Maybe we hit them.'

Manoeuvre, commented her mind, adding another unhelpful element to the mix again.

'Unless they're not out there,' she added, sullenly, the silence of the radio network weighing oppressively on her shoulders. She paused, thinking for a moment.

Shit. Manoeuvre.

'An emergency manoeuvre. Someone could have executed an emergency burn. Accelerating us away. To a safe distance. We cou–'

We could be carrying a shitload of speed in a godforsaken direction.

Johansson's pulse skyrocketed raggedly, and she flung herself towards the communications console. Its screens were not blank but instead displayed a single warning in the top-left corner: *CPUCPUCPU*, terminated by a rotating backslash.

Something might get out.

She touched a finger to her communicator, making sure it was locked in broadcast mode, clicked a button that tied it into whatever was left of the ship's communications systems, and drew in a long, controlled breath, trying to compose herself.

'Mayday, mayday, mayday, this is the RSF *Hard Targ*–'

No, you idiot, that's your ship, not this one.

'Right, right, mayday, this is the RSF *Prompt Excursion*, the RSF *Prompt Excursion*, the RSF *Prompt Excursion*. Last known position … unknown, but may have been around Mars or an orbit around Helios, with two other ships and a station.

That's all still a major blank, she thought, frustrated. *Around Helios, yeah, like everything else around here. Good job, moron, back to the academy with you. Still, better than nothing.*

'Departure, departure, departure, ship has been damaged, extent unknown. We require immediate assistance. One survivor, injured, remaining crew status unknown. Possible magazine failure. Ship is armed, exercise caution. Over.'

Maybe. Better to be cautious than not, at any rate.

She leant against the console and drew a ragged breath.

'I intend to attempt to restore control of the ship to prevent collision, irrecoverability, and further damage or the loss of life. Over.'

The subduing sound of nothingness poured directly into her ear as the fog crept slowly back into her mind.

'Mayday, mayday, mayday, this is the RSF *Prompt Excursion*, transmitting in the blind, we require immediate assistance. The ship is armed and may be departing towards other vessels or an unrecoverable position. Over.'

Silence. She was conscious of her body sagging, as a pronounced pain began to work its way up and down her arms.

'Mayday, mayday, mayday. This is the RSF *Prompt Excursion*. We are uncontrolled, may become unrecoverable, and pose a risk to others. We require immediate assistance, over.'

Johansson was struggling to remain awake.

'Mayday, mayday, this is the RSF *Prompt Excursion*. I require immediate assistance, over?'

She held the broadcast button down for fifteen seconds and then released it. A single click, maybe a hollow *pop!* from the speakers, then nothing.

Johansson swooned, her vision blackening as the assisting chemicals abated, leaving her on her own.

'Mayday, this is the *Prompt*, departure, departure,' she said, ever more slowly. She found herself fumbling with the controls, her fingers feeling numb and becoming sluggish. The console's seat felt soft, supportive. The air was warm.

We could just go to sleep.

Her head rolled forwards and then snapped upwards, her eyes widening for a moment.

What was I doing? she thought, uneven, her mind rambling. She looked at the controls in front of her; the text on the panels' surfaces and switches had been dulled, worn away by countless fingers passing over them or pressing on them, and the displays refused to reveal anything of use.

'All these need replacing,' she said, unevenly. 'This looks like a ship that's been in service for fifteen years, not one that's fifteen months out of Lunar S1.'

Trigger the EPIRB! snarled her mind, a cursory snippet from some bygone training session momentarily crowbarring its way into proceedings. *Don't go to sleep!*

'Don't go to sleep,' said Johansson, lazily. 'Trigger the EPIRB.'

Her eyes scanned the panels until she found a large button marked EPIRB. She pressed it in, feeling it click satisfyingly, and waited. Above her, Local and Last Line coerced the Emergency Position-Indicating Radio Beacon to life, and the ship began to automatically signal its distress, over and over, hurling waveform after waveform outwards, yelling for help.

But the bridge remained hushed, restful, the displays empty. Johansson closed her eyes, just for a second, and exhaled heavily through her nose. She felt her pulse slow and her shoulders lighten, her mind and body alike revelling in the inaction.

I'm going to have to go back to engineering, she realised, a frown flickering over her face. *Emergency bridge. Repair droids. Assert control. Find the crew!*

'Ship's dead, departure, status unknown, crew status ... unknown,' she whispered, as a dull but hot ache slowly crept across her chest. 'Need medical attention,' she added.

But I just need a moment, Johansson thought, pushing her head back into a cushioned bolster softly. She wearily unclipped her gloves, rotating their locking collars free, clipped them to her belt, and leant back into the communication station's seat. She closed her eyes and, this time, let them stay closed.

At least it's me here, and not my daughter.

She smiled softly and unconsciously tucked herself into a ball, tight and small, her breathing deepening, abating, her thoughts wandering.

I'd like to see you again. It's been, what, six years? Seven?

Johansson stretched and floated free from the couch, around the desolate space, like a speck of dust highlighted by the sun shining into a room. She tried to lift her eyelids for a moment, but they felt pinned to her cheekbones. The ship hummed quietly around her, softly, and the warmth weevilled its way into her suit, cosseting her, soothing some of her aches.

We have a lot to talk abo–, she thought, fleetingly, as her mind succumbed to slumber, like the remnants of a sandcastle being swept away by a wave.

Johansson dozed, her sleep deepening as the minutes ticked by.

In the distance, something metallic clanged against the hull.

In the distance, an alarm barked into life.

CHAPTER FOUR

The doors leading to the crew quarters swept open effortlessly, leaving thin trails of ash in their wake. Johansson waited, rubbing her eyes and massaging her still-sore wrists, as the debris slowly followed the path of the panel from which it had detached; jet-black grains of incinerated plastics, previously liquefied metals, and scorched paints, moved like oppressive and leaden raindrops in either direction. As the parting waves of ashy materials receded, the crew quarters beyond came into focus.

Johansson rolled her head left and right, looking for anything of concern that lay beyond, but the compact section looked safe and intact; a lighter, welcoming corridor led away from her, with entrances on the left and right granting access to larger rooms such as the kitchen, sleeping area, medical bay, private bunks, and relaxation zones. Each doorway had a rail running around its perimeter, allowing the crew to move easily about, regardless of their orientation, while main rails on the floor, ceiling and walls granted the ability to traverse the wide corridor without fuss.

We're still here. For now. Suit must have decided that rest was essential.

She tapped the suit's thigh plate, double-checked the switches on her communicator, gripped the frame of the door firmly, and cleared her throat.

'RCOM, this is WSO Johansson of the RSF *Prompt Excursion*. Time unknown, location ... unknown. We require urgent assistance and I have triggered the EPIRB, and I am attempting to locate the crew and establish control of the ship.'

At least this area looks intact.

'The main bridge is inoperative, the secondary is out, and I believe the ship may be in an uncontrolled roll and a state of departure following a catastrophic event, and there is a risk of collision or the ship becoming unrecoverable.'

We could simply drift off into the black. Or something else packs up and the ship finally lets go. Or I miss something obvious and vent myself into space.

She made her free hand into a fist and pressed her fingertips into her palm, trying to force the thoughts from her mind.

'I am injured but attempting to make my way to the emergency bridge in engineering, to establish control. Many systems are down, while those remaining are malfunctioning, and the rest of the crew are unaccounted for.'

They could be in engineering, tackling this. I hope so.

'Broadcasting in the blind, presumed off air, but I will continue to relay updates as I go. Over.'

Going to need strength. It's a long way to the back of the ship.

She grabbed the nearest rail and carefully swung herself into the kitchen, the suit's internal motors aiding her ingress, and made a beeline for a battery of vending machines that were integrated with the wall. *Noodles, hot,* she thought, mouth watering in anticipation. Johansson scanned the keypad, entered 28, and the machine obliged: noodles, hot, in a cup and with a plastic fork. The next machine served up a syrupy cold drink, in a squeezable plastic container, while the last proffered myriad coffees and teas. The machine appeared out of milk, so Johansson settled on a black tea; it was the gentlest caffeine-containing option on the menu.

Her options orbited around her as she floated by the machines, occasionally drifting into them, and she wolfed down the noodles.

How long has it been? Has it even been an hour yet? Two?

The thick beef-flavoured noodles lifted her spirits, as did the drink, and she took a moment to stretch and gather her senses in the illuminated, temperate room. She looked down at the unhelpfully blank display mounted on her wrist, tutted to herself, and then checked the suit's front panel. It wasn't obvious how much power or medical support was remaining; a few emergency status lights still shone green on its front, but there seemed to be more amber ones than there had been earlier, and one red flashing light. She tapped its display and status panel, inquisitively, hoping something might change for the better, but nothing did. But all it had to do was keep her upright and alive and, now, at least, it wouldn't have to rely on electrical power or emergency chemical heating to keep her temperature up; the ship was now taking care of that.

But that might not last, she realised, after a moment's reflection, eyes roaming busily around the crew quarters. *Best get moving.*

Refreshed, Johansson moved slowly into the medical bay. There was a plethora of supplies but nothing for the suit's own medical pouch. She took a handful of painkillers from a sealed tub and swallowed two, rather than waste one of the green syringes she now carried. There was a lot of equipment that could probably help her, but none of it was familiar. The numbing effects of the tablets were helping to quell the worst of the pain, anyway, and the sustenance was bolstering her energy.

My issues will remain a problem for later, she decided. *The others could be in a worse way, and I'll probably not remember my own problems in short order.*

She spotted one of the shower cabinets, a light blue panel on the front displaying *Hot Water Available*. The temptation was overwhelming; Johansson could feel sweat wicking down her fitted leggings, through her top, and aches permeating every joint and muscle, her body still struggling and battling against fatigue and its injuries.

I'd kill for a shower. But it might kill me.

'My suit is heavily damaged,' she said out loud, imagining a rescue ship blazing towards her, listening in to her communications, simply unable to get a response to her, the thought alone warming her. 'I don't think I can remove it without breaking it, and the modicum of support and protection it's offering now might come in use if other areas of the ship are in poor condition. Over.'

And I don't want to really see what lies beneath, added her brain. *Thanks.*

Johansson quickly traversed the living quarters, exploring all the other rooms, but it was desolate; there were no signs of any other crew, no signs of issues, no signs of conflict. But all the signs of everyday life, the unfinished mag-card games, the unmade beds, the half-full drink containers, the partly read books and well-thumbed technical updates, the annoying guitar that Brierly would inevitably try to play in front of everyone come the evening, everything she thought she might readily recognise, was gone.

It's like this place has been cleaned out, she thought, an unpleasant veil of nervousness slipping over her mind, as she finished her sweep. The area wasn't entirely barren, though; some of the terminals remained, floating freely, but their thick rubberised power cords were stretched, distorted, as if yanked by a giant unseen hand. A few storage units loaded with personal clothing and equipment were still present and correct, too. One of them was jammed in the doorway of a bunk room, its plasticised casing embedded solidly in the steel surround of the door.

Maybe this got vented, too. Whatever happened, it beat the ship up. And me.

The urge to touch her battered forehead was overwhelming, so she instead ran her hands over her suit again, checking for anything new that was amiss, and rifled through her pockets. There was nothing in the trouser section of the suit, nor in its shoulder pouches. She lifted the remaining pocket cover, embroidered M. JOHANSSON, on the right of its chest plate. Inside was a security pass, her identification, some loose bits of paper, a clean cloth, and a photograph of a silver corvette. She looked at it, blankly, then stowed everything back safely in the pocket.

Johansson cocked her head again, listening. The only sounds now were far-off pump and fan noises, air and fluid being circulated, contactors shunting fore and aft; the signs of Local Base Processing, its associated systems, and the standby reactor, all doing their thing. Nothing ominous, nothing alarming, no mechanical indication of electrical distress. The lack of clutter aside, there was no indication of a catastrophe, past or ongoing.

'The crew quarters are clear and relatively undamaged,' she announced. 'Based on what I've seen so far, the damage must be focused on the rear of the ship.'

At least it's me here, and not my daughter, she fleetingly recalled, her eyes swivelling around the room again, scanning for anything of use. *She's been burdened with enough.*

'I ... if able, please relay an update to my daughter and let her know that I am okay. She is serving, or was serving, on the *Lucky Breeze*. Appreciated. Over.'

Johansson nodded, feeling a light sense of relief, and worked her way to the rearmost section of the living quarters, which featured two short tunnels that led to identical heavy-duty doors. Each door opened into a redundant safety area, for pressure and fire control, the blast doors of which would then allow access to the ship's main station beyond. From there, she could access the rest of the ship, using its compact transport trains to roam along the length of it.

'If anyone's left, they're bound to be in engineering,' she said, trying to maintain a more positive tone, while gazing in the direction of the station. 'Stephenson, Phillips, hell, I'd even be happy to see Brierly. Maybe they're putting the stops to whatever is going on.'

The names effortlessly rolling off her tongue caught her off guard.

Okay, I've got some names. Progress. But no faces. What is going on?!

She turned back to the accessway to the bridge. Above the door, emblazoned in gold text on a black background, was the identifier 00046.XP / RSF PROMPT EXCURSION again. Johansson blinked, slowly, thoughts tumbling in her head. She could see marks where the numbers had been lifted, and shifted across, to make room for the XP.

The digits are the Force's fleet ship count. But XP is …

Another blank. Johansson massaged her unbruised temple again, but a dull and increasing throb steered her from trying to squeeze more out of her memory. *Maybe concussion, maybe medication, maybe both are to blame for my turbulent memory*, she thought, hitting the button to open the doors to the platforms. *Don't bang your head again.*

Johansson pushed herself through the doors and into the station. The grey-panelled hallway around her fanned outwards, and four walkways, demarcated by yellow bands, stretched outwards, terminating in another large bulkhead. Between each walkway were two rails, a bright silver, which disappeared into small automatically operated doors, set into the bulkhead, which led into compact tunnels beyond. The lighting was working properly and the air was fresh, circulating.

The destination board for the train from the leftmost platform, facing aft, showed that it would take her past the fuel and oxygen tanks that straddled the starboard side of the ship, and then past the first reactor plant, mounted out from the central core of the ship on a sponson, and on into the starboard station for the engine and power section of the ship. The central tunnel seemingly ran straight down the spine of the ship, into a section that was only signposted as Buffer. It was evidently inaccessible without the proper clearance; the door to the tunnel even had adhesive security tape on it, which would tear and mark its surfaces if anyone opened it. Johansson scowled at it, the pulsing in her head intensifying.

I don't remember that. But the digits are the Force's fleet ship count. And forty-six is an old one.

She rapped her fingers against the edge of the board, confused, and turned to face the tunnel on the right. It followed a similar path to that of the left, terminating in its own station at engineering, but it had two distinct branches to it that would take crew directly to the front and rear defensive rings. These structures, which wrapped around the ship, were made from thick bands of radiation-absorbing materials, staving off the oft-high background radiation of stellar environments, and substantial stacks of inert ablative and reactive armour, which bore the brunt of impacts from debris or any weaponry that might be cast the ship's way. Anything that did punch through would then have to take on a mix of conventional multi-layer armour, which was packed with titanium, graphene, ceramics, and shrapnel-catching meshes.

Makes these things a real Hard Target. Doesn't help much if the bang comes from inside, though.

Johansson hovered. The station was practically silent, and the space was bright enough, its light grey composite panelling more welcoming than the harsh metals of the bridge, but the absence of sound and activity was making her even more restless. Doubly so because, in the large, uncluttered space, nothing appeared amiss. Everything seemed fine, but at the same time not. She peered a little more intently into some distant corners and shadowy spots, checking for concerns that weren't there, and lingered, sensing something cataclysmically amiss.

'Hard Target,' she said out loud, as the gears in her managed to mesh properly for a second.

Clulite. Old code. Desolate quarters. Worn paint. Unfamiliar marks. Different loadouts. Buffer. Three rails. Forty-six. Low number. Wrong number. Not th–

'Oh, fuck,' she shouted, spinning around on the spot. 'Oh, fuck, fuck!'

This isn't my ship! This isn't my Sark!

'What the actual fuck?!' she yelled, her voice echoing around the station, her arms spread wide, head tipped back, her face a mess of confusion. 'This isn't the *Hard Target*!'

I should have stayed on the beach!

Confusion saturated her mind as she inadvertently pushed herself backwards, surprised, bumping into the wall awkwardly. Her eyes tore around the station, flicking from one corner to the next, her heart hammering away. Johansson's head rocked in uneven motions as she tried to subdue her panic, some of the lights on the front of her suit flickering in alarming colours and patterns. The sole comfort of familiarity flushed from her entirely, leaving her feeling entirely exposed and alone; she gasped for breath, gripping the defunct display on her wrist, her free fingers clenching and unclenching, and pounded the wall in frustration.

I knew this posting was too good to be true. I knew I shouldn't have trusted RCOM.

Johansson banged her head against the panelling, and let out a shriek, the noise echoing around the deserted platform.

I knew it, I knew it, I knew it.

A poking sensation tiptoed its way up her spine, making her back tingle, and she sensed a blooming sensation of calm, of softness. She nodded unthinkingly in the direction of the suit's chest plate, thankful, the fright and fear being mitigated by whatever it had released.

But I needed the money. I need the money. So I can stop doing this.

'Okay, okay,' she said, faintly, 'I don't need reminding.'

One, two, three, four …

'Onetwothreefour,' she said, hurriedly, as if testing herself. 'One two three four, one two three four, one two three four, one, two, three, four, one, two, three …'

And at least the Hard Target might be okay. The crew, they might be okay. It might be okay.

She felt the tension in her body fade a fraction more, and some composure crawled its way back in.

And this is just a ship. And it's a type of ship you know.

'And we're both still here, so I'm not entirely alone,' she said to the suit. 'The board might have changed but the game is still the same. Still in this thing.'

Observe.

'This is WSO Johansson of the *Hard Target*, broadcasting in the blind,' she growled. 'I find myself on an unknown RSF ship named the *Prompt Excursion*, identifier 00046.XP. It has been damaged, and the status of the *Hard Target* is unknown.'

Orient.

'I can only assume the *Prompt* was the ship we were sent to disarm, and I must have been on it to oversee the unloading process, before the incident. Any prior reports now relate to this ship.'

Decide.

'I am proceeding towards the engineering section of the *Prompt Excursion* and I will attempt to assert control and locate the crew. This might not be my ship but it's definitely my problem. Over.'

Act.

Johansson tried, but couldn't bring herself to turn back towards the trains. Something was stopping her, she realised, something that she had seen, amid her panic, something that was now gnawing at her, like wondering if you'd left your front door unlocked fifteen minutes after leaving home. The ugly sense of comprehension continued to grow, squeezing her brain against the inside of her skull, increasing with every minute it went unstudied. She pressed her thumbs and fingers together, and let fly with a solitary, loud *click*, trying to free herself from the cyclical loop.

Fine, she finally thought, relenting. *Just make it someone else's problem.*

'RCOM,' she said, 'all three trains are present at the station. Over.'

The existence of the Buffer train was a surprise, admittedly, but its presence wasn't, given the intact security tape over the tunnel opening. But the presence of both port and starboard trains did surprise her; no one was up front, so all must have used the trains at some point to reach the other sections of the ship.

But why had the trains been returned? speculated Johansson, agitated. *Can they return on their own? Why would they return on their own?*

She glared at them, taking no consolation in the fact that all three of the small silver three-seater trains, which had cargo beds in the back, appeared to be completely normal. She made her way over to the leftmost train, looking for anything of interest, only really registering the fact that it had wheels on top of and underneath the rails, securing it in place.

'I ...' she said, trying to come up with some way to diffuse her worry about the trains, and the readily growing stack of odds that were not in her favour. She felt herself falling into shadow, the disarray distracting and tormenting her.

A solid, comforting concept popped into her mind again: *Act!*

Johansson tossed a mental coin and quickly lowered herself into the seat of the leftmost train, and clipped its security belts to her suit. She scratched at her lower back, one of the suit's harnesses digging into her and irritating her, and felt a familiar series of scars, ripples beneath her fingertips.

The joys of the service, she thought, pressing the button for the engineering platform. *Thirty-seven years, most of them rough. Such is life in the RSF.*

The unobstructed recollection surprised her. But, before she could reflect further, the train hummed loudly; the access portal in front of it swept open, her chair rotated to face the direction of travel, and, with nary a jolt, the train set off.

CHAPTER FIVE

The track stretched out in front of the small train for hundreds of metres, most of which were required simply to get past the *Prompt's* propellant and oxygen storage tanks. There were several small platforms along the way, allowing access to key machine areas, and further down the line were two bespoke platforms that provided access to each end of the reactor sponson on that side of the ship. At the far end, the final stop: Engineering Access.

Johansson nodded to herself, as the train hummed along, busy with the process of paring back and associating snippets of memory, all while trying to dodge those that prompted a feeling reminiscent of a hot poker being inserted into her brain.

Start small, she thought, *start local*, as she tried to recall the configuration of a Sark-class ship. There was the heavily armoured bridge, then there was the secondary bridge, living quarters, and main access station. All checked and inspected. Then there was the front ring, a protective structure that shielded the larger, but more lightly built, crew quarters and station. It was dotted with offensive and defensive systems, and it also covered the first of the fuel and oxygen tanks. These stretched far beyond the front ring, but protecting a handful ensured some degree of survivability and kept overall weight and cost down.

Johansson's train cleared the station's portal and made its way into the backbone of the ship. The trains didn't move at high speed, for safety's sake, but they were less risky and more convenient than manually traversing the length of the ship. She peered ahead, registering little but a clean, well-illuminated tunnel, her view only occasionally blocked by automated safety doors that opened and closed as the train made its way along. The train cruised quietly past the first station for the storage tanks, then the second, unprotected by the ring, and third, and then on into the long section that separated the crew and tank section of the ship from the engineering section and larger defensive rear ring. In between the rings, countless cargo-hauling frames, cranes, and endlessly configurable stowage platforms, jutted out from the core of the ship.

From afar, these Sarks sometimes look like Christmas trees, thought Johansson, smiling weakly. *Albeit ones dotted with more weapons than you can shake a stick at, not baubles.*

The next platforms, in the distance, provided access to one of the two main nuclear reactors that helped power a Sark. The reactor structures, mounted away from the core of the ship to provide a degree of separation and safety, were elegant, frail-looking affairs. Each resembled a bright metallic dart, at the tip of which was the reactor itself, its core blossoming outwards in a complicated maze of gold and black piping; sodium-based liquid metal coolant, turbines, generators, the massive shunt assembly, the array of heat radiation panels, all working in elegant unison to calm and care for the fission at hand. And while the reactors looked svelte and dainty from afar, the combined length of both was comparable to a small tower block.

The heat radiation panels always looked like shuttlecocks to me. Beautiful shimmering surfaces, always shifting to face cooler space.

'But they're just the biggest booster packs in history,' said Johansson, the ship becoming more tangible in her mind. She coughed into her hand, recalling her hot microphone. 'No obvious internal damage to the central core of the ship, up front; I'm proceeding rearwards towards the reactor stations.'

Over. Over? Out. A response will come when it comes. To hell with it.

Beyond the reactor, the line Johansson had picked ran straight into Engineering Access. Its name didn't really do it much justice, as it was far more than simply an accessway. The facility was a compact but complex multi-level structure, located within the rear ring, which was both the heart and nerve centre of the ship. Slung beneath it, the Sark's primary power source: a tokamak fusion plant, which powered the energy-hungry shielding systems and four plasma propulsion drives.

'Praise be for fusion,' said Johansson, wiping her brow, the temperature increasing as the train progressed along the track. 'And Environmental is struggling a bit here, so maybe Local's not faring too well in the ship.'

What felt like the correct twenty-odd degrees suddenly felt closer to thirty, and rising.

Getting pretty warm. Like Earth did, and now look at us. Clashing over the few options, squabbling for the scraps, while the rest of the forces strive to keep everything in check.

The tunnel stretched onwards and the train forged ahead. Johansson kept her view forward, watching for obstructions and issues, but beneath, on her chest, the pattern of lights on the suit's status panel was changing. Ones that had been previously inactive were now yellow, registering something new.

And if you're one of the several billion unskilled, unemployed, devoid of cash, well, get used to the odd boot in your face. But we're stretched thin, thinner than ever.

'Ambient temperature is rising. I hope we're not coasting towards the sun,' she said, offhand, in something she thought hopefully resembled a joking tone.

The train rolled on, unconcerned, and approached the first station, near the nose of the starboard reactor sponson.

And so's the Fleet, and its expeditionary forces. Creeping ever outwards, at a glacial rate, but too small, too slow, its resources and funding sloughing away.

'I mean, that would be a pretty surefire way to take a damaged and potentially dangerous ship off the board, though,' she added, the warmth permeating her suit, seriousness creeping back in, as the train entered the station and more dim yellow lights appeared.

I mean, I'd try that, if the situation was desperate. Even if it meant manually pilot–

Johansson shifted in her seat, bothered by the warmth, as the train rolled along the platform. Nothing looked amiss, and the train ambled forward unimpeded, approaching the first of the heavily shielded doorways leading off the platform towards the reactor. Some of the yellow lights became red.

I can't remember wha–

For a fleeting moment, a sad emoticon appeared on her suit's wrist display, followed by an incomplete trefoil. She caught it, out of the corner of her eye, and frowned. Johansson tapped the screen, curious, as the train passed the first doorway; on the suit's chest panel, dim red flashes. The panel on her wrist remained unresponsive, only its green backlight shimmering occasionally as she moved her hand, smoke hovering around its damaged wiring.

Intermittent at best. Add it to the list.

Nothing appeared out of the ordinary with the first door, adjacent to the reactor itself: it was closed, locked, intact. The emergency lighting and warning lamps around the door and on the platform, however, were off. Johansson squinted, unconvinced, the complete lack of activity, light or electrical power implying that something, somewhere, had gone sideways.

Probably another issue with Local, she thought, her attention swinging back to the track in front.

The train moved on and approached the doorway to the reactor station's second gantry, the one that struck outwards into the shunt assembly. Johansson eyed it cautiously; the blast door was marred, the paint on the platform side scorched by intense heat, and a thin cloud of dull, unmoving grey smoke was lingering around the door. But the door looked closed, the area inert. Johansson hesitated, her mind more interested in how the smoke looked like footage she'd seen of waterfalls.

The train rolled onwards, automated, drawing closer to the door.

Five seconds out.

Johansson opened and closed her mouth, tasting something bitter.

Four seconds.

Shit, she thought, attention swinging wildly back to the platform.

Three seconds.

There's a shado–

Two seconds.

The train rolled towards the door, which had been jarred open a few barely visible centimetres.

One second.

'Shi–'

Johansson's hand moved towards the emergency controls, but it was moot by that point. The train drew level with the opening and the unshielded, unrelenting force of the nightmare inside poured forth, like a laser cutting through plate steel, highly radioactive materials set free by some catastrophic failure. Johansson blinked, the temperature spiked, and the train passed the doorway.

She wiped her forehead again, shifting in her seat nervously as her heart tried to escape from her chest. A slight stabbing sensation in her waist; the suit administering something new, possibly.

'Shit,' she muttered regretfully, as the train quietly swept into the next tunnel, its motors humming quietly, unperturbed. Johansson cast her eyes to the ceiling, bit her tongue, and mentally lashed herself for her lack of care. *No point rushing if you're just going to inadvertently unalive yourself*, she thought, chiding herself. *More haste, less speed.*

'Uh, it, ah, looks like the port reactor station has been damaged. Advise caution if the intent is to board.'

Yeah, let's not tell them that we might have just fucked ourselves. Maybe it is just heat and stress, though. Okay. Yeah.

The train bumped slightly over a joint in the rails, indicating a section change. From a distance, it appeared to be approaching what looked like a solid wall. However, the track twisted sharply right then left, swinging the train around the interjecting obstruction. The same sequence followed just a few metres later, but reversed: a wall, a swing to the left, then a swing back to the right, and onwards. *Like the munition storage sites*, thought Johansson, her focus returning. *Blast mitigation, should the worst happen.*

Her head was starting to ache again, but she pushed the thought of its cause to the back of her mind. Johansson could feel the suit releasing something else into her bloodstream at its usual wrist and neck injection points; her vision cleared a little and some of the pain drained away.

'I hope there are some more support packs in engineering for you,' she said, voice wavering. 'You're about the only thing keeping me up and mobile.'

The suit didn't respond, audibly or visibly. She automatically patted her chest plate again, regardless.

Good suit. But its resources are finite.

The train rounded another series of blast-mitigating walls, made its way through a final portal, and entered a loading gate. There were platforms on each side, level with the train, hardware for loading and unloading the vehicles that came and went from engineering, and some accessways leading off to the left and right. In the middle of the track was a crash buffer, behind which the platform wrapped around, for stopping the train, and beyond was a wide and heavily armoured door that led directly to Engineering Access.

Everything had one thing in common: it was completely unlit, electrically dead, and as silent as a crypt. The only source of light was the battery of four lights on the front of the train, which illuminated a sharp arc ahead, revealing that the blast door was closed.

Another ominous tell-tale caught Johansson's attention. The entire surface of the blast door was painted with red and white stripes, interspersed with fluorescent strips for visibility in the dark, and these finishes extended over the large rotary locking plugs that were operated electrically. Usually, the door was down for safety reasons, but it wasn't locked; opening it could be done quickly with hydraulic power and, in this configuration, the paint and striping that covered the rotary locking plugs would be at an angle compared to that on the rest of the door. The headlights of the train, however, revealed that all the lines and markers on the door and the locking pins were all neatly aligned.

Fuck, thought Johansson, and she grimaced. *Not getting through that easily.*

The train rolled a few more feet, sidled up to the buffer, and came to a stop. Johansson cocked her head, still strapped into the seat, and listened.

Absolutely nothing. Dead.

'I've reached Engineering Access,' she said, quietly. 'There's no power at the gate and the doors are all closed and locked.'

She stayed in her seat and frowned at the blast door. The locks needed power to operate, as did the pumps for the hydraulics that opened the door. *The rails are being powered by the standby reactor up front, but why not the door and the lighting in here?*

Johansson unpinned her suit from the train's chair and stood up. Nausea rippled through her, her stomach rising, cresting and falling, like a wave, and she vomited over the side of the train. She grabbed its railing, steadying herself as she doubled over, and heaved again. Her stomach convulsed, and her body shook; she pressed her forehead against the cold metal of the train's guardrail and shuddered, bringing up nothing else but a little spittle and acid.

She slumped back into her seat and groaned, weakening. Her hands made their way to her stomach, in an attempt to soothe and settle herself, and she lay still, watching the gloom above.

Just another obstacle and more question marks.

'Tell me this isn't happening,' she uttered to the void.

Silence.

'Torch.'

Bing!

She smiled a little. But still no crew, still no conversation, still no help. Still no idea what was going on, where they were, or what the status of the ship, but not her ship, was.

'Maybe this isn't really happening, torch,' said Johansson.

Bing! went the torch, merrily as ever.

'Maybe I'll wake up in a minute, torch,' she said.

Bing! it responded.

Johansson continued staring into space. It was warm at the loading gate, almost balmy, and slightly humid; she could feel the need to sleep creeping in again, exacerbated by the nausea which, at least, was subsiding.

Assume control, help this ship, said a quiet voice in her mind, her ingrained training poking her again. *Find the crew, help them*, it reiterated. *See your family, get paid!* it added, sounding like one of the dire infomercials that streamed constantly on the boards in the streets, the ones that had an unpleasant habit of targeting you by name and social position.

She rolled her head forward and glared at the door. It glared back, its locking pins obstinate. 'No rest for the wicked,' she murmured, as she put her gloves on and dragged herself out of the train.

Starting from the left-hand side of the station, she milled along the platform, taking in everything in earnest, seeking anything of use, using the torch's crisp white light to pick her way along. Like the living quarters, objects were floating everywhere: tools, parts packages, crates, odd bits of debris, and lighter machinery. The train was affixed to its rails but the smaller loading tools, which were usually magnetically adhered to flat surfaces, had obviously failed or depleted their batteries, causing them to drift free. The bigger stuff, the hydraulic loaders and carts, appeared to still be in contact with the deck.

Perhaps their batteries still have some charge.

At the end of the platform was a short walkway in front of the train, bridging the two sides, directly past the Engineering Access door. Johansson flashed the torch around the perimeter of the door and saw nothing. The solid-steel blast door didn't appear damaged. She touched it again but sensed nothing. It was probably half a metre thick and, given how warm it was in the tunnel, its temperature probably wouldn't reveal much about what was on the other side.

Johansson pictured things occurring on the other side of the door: machinery running, heating systems working, the harsh vacuum of space remaining safely and sensibly outside. Perhaps even people were in engineering, striving to revive the ship and get it back to where it was supposed to be.

'You're in there,' she murmured, nodding to herself. 'And I'm on my way to help.'

Johansson turned away from the door and set about investigating the other side of the platform. More spares, more loaders, and another heavily armoured door. Behind it, a munitions lift that stretched across the ring. The warning markings were chipped and scratched, but the viewing port was undamaged. Johansson pressed herself up against the glass and looked inside.

Pitch black. What a surprise.

She drew the flashlight up, squeezing it into the corner of the viewing port, so it could cast its light inside. She peered inwards, seeing nothing but an empty shaft. Johansson rotated the light a little, revealing more of the lift's interior; the door led to a small platform, suspended in a vertical tunnel, which was connected to a rail at each corner. The tunnel went both up and down, at least relative to Johansson and the orientation of the platform, and stretched in either direction far beyond the partially obstructed and diffused beam of the torch. Conduits erupted from the walls in places, and disappeared into the dark, breaking up the dull metal surface.

Johansson backed away from the door and explored around it with the prying beam of the torch. There were no obvious cables or panels that led to it, no locking mechanisms or indicators, just unyielding and grey metal. She glanced over her shoulder, at the lifters and machinery scattered around the station, and sighed.

'This is a much older Sark,' she grumbled, vaguely remembering the board at the main station. 'It doesn't have dedicated crew access lifts on both rails. Just the automated munitions ones on this side.'

Haste makes waste ... we could go back?

'I'm not going anywhere near that reactor to see if there's a crosswalk still accessible,' she protested. 'This, I bet this can still be used in a pinch.'

She flicked the torch around, looking for inspiration, and the ugly shadow of a jagged edge on the ceiling caught her eye. Scorch marks marred the panels around the gap, stretching for several feet in several directions, creating an ominous blotch. Johansson pushed herself off from the floor of the platform and drifted up to the panel, bumping gently against the ceiling. It wasn't an access panel, just a blank plate, albeit one a good few inches thick and four feet long and wide. Something had exploded behind it, tearing the mounting bolts completely in half on one side and shattering the thick graphite–epoxy composite panel, causing chunks of it to drift away.

'Seems to be a recurring theme today,' muttered Johansson, acerbically. Cautiously, the gloved fingertips of one hand digging into the gaps between the panels, she pivoted her head and shoulders into the gap, holding the torch ahead of her. The light revealed chaos; within was a near-spherical void where previously there had been feet-thick power cables, conduits carrying communications and control data, pipework and electronics, all seemingly vapourised.

Johansson cast the beam of the torch in the direction of the bridge revealing, not that far short of where the panel had blown out, a suspended quagmire of melted, incinerated and scorched wires and power lines were sprawled around the interior of the duct. Casting the torch's light in the other direction revealed the same, a few feet further down the duct.

She swung her upper body into the duct for a better view. A bobbing cable clipped the wall and arced furiously, sparks cascading around the duct. Johansson grabbed the tattered edge of the insulated composite panel for stability, taking care to avoid the cable and anything else that looked remotely suspicious, and carefully inspected the interior of the space. The energised and sparking cable, some six inches in diameter and composed of countless bundles of fine copper, originated from the front of the ship; those on the other side, from the rear, appeared dead.

Power from the standby, she guessed. *This must be why everything's out down here.*

There were no signs of anything having struck the duct; although it would need a lot of fresh panels and bracketry to be returned to its original condition, the explosion had seemingly originated from inside it.

Maybe there was some kind of battery assembly here, something that let go in a really big way.

Johansson rotated slowly. On the side of the vent nearest Engineering Access, there was a small hole. It was countersunk and neatly machined, so it wasn't from something that had hit the ship. The panel around it was severely burnt, and buckled inwards around the hole, almost as if the explosion had originated at that point.

Maybe a strike on the other side of that panel, blowing out through here. Maybe.

'Johansson. The *Prompt* has taken some significant damage to at least one of the prime conduits in front of Engineering Access, and no auxiliary power is making it back here. I can't ascertain the state of the other reactor, but maybe the fusion plant is running.'

Interesting, but this isn't getting me anywhere, she thought, the conduit starting to feel like it was shrinking around her. *Fuck it*, she added. *Keep moving.*

Johansson pushed herself back towards the deck and again turned her attention to the door leading to the ring. It obviously wasn't going to get any power from the front of the ship, and it seemingly didn't seem to be getting any power from the rear, and there wasn't any obvious way to operate it otherwise.

'If I can get into the rear ring,' said Johansson to the empty platform, as if asserting and justifying her thoughts, 'I can perhaps take a look outside and get a better handle on the situation, and also advise if we're approachable.'

External optical systems in weapons mounts, redundant communications arrays, sensors, lasing equipment, hardened, all the toys, up for grabs. Come and get 'em!

'And if I remember correctly, even in these early Sarks, the rings pull their power directly from the fusion reactor. If it's still up, then everything in the rings might be as well.'

My domain, at last, Johansson thought, feeling more confident by the second, nodding to herself eagerly. *Get in there, identify what's going on, start unpicking the mess, track down the crew.*

'And I think I've got a way in,' she said certainly, rolling her left shoulder and flexing her fingers. She bobbed over to the heavy loader that was parked on the corner of the platform, landing softly alongside it. Like most heavy equipment, it was painted bright yellow, for visibility's sake, but it was still a surprisingly slender and elegant machine. It was almost insect-like, with its four long articulated legs meeting in a small central turntable, a compact and heavily protected cabin atop, and a long, compound-jointed arm. The arm was tipped with a powerful jaw, the fingers of which could be automatically swapped for pallet forks affixed to the side of the machine. But, like everything else on the platform, it was dead.

'Can't have been out for that long,' mused Johansson, running her fingertips over its cold frame. 'It's still on the deck, not floating free.'

She opened a small port on the tail of the machine and unclipped the portable generator from her waist. It looked like a true token gesture, connecting the shoebox-sized box to the heavy loader, but she didn't need it to power the machine for long, or properly; it just needed to run for a few minutes, if that.

I haven't used one of these since munitions handling at the RSF depot on Mars. But at least I can remember doing that, so, hopefully ...

The loader's lightweight looks concealed its true power but, unlike the smaller machines, it wasn't designed for manual operation and would normally look after itself, following instructions from Local and Main. But there were always instances where having a human at the helm would better keep things in check; the self-operation systems were good, but the real world sometimes threw curveballs that could confound even the most advanced machines.

Various warning messages flashed across the screen of the portable generator as it awoke, but it begrudgingly accepted its fate and began producing power. Water dripped from it as its fuel cell went to work, using oxygen from the ship's atmosphere and ultra-compressed hydrogen to generate electricity. Lights in the loader flickered in response, then brightened as the generator worked out its immeasurable load and set about doing its best to meet the demands.

Johansson pressed the button to switch the jaw to the loader forks, and the hydraulic pumps of the machine whined into life. It rose upwards, straining and grumbling, as the tools changed over, and then dropped into a pronounced, if slightly faltering, humming idle. The portable generator began flashing amber and protested quietly. Johansson backed the machine up, bringing it level with the door, its feet clanking loudly against the deck as their magnets drew them into place. She rotated the core of its body, swinging the arm towards the door, and pressed the button marked LOAD. The machine squatted and assumed a poised stance, like a runner set to sprint from a trap.

The generator flashed red. Johansson pushed the stick for the boom control forwards, thrusting the forks of the machine into the gap between the panels of the door. The forks screeched horrifically, rendering small strips of metal from the panels, echoing into the tunnel, before jamming firmly between the door's aperture.

The generator flashed white and red as Johansson's index finger pressed down on one rocker button on the stick, while her middle finger pulled upwards; the forks of the machine strained, responding to the controls, trying to move in opposite directions. The generator was still flashing, its ever-changing light making shadows from the machine's legs and boom dance and strobe around the access hall.

Johansson watched the pressure on the gauges climb up to the red section, stabilise, and then climb no further. She reached down alongside the seat and felt for a small handle, shaped like a tee, protruding from the floor; she pulled it upwards, rotated it 180 degrees, and pushed it down. The pressure gauges resumed their climb, deep into the red, and the forks twisted and the legs strained as the machine battled against the door. Johansson tried to focus on the centreline of the door, as the machine heaved and bucked, and pushed the joystick forward. The loader, like a rugby player in a scrum, put its shoulder forwards and dug in with its legs.

Something has to give. Not me!

The machine lurched forward alarmingly as the forks slid into the seam of the door's blast-resistant panels, and its lights dimmed and gauges faltered as the forks began to travel in opposite directions, forcing the door's hefty panels apart. Machinery and mechanisms within the wall and above the door clanged, snapped and crunched in anger. Ten centimetres, fifteen centimetres, thirty, forty, fift–

The machine dropped dead. Johansson quickly reached down for the handle alongside the seat, lifted it and rotated it several times, locking it back down, in an effort to stop the forks from closing. She hopped from the cab, swinging herself along the rails on the machine, and cast a quick eye over the portable generator. It was completely spent, its housing distorted by the heat and demands. 'One less thing to carry,' she said, discarding it.

She rushed to the front of the machine and inspected the opening it had created in the door leading to the ring. It was just big enough to squeeze through, and the forks appeared to be unmoving. She flashed the torch around the platforms one last time, just in case, and then clipped the torch onto her suit's shoulder mount. Johansson used the lowest fork as a step, towards the gap in the door, and grabbed hold of the upper fork. She then pulled herself up and swung her feet between the door's panels, like a gymnast working on a pommel horse. A gentle push and she would arc gracefully and slowly through the opening.

A hollow *pop!* rang out across the platform. She tipped her head back, looking for the source of the noise. A beautiful iridescent rainbow was erupting from the boom of the machine.

Hydraulic oil, fuck!

The rams that operated the forks sagged a little as the machine's stored pressure and fluid began to fade.

'Oh, shit!' she shouted.

Johansson waved her arms around but, as she had looked back at the source of the noise, she had drifted from arm's reach of the forks. She was barely moving, but her feet and ankles were within the opening of the door created by the loader. The failsafe mechanisms of the door began to win their argument with the depleting hydraulics of the loader and the upper panel of the door lurched downwards a fraction, dust sleeting from its thick metal edge.

Her knees drifted into the gap.

She reached down past her waist, clawing at the underside of the falling top panel, seeking any finger hold.

The lower panel bounced upwards an inch, closing on her, rubbing against the suit.

Her fingertips grabbed some kind of locking assembly within the door, just as the loader sighed, plaintively, and its hydraulics gave out entirely. She pulled, with all her force, propelling herself through the rapidly closing gap. The suit's buckles and fittings bumped and snagged on the door's metalwork as she accelerated between the closing panels, the gap shrinking as her speed increased.

Johansson closed her eyes and screamed. She rocketed clear of the door, into the lift shaft, and crashed into the wall on the opposite side. A deafening and drawn-out *bang* erupted as the two heavily armoured panels cinched together tightly behind her.

The loader, its work done and life force expended, crumpled into a pile amid a pool of hydraulic fluid.

Silence descended in the shaft, only to be broken moments later; the noise was a strange combination of laughter and sobbing.

CHAPTER SIX

Blood pooled at the corner of Johansson's mouth. The occasional drop would free itself from the corner of her lip, as she floated around the shaft, and join the murk of sweat, blood and spittle already clouding around her.

She shifted, in pain, and unconsciously wiped the blood away. Her chest heaved, as she stuttered into life, and she let out a yelp as her inrush of breath was suddenly brought to a grinding, painful halt. Johansson stopped dead and rolled her head around, experimentally, orienting herself. She'd come flying out of the gap in the door and straight into one of the main uprights of the shaft, a substantial and unyielding beam of titanium.

Johansson steadfastly refused to open her eyes; her head was pounding, her face scrunched up in splitting agony, and the dark was infinitely easier to contemplate and tackle than whatever was around her. Tentatively, she ran her left hand down her right side, probing.

Touch, nothing, relief.

Touch, bruised, wincing.

Touch, agony!

A sensation like a hot electrified poker being rammed into her chest ripped through her when she touched the area just behind her elbow. She moaned, rotating slowly in the dark, trailing bodily fluids.

Johansson slipped her hand down to her waistband and fumbled around for the medical kit. *One of the three red ones*, she thought, urgently. Moving her right arm seemed like a no-go, as even rotating her wrist sent stabbing pains up into the base of her skull, so Johansson instead pressed the cylinder to her neck and thumbed the button on its base. It hissed slowly, stopped, and then she tossed the now-spent cylinder into the shaft.

She opened her eyes as the more aggressive battery of chemicals assaulted her, sending stars through her vision and obliterating the pain in her side. The embers in her eyes ignited, erupting into glowing fires, but a tremendous sensation of dizziness inundated her as the compounds sought to chase out the radiation, the fatigue, the stress. Johansson reached out and grabbed one of the columns that supported the lift, pulled herself tight to it, and waited for the dizziness to pass. She looked downwards, the lift shaft stretching away into the gloom, dim blue strip lights at its corners tracing to a distant illuminated point that suggested some kind of end.

'RCOM, Johansson. I can get up to the ring,' she said, her voice cracking but pleased. 'The blow-out panels are all intact, and none of the emergency portals are closed. Nothing's hit this shaft, and nothing's cooked off in it, either.'

RCOM, Johansson. Who else is it going to be, exactly?

A wry smile spread across her face.

Fine, be gone with it!

Johansson spun slowly, awkwardly, getting her bearings. The beam was straddled by two substantial conduits, leading away from her in both directions, thick blue ribbing protecting them from impacts. One was marked XP, the text repeating every metre or so. Johansson blinked, looking at the conduits with slightly freshened eyes.

The one marked 'XP' is newer. Fewer dings, fewer scratches, less age-related wear and tear.

She blinked again, her mind swirling.

'XP stands for experimental,' she said, her voice quiet, as her memory flickered. 'This is an experimental ship. That's why the identification plate had been altered.'

It doesn't seem that different from other Sarks so far, though, that Buffer line aside. It's just, what, maybe fifteen, twenty years or so older than the Hard Target.

Her vision greyed a little, distracting her. The lift shaft was pressurised, but not to the same standards as the rest of the ship. The oxygen content was just some 10 per cent, half that of the habited areas of the ship, and the pressure was lower.

Not ideal for a human. Got to keep moving, get out. But more hast–

She reflected on what she had seen for a moment; the fore and aft electrical systems of the ship, among other things, had been effectively severed in at least one place. Ancillary power from the standby reactor up front was making it to a few areas, but not beyond, making Engineering Access inaccessible, at least on her side of the ship. Power from the main reactors and fusion plant was however directed into the engineering areas, and then back into the spine of the ship to be transmitted forward.

The ring could, hopefully should, be up, she thought, looking towards one end of the shaft. *It better bloody be.*

Communications, flight controls, weaponry, and shielding; all of the main controls were also channelled through similar ducts that ran along the central backbone of the ship, and significant damage could cause failures elsewhere.

Like that on the bridge, realised Johansson. *But there are redundancies.*

'But only with adequate power and some degree of Main,' she said to the void, mind broiling. The ship was like a tower block, in

74

that respect. Local Base Processing could handle the simple things, like keeping the air breathable and the doors opening on every floor; however, for communications and control throughout the proverbial building, and for the major systems to function properly, Main Base Processing had to be in effect, which entailed the ship having constant and substantial power.

'I think Main is entirely out, due to the damage, outages, and whatever else is going on,' she said, conclusively. 'And I hope you're well on your way, because we need your assistance sooner, rather than later.'

Help's not going to be just down the road, though. It's going to take time.

Air hissed through Johansson's clenched teeth. Firing one engine for one second on the ship, for example, required a complex degree of cooperation between the propellant storage system, the intermix system, the nacelle structural and orientation systems, communication array orientations, shielding orientation, weapons orientation, storage tank slosh controls, exterior cameras, all manner of things. Local couldn't do that, and Main could only do it if everything it needed was operable and talking to it. There were workarounds, as always, but the results were often suboptimal.

'This thing's not going anywhere in a readily controlled fashion,' asserted Johansson. 'It's dead as it sits, but its crew might not be.'

And what if the fusion plant is shut down, or damaged?

The starboard reactor had clearly seen better days. The status of the port one was unclear, as was the status of the compact standby reactor in the rear of the ship. It was like the one near the bridge but envisioned primarily for keeping the engineering spaces hospitable to human life, and for providing power to start and control the main reactors and fusion plant.

If accessing reactor stations directly, remember to wear the proper protective equipment, warbled her mind unhelpfully.

Johansson's skin prickled, recalling the tunnel and the heat from the door, and the dizziness rushed back in; she clenched the upright as a stabbing pain tore through her belly, forcing her to double over, her muscles quivering and hot. The painkillers blunted the worst of it, but Johansson still felt like she'd been hit by a truck.

Get yourself together, she thought, closing her eyes again. *Head aches. Dizzy. Short breath. Low oxygen here. Trained for this.*

Johansson reached back down to her belt and freed one of the blue cylinders from its bag and pressed it against her neck. Oxygen intravenously flooded into her system, settling her view and mind a little. Three quarters of the blue cylinder remained coloured, so she clipped it back into its pouch.

This way or that, it doesn't matter. Press on.

She dragged herself onto the lift platform, the control panel of which was completely dead. Johansson craned her neck upwards and found the view to mirror that of the downwards-oriented direction: marker lights, tracing to a distant point, and no obstructions.

Just the one platform in the shaft. Nothing to hit.

Johansson crouched a little, then pushed off from the platform, springing upwards towards the light. Five metres, ten, fifteen; the lights kept passing, ticking by.

Better not be another door up there, her mind contemplated, distressed.

Thirty metres.

How am I going to stop myself! she realised.

Johansson swore the tunnel shaft was widening slightly.

Might have been a bit hasty.

The lights kept passing by.

At least I've still got another two red cylinders.

Johansson drifted from the exit of the shaft into a smaller version of the loading bay she had come from. It had a horseshoe-shaped platform that loaders could drop their payload onto before returning down the shaft, and space for one loader to be parked within the ring for quick access and use. Three doorways led off the platform, illuminated by dim blue combat lighting, and there was the distinct smell of smoke. Some debris lingered in the air, occasionally catching the light as it rotated.

She braced herself for an impact with the ceiling but it never came. Instead, Johansson drifted into thick cargo netting, suspended several metres from the ceiling, which arrested her ascent and brought her to a stop.

Always preferable. Better than loose munitions bouncing off the roof.

She crawled over the netting and pushed herself onto the decking. Her breathing still felt short, but less so than it had done in the core of the shaft.

A positive, at last.

One of the large doors on the left, which led to a munitions storage and relocation area, was wide open. Within its aperture stood a loader, inert and unpowered, with a pallet of ammunition on its forks. Everything effectively appeared intact and undamaged, otherwise.

Johansson used the loader's legs to slowly manoeuvre herself into the munitions bay. It was filled with enclosed blast-proof racking and storage bins, all painted a dull grey colour. The residual tritium illumination present in the room, amplified by the harsh beam of her torch, revealed a thick grey murk lingering in areas. *Chemical fire suppression*, realised Johansson. *But there was no fire in here. What a clusterfuck.*

Conveyor systems carried the cannon shells, missiles and decoy devices away from the storage and relocation area to the individual weapon system caches around the ring, the black-and-yellow chequered panels in the wall indicating the areas that would open up for munitions transport when required. Some were ajar, ammunition lingering on their ramps, as if all the electronics in that small area had just given up the ghost simultaneously.

Johansson peered at some of the rounds on the belts, curious, and noticed that the only marks on them were from the rails in the storage bins.

These rounds are new. So why are they out of the bins now? We were unloading everything, not loading it.

'Quick update. I've managed to make it into the ring; it looks like something triggered a loading cycle,' she said, voice sounding more settled, the familiar environment and equipment pacifying her. 'Maybe a bit flipped in Main or Local. Anyway, there could be live munitions in some of the weapon stations, so don't park by touch.'

She propelled herself over to the mechanical access doorway, designed to allow technicians to enter the mechanical area to service broken equipment. It would lead into the central and habitable corridor that looped around the front of the ring, providing access to the various stations and sites dotted around it. For once, it was already open.

Another positive. Things are looking up. That must be where the oxygen is flowing in from.

She coasted into the ring's corridor; it, like the elevator shaft, was dark. The only light came from emergency strips, running along the perimeter of the suggested floor of the corridor, that led away to the right. Johansson flashed the torch in the direction that the strips led, revealing junctions and other doors that granted access to other areas of the ring.

Johansson rotated herself, using the guide rail around the door, and turned her gaze and the torch's to the left. The corridor ran on for a few metres, then terminated in a heavy yellow-and-black striped door. Its paint was bubbled, the areas around its edges charred, black streaks reaching out from damaged seals to mar the dark grey finish of the corridor. Johansson drew herself up to the door and sidestepped her way over to the first of two hardened viewing ports mounted within it. The toughened glass was scorched black, like a long-neglected oven, and offered no view of what was beyond.

She shuffled over to the other viewing port and pressed her face up against it.

Johansson gasped.

'Holy fuck,' she added.

On the other side of the door, bedlam. The corridor was practically unrecognisable. The marker lights stretched outwards a few metres and then the floor simply disappeared. Above, twisted plating and structural beams, interspersed with shattered electronics, obliterated wiring harnesses, sagging conduits, and shattered pipes. It was like the corridor from that point on had been squeezed, twisted and torn by some unseen and almighty force.

Ammunition from damaged feed trays drifted around, along with the unidentifiable remnants of other machinery and equipment. All of it was heavily charred and distorted, as if an immense amount of heat had instantaneously materialised within the hallway. And yet, occasionally, vapour and gas would vent into the crippled corridor, along with an intermittent shower of sparks, one or two live systems somewhere within the section still trying to maintain some fractured resemblance of functionality.

'There's power up here, I think,' she said, trying to suppress the sudden hopefulness that washed through her. 'Unless something on this Sark has changed, there are no standbys in the ring, so the fusion plant must still be up.'

Projectiles and plutonium don't mix well, after all.

Johansson lowered herself a little, trying to improve her view of the corridor. She squinted, struggling to resolve and recognise what she was looking at; long black tendrils descended from the ceiling, occasionally interspersed by large chunks of a rubbery-looking material. Shattered pieces of a darker, more solid-looking substance orbited among them, and the whole lot was wrapped in a mist of thousands of angry white shards.

That's ballistic nylon. Graphene. Ceramic.

'The ship's armour has been penetrated,' said Johansson, slowly, chewing on her bottom lip, pushing herself away from the viewport for a moment. 'No wonder everything's in such a mess here. Only anti-ship weapons wreak that kind of havoc.'

We didn't lose a magazine. We didn't collide with something.

'This ship has been attacked, and whatever came for it hit it hard,' she said, sullenly, her shoulders slumping. 'I think someone just put another few chips on that stack of odds that's against me.'

I hope the Hard Target made it out.

Johansson pressed herself lower still, trying to get a view of what was beyond the shattered armour, but it was so thick, and her viewing angle so poor, that nothing else could be seen. Johansson tapped on the door unconsciously, reassuring herself that it was solid.

She stared at her feet for a moment, trying to recall what had happened. Events long past flashed through her mind, followed by some very present, but this ship, her ship, the essential priors and posts, obstinately remained enshrouded in some kind of painful clag.

It could take weeks for that to come back. We're almost there. Observe, orient, decide, act.

She dwelt on the matter for a moment.

'I need to find a weapons station. Communications, cameras, system controls, they'll all be there,' she muttered, looking to her left and right.

Johansson pivoted and started making her way along the safe and secure section of the corridor. The floor was gently curved, following the profile of the ring, and the view down the corridor was significantly restricted by its curvature.

She brought herself to a stop by a door marked MLR.CON.T1. The security pad by the door beeped at her, to Johansson's surprise, in recognition; she pressed her access card against it, entered her code for physical security systems, and the door unlocked, clanked, and disappeared into the wall. She pressed and held for five seconds a flashing icon on the door, locking it into a service mode in which it would not shut unless a new alarm sounded.

The cramped and unlit room was small and devoid of anything of note, aside from a small metal table, integrated into the wall, and a host of large panels, each of which covered myriad network and power system controls. Beneath the table was a lockable drawer with a nine-digit keypad along its front. Johansson entered her code again and the drawer released, ejecting a few inches from its housing. She pulled it clear, revealing a small computer, housed in an armoured case, with two cables wrapped in loops taped to the back of its screen.

Johansson placed the compact computer up on the desk, checked its battery using the in-built status monitor on the side, opened up the screen, and set about unbolting one of the panels on the wall. It was littered with markings, including WQA.1 and WMA.1, and all manner of cautionary notes and alerts, including: UNAUTHORISED OR INAPPROPRIATE REMOVAL OF THIS PANEL WILL RESULT IN IMMEDIATE EXPULSION FROM THE SERVICE.

'I don't think you'll mind, this time,' said Johansson, as she freed the panel. Beneath were myriad connectors and ports, along with a handful of flashing lights; Johansson traced her fingers along the wiring harnesses, and between the ports, and settled on one in the upper-right corner. She unwrapped one cable from the computer and inserted its free end into the port behind the panel, then switched the computer on.

GMD REMOTE WEAPONS STATION, proclaimed the computer, before asking for more security information.

Johansson obliged.

PRIMARY POWER ONLINE, said the computer.

'Praise be,' uttered Johansson. 'The fusion plant lives.'

SECONDARY POWER OFFLINE, added the computer, unhelpfully.

'But not the port reactor.'

BACKUP POWER OFFLINE, read the display, annoying Johansson.

'I don't want to run the ship,' she griped, stabbing the keys, 'I just want to look at it, or talk to someone.'

EXTERNAL CAMERA NETWORK INOPERABLE, replied the text on the computer's display.

'The cameras or the network itself,' said Johansson, typing in the question. 'It's not like I can just look out of a window.'

The computer did nothing for a moment.

EXTERNAL CAMERA NETWORK INOPERABLE, it responded. *EXTERNAL CAMERAS INOPERABLE.*

'Maybe I should just ask for a list of what's working,' said Johansson. 'It might be quicker.'

She stabbed the keys and the computer displayed a progress bar that slowly began filling up. As the bar progressed, text began appearing in a new box alongside, showing what was responding and what was not. All of the external main communications and visual equipment was toast, according to the computer, along with all the countermeasure systems, defensive shield generators an–

Two functioning ring systems popped up on the screen: *M.SR.*3 and *M.SR.*4, which Johansson recognised as short-range missile batteries, usually on the underside of the ship.

Maybe the damage is confined to the upper section of the rear ring.

'I can work with these,' Johansson said to the computer, authoritatively. 'When is a missile not a missile?'

The computer beeped once, prompting her for input.

'When it's a drone,' responded Johansson, grinning.

She moved the cursor on the screen over *M.SR.*4 and pressed the button to select the battery. Nothing happened, and the display remained unchanged. Johansson tried to select it again; the display broke up for a moment, then returned her to the original menu.

'Come on, we're so close,' she said quietly. Johansson crossed her fingers under the desk and hovered the cursor over $M.SR.3$. A box appeared around it, indicating a potential selection. She clicked, and the display immediately filled with a three-dimensional representation of the launcher and myriad system readouts.

'Sweet.'

She went to move the cursor and a message appeared, crushing her enthusiasm.

PRIMARY POWER UNAVAILABLE – REALLOCATING – 0882.0.

Johansson thought she saw the lights dim for a moment.

'Oh, just work with me, for one time,' she shouted, shaking her head.

She pushed herself away from the desk and stuck her head out of the door. Using the torch, Johansson slowly inspected all of the panels on the ceiling of the surrounding area. The beam, as it travelled along the roof, revealed what she was looking for: EMER14. She flashed down the corridor, using the rail, swung under the panel, and pressed its recessed corner. It dropped down, revealing its bounty, and Johansson grabbed a fresh and undamaged portable generator from the cargo netting, along with more food and water.

Johansson hurried back to the exposed cabling by the computer, cramming more chewable tablets into her mouth while gulping down fresh water, and fished around among the loose cables for one with a large lockable coupling on the end of it. Unsurprisingly, it had worked its way to the back of the cabling box; it probably hadn't been touched since the ship was built. She fished it out, connected and locked it to the portable generator, and switched it on.

The display on the computer updated to reflect the new, albeit comparatively small, source of power.

'Doesn't take much to put a missile out there,' she said, looking at the increasingly recognisable interface, almost pure muscle memory allowing her to flit through the displays, options and command systems, the computer chewing through her rapid inputs. The speed of her inputs surprised her, old habits and training rushing to the forefront of her mind, the familiarity of the experience pushing the clouds in her memory aside.

They must have been using this thing as some kind of test bed.

'For what, I wonder,' she said, absent-mindedly. Johansson stopped her inputs for a moment and then selected the tab to show the overview of the ship's weapons system, available or not. The screen updated and she let out a long, loud whistle.

Oh, that could well be it.

The start of the list was unsurprising, detailing a small complement of turreted twenty- and forty-millimetre autocannon, fore and aft, along with compact laser arrays. For the most part, given the routes Sarks generally took, all were often engaged in just obliterating or degrading incoming stellar debris. Given the scale of the ship, few were really a problem, but staving them off did help the ship's ablative armour, radiators and optical systems last longer in the harsh environment of space. And, like all Sarks, it had the regular complement of four short-range missile batteries, and two long-range batteries, for engaging more substantial or harder-to-hit targets, those that might prove too problematic for its cannon to handle. All were flanked by countermeasure projectors, designed to make the ship harder to see, target, and track.

Virtually all were greyed out because they or their communication systems no longer existed. But the list continued on another page; more countermeasure systems, some Johansson didn't recognise, more short-range missile batteries, an extra pair of long-range batteries, chaos-inducing quad-mounted 40mm turrets, which could throw up a defensive wall of flak in a second, or rip a target to shreds with nary a thought, and–

Wow.

Johansson whistled in awe again as she clocked two substantial greyed-out sections near the bottom of the page: a pair of ultra-high directed energy plasma railguns, the cumulative result of research started back in the 20th century, mounted on the outermost points of the rear ring. Each drew its power directly from the fusion plant of the ship and could provide fire for as long as the plant was operational and gas was available, their projectiles dealing significant thermal, mechanical and electronic damage.

I guess someone didn't like the idea of this thing being out in the wild.

She clicked on the railguns instinctively but the console baulked at her, reporting that there wasn't even power enough to heat and engage with their systems, let alone bring one into anything remotely resembling fireable condition.

Johansson briefly tabbed to the shielding configuration display to see if anything was still up. The technology wasn't exclusive, but military-specification Sarks were outfitted with a battery of shield grid generators, linked to the fusion plants, which employed a blend of laser matrixes and plasma emitters to shield sectors of the ship from incoming projectiles. The console would let her click on the shield menu, but it then seemed to lock up, dropping her back at the weapons interface.

No matter. The firefight is long over, hopefully.

The generator pinged at her, and she navigated her cursor back to the M.SR.3 battery. Her fingers pounded at the keys, powering up the missile launcher using the portable generator. She kept the power-draining positioning and tracking motors off, as well as the conditioning systems for the entirety of the missile battery; she just needed to open a door and get a missile into space.

She cycled through the options on the computer's display and a diagram of one of the responding missile batteries appeared on the screen. To the right of the keyboard on the computer was a shielded cover, again marked with red-and-white stripes; she popped the cover off, revealing a pair of small joysticks and several other buttons.

Let's go take a look outside.

There were nine missiles in the launcher, out of a possible forty, but only four reported as functional. Johansson selected the first, rotated a dial to PASSIVE, instructed the launcher to open its hatch and release the missile, and waited.

It doesn't need to work properly, it just needs to work.

Nothing happened.

'That one's dead as a doornail,' she said to the computer.

She cycled to the next and instructed the launcher to fire it. A small illustration showed a pair of locking devices, flashing, unyielding.

'That one's stuck to the pylon,' said Johansson. 'Contact welding, maybe, due to the cold.'

The next missile was lower down in the launcher, closer to the ship itself.

'Third time's a charm,' said Johansson.

Beneath her, in the void outside the ship, a five-metre-long missile was released from its pylon. Its motor did not fire; instead, a small hook in the pylon gave the missile a gentle push, shunting it slowly out of the missile battery.

The display on the computer updated, the text boxes and diagrams being replaced by a live feed of the camera from the missile. The missile was alive, and talking to the battery, and the battery was relaying everything to Johansson, through the ring's tattered circuits, using the emergency remote weapons system.

ClickclickclickclickPOP!

She grinned, revelling in the noise of her personal fanfare, and pounded her clenched fist gently on the desktop twice. Johansson winced a little, the jarring action sending sputters of pain through her side. She clenched her teeth and focused back on the display.

The feed from the camera wasn't showing anything. She stared at the screen, looking for any sign of detail, the data stream showing that, yes, the missile was outside and moving, coasting along, rapidly putting distance between itself and the *Prompt*. Johansson puzzled over the display, watching it, and then the missile ceased to be.

Johansson tapped the side of the screen, annoyed. She flipped back to the live technical feed; battery power, fuel flow, communications status, internal pressure, internal temperature, skin temperature, release status, all had gone dead.

Shaking her head, she selected the final missile that was reporting in; passive, fire, released. The launcher reported the pylon clear and the tube empty.

'That missile is definitely outside,' she said to the computer, as she used its thrusters to bring it to an almost immediate stop, close to the ship. But its view was still blank, showing nothing of the universe beyond the ship.

'Maybe there's some kind of communications issue,' said Johansson, watching the data streams intently and cycling through the display modes for the missile's nose-mounted camera. The standard view displayed nothing but, when she cycled to infrared, the underside of the ring immediately popped into view.

She breathed a sigh of relief. 'Thank you,' she said, foot tapping on the floor nervously, as she took in the superbly detailed view. The missile's thermal imaging capabilities were excellent, to allow it to track even cold, small and fast-moving objects, and Johansson could see the underside of the ring, just ahead of the launcher, in terrific detail. Sure, it was presented in the strange primarily purple-and-black cast of the thermal system, with only hotter items showing up as brighter colours, but Johansson was just grateful to see something other than the inside of the ship for once.

'Let's get a good look at this beast,' she murmured, pulling back on one of the small joysticks slowly. The missile responded eagerly with a smooth 180-degree flip, and the new view revealed an intact launcher that the missile was well clear of. Johansson flipped the missile again and pressed one of the buttons alongside the joysticks, and the missile's motor coughed in response. It was a short burst, but enough to get the impromptu drone moving away from the ring, and Johansson carefully guided the missile along the centreline of the ship, travelling from the rear ring to the nose.

I won't venture far from the ship, just in case. I won't be able to see everything, but something is better than nothing.

The missile arced gracefully along the length of the *Prompt*, plotting a smooth flightpath thanks to Johansson's careful guidance, and then halted. She then spun it around, its camera focusing hurriedly on the new view presented to it.

Johansson stared in disbelief.

'VSF,' she muttered, shaking her head, 'VSF.'

CHAPTER SEVEN

The *Prompt Excursion* had suffered a massive onslaught. Oxygen and propellant were venting from tanks on its starboard side, spinning the ship slowly around its central axis, and the ship was shedding debris, like a dandelion caught in a gust of wind. Its engines were dark, all of its marker lights out, and vital fluids were seeping into the void from its nacelles, reactor sponsons and engineering structures; left unaided, it would bleed out, shut down entirely, and take its crew with it.

Or, at the very least, thought Johansson, *me.*

She grimaced as she peered a little more closely at the screen, slowly taking in the scale and extent of the damage, which had torn from the *Prompt*'s bow to stern, and recognised the signature of the impacts.

Telegraphs. A wave of them.

The heavy-duty anti-ship weapons were dumb but deadly; each was a single tall pole, forged from depleted uranium, and that was it. There was no engine, no manoeuvring thrusters, no targeting hardware, nothing. Their launchers simply pointed them in the direction of the target, flung them into space, and left them to be the problem of whatever they eventually collided with. And, because of their inert nature, they could be difficult to detect; a hit was often problematic, at best, for a large ship, and often terminal for a smaller one. But their unguided nature meant they had to be fired en masse, at least if you were shooting at a moving target, to ensure a decent chance of an impact.

A glint on the screen confirmed her suspicions; the remnants of a Telegraph were visible, jutting out of the rear ring, embedded deep within the outer layers of armour. It stuck upwards, like an errant twig on a perfect lawn, the area around it buckled and blistered.

Very severely fucked, thought Johansson again, slumping in her seat, the edge of the console sinking into her elbows. Her head suddenly felt like it weighed a tonne, and a cold, dank sensation closed around her, her vision greying again in response.

'*Prompt* to anyone,' she said, voice faltering. 'This ship's been hit by numerous Telegraphs. The damage is extensive, uncontrolled. Engines all look to be out. We're venting. Not under command. Crew status ... unknown.'

We're not going to last much longer. I'm going to give out, or it will. Who goes first?

She felt something wet in the corner of her eyes and blinked, repeatedly, trying to keep them clear. She jutted her thumbs up to her face, squeezing the offending moisture away, and then pinched her cheeks. Johansson realised that her jaw was clenched closed, but her teeth were chattering slightly over the deathly silence of the communications channel, her muscles teetering on the edge of–

I'm sorry, sweetheart.

She sobbed, fleetingly, and shook her head, the pooling tears flashing away from her face.

Another year, another failure. And now this. This is it.

'I hope, I guess, someone is receiving this, be it now or later,' she said, haltingly, trying to bring herself back into line, to obscure her sobs. 'I am WSO Johansson, from the RSF *Hard Target*, aboard the experimental ship *Prompt Excursion*. I was here to aid in the unloading of the ship's munitions but it appears to have been targeted by an unknown force and heavily damaged. The crew is unaccounted for, location unknown, the ship uncontrolled, damage ongoing, and I believe it will either fail totally or become unrecoverable in short order.'

Yeah, that's about the long and short of it. And now for me, while I can.

'I'm hurt, but my suit is just about keeping me up. It's also damaged and unresponsive. I can't remember what happened; I just woke up on the bridge of this thing and, well, now I'm here. But probably not for much longer. I think I'm going to go to the beach.'

She smirked, and rubbed her arms gingerly, but the waves and the sand didn't follow.

I suppose there is more still to say. And now is my last opportunity. Stupid of me. And now here I am.

'Just ... please, I implore, whatever happens, whatever gets slapped on the file for this, please get a message to my daughter for me. I don't care how you want to dress it up. I just want you to tell her that I am sorry. That I should have made time for our relationship, not for more deployments, contracts, ships. That I should have put in more effort, not shied away. If anything, just tell her, like I haven't done for years, that I–'

The console beeped noisily, demanding input. She cast her eyes downwards at the screen and thumbed the remaining tears from her eyes, the gritty textured feel of the suit's gloves forcing her to squint, steeling herself a little, pulling her mind back into action.

Johansson's drone-slash-missile was lingering a few hundred metres away from the *Prompt Excursion*, slightly off to its port side, resting above it and parked looking back along the length of the ship, from somewhere near the secondary bridge. She baulked, taking the image in, processing, the heat from her face flushing away.

'What is that?!' she muttered, quietly, leaning towards the screen.

At a glance, the ship appeared to be a conventional Sark, the kind that would usually haul whatever the military and government needed at the time: minerals, gases, liquids, munitions, equipment, and other ships, from the planets to the main asteroid belt, to the bases on Moon and Mars, and to the outposts beyond. Or, in its less civil role, it would be used by either to bludgeon its way into wherever they saw fit, and it could protect those positions until told to do otherwise. But, on closer inspection, at the nose of each reactor station, and on the upper and lower leading edges of Engineering Access, were large, angled panels, spreading outwards. The thermal camera reported the unfamiliar panels as being warm, their surfaces strangely uniform and uninterrupted. Behind each of the thick panels, only one of which seemed to have received any significant damage, was a substantial frame and an underlying armoured enclosure.

'Some kind of new radar, LIDAR or shielding array?' said Johansson, uncertain.

She thought for a moment.

'Or something designed to defeat detection systems?'

Maybe it wasn't the armament. Maybe this is why the ship has drawn all this flak, she realised, eyes boring into the feed from the missile. *Maybe someone took real offence to whatever that is and decided it needed to be off the table, pronto.*

'Well, it makes sense to use a big ship if you were going to spin up something like that for trials,' she mused, leaning back, the computer unresponsive to her chatter. 'Old, but not obsolete, and with a big return.'

One of the ship's low-visibility identifying roundels, a dark grey circle with a lighter grey band around it, distinguishable in all imaging modes, began to creep into view; the *Prompt* was moving slightly, relative to the missile. Johansson put her hand back on the controls and nudged the missile sideways, and a little more of the secondary bridge came into view in the corner of the screen. A few deep gouges were torn in the armour on the sides, suggesting glancing hits, but, aside from the usual wear and tear imparted by space flight, it looked sound. A large heat bloom gave away the position of the standby reactor, which seemed to be operating normally.

She watched, a degree of morbid curiosity arising, as the camera picked out new details. The forward ring showed signs of more significant damage, and in places entire plates of its armour had been smashed to pieces, leaving the structure underneath exposed. No intact offensive emplacements were visible; mountings remained in a few places, and just craters in others. One splintered Telegraph jutted out from a union point, where the protective elements of the front ring joined over the main elements of the underlying structure. It had made its way through the outer armour, dispersing its energy violently as it went, forming a huge crater, but its remainder had only been enough to wedge it in the structure of the ring itself.

But the rings did their job. And at least the core of the ship dodged the worst of it. One solid hit there and we'd probably have two ships, not one.

The incoming munitions had marched rearwards, doing a fine number on the starboard tank assembly but seemingly missing the port, and onto the rear ring. The leading edge of the rear ring, on the starboard side, had been shattered; the debris expelled from it, or perhaps the impacting weapon itself, had then hit the starboard primary reactor towards the tail of the reactor housing. Violent heat blooms erupted from the structure, smearing across the missile's infrared view.

'The core shield has been compromised,' said Johansson, her

stomach twisting into a knot, the sensation of heat and discomfort of her train ride surging back through her body.

Even the little of the fusion plant she could see appeared in some distress. Odd shading in places, where there should otherwise only be flat surfaces, suggested impact damage, and inconspicuous but foreboding thermal signatures, present where there should be nothing, indicated more issues. The only saving grace was that, from this angle at least, the port reactor station appeared free from heavy damage. But it was cold, not operational, and a faint haze around its nose suggested that it, too, had not escaped unscathed.

And I've never been involved with the mains. I just put holes in them. Mobility kills. Minimal casualties. But I don't know how to make them go. And I can't go out, can't fix that.

It appeared that the incoming fire had then shifted across the rear ring, obliterating much on its upper surface. Weapons stations, the second row of shield emitters, communications arrays, the works, were all either gone or damaged. Some had been hit so hard that they were practically unrecognisable.

Still very severely fucked. Just like me.

The ship's engines, which just protruded beyond the comparatively safe enclosure of the rear ring, had seemingly taken a beating as well. The image didn't show much of them, as the ring obscured practically everything but the tails of the large drive cones from the image's angle, but there was a faint and gritty-looking fog visible around the structures.

Could be coolant, argon, oxygen, or all of those. Or perhaps shattered armour.

It had obviously happened quickly. The remaining upper batteries on the rear ring had seemingly set about swinging to meet the incoming threat, but the response had been too slow, the remaining barrels and launchers pointing vainly in erratic and unrelated directions, like trees in the aftermath of a forest fire.

'That's why there was fresh ammunition heading up the conveyors,' she cheered. 'We were firing back!'

She felt a surge of pride and enthusiasm; an old Sark, caught by surprise, but it still set about slinging lead, just like they always do, until its last gasp.

'*Prompt*. One last thing. Whoever launched the attack knew our specifics. They used Telegraphs, so they must have known our position, vector, and timings, there or thereabouts. And our guns were up, in track, trying to put some metal out there.

'WSO Johansson,' she added, quietly, 'out.'

She lingered, the display burning its pattern in her eyes, as the dark of the room closed around her. The missile lingered, too, hovering off the beam of the *Prompt Excursion*, its scanners and imagers condensing the grim details to unerring ones and zeros, transmitting them through the void, unrelenting, the disheartening image unchanging on the screen. The ship, alone in space, captured for one last time from the outside, like the final photograph of a solitary being of a near-extinct species, on the brink of disappearing in a blink.

Johansson didn't need to see any more. The *Prompt* was dead in the water, its heartbeat slowing, and the sharks were circling. It was done, and she was done, she decided. She slumped in front of the display, a long, heavy breath escaping from her chest, her battered body starting to give way now that all seemed said and done.

The faint murmur of remaining hardware in the ring calmed her a little, like the ticking of a distant clock. The final dregs of the red cylinder were fading, like coals on a cooling fire, and the pain was intensifying. The heavy-duty blend of chemicals had staved off the worst of the pain, tiredness, nausea, and lord knows what else, but, as it faded, her temperature began to creep upwards, her burns began to ache, her pulse ran up and down like a yo-yo. The amalgamation of advanced silicon elements in the cylinder was at least helping to stitch her ribs back together, but it would only work if she stopped moving for a while.

'Thanks for the ride, suit,' she said sombrely, her index finger brushing the corner of one of the flexible protective plates embedded in its fabric.

She felt her muscles slacken slightly.

'Thanks,' she murmured, guessing the suit had expended some kind of relaxant, something it still had in reserve, just in case. It wasn't much, but it blunted a little of the agony.

'Maybe I should just fly the missile into the ship and end this charade,' she said slowly, as she tried to work out if she was joking or not. Her fingers followed her thoughts automatically, typing the words into the computer.

No, that'd be the easy option. They'd probably judge me more of a failure, then, as would she, and my records and remaining family benefits would be panned for eternity.

Her hands made fists.

No. Till death do us part, ship.

Johansson closed her eyes for a moment, the cool tungsten-carbon alloy of her suit's neck protector being the only thing that registered with her senses. She felt her breathing shallowing out, gently, almost comfortingly, her body slowing.

The computer beeped again, insistently. Johansson sluggishly lifted one eyelid, her head slumped on her chest, and then the other, before rolling her eyes towards the offending and intruding noise.

The display read, in luminescent green text: *PAYLOAD SUFFICIENT*.

'Tell me something I don't know,' she muttered, 'and leave me alone.'

Her eyes flashed across the display as she closed them again.

Something had changed.

She raised her head, her eyes widening, and dragged herself close to the terminal. Something was different; there was a tiny heat source, on the cool and idle port reactor station, that was moving. It was slowly working its way around the reactor's radiator panels, like a bee scouting the perimeter of a flower.

'A drone?' said Johansson, quizzically, her head jolting upwards a fraction.

If it can fix that reactor and it restarts, or if I can start it, then perhaps I can get access to engineering, she thought, her mind flaring. *Perhaps there's still a chance.*

'Investigate the drone, and potentially get out of here,' she mumbled, 'or die.'

Act! went her mind, jarringly. *Ship! Crew! Family!*

'This thing's done!' she hissed at the void, angrily. 'Look at it! There's no one here! It's not even my ship! It's just me! And look at me! Let me spend my last moments in peace.'

A memory flashed into her mind, out of the smog, clawing upwards like a mole out of the ground: *Not Your Problem.* Johansson rolled her head back, exhaled, and gritted her teeth. Her head fell, and she nodded, glowering, her body sweating and shivering a little as the now-uninhibited radiation set about freshly corrupting her cells.

'The *Not Your Problem,*' she repeated.

I don't want to impose that on her, she realised, a shudder flitting through her body briefly. Johansson closed her eyes. *A bright silver corvette, flitting through the stars, its shield arrays glowing a beautiful teal. She deserves better.*

The recollection ended, fading out. Her mind butted back into the conversation: *Idon'twanttofuckingdie!*

Johansson tried to take one long, calming breath but failed miserably, the jutting pains in her chest stifling her motion. She cackled quietly, at the desperation of it all, and raggedly yanked another red cylinder out of its holster. Johansson drove it into her neck, unforgivingly, and shunted the button on the end. She followed it up with a shot from a blue cylinder, discarding it, even though half remained.

Her head and vision exploded, and everything resembled a kaleidoscope for a fleeting, thrilling moment. She could feel her heart trembling in her chest, pushed to its limits, as another relentless mixture of animating chemicals saturated her veins.

Johansson threw up, convulsed, and slumped.

'Fuck,' she shouted. 'Fuck that.'

She heaved again, her body struggling to assimilate everything, and banged her hand heavily on the desktop.

Silence descended and Johansson didn't move for a minute. She coughed, arched her back a few times, stretching cautiously, experimentally, and slowly rotated herself to view the computer's display. Her head swam, the light from the screen blurring across her vision.

The last one of those lasted me, what, a few hours? she thought. *More in the bin outside, but I'm not sure I can take more.*

She waited for a minute, gathering her senses, and just watched the display. The missile had not moved, she noted, but the heat source had. It was getting warmer, too, as it went about its business. A rough cough escaped from her throat and she sat up, shaking herself down.

'RCOM, this is Johansson on the *Prompt*. I think I've spotted a drone working on the remaining main reactor,' she said, sounding like she didn't quite believe it herself. 'I'm going to roll the dice for you ... one more time, and keep at it until this monster breaks apart.'

Fuck them. I'm not doing it for them. You've been jacked around by them enough.

'Just promise me one thing, you pr– ... well, please, you have to, whatever way this spins out, tell her what happened. Don't leave her hanging. She needs to know I died, and where, and, if you're ever going to go to bat for me, do it then, and tell her what happened. I don't want her to have to carry those question marks for life, like I did. Over.'

Johansson nodded snappily and pressed the button on the pad to ignite the missile's rocket motor. The screen vibrated for a moment, then smoothed, as the motor lit, settled, and then cut out again. A few metres per second, nothing aggressive, just practically coasting along. Johansson touched the joystick softly; thrusters on the side of the missile puffed momentarily, steering it towards the bogey.

The camera slowly began to reveal more of the port reactor's details as the missile closed on the sponson. It was intact, but the camera revealed shrapnel had clipped some of its supports and housings, causing something to weep from it, and the thermal camera indicated that the reactor itself had been offline for some time.

Pump failure, perhaps, and scrammed automatically. The ship's electrical systems are pretty jacked, to say the least.

The missile continued its approach. Subtly, as if someone were watching, Johansson checked again that it wasn't armed. The marker still had a vivid cross through it, indicating the warhead was not in play. *That would be quite the mistake,* she thought, smiling a little. She cycled through the arming menus anyway, seeking reassurance, and changed the greyed-out and inactive *Proximity* option to *Remote trigger*.

'Easy does it,' she said, slowing the missile as it passed the strange array, at the tip of the reactor, and cruised towards the radiator section. The small heat bloom was there, on the perimeter of the radiator assembly, shifting a little.

'What are you?' added Johansson inquisitively, as the missile puttered to a stop, its thrusters puffing gently from its nose.

The optics blurred for a moment as the missile shifted to a lensing system capable of resolving such a close object.

It wasn'–

Johansson screamed, joyfully, and threw her hands up in the air.

'It's a fucking person!' she shouted. 'A fucking person in a spacesuit!'

Johansson's eyes goggled at the display. The person in the spacesuit continued inspecting the radiator section of the reactor, unaware of the missile's presence. They were struggling with a tool, trying to release a union of some kind on the reactor station. A small box, tethered to them, bounced around freely.

She watched intently as they went about their business. Occasionally, they would turn back, casting their torch in the direction of the gantries to the reactor, causing the tethered box to swing around them. Eventually, it would clash with the ship and bounce off in a new direction, its tether sometimes wrapping awkwardly around the astronaut. They would fiddle with it for a moment, returning it to a relatively still and safe position, and then turn back to the reactor.

Johansson cocked her head.

No. No, I'd never hear that from here. But they're there! I can see them!

She lit the missile's engine for a split second, bringing it closer to the cooling section of the plant. Johansson carefully guided it sideways, making sure it would pass the astronaut rather than bump into them, and yawed the missile, ensuring it would be side-on to the viewer, maximising their visibility of it.

The astronaut continued working.

No sound, no vibration. Can they even see it?

The thermal imaging system obfuscated what natural or artificial light there might be, making it impossible for Johansson to judge what was illuminated and what wasn't. If the astronaut was in shade, it would be practically impossible to see the missile drifting alongside.

Johansson carefully brought the missile closer to the astronaut, and flipped it, orienting its motor towards them.

If they don't see this, it's nudging time.

She cycled the console switch for the motor's ignition system to INACTIVE, ran the missile through a start-up sequence, and then reset the ignition system. A small cloud of propellant hovered behind the missile, waiting.

Johansson tapped the RUN key on the console. The igniters in the missile sparked and the cloud of propellant lit instantly. It burned rapidly, its bright cocktail of blue and yellow light unmissable in the sea of black. She flipped the missile, pointing it back towards the astronaut.

They were no longer there.

She waited, eyes darting over every inch of the screen.

A hand slowly appeared over the back of one of the radiator panels, followed by a shoulder, followed by an inquisitive helmet. Johansson could see a hot spot moving around as well, sweeping back and forth. *The torch*, she realised. *They're looking around with their torch.*

The astronaut pointed the torch directly at the nose of the missile. They clambered back over the edge of the radiator panel, cautiously, and then sat on its edge. The protective solar and thermal shield of their faceplate concealed their face, but Johansson knew they must be smiling.

A hand went up, slowly, and waved at the missile.

Johansson bobbed the nose of the missile, curtseying in acknowledgement.

A thumb went up. The hand then gestured downwards, at the reactor station, and the astronaut drew their fists together, and rotated one in a circle, like a fisherman winding in a reel.

Repairing, realised Johansson.

The astronaut then touched the side of their helmet, and then waved their hand left and right.

No comms. Figures.

The gesture changed again. An open palm, the other, with outstretched fingers, rapped against it twice.

Ten. Ten minutes.

Johansson watched with interest as the astronaut worked. Using a heavy adjustable wrench, they freed a panel from a break between the outstretched radiators. Underneath was a tangle of cables and pipework, leading to an assembly buried deeper within. The astronaut reached in, pulled a smaller spanner from their tool belt, and set about freeing something. A cloud of pressurised coolant erupted into space as couplings sprung free, momentarily making the astronaut appear trapped inside a vigorously shaken snow globe.

The astronaut tugged on the rope securing the box to them, bouncing it along like an errant puppy on a leash. They grabbed at it, opened it, and removed a bulky electric motor and pump unit. They reached back inside the machinery, and yanked the old assembly free, throwing it over their shoulder and into space.

I see that you're having the same kind of day.

Johansson could see that there were only a handful of connections that needed to be attended to. Three minutes later and the new pump was safely ensconced within its housing, and the astronaut quickly replaced the exterior panel, pounding on each corner once just to make sure it was secure.

They turned back towards the missile, taking a moment to reacquire it.

A hand went outwards, palm down, making a motion like riding a rollercoaster.

I want to return to the ship.

Johansson shrugged.

Well, you got out there somehow. Back the way you came!

Johansson waved her hands in the air, confused.

The astronaut made the gesture again.

Do I look like a taxi?

Johansson thought for a moment, as she looked at the astronaut sitting on the panel.

Have you been out there since the beginning?

The astronaut waved their hands in the air, looking for some kind of response.

Johansson made the nose of the missile bob erratically, its seeker tracing a figure of eight, hopefully expressing something resembling confusion.

A new gesture: a closed fist, pumped towards the chest, and then down towards the astronaut's feet.

You want me to come closer.

Johansson gently rolled her fingertips over the joysticks, and tapped the controls softly, caressing the missile into a closer position. All its camera was showing now was a radiator panel, nothing else. The astronaut was out of sight.

The missile suddenly rolled hard to the right, its nose scraping against the radiator panel. Johansson instinctively reversed it, countering the roll, getting the missile into a safe and stable position.

A hand appeared on the display, immediately in front of the missile's optics.

That crazy fucker, thought Johansson, grinning. *I am a taxi.*

A single finger jutted out, then made a spooling gesture.

Johansson laughed, understanding, and then ignited the rocket motor at its lowest possible output. The missile began to creep along, away from the nose of the reactor. The jutting finger moved upwards on the display, so Johansson followed suit, pulling back on the left joystick slowly; the jutting finger disappeared and was replaced by a hearty thumbs-up. The astronaut then pressed their palms together and made a small clapping gesture.

Towards the ring. Okay, and keeping close.

She pulled back on the stick a little more, ensuring the missile would fly out to the leading edge of the ring while hugging its contours.

It will pass near me, she realised, as it travelled along the length of the loading shaft.

The hand reappeared in the display, making a curving gesture.

Up and over. Okay, sticking close.

The damaged section of the ring appeared in the display as the missile traced a path along the ring and around its edge. The scale of the devastation was impressive; it looked like several Telegraphs had impacted in the same area, shattering a huge chunk of the ring, blowing it into space and the reactor station below. The obliteration revealed all the different levels in the ring, its corridors, power and ammunition loaders, all now exposed to the harsh vacuum of space.

How are you going to get in? wondered Johansson.

The hand reappeared, and pointed further around the ring, closer to its munitions shaft. Johansson peered at it, realising they were heading in the direction of where she had entered the structure. She cut the missile's motor, waiting for instruction.

The finger shifted towards a blackened area on the ring's surface. It looked insignificant but as the missile closed on it, Johansson realised it was a yawning gap in the upper surface of the ring. It looked like a Telegraph had driven clean through the upper armour and, having struck what must have been a comparative weak spot, it had passed clean through and on into the ring itself.

That's what I could see, she thought, *on the other side of the emergency door outside of the lift.*

A fist appeared, prompting Johansson to stop the missile. The camera bobbed as the astronaut disembarked, pushing themself off the missile and down to the opening on the hull.

They're free-floating, she realised. *No thrusters or ties.*

What a lunatic. Or the bravest person I've encountered.

The astronaut popped back out of the chasm, anchored their foot in a cable protruding from the gap, turned to the missile and shrugged. Their finger traced a vertical line, moved across a little, and then back down. They then banged their fists together.

Closed door. No shit. What about the airlocks in the crew quarters?

She turned the missile slowly and made it nod in the general direction of the nose of the ship. The astronaut moved in front of the camera, pointed at the crew quarters, and held up a fist, then stuck three fingers up, their torch casting erratic shadows as they moved.

Hydraulic, electrical and pressure failures.

'I guess you've already tried to get in everywhere,' she mused.

Johansson pivoted the missile in the direction of the airlocks in Engineering Access and the drive section. She repeated the nodding gesture.

The astronaut threw up both hands, then made a fist, and then stuck up the same three fingers.

Hazard. And hydraulic, electrical and pressure failures.

She racked her brains.

'There had to be a way to get someone into the ship without blowing more holes in it or depressurising the remaining areas,' said Johansson, rolling the tip of the joystick between her finger and thumb, thinking.

The ship was venting oxygen and bleeding more off seemed like a poor idea at the best of times. There was no way to judge how much was left, without Main Base Processing or visiting the oxygen stations themselves.

She racked her brains again and turned her attention back to the emergency weapons station.

Weapons station.

Johansson rocked the missile, grabbing the attention of the astronaut. They clambered aboard and she lit the motor, propelling the missile free of the ring. Heeding the astronaut's warnings, she flew the missile around the front of the ring, down to the launcher it had been fired from. Johansson brought the missile to a stop, just a few metres from the hatch it had been released from.

I hope you get the idea.

A diagram of the launcher popped up on the display. She tabbed through the options and commanded the launcher to open the tube the missile had been fired from. The hatch moved aside, on the screen, reacting quickly to her input, and the beam of the astronaut's torch fell across it.

Johansson rocked the missile back and forward a few times.

A finger appeared in front of the camera again and pointed at the tube.

Johansson pitched the missile forward again.

A thumbs-up, followed by a middle finger, flashed across the lens.

'Yeah, I'd be nervous too,' she said, smirking, pressing a button marked V.HOLD.

The astronaut pushed off from the missile, floating free towards the launcher, and grabbed the edge of it as they sailed by. They clambered into the open tube, head-first, and then lay still.

Johansson commanded the hatch to close, sealing the astronaut in the launcher. The portable generator pulsed as she shunted its power around to new hardware, activating dead sections of the missile station and its supporting hardware.

'I don't need much,' she said to it calmingly. She scrolled through the options on the display and selected a new type of missile for the tube. Hundreds of metres away from her, machinery graunched into action; sealed hatches began to open and close, and automated arms and conveyors began to move, pulling a different type of missile from its adjacent ammunition stowage and escorting it to the launcher. The mechanisms emptied the tube, foisting its contents onto a return track to the ammunition storage area, and loaded the fresh missile into the launcher. The display updated, indicating the new missile was up and on its pylon, ready for commands.

Moments later, in the corner of the display, the ammunition storage counter updated. It incremented by one, and then quickly reverted to its previous reading. Something in, something out.

They're in.

'I am fucking brilliant,' she said to the computer, beaming.

It beeped, confirmingly.

CHAPTER EIGHT

Adrenaline pumped through Johansson's veins as she bounded from the control room, swung from the handrail by the door, and fired herself into the ring's central corridor. She rocketed along, head still reeling and hammering, elation driving her towards her destination.

The rear ring was relatively undamaged on the underside. The central corridor was intact, and only the odd cloud of debris and collection of loose equipment impeded Johansson's downward arc. The air smelt acceptable, breathable, and the climate was tolerable. Johansson appreciated its comparatively sane environment, its safe feeling boosting her spirits further as she tore along.

A corridor speared off to her right, leading to an armoured bulkhead. The sign overhead said M.SR.CACHE, but the numbers next to it had long been rubbed off. Johansson wrapped her hand around the rail by the opening as she passed and swung herself into the short corridor. She slid along the wall, bleeding off speed, and brought herself to a jarring halt alongside the main access to the ammunition storage area. The pain in her side flared for a moment. *A little more careful, please.*

She stabbed her card and access code into the door, which had already detected her approach, and grabbed the access handle. She twisted, rolled it, and pulled it towards her, and the blast door quietly and effortlessly retracted upwards.

There was blood in the air.

Never mind that, she thought, suppressing panic.

Johansson flashed down through the weapons cache, row upon row of locked and secure dull green boxes containing missile after missile, the machinery between them inert. Markings on the floor: M.SR.3 and M.SR.4. She clipped the corner of the rail with a fingertip, changing her trajectory to follow the yellow hatched markings.

The conveyer and crane ahead were stained with blood, small arcs of it cast this way and that.

'I'm coming,' she shouted, pushing off anything she could get a foothold on, building speed.

One last corner. She hooked her foot into the pylon at the corner of the racking, spinning herself around it, slinging her body into the missile storage area for short-range batteries three and four.

Her astronaut was slumped in the corner, a cloud of coagulating blood hovering around them. Their suit was in tatters and an ugly gouge ran from shoulder to hip. The material was blackened, filthy, and the tears in its outer layers exposed angry bruised patches of flesh and small pools of blood.

Johansson landed, crouching, by the astronaut, and placed a hand on their undamaged shoulder.

'I'm here,' she said, 'it's okay.'

The body rocked slightly.

They're nodding. I hope.

Johansson carefully unclipped their helmet, rotating it slowly, so as not to twist their body, and lifted it clear. Piercing, vibrant eyes stared back at her.

'It looks worse than it is, but that was a terrible idea,' said the astronaut, swallowing hard. 'That machinery run is definitely not designed for handling soft items.'

She pressed a green cylinder to her neck, thumb popping the safety cover clear and pressing the button. Johansson just gawped, frozen, her mind struggling to comprehend the presence of another person, busy with the process of flushing away the sensation of hours of desperate isolation.

'I need to get out of this suit,' she said, gruffly. 'Some help, please, and bandages if you've got them.'

Johansson shook her head, bringing her senses back, and pulled the remains of her medical kit out of its storage pack on her belt. She helped the astronaut out of her suit, slowly removing piece by piece, trying to cause the least pain possible. Boots, ankle protectors, leg and knee sections, waist and hip modules, light and power, oxygen storage, shoulder supports, and arm modules, all drifted free, the damage not inhibiting their removal.

Johansson still hadn't blinked but found her gloves slipping off and her hands automatically tending to wounds, wiping, cleaning, spraying anti-coagulant gel, adhesive, protectant, and applying bandage patches. The astronaut nodded in thanks, settling as the green cylinder's contents pumped around her system.

'Pretty wild ride you put on for me there, but the timing was perfect,' she said, confidently, as Johansson cautiously wiped blood, sweat and dirt from the astronaut's face. She looked back at her, eyes narrowing for a moment. 'And you are?'

'I'm Johansson, from the *Hard Target*,' she said, trying to sound calm and composed. 'I am its Weapons System Officer. Or was.'

'I see,' she responded, her brow furrowing a fraction. 'Okay. You can call me Law.'

She extended a bruised hand and Johansson shook it gently, the sensation of warm skin against hers causing a calmative haze to descend for a moment. She paused, their eyes locking for a second;

they nodded at each other, silently acknowledging the day's turmoil and trials.

'How long have you been out there?' said Johansson, resuming her wiping.

'Right from the very start of this escapade,' Law responded, rolling her head, testing herself. She looked down at the display on her wrist. 'Three hours and forty-two minutes.'

'That's quite the spacewalk,' said Johansson, binning the now-filthy cloth and grabbing another.

She cocked her head, her motion slowing for a second. Law put a hand up, preemptively. 'No questions. Where are we, what's going on, that kind of thing. You know the drill.'

Yes, but. And do I?

Johansson frowned, and then nodded, but she sensed intrigue was written all over her face in sky-high flashing red letters.

'Maybe later,' said Law, casting a wary eye over her. Johansson's close-fitting in-ship suit was battered, its blue outer fabric surface marred, singed and torn at multiple points, its external components heavily damaged, dark patches in places, and fresher blood had seeped through in several areas. Her head and neck were bruised, mottled and bloodied as well, and her cropped hair was flecked with blood, oil, grease and debris.

'You look like how I look and feel,' said Law, a blunt smile creeping across her face. 'Suffice it to say that the day hasn't gone to plan?'

Johansson nodded, looking back at her, studying Law's suit. A dull silver-grey colour, not a flight or engineering get-up.

'What is your role on this ship?' said Johansson, curiosity finally overwhelming her.

'Operations Executive,' said Law. 'I'm your new higher-ranking worst nightmare.'

Set myself up for that one. Add it to the pile.

Johansson looked away briefly, shoulders slumping, as the

fleeting joy of discovering another crew member was suddenly over-written by an overwhelming urge for food, sleep, medical attention, and to be in a space that wasn't trying to kill her every ten minutes. She sighed, exasperated.

Law rose, testing her movement, and put her hand on Johansson's shoulder.

'Look,' she said, pausing for a moment, mulling her choice of words carefully, practically chewing on them. 'The situation isn't great. But it is salvageable. I'll get us out of this.'

Johansson's chin dipped a little, acknowledging Law. She leant back against the wall, revelling momentarily in the support and sensation of not having to move, and then shrugged.

'What happened?' she asked.

A scowl flashed across Law's face. 'We were attacked. You've seen the state of the ship, the damage inflicted.'

'Wh–'

Law cut her off. 'Look, don't waste your time. If you ask more questions, I might as well put you in that loader and fire you into space. If I start talking, I might as well load myself into it instead.'

Johansson grimaced, then sighed again.

Great. But at least you're not on your own. Just do your job: observe, orient, decide, act.

'Okay. I've skipped the dying part of today several times, so I might as well continue that trend. What do you need, how can I help?'

Law nodded. 'Good. Tell me what you know about the status of the ship and its crew.'

Johansson baulked for a moment. *You're relying on me for that?* she thought, surprised. *I'd hope you know more than me.*

She lowered herself onto a bench and anchored herself to it, seeking more respite for her weary body, and paused for a moment.

'Okay,' said Johansson, trying to push the clouds in her mind aside. 'From inside, the bridge is intact but inoperative. The secondary bridge might as well be considered a total loss. The crew quarters, living spaces, those all seem okay. There's a standby reactor up front which is running, and the batteries are charging.'

'Good,' said Law, her face expressionless.

'Local is seemingly okay up front as well,' added Johansson. 'There's no Main in effect but air, heat, power, that's present and correct in a lot of places.'

Law nodded, ticking mental boxes.

'Things get pretty ragged, pretty quickly, once you get beyond the bridges. The front ring has been hit, the oxygen and propellant tanks and facilities have been damaged on the starboard side, and the ship is venting, maybe enough to put us in this spin.'

'I've seen that. The port ones are okay and don't appear to be venting. Looks like the self-sealing systems have done their job in a lot of instances.'

Johansson hesitated for a moment, unsure if she should continue. Law wagged her hand at her, prompting her.

'The starboard reactor, that's just gone. It looked like it took a cloud of debris, or what was left of a Telegraph, straight to the rear of the reactor assembly. I actually passed it earlier; one of the blast doors had been compromised and it looked like the whole sponson had suffered from fire. It's hot down there, too.'

'Temperature or radiation?'

Johansson's stomach did neat flips again.

'The latter,' she said, blinking. 'But I wasn't paying attention to that, at the time.'

Law cocked her head, lowered herself, and looked at Johansson directly. 'There's nothing to be done about that right now, if that's the case.'

Johansson felt giddy, her stomach still churning violently, and put her head between her knees. *Such a stupid mistake.*

She ran her fingers through her hair again, trying to focus and clear her mind. *Concussion*, she thought, trying to console herself. *My mind's all messed up. Errors are inevitable.*

'Can you get me some coffee?' said Law, out of the blue. 'I need a drink.'

Johansson dragged herself back to the emergency bin and rifled through it until she found some of the self-heating drinks. She took the warm juice for herself, and a single coffee for Law.

'Where did you get this?' said Law.

'From one of the emergency bins in the corridor.'

'There are anti-rad tablets in there,' she responded, indifferently. 'I take them when working in the fusion and fission areas. They might take the edge off.'

Johansson exhaled through her nose, her shoulders slumping for a moment, and then clambered back to the emergency bin in the corridor. Silver foil packets lined one pocket, which had an orange trefoil stitched into its outer side. She inspected them and extricated two coin-shaped pills from their packaging, and then placed them on her tongue. The acidic taste startled her slightly, so she washed them down with the warm drink. Johansson bowed her head and tried to breathe in a controlled, steady fashion, before making her way back into the room.

'You were telling me about the situation behind the front ring,' said Law, her voice firm.

Johansson nodded. 'Starboard reactor, scratched. The upper area of the rear ring is devastated; I know you've seen some of it, but the impacts extend all over its surface. I haven't had a chance to inspect them yet, but the nacelles look like they've taken some hits, too. The view from the thermal imaging system wasn't great but I could see clouds around them. Probably ablative armour that's been vapourised, but it could be propellant or coolant.'

Law didn't seem that surprised.

'I can vouch for the damage to the rear ring,' said Law. 'Munitions were cooking off in some areas, and we definitely lost a magazine or two, but there hasn't been a detonation for a while now.'

Her hand waved from side to side, and then she made a little popping gesture.

'That must have been what I felt earlier on,' said Johansson, remembering the dust lifting from the deck.

Law nodded at her. 'What about inside,' added Law. 'Where have you been? Tell me what you've seen.'

Johansson parted her hands and shrugged. 'Power and Local from the front extends down to Engineering Access. Just before engineering, on the starboard side, it looks like there was some kind of explosion or impact in the main conduits. The ship's acting like it's severed in two, for the most part; no power or control from the front reaching the aft, or vice versa, but it's a bit patchy. I was trying to get into engineering but the main blast door on the starboard side is unpowered, closed and locked.'

Law's face darkened. 'You didn't go to the other side to check for access?'

'I didn't want to go anywhere near that reactor again, so there went the crosswalks; I figured I'd cross over using the ring, if need be.'

A nod, albeit one paired with an annoyed look.

'There seems to be some power up in the ring, though, so the fusion plant must still be up,' said Johansson, thinking. 'So, I don't know why the door's completely out.'

'We've fusion power, yes. But ... I'm not sure it's able to be distributed that way at the moment. Anyway, you couldn't get through that door if you wanted to. Coded.'

It was Johansson's turn to nod with an annoyed expression. She made sure to do it slowly, ensuring Law caught a glimpse of her frustration.

'Oh, and there are no internal or external comms, either, and none of the external imaging systems are working,' she added, inadvertently sounding slightly snide.

'How did you get into the ring?' said Law, ignoring Johansson's tone.

'I forced the munitions elevator on this side open with a loader and jumped. And up there, well, the distribution might be all over the place but some power appears to be making it to the ring, or it's residual emergency power, and my codes are still working, so some processing is going on back here, too.'

'You took the loading shaft up to the ring?'

'Yes. I didn't enjoy it,' said Johansson, snorting a little.

'That makes two of us who have been places we shouldn't today,' said Law, her face warming a little. 'And the missile?'

'Two of the short-range batteries reported back when I polled the ring's systems. I figured it was the easiest and safest way to get out and see what was going on. There were four missiles on station: two wouldn't launch, the other failed after several hundred metres. Only one missile was flyable, and stayed that way, but its main conventional camera was out. There might be others in the caches that we could bring into action, though. I've been using the portable generators to get things going, when needed.'

'Nice to see that someone still knows about the remote stations and how to put the ship to work,' said Law, her head bobbing up and down appreciatively. 'You've served on Sarks before?'

Johansson squinted and rolled her eyes as she tallied the years. 'Probably about nine years in total, with the RSF,' she said. 'A year or two on commercials.'

Law patted her thighs, put her hands on her waist, and looked in the general direction of Engineering Access, her brow furrowed.

'Good,' she said, without turning to face Johansson. 'That could prove useful.'

'Do you know anything about the rest of the crew?' said Johansson.

Law shook her head and shrugged. 'I've not seen anyone but you. Doesn't your suit have anything to say about the matter?'

'My suit has fuck all to say. It's been mute since I regained consciousness, on the bridge, apart from one single tone,' she said, annoyance flashing through her voice. She pointed at her side. 'And I think it needs a hard reset, anyway. Some techs patched a few glitches and, yeah, standard, a load of new ones got introduced.'

Law swung down, looking at the damage to the side of Johansson's suit. Tape covered bundles of split wires and damaged pipework, and the flexible armour woven into its structure was split and torn. Law could see that the suit's underlying components were also damaged, thin but strong slivers of metal jutting outwards in unnatural orientations. Beneath, tattered flesh and the mother of all welts.

'That interconnect's taken a hell of a blow.'

'I think I got thrown about pretty hard when we were attacked,' said Johansson. 'It's not completely wrecked, though; it's been dosing me, I can feel it. I think it's about spent now, medically, but it's still got some power. Motion augmentation still works.'

'I'm not sure,' said Law, glancing over it. 'Is all of this yours?'

'What?'

Law was waving an index finger over the fabric on Johansson's suit. She looked down, following, seeing dull red blotch after dull red blotch.

'Oh, yeah,' she said. 'I didn't need it any more, apparently.'

A realisation dawned.

'You're just wearing clothes,' said Johansson. 'Not a suit?'

Law arched an eyebrow and then nodded. 'I'd only just transited to the ship; I got called out for an inspection on the drive section so hadn't suited up yet.'

Johansson sucked down more of the warm and comforting, albeit sickly, drink. *Plausible*.

They floated in silence for a moment, contemplating.

'What about the exterior of the fusion station,' asked Law.

Johansson shrugged again. 'I didn't really get a good look at it. I saw some hotspots, but I was focused on you at that point.'

Law's eyes narrowed. 'Did you see anything else on your little sightseeing trip?'

'You mean the trip where I saved your life?' retorted Johansson, vexed. 'Yeah, I somehow couldn't miss those six big black panels. So shoot me.'

'Six?' said Law, unthinkingly.

Johansson's head bounced up and down. 'I came in from near the front of the ship, alongside the secondary and crew quarters. I wasn't going to go much further but then I saw you, and off we went.'

'Anything else?'

'What, apart from the ship spilling its guts into space? No.'

'Okay,' said Law, pursing her lips, then relaxing. 'That missile stunt was a good idea.'

Johansson smirked. 'I'm not sure if I've got any of those left. What's yours?'

Law pointed in the direction of the nose of the ship. 'It's imperative that we make it to our destination. But the ship's effectively not moving, and without controlled power it's going to get harder to corral and rescue as the battery backups in other sections fade.'

Johansson nodded, intrigued.

'If we get the port reactor going, and get some regulated main power back, then I can get us into Engineering Access. From there, we can restart Main and reestablish some continuity and control. And then, at all costs, we have to get some propulsion up and get down the road, to safety. What we can't do is just sit here and let the ship die.'

She glimpsed at the timer on her wrist again and mouthed something to herself.

Incremental counting, clocked Johansson. *Duration? Time left?*

Law grunted, annoyed, her display panel showing little else but question and exclamation marks as she cycled through its modes. 'I used to be able to run and fly this remotely, before it all got jacked to the nines. Now, this is just practically a toy that can only flip light switches.'

Pretty bespoke, in any case, mused Johansson. *I've not seen something like that before, not for a ship of this scale.*

'Can you do what you're saying?' she said, concerned. 'And do you genuinely think that we can bring this thing to heel?'

'Yes,' said Law, sounding extremely assured. 'We'll have to do without some automation. But the *Prompt* still has its older chemical engines, alongside the plasma nacelles. If I can get fuel and oxygen to them, they'll go. Even a brief burn would suffice. We only need a decent shove in the right direction.'

'Not the plasmas?'

'We can't employ those, no.'

'Why?'

'Too complex, especially now.'

Okay, thought Johansson, lifting her chin. *It's possible.*

Law continued, her pace quickening. 'Getting into Engineering Access and firing up Main should also bring the ship's automated repair systems back, so its drones and machinery might resolve some of the issues we're not otherwise aware of or capable of fixing.'

'And we might find the crew in there, too,' added Johansson.

Law shrugged. 'Maybe. At the very least, if you're going to be of help, we should get you some medical attention.'

Johansson glanced downwards, thinking, straw still firmly embedded in the corner of her mouth. She then looked up, straight at Law.

'Can you at least tell me how I ended up here?'

Confusion washed over Law's face.

'What do you mean?'

'All I really remember is that we arrived at a station, a Transit

Station, and that I was to aid in disarming a Sark, presumably this ship,' she said, her inflection questioning. 'And since that point, I've just been trying to find the crew, stay alive, and get us back to some kind of normality.'

An undercurrent of distress appeared in her voice. 'But I don't know why, I can't recall how I got here, or what's going on.'

Law crouched down in front of her and placed her palm on the side of Johansson's face. She recoiled, bewildered.

'Look at me,' said Law, her voice more assertive and harder.

Johansson shifted her gaze, catching, and then focusing on, Law's eyes. She was holding a small torch and started flashing it across Johansson's view, watching her response.

'Do you remember signing on for this mission?'

Johansson shrugged, exasperated. 'Flashes, if you press me for them. I remember being on a station, looking at a military contracts board. I think I spoke to someone. And I remember some things from before then. But it's all hazy, erratic. It's not like I've had many moments to think or recover today. And don't ask me when that was. One minute it feels like ten days ago, the next it feels like minutes ago.'

Law moved the torch across Johansson's face at a slower speed. Johansson could see the dark centres of Law's pupils occasionally, shifting inwards and outwards as she studied Johansson's own.

'Do you remember the risks, requirements and benefits?'

Johansson shook her head. 'I get the impression that I felt it wasn't going to be conventional, but I didn't envision this.'

'I don't think any of us wanted this,' said Law, as she continued to move the torch back and forth. Johansson felt woozy, and bile started to rise in the back of her throat.

'You've got a serious concussion,' said Law, flatly, stowing the torch. 'And those reds probably aren't helping your recovery. And the stress.'

'My suit's been doling stuff out, too,' said Johansson.

'That'll contribute,' said Law, casting her eyes up for a moment, and then nodding. She helped Johansson up and propped her against the wall.

'I am not sure why you are on this ship but, presumably, there was some kind of issue that required your hands-on expertise. Regardless, you are here now, and I need to brief you on some key points before we continue,' she said, her tone sharpening.

'The *Prompt Excursion* is experimental and highly classified. You will not speak of it to anyone. You will not so much as make a mental note about it. You see nothing. You hear nothing. You feel nothing. The Buffer area and central track are off-limits. You cannot enter Engineering Access without me and my explicit authorisation. And no more unauthorised external ship activity; if you fail to comply with that, or anything else, the result will be immediate expulsion from the RSF.'

She paused, thinking for a few seconds.

'And maybe even the ship.'

Johansson's head cocked as her eyebrows climbed skywards.

'One more point that you might need reminding of: O, E. As the Operations Executive, I have final authority. You do what I say, and if you disobey my orders, out you go.'

You don't say. Yeah, I remember that.

'I hope there's a good benefits package for this,' said Johansson.

'I can't speak to your contract, but I know that most involved with supporting this activity are effectively getting a year's pay and benefits for an outbound and inbound trip, some of which are just a few days' work. It's good money, and often straightforward.'

Johansson stifled a laugh.

'Well, it was going to be, at least. We're a bit beyond that now.'

'I'm not sure I'll be of much use,' said Johansson, quietly, 'but I know these ships, to a degree, and I'll do what I can to assist.'

Law crossed her arms and stepped back.

'You do that,' she said, 'and we might stand a chance.'

She tapped her feet on the deck for a moment, studying Johansson.

'You and I need to ensure that this ship stays powered. And I cannot stress how much we need to get it to its destination.'

Johansson was unmoved.

Law blinked, thinking, and then leaned forwards, a shadow falling across her face.

'If we don't, we'll change the course of humanity. And not for the better.'

CHAPTER NINE

'We've got to get into Engineering Access as quickly as we can,' said Law, launching herself into the ring's corridor. Johansson drifted awkwardly behind her, muscles not complying willingly with her commands, as they made their way through the corridor. She couldn't help but admire the way Law moved: no suit, no aids, but strong, balletic, and quick.

Not to be fucked with, she thought, as Law powered from railing to railing, traversing the ring with ease. The only thing that really suggested anything was amiss in its lower section was the occasional status panel, dotted between the offshooting corridors and access-ways, that was either garbled, inoperative, or displaying a dazzling array of red and amber lights.

I bet she knows what she's doing, too. Driven, like my daughter.

'How will we get back to Engineering Access?' said Johansson.

'We can't go the way you came in,' said Law, bluntly. 'Even if we could get another loader in that shaft, there's no way to extend its arm and stabilising legs to lift that door.'

'How about some explosives,' responded Johansson, half-jokingly.

'No,' said Law, firmly. 'The blow-out panels would let go and we'd decompress the shaft, and we might get stuck on the wrong side of an emergency portal.'

'And I figure going outside is probably out of the question, too?'

Law nodded. 'My spacesuit is too damaged and even though there are spares, we've no way to safely egress or ingress. I can't risk getting stuck outside again.'

Maybe we should just try it without suits, thought Johansson, smirking to herself.

'We're going to try the crew lift on the other side of the ship,' said Law, as she hammered along, Johansson lurching from hand-hold to handhold behind her. 'It's unknown, yes, but the lower ring is in better condition, and I should be able to make it work, so we can get to the other accessway into Engineering Access.'

'And if that blast door is closed as well?'

'That's what we need the port reactor for, among other things. It feeds power straight to the engineering section, so we should be able to sidestep any damage and actuate the door.'

'And the train should be working and available already on that side, which will make things easier,' said Johansson, smiling. 'Maybe the ship will play ball with us this time.'

'It'll do what I tell it,' said Law, snappily, throwing an angry glare back at her, barely interrupting her stride.

The response surprised Johansson as much as the dull blue glow that was illuminating the next corner. The pair sailed around it and slowed to a stop in front of another doorway. The door was open and, behind it, a lift designed for accommodating eight people was waiting. But the interior lights were off, the control panel dark.

'I'm glad we doubled up on the lifts on the later Sarks,' said Johansson.

Law grumbled under her breath and turned away from Johansson. She pulled a multitool from her pocket, flipped out a blade, and jammed it beneath the panel, prying it free. Johansson could hear harnesses being unclipped and clipped, and cables snipped, and then Law focused on her wrist. Johansson couldn't see what she was doing but it didn't take her much to figure it out.

Using that remote. That's pretty impressive access, if she can control the power regulation all the way to one relatively insigni–

'Don't hold your breath,' said Law. 'I can send commands to some fragments of the networks that are left, bu–'

The lift's lights popped to life, and a steady hum arose from the motors mounted in each corner of the shaft. Law shrugged and gestured to Johansson, and they stepped forward into the cage. Law didn't even touch the now-illuminated panel on the wall; she tapped at her wrist and, after what felt like too long a wait, the lift started to move towards the station.

'It's nice to have the *Prompt* on my side for a change,' said Johansson. 'Thanks.'

Law glanced at her and gave a quick, sharp nod as the lift's cage reached the core of the ship, easing to a halt with a soft *clang*. They stepped out into a short corridor, the air breathable and the environment normal; Law waved her hand downwards, slowing, and then made a gesture for silence. Johansson brought herself to a stop just behind her, head cocked, listening.

Around the corner, the corridor split into two. One, marked by a dotted red and green line, turned into a walkway that led to a small platform on the main rail line to the bridge. The other, marked by a dotted white line, led down a corridor directly to the port station for Engineering Access. Law drew herself up to the padded corner of the junction, designed to protect absentminded or inadvertently propelled crew from hitting something sharp and unpleasant, and hovered by it, fingers wrapped around the guide rail, listening. Quickly yet smoothly, she pushed herself forwards and glimpsed around the corner. Just enough movement to expose half her face and get a look towards the station, unobtrusive and rapid.

Johansson shrugged at her, arms up and palms upturned.

Maybe she's not quite right in the head.

Law drew level with her, eyes darting around the corridor and accessways.

'I can't see anything that looks like a hazard from here. You go in first and take a closer look,' said Law quietly. 'No point in us both venturing in there and getting fragged. Your suit can at least soak up some punishment, and I'm guessing you've some combat experience.'

Johansson scratched her head, perplexed, but responded with a shallow nod. 'Alright.'

Law's eyes narrowed a little. 'You've made it this far, but we don't know the full story, or what's pitched against us. A little caution won't do us a disservice.'

Less speed, recalled Johansson hazily, *more haste*.

She nodded in agreement again, exacerbating the motion, and started inching her way down the corridor to the train station. There wasn't much distance between the port rear ring station and the reactor sponson, so they could at least traverse the distance unaided, if need be.

I just hope it's not hot, thought Johansson, remembering the coppery taste on her tongue. She pulled her glove off, out of sight of Law, and looked at the upper surface of her hand attentively. It was blotchy and red. Her fingers were shaking as well, a subtle but intense vibration, but she couldn't work out whether that was a trick of her vision or an actual issue. Johansson tutted, flexed her fingers, and pulled her glove back on. It wasn't much, but it felt better than nothing at all.

She stepped forwards onto the station at Engineering Access, which was almost a mirror image of the starboard-side platform. It was dark, like its counterpart, and the torch revealed it was also empty, unthreatening, save for a similar complement of inert loaders and storage crates. A panel near the train track was dimly illuminated but the heavy blast door was closed and locked, its controls dead.

Quelle surprise.

Johansson made her way back to Law. 'Quiet as a mouse in there,' she said, nodding in its direction. 'No signs of anything, and there's no train, which tallies. No joy with the door, predictably, but I think the transport system is okay. Must be getting something from up front, through the rail system.'

'Can we get off the platform?'

'We can make our way down to the sponson manually, but I'd prefer to call the train from the nose of the ship. We can ride it to the reactor, and then back here. It'll save time, for one thing.'

Law nodded in agreement. 'And your energy.'

I'm dead tired, thought Johansson, wilting for a moment. *But not dead!*

They wandered out onto the platform together and floated above it. Johansson moved over to the transport panel and pressed a few buttons; the standby reactor was still ticking along in the nose, and the system confirmed that it could shift the required power from the track system on the starboard side to the port side.

'It'll be a few minutes,' said Johansson, as the panel beeped. 'At least something's working as intended.'

Law glared at her. 'You can hardly fault the ship for this. It's doing its best.'

'I'll reserve judgement,' said Johansson, looking around the station again as silence descended. Only a subtle and gently increasing hum, from the rails, indicated anything was happening.

'What is going on?' said Johansson, ambivalently.

Law let out a long, agitated breath, and stared at her.

'If I told you, it wouldn't make any difference. Aside from the fact that, shortly afterwards, I'd have to break your neck.'

Johansson edged away a little, using her toe to push herself back along the deck, and then stopped. Frustration flashed over Law's face momentarily, some internal battle coming and going at a lightning rate. She shook her head.

'I need your help, and I'm going to continue to do so, until we're home and safe, or we're dead.'

Her voice was cold, sharp.

'Well, I apparently signed up for whatever this is, so I'm going to carry on hel–'

Law waved her hand, interrupting.

'I appreciate that. But all you need to know is that it is imperative we regain control of this ship, and get it to its destination, at all and any costs.'

'It's that important?' said Johansson, Law's comment about humanity ringing in her ears.

'It's that important.'

Johansson huffed, turned away, and shook her head.

Suck it up, she thought, berating herself. *You're RSF. This is RSF. And you signed up for a mission. And, yeah, like some, it's FUBAR. Deal with it.*

'Fine,' she responded, agitated. 'All I'm really interested in is saving any crew and getting out of here. But I'd prefer to know what your role in this is, too.'

Law stared at Johansson, thinking. The rails began to sing a little more intensely. Law muttered something under her breath, slowly caving in to the need to relinquish something.

Got to give me something to go on.

'Okay,' said Law, her tone softening. 'As Operations Executive I'm responsible for overseeing the ship in these trials, primarily monitoring both its performance and the performance and condition of the crew. And, yes, that involves me getting my hands dirty, and occasionally injecting orders and commands that supersede those in control.'

'But this isn't a new ship to be assessed, is it?'

'The *Prompt*? Lord, no; it was getting on for thirty years in service before we initially recommissioned, up-equipped and renamed it, and that was, what, ten years ago?' responded Law. 'Hence the archaic layout and access in places. It's just a fudge, kit-bashing with military gear, to get it up and working. Don't look too closely at the details, that's all I'll say.'

Like the roughly updated nameplate, I guess.

'Why use an old ship, then, if it's so compromised?' said Johansson.

Law lifted a finger, just as the doorway from the station to the track began to open. She nodded in its direction, the doors parting to reveal the small silver train. It hummed up to the platform and drew to a stop next to them, its electronics purring gently. She slipped into the front seat and looked back at Johansson on the platform.

'Think of it like this: if a nobody steals a junker out of a scrap-yard, hacks around with it a bit, and then disappears, would anyone care?' said Law. 'But if someone builds a bespoke sports car, and puts it front and centre in a showroom with a famous driver, and then both vanish into thin air, well, that's going to raise a lot of red flags.'

Great, thought Johansson. *Fucking great.*

'And it was cheaper. We could equip two or three of these to suit for the price of building one new ship. Much easier to justify and sign off.'

It gets better, thought Johansson, smirking to herself. *To the lowest bidder, the spoils!*

'And funds weren't exactly forthcoming,' continued Law. 'Anyway, get on my train.'

Johansson exhaled, shaking her head, and clambered aboard the train. They both clipped in and Law pressed the button for the port reactor's shunt module; the doors opened again, and the train set off smoothly and quietly away from the platform, into the dimly lit access tunnelway. It was cooler in the tunnel, away from the warmer engineering and ring spaces, providing a little relief.

'How long have you served on this?' said Johansson, as the train cruised through the tunnel.

'First time out, on this ship' said Law, unabashed.

Well, that's fantastic. An unproven quantity on an unproven quantity.

'What di–'

Law waved a finger and shook her head. 'Enough questions. Task at hand, please, before we lose this thing entirely.'

The train sidled up to the aft platform of the reactor station. The sign over the door read R.SHUNT.P1. Law unclipped and vaulted from the train, making a beeline for the access panel and status display by the heavy metal door. Johansson squinted in discomfort for a moment, recalling the warmth and taste of the other platform, something in her head pulsing dully in response.

'It's still up,' said Law, sticking her thumb out. 'Power and some Local, so we can make progress here.'

Johansson lifted herself wearily out of the train and pushed off in the direction of the door. It was brown, wide, with white stripes and large red radiation signs on it. Above was an indicator designed to flash if excessive radiation was present in the corridor beyond, but it was completely unlit. Even the test light was out.

Just like the other. Lots of unconnected and erratic failures.

Law cycled the door controls. An empty gantry stretched outwards from the opening door, leading to another sealed portal that led directly into the reactor's shunt module. Law moved up to it, Johansson drifting along behind, and worked the controls. The door behind closed them, and then the door ahead opened.

A gesture from Law. *You first*, thought Johansson, sarcastically, as she swung herself around the door's frame and into the module. It was a little warmer, and the air tasted stale, but it seemed safe. Law poked her head in, slowly, and then followed her in, closing the door behind her, the marker lights on the adjacent board all shifting to green.

There wasn't much to see inside of the shunt module itself. There were a pair of seats, with semi-circular control panels around them, in the centre of a square room. Heavy panelling, a dark graphite colour, littered the walls, interrupted by substantial cable runs and pipework. Johansson craned her head back, looking at the mire of metal, plumbing and wiring. In front of the control panels was another heavy door, providing access to the gantry that led to the reactor itself, in the nose of the assembly. There was no noise, aside from the scuffling of Law moving around. She manipulated the controls and touched the screens, experimentally, investigating.

'Have you ever tried a cold start in a situation like this?' said Johansson, cautiously.

Law's hair formed an S-shape, the absence of gravity leaving it hanging in the air, as she shook her head. 'I've shut down, or scrammed, and started reactors on ships before, in flight, but not on ones that have taken as much punishment as this.'

Johansson bit her tongue, sensing a question about the attack would result in a lashing of some form.

'Is it possible without Main Base Processing?' she asked instead. 'My speciality is offensive and defensive systems, so this is well outside of my wheelhouse.'

Law's hair flowed in a pattern resembling an infinite symbol as her head bobbed uncertainly. Johansson could hear air being drawn through teeth again.

'It's not ideal, but we can do it.'

'And what are we going to do?

'These shunt assemblies soak up any excess output from the reactors, using heat exchangers, water storage, capacitor banks and batteries,' said Law, bringing up complex-looking control charts on the console, her eyes flicking back and forth. 'It saves us wasting it, eases the load on the exchanger panels, and provides us with a reserve and a way to protect the generators from spikes in demand.'

The console made an unpleasant clanging noise, so Law touched another section of the display, and it beeped in a more tolerable fashion.

'And it's that reserve I intend to use, to bump the reactor back into life.'

'Alright,' said Johansson, appreciatively. 'What do you need from me?'

Law indicated at a panel off to her left. 'Break that out, will you?'

Johansson brought out her driver and started undoing the bolts that were captive in the panel's frame. The driver seemed sluggish, but it metered out enough torque to break the bolts free.

'Underneath is a series of controls that we can use to divert the stored power in the shunt to the reactor ancillaries and control systems,' said Law, her arm waving up and down and left to right, as if tracing some unseen map.

Johansson nodded, freeing the panel from the wall, and set it safely to the side.

'I've got six rotary switches on the top, six breakers underneath.'

'Set all the switches to the rightmost position, then close all the breakers.'

Click. Click. Click. Click. Click. Click.

'Switches set,' said Johansson.

Clunk. Clunk. Clunk. Clunk. Clunk. Pop!

'Sixth breaker won't close.'

Law leaned into the screen for a moment, her hand flashing to her wrist for a moment.

'Try it again.'

Pop!

'Of course,' she said. 'Just perfect.'

'What's wrong?'

'Breaker six is the controller for Automated Reactor Supervision, the integrated system that helps power up and regulate the reactor. I was investigating some leaks and replacing its pump when you flew by,' said Law. 'The pump was blown out but there must be damage elsewhere that I couldn't see. It's probably a severed harness in the gantry somewhere.'

'This thing was cleared to fly with that damage?' said Johansson, surprised.

'I was against the clock and we had plenty of redundant power. I could easily fix it once in transit, which is why I was subsequently out there.'

Unconventional. But then what's conventional about this?

Law looked to the bulkhead doors in front of her.

'Let me guess,' sighed Johansson, a frown spreading across her face. 'We can trigger it from in there.'

'It's only a short walk,' said Law, a reassuring tone seeping into her voice. 'It will be perfectly safe behind the environmental shield. A few panels, a few plugs, done.'

Not the glow-up most would desire, thought Johansson, stomach swirling.

Law gestured in the direction of the doorway. 'You head on through and I'll cycle the access chamber, which will let you into the gantry. Proceed to the end of it and there will be another rotary door. You should be able to operate that yourself.'

'How am I supposed to know what to do when I get in there,' said Johansson, tapping her ear quizzically. 'There are no in-ship comms.'

Law looked at Johansson, exasperated. Johansson held up her hand, in realisation, and reached under the nearest console. Her hands roamed around for a moment and then pulled out an emergency manual stowed under the desk. It was captive, a plastic strap holding it to the metal frame, but a sharp tug freed it from its confines.

She held it aloft, triumphant. 'Scratch that.'

Law teetered backwards from the brink, the redness and anger flushing from her face, and cycled the first door.

'Alright. All you have to do is get in there and set the ARS to its run mode. That's it. Once you're back in here, I'll set about starting the reactor.'

The door hissed as its cylindrical body rotated, warmer air drifting out into the surge room. Johansson nodded at Law, shook herself down, and swung into the door's core chamber. She braced herself against the wall and gave a thumbs-up. Law repeated her input and the door assembly rotated, its opening now exiting into the gantry to the reactor door.

Johansson looked back through the glass and watched Law return her attention to the display panel. The gantry was warm, not hot, but the air was still and had a vague and slightly disconcerting taste of ozone to it.

You're not even in the reactor assembly, she reminded herself, *and you're behind the environmental shield.*

The inside of the gantry was illuminated with dull amber strip lights, positioned in the corners of the square shaft, which led to a substantial blue door. It was littered with warning signs, including the oft-repeated three-bladed sign for a radioactive source.

And what a source it is, thought Johansson, as she hauled herself along the gantry.

The door controls were active and responded immediately, the big blue door splitting from the middle, revealing a matching pair behind. Johansson guided herself into the chamber between the doors and pressed the panel in between. As the outer door closed, a gentle hissing, and a series of mechanical actions beyond both doors, made themselves heard.

A few more of those pills wouldn't go amiss now. But at least that red is doing sterling work.

The inner door opened and even-warmer air rushed in.

Johansson swallowed, hard, and stepped out onto the dark walkway. Her eyes adjusted, slowly, revealing a giant spherical shield in front of her. She could only just see the upper portion of it if she tipped her head back, its remarkably unbroken surface marred only by a single staggered seam down its centreline. Below her was almost nothing, just a void, stretching down to meet the lower reaches of the shield. It was made from compacted regolith, lifted from the Moon's surface, and metres thick, saving construction costs and time. Beyond it was even more shielding material, including thinner layers of lead and isolated layers of water, all of which were designed to protect the areas fore and aft from the core's continual radioactive output.

Machinery littered the expanse surrounding the walkway, most of which was confined to the same level. Pipes and cables stretched beyond view, under and over the shield, creeping their way closer to the core buried in the centre of the biological protection structure. Illumination was scant; this wasn't designed to be readily occupied on a routine basis. Johansson shook her head, trying to focus her mind.

Still a mess, still feeling out of it. Sort that later, not now.

A vague prickling sensation made her heart race.

Time is of the essence.

Johansson set down the manual on the walkway and opened the section marked MANUAL AUTOMATED REACTOR SUPERVISION (ARS) OPERATION. She started reading, occasionally pausing to rub the sweat from her eyes.

'3346.1I: Manual Automated Reactor Supervision (ARS) operation: Physical damage or outages may necessitate the manual operation of ARS. This can be accomplished through manual actuated controls within the reactor assembly, permitting safe start-up of an otherwise non-functional reactor. Please wear appropriate safety equipment and consult your ship's physician to acquire appropriate anti-radiation medication beforehand.'

Great. And here I am with a duff suit and a laminated manual.

'3346.1S: Manual Automated Reactor Supervision (ARS) operation: Proceed across the gantry to the reactor assembly. Remove panel marked ARS# and cycle the rotary encoders to positions three, three and three. Inspect for any other issues before replacing the cover and exiting the structure.'

This bit seems easy enough, at least.

She steered her flashlight around the room, trying to ignore the looming biological shield. More pipes, more conduits, more pumps, more pressurised covers, but no suitably marked panel. She turned around, looking at the furthest reaches.

There, at the very top. Great.

Johansson pushed off from the walkway gently and floated up to the panel. MAX COMP. WEIGHT 35KG, it proclaimed. Her suit's driver strained again, its motor hunting up and down, but it pulled the six captive bolts free. Three encoders were below the panel, just as the manual suggested. She thumbed them, slowly and cautiously, rotating each to its third position. Her hackles stood on end as something clicked over her shoulder, machinery in the chamber crackling into life.

The panel had drifted off, closer to the shield.

'Fuck that,' she shouted in the general direction of the reactor.

Fuck, I'm going to have to get that.

If the ship accelerated or decelerated quickly, the unsecured panel would turn into a lethal projectile and tear through the machinery of the reactor assembly.

Fuckfuckfuck.

'Alright, let's be quick about this,' she said.

Johansson placed her feet against the wall, squatting, and pushed off gently towards the panel. As she sailed past it, she grabbed the panel, wrapping herself around it, and stretched her legs and feet outwards. She felt her soles come into contact with the gritty-feeling outer surface of the biological shield, felt the imaginary heat, felt the immense power lurking beyond, and braced herself, eyes scrunched shut, pushing away again.

She bounced against the rear wall and released an almighty breath. Her entire body was shaking. Johansson struggled, securing the panel, concentrating on what was in front of her. She looked down, orienting herself to the gantry, and her vision suddenly blurred and warped, the height causing her mind to spasm briefly.

Or it's the radi–

She wretched, hard, one hand instinctively reaching for her stomach.

Got to get o–

She shuddered, breath ragged, and collapsed on the gantry. A minute passed, then two, the warmth of the chamber saturating her still body. The dull sounds of pumps and machinery coming to life, from deeper and deeper within, made her twitch back into action. She dragged herself to the door, down the walkway, shattered and spent, and feebly cycled the controls for the last door. Johansson tumbled into the shunt, the door closing automatically behind her, and clattered noisily against the wall, her head lolling, arms limp.

Something mov–

The silver corvette tore towards her, its engines ablaze, missiles springing from its launchers.

Her eyes fluttered, and a gentle smile spread across her face.

The Not Your Problem.

A shadow passed over her.

Miss you, too.

The world went black.

CHAPTER TEN

A feeling like a fresh breeze, on a hot summer's day, swept across Johansson's cheek. She sensed that she was lying on the floor, on her side, bobbing up and down, touching the cool composite panelling occasionally. Someone, in the distance, said something about how her vitals were barely registering. It had been hot near the core, and the background radiation was higher than it was elsewhere in the ship. Not dangerous, to someone fit, healthy and unstressed, but–

Her limp body was suddenly moving again. Up and off the floor, being pulled along, manoeuvred carefully into the cargo bed of the train.

Snippets of speech floated past her.

'–w more minutes and we'll get you patched up. I'm going to need you t–'

The train bumped over a joint in the track, and silence fell. She could feel the train's motors vibrating gently, her body heat soaking into its decking.

Great, thought Johansson, fading in and out like an expiring bulb.

The train slowed as it approached Engineering Access.

Johansson glimpsed, from a bloodshot eye, a different picture from before; the platform was bright, illumination streaking down, and the displays on either side of the imposing door were bright and alive.

Johansson's body moved again; Law was lifting her from the train and setting her down by the door. The red and white locking pins were still firmly in their closed position, but she occasionally discerned Law prodding at the displays, entering codes, and accessing the security and control subsystems of the ship.

Definitely has authority, she thought, swallowing dryly, trying not to move. *Definitely knows what she's doing.*

The locking pins rotated with a graunching, jolting motion, forged pieces of steel being retracted from one another to clear and free the door mechanism. Dust shook from the mating edges of the panels, pressure blowing it outwards from the door, into the platform, as the edges began to creep apart. The almighty steel panels of the door began to drift clear of each other, their interlocking teeth and linkages clanking as the electrohydraulics of the system, powered by the ship's port reactor, made lifting the door's tonnage look effortless.

What's behind door number one, pondered Johansson restlessly.

She could hear a panel being opened, small hydraulics pressurising, and packets and packages being torn asunder. Fleeting glimpses of arms moving over her, casting objects here and there, manipulating her body awkwardly and quickly. She tried to mouth thanks, but something was slowing her, softening her, taking the edge off.

'–eal bad day if we get back, but so be i–'

Johansson felt a stabbing sensation, and her body rolling. Some odd metallic noises, composites scratching. *Looking at my suit, are we*, she thought, as Law poked around, trying to extricate some kind of response from its battered electronics. She heard tape being pulled off gently and metallic scraping noises; Law was digging deeper into the fitted in-ship suit, occasionally bumping the servo-motors and their linkages with whatever she was exploring with.

'–oing to need you as much as I need her,' muttered Law. 'Just keep it u–.'

Johansson's head rolled as Law manipulated her, and she caught a view of another shuttered and locked door.

We're in the containment area between the platform and engineering, she thought hazily, eyes opening wider, pupils focusing.

'We're going to rest here for a minute,' said Law, sensing a degree of consciousness. 'Something's fouled the air up in there, so I've reset and started the scrubbers.'

Johansson tried to speak, to express concern about those who might be or might have been in there, but she couldn't. Law pressed a cold compress to her head, slipped some anti-radiation tablets under her tongue, and poured fresh water into her mouth. Johansson watched as snippets of bandages drifted past, old and new, along with patches designed for treating burns and gashes.

Thank you, she thought, blinking erratically and slowly. *Finally, some care.*

The world went red for a moment, and then black, silence flooding her mind, peace descending. She did not move or think, and could not, but the *Prompt* continued to spiral around her, creeping towards its end like a spinning top inching towards the edge of a table.

Stimulants steadily crept into tired but willing receptacles, and she startled back to reality, her head thudding against the floor as she tipped it back, her senses muddled and diminished.

Still going, she thought, surprised.

'How long have I been out?' she said slowly, only for no one to respond.

Johansson pulled herself upwards, her fingers struggling to make meaningful purchase on the sheer metal frame of the door, until she was in a pose vaguely resembling standing. Sweat was dripping off her brow, soaking her suit, blood was seeping from her nose, and Law had gone. It was deathly warm, and still, but there was a new noise in the background, coming from somewhere else. It was a shrill, angry racket, like the noise a train made when slowing from speed for a station, but it was persistent, unchanging in its volume or pitch.

She touched her fingers to her neck, sensing new injection sites. One of the green cylinders, and one of the blues, were missing from her pack. Fresh bandages had been applied to the obvious wounds, and some kind of gel had been smeared over the worst of her burns and marks. New tape had been applied to the suit's exposed internals, too, but both the battery and medical packs remained unchanged. She smacked her lips together: a strange taste, some unfamiliar pill, perhaps.

At least that's all something, she thought, feeling a little steadier.

Johansson scanned her surroundings briefly. There was the edge of a heavy blast door to her right, and one to her left, and she was in the space between the two doors. An emergency panel had been popped from the ceiling, offering up supplies and tools. She staggered upwards, like a fawn finding its footing, stretched to it, and freed some water and energy tablets.

She muttered, wishing for something more substantial, but was quietly glad for the sustenance and refreshment. The water, for one thing, helped clear the acrid taste and chalky energy pills from her mouth. She swilled with it, briefly, and spat out some blood and mucus. *Delightful*, she thought, as it painted a gruesome picture on the wall.

Johansson rested against the bulkhead, breathing slowly and a little deeper each time, testing her ribs. The bonding agents appeared to have done their work; there was some residual pain, but not the sawing, splitting agony of before. No doubt some of the painkillers were helping neutralise the worst of it, too, along with whatever the suit might still be putting out.

'Cheers,' she said to it, brushing her chin against the neck guard. 'At least it doesn't feel like we're at death's door now. But I'd quite like to go home.'

Engage until expended. That's what the instructors used to say.

Johansson shifted and started patting herself down, tentatively and gingerly exploring. The torch was still present on her shoulder mount, and the remnants of the medical kit bag were strapped to her waist. A few loose bits of paper in her pockets, a clean cloth. The driver was still installed in her wrist mount, along with several bits and adapters. Johansson rolled her wrist over and looked at the display embedded in it but it was still blank, more wires from its harness pulled out of their connectors and severed, and the few remaining status lights on the suit were dim to the point of almost being unnoticeable.

Okay. Engage until expended.

She used scissors from the medical kit to cut the corner off a self-chilling pack of orange juice and sipped at the contents. The coolness rushed to her core, settling her, helping clear her mind and steady her further.

Both doors are open, mentioned a voice, in passing, in her mind. *Engineering Access is open.*

She closed her eyes, idly wondering where Law was, and listened to the ship, her breathing slowing and deepening. The odd screaming noise persisted, afar, but up close, nothing but the gentle hum of pumps, the murmur of distant circulation fans, an–

Both doors are open! went the voice again, louder.

Johansson rolled her head to the right, slowly; the station outside engineering, the silver train sat at the platform, lights on, air moving, everything else still. She rolled her head to the left, but her eyes did not want to follow beyond the yellow hatched marking on the floor that indicated that, yes, the door to engineering was wide open.

It's just another chamber in this ship, get a grip, she thought, reassuring herself. *Law will be in there, maybe others as well, trying to save the ship.*

Johansson rested her chin against her chest plate for a moment, composing herself, her eyes pressed closed, shielded by the darkened hallway between the doors.

Just a moment's peace before I continue. I think I've earnt that.

Something wet touched her cheek. She opened her eyes, looked up, and an arm tumbled slowly past her, a cloud of coagulated blood and splintered bone following in its wake.

Johansson's eyes bulged. She screamed, her arms pumping against the wall behind her as she struggled to get up, to get away. An unseen force yanked at her collar, pulling her clean off the floor and towards the train. She choked for a moment, jolted into motion, and yelped. Her vision was a blur; whatever had grabbed her was moving quickly, without hesitation or thought. She moved her arms, weakly, but couldn't reach or touch whatever was dragging her through the platform.

The seat of the train impacted her lower back, causing her to arch in pain and sending stars through her view. Something tugged at her again, yanking her sideways. Johansson felt her suit tightening, clenching harshly around her waist and shoulders.

'We're getting the hell out of here,' shouted Law, her face and suit dotted with blood. Johansson recoiled, her aching muscles springing into adrenaline-shocked life and bulging against the seat's taught straps.

Jesusfuck.

'Jesus, fuck!' she shouted, coming to her senses, her arms and legs flailing around the carriage in alarm.

Law smashed her fist through the transparent red cover under the control panel of the train and jammed the lever to full power.

The train bucked aggressively, sparks showering from the rails as it accelerated, its motors whining in protest, the tunnel doors whipping open with a deafening *Bang!*

Johansson turned in her seat, back towards engineering. Two bludgeoned bodies, shrouded in thin clouds of blood, were drifting outwards from Engineering Access, towards the train. Their grey suits were torn, shredded, their eyes hollow, lifeless.

She choked back the screams as Law started yelling anew, as the train rocketed away.

'What the fuck happened to the–' shouted Johansson, knuckles whitening as her grip on the train's seat intensified, the crew still looming in the distance.

'Who knows,' interrupted Law, her voice loud but trembling wildly.

She was still pulling on the lever to accelerate the train, bending it backwards, distorting its mounting frame, but the train had no more to give.

Fuckfuckfuuuuuck, went Johansson's mind. All she could see was their contorted and blackened faces, the gashes in their suits, and the viscera drifting around them like a godforsaken heat haze in a desert's glare. *And their eyes. Pure terror, locked.*

The train screamed, its motors red hot, as it blasted past the port reactor gantries and on towards the tank area.

They're just specks on the horizon now, thought Johansson, mind trying to find some facet of respite.

'What are we doing?' shouted Johansson, over the roar of the train.

'I'm putting as much distance between us and that,' said Law, gesturing backwards with her free hand, 'as I goddamn can.'

Seems a bit moot. It's not like they're coming after us. I hope.

The train barrelled past the port fuel and oxygen tanks, pegged to its maximum speed, tipping precariously on its suspension as it hit a minor jink in the line before the platform leading to the living quarters and bridge.

Law yanked the lever under the dash rearwards, stabbed the button for the platform, and let the train's braking system take over. Heavy shoes swung into contact with its wheels, throwing ceramic materials and sparks away from the train, and smoke plumed from its underside. It slowed, bit by bit, and thudded into the buffers at the end of the track.

The train had barely been stationary for a second but Law was already making a beeline for the platform's bulkhead door, gesturing frantically at Johansson to follow her. She unclipped, scrambled free of the train, and pushed herself towards the door. Law reached it first, swinging around the corner into the living quarters, mashing the emergency close switch with her fist as Johansson barrelled past her, the train ticking noisily as its brakes, wheels and motors started to cool.

The door hissed angrily, slamming to the floor, and its locking pawls banged noisily as it secured itself. The access panel changed to showing red with white stripes, confirming the door was locked.

'What the fuck,' groaned Johansson, her voice harsh.

CHAPTER ELEVEN

The crew quarters were pallid, quiet, offering no relief or distraction. Law and Johansson hovered by the door, their breathing irregular and fast, sweat beading down their faces, pooling around their collars. Law leant back against the wall, staring at the ceiling; Johansson put her head between her knees, gathering herself.

She glimpsed upwards and saw Law's head tilted back. She was unmoving, frozen. The colour had drained from her skin, and her fists were clenched so tightly that her muscles looked like they were trying to tear through her forearms. She said nothing and didn't make a sound.

Her mind's probably replaying the past minutes over and over. Lord knows that mine is.

Johansson pulled herself up and made her way over to the counter. She extricated a cup of hot coffee from one machine and followed it with another cup of black tea. Still trying to process what happened, she proffered the coffee to Law.

'You'll feel better,' she said numbly, sipping on her own tea.

Law took it from her and quietly thanked Johansson. They sat in silence, unmoving, and drank. Law crossed her legs, and pushed herself down to the floor, in front of Johansson, lips pursed. Her eyes were red, but ablaze with more than fear and distress.

'Things are ...' she said, tailing off.

She shrugged, exasperated. 'Fuck!'

Johansson raised an eyebrow at her.

Law stared intently at the bottom of her cup of coffee, fingers drumming around its edge, thinking.

'Things are not going at all to plan,' she said.

'Understatement of the fucking century,' responded Johansson curtly, voice gritty.

Silence filled the void. Johansson stared at Law, unsure what to say or do, mind still obsessing over the grisly scene. Law looked back, her expression softening, shifting from stony to sad. Her shoulders slumped and her head rolled forward, eyes locked on the floor.

She said something inaudible, her head shaking back and forth. Johansson could see droplets of water in the air, drifting away from her like tiny droplets of solder, warping the view of the world behind them.

I'd expect better from senior command, thought Johansson, rolling her eyes. *But then you were doing similar, earlier. Don't be so harsh.*

Johansson pushed off from the wall softly, propelling herself over to Law. Tentatively, cautiously, she reached out and put a hand on her shoulder. Law's head tipped a little in the direction of Johansson's hand, so she lowered herself further, and put an arm around Law's shoulders, squeezing her softly.

Law swore under her breath, shuddering, the rest of the adrenaline wearing off. Her hair had matted to her face, a mixture of blood, not hers, and sweat plastering it awkwardly over her forehead. Cautiously, Johansson brushed the hair from Law's face as she pulled out the clean cloth from her own pocket. She dabbed here and there, shifting tears and blood, and sensed Law's muscles slackening, her breathing slowing.

She looks a bit older than me. To still be in the service, fair play.

Law's hands suddenly appeared below Johansson's neck and clenched the fabric beneath the locking collar for her helmet. Law muttered something and tensed, pulling Johansson closer.

Johansson lifted her hands, palms outstretched towards Law. Her eyes were strained but intense, darting around until they locked firmly onto Johansson's, becoming focused and still.

'We are going to go back there,' snarled Law. 'We are going to fix this.'

Johansson stood up, backed away a little, putting a little distance between the two of them, and pushed herself against the wall, upright. She rubbed her fingers into her eyes, tipped her head back a little, and listened to the ship for a moment.

Great, just fucking great.

She cleared her throat and locked her eyes on Law, who was slowly rising off the floor.

'What's going on?'

'I don't know what happened in engineering,' Law responded, voice dull and cold. 'And remember my rank and your obligations, please.'

Johansson grimaced, eyes throwing daggers at Law.

'What happened to the crew?' she said, insistently. 'What's going on with this ship?'

That's feeling like more than a secondary concern now, realised Johansson.

Law laughed dryly, her head thumping against the panel behind her as she rocked it back, striking it a little harder each time.

Johansson was tired. Law's laughing grated, its increasingly staccato nature jarring amid the silence of the living quarters.

To hell with this.

She slapped Law, hard, her palm cutting a crisp, clear line through the cloud of tears still circling her head. Law's laughter died immediately and, with two aggressive sobs, her chest heaved and she went quiet.

'Tell me what the fuck is going on!' barked Johansson.

'Oh, there's that bullish streak,' snarled Law, sneering. She prodded Johansson's breastplate firmly, sending her drifting backwards, putting some distance between them.

Johansson recoiled, confused.

'I took the time to flit through your records while you were out,' she muttered, aggrieved, throwing up her arms in defiance. 'And I know you get your hackles up when you don't like what's going on, when you're not in the loop, but you don't know the first iota about what I've done, and what I've sacrificed, to create this, to get here!'

Her eyes were shooting an unrelenting stream of daggers at Johansson.

'Oh, so you had time to sort through my files amid, you know, dealing with the small problem of being stuck on a dying ship with a slaughtered crew?' snarled Johansson. 'I'm starting to question your priorities!'

'God damn it!' screamed Law, fists clenched. She turned away, fell silent, and stared angrily in the direction of engineering.

Johansson let her boil for a moment, detaching herself from the unfolding disaster, and made some fresh tea. She watched the loose oddments floating around the room, but they only reminded her of the corpses in engineering.

She found herself rubbing her forehead again. It felt like the knives were slowly being pulled from her brain, the pain of recall lessening by the hour, the fog around previously obscured memories lifting slowly.

The concussion is lessening, maybe. Memory's still pretty abridged, though.

Law tapped the deck, distracting Johansson. Her face kept flashing to anger, then to a more sombre gaze, and then back, but the duration of the calmer expressions extended as she cooled a little. Johansson sensed her mind running at ten to the dozen, and passed her more coffee, carefully, then let her be.

I need you as well, she thought, sipping on her drink slowly.

Law turned to look at her, eyes roving up and down.

'Can I help you?' said Johansson, sardonically, the sensation of being under the microscope making her uncomfortable.

'What have you endured in the service, in your time in it thus far,' said Law, eyes narrowing.

'Thus far? You make it sound like I'm getting out of this situation,' snorted Johansson, her head rolling. 'But I'm sure you know that particular drill,' she added, waving her hand from head to waist. 'Starting with being glossed over for promotions, fewer opportunities, weaker benefits, ignored at points when I really shouldn't have been, the usual quagmire.'

Law continued to stare at her disconcertingly.

'I gave up hammering the ladder pretty quickly, to be fair; I just did what was right by me, which, well, didn't go all too well, ultimately. It all compounded in an ugly fashion. But at least I felt better about it.'

Johansson shrugged, unsure, unwilling to expand.

I don't know you. You just outrank me.

Law cast her eyes off to the side, looking down the length of the corridor.

'All of this,' she said, gesturing around her, 'is because of me.'

'By that, you mea–'

'Yes, the ship,' she clarified hastily. 'I'm responsible for this. It's taken almost twenty years to get this project to this point, in total. And you can imagine what that's involved.'

Johansson shook her head slowly, her shoulders lifting.

How can I? I don't even know what this is.

'I'm not sure that I can,' said Johansson, feeling like the floor was about to open up and swallow her. 'All that work doesn't just land you with a Sark that looks like it's crashed into an arms depot, does it?'

Law laughed as she crushed the coffee cup and tossed it to her side. 'No. You didn't sign a short-service contract with a six-figure paycheque attached just to support an old Sark-class ship that's been up-gunned. The non-disclosure agreement and operational behaviour requirements were almost sixty pages long apiece; condensed, we effectively told you to not look at anything too closely, if at all.'

Johansson swallowed hard, the tea suddenly tasting excessively bitter and harsh.

'So, there is more to this,' she said, weakly.

Law nodded, once, assertively.

'And, having foreseen some potential second-thought cases, we took a lot of collateral, just to be sure, for anyone even remotely involved. Your career, your qualifications, your home, and all your records, that'll all cease to be if you go sideways on me,' uttered Law.

No, thought Johansson momentarily, her insides cartwheeling suddenly. *Not again.*

Johansson baulked, the recall jarring and violent. She weakened and grabbed the edge of the table, trying to steady herself.

Law's voice continued in the background, her tone softening as Johansson visibly withered. '–o do what I say. I know it's a lot to take in.'

Not again, shouted Johansson's mind again, her stomach and mind still pirouetting unpleasantly. *I can't do that to her, too.*

Law had stopped speaking. Johansson closed her eyes and tried to regulate her breathing, tried to extend her memory's reach. The room felt to be shrinking around her, the ship collapsing inwards on itself, into blackness. No clarity; irradiation, corruption, concussion, medication, all conspiring against her, muddying her thoughts and feelings.

This is a nightmare. It must be.

'Still with me?' said Law, frowning.

Johansson shook her head violently, in the negative, struggling.

'This ship looks like a lost cause, and I'm starting to feel that way too,' she stuttered, pain and confusion wracking her body. 'And you're not helping.'

The deck plates shivered momentarily, in agreement, a judder running up and down the length of the ship. Law spread her arms out, placed her hands on a table, and bowed her head for a moment.

'This ship is far from a lost cause, and with the proper investment it will become our saviour,' said Law, 'I can guarantee you that.'

'You've got to give me something more meaningful to go on,' said Johansson feebly, followed by a single hoarse laugh. 'Otherwise, I'm not sure I can.'

Law nodded, and tipped her head to the side, looking away. Her fingertips rapped the tabletop rapidly, incessantly, and then the pace began to slow. A deep breath, then a slow exhale, and the clattering stopped.

'There was a project, started about sixty years ago, designed to push the envelope of space flight. Everything was on the table, as a means to extend our reach.'

Johansson raised her head, listening intently, the distraction starting to flush the desperation from her system.

'The biggest facet of it was drive technology,' continued Law. 'Direct nuclear, ion, plasma, pulse propulsion, the works.'

'All of those are pretty insignificant, in terms of the scale of space,' said Johansson, bluntly, agitated.

'Exactly,' said Law. 'Which is why, as the project developed over the decades, more outlandish and extreme concepts were floated, milled up, trialled, pushed out there.'

'And I guess a modicum of desperation was creeping in by that point?' said Johansson.

'Exactly, again. Anything that could get us away and out to more liveable, usable planets, anything that could ease the conflicts, the clashes over resources, and give us a more meaningful foothold in space. Anything to help get us out of the mess we'd driven ourselves into, basically.'

'And the *Prompt*'s part in these developments?'

'The *Prompt Excursion* has been a test bed for a long time now. That's why it's a bit of a patchwork of different eras and types of hardware. That's why it's got more recent advanced plasma drives instead of older nuclear thermal rockets, for one.'

'And now?'

Law shook her head. 'I can't sa–'

'Something beyond those capabilities?' proffered Johansson, cutting in, sensing the avenue coming to a close.

'Something beyond those capabilities, yes,' said Law, appreciating the out.

'And those panels outside?' said Johansson, opportunistically.

'Those are an integral part of the system,' responded Law, nodding. 'They are not offensive; they are key to protecting the ship in flight.'

'Okay,' said Johansson, acceptingly. 'And the reason the ship is now riddled with holes?'

Law tossed her head back, a disconcerting grin stretching across her face.

'This technology has not been perfected yet, and there are many question marks about its efficacy and capabilities. But, even so, if it can be made to work, it will transform space flight and our ability to travel.'

'And whoever doesn't have it will be left in the ashes,' said Johansson, reflexively.

'Which is why, I'm telling you, we find ourselves here. Disable it, destroy it, take it over; any of those would be preferable outcomes for those minded to suppress it.'

Johansson frowned. 'But how do they know about it?'

'Like all experimental technologies, there have been hiccups,' said Law, shrugging. 'There was an incident near Io, in which we lost a station and several ships. Despite our best efforts, it still drew a lot of eyes. Space might be big, but it's hard to miss that kind of maelstrom.'

'That's a heavy loss to cover up.'

'In material terms, yes, in crew terms, not so much. The numbers were ... limited.'

Johansson squinted. 'What are the Transit Stations?' she said, the memory springing forth.

'They are the sole hubs for ships with this technology. You don't remember arriving at Transit Station T1, at the L3 Lagrange point on the opposite side of the sun?'

Johansson rocked her head, uncertain. 'I remember being en route to a station, that much is true. All I otherwise effectively recall, in recent history, is waking up on the bridge, after whatever this was,' she said, pointing at her surroundings. 'There are some fragments, but they're mostly nonsensical.'

'And before?'

'Well, I remember who I am, sure, at least now, and I remember my past, my experience, my training, but even some of that's fractured. Or, I don't know, maybe some is missing. Hell, it's not like I've had much of a chance to reflect on it.'

'I'm sure you'll sort it all out, in time,' said Law, dismissively. 'But we first have to get the *Prompt* under control, under way, and to safety. After that, it will be someone else's problem.'

'I've nothing better to do with my time,' said Johansson, glancing at the bottom of her now-empty cup, some conviction creeping into her voice. 'Anything will be better than just being a sitting duck, and if you're serious about what this can do, then let's get it home.'

'That's the spirit,' said Law, breaking into a smile. 'And no more questions,' she added, tapping a single upright finger against her lips.

Johansson returned the gesture, using her middle finger, and laughed.

CHAPTER TWELVE

Law swept elegantly around Johansson as they busied themselves emptying the emergency locker in the crew quarters of anything useful. The few remaining tools, packets of food and bottles of water all made their way onto clips or into bags. Johansson even unhooked the fire axe from its mounts; it was a short but light titanium affair, with a dull grey finish and a finely machined, blindingly sharp leading edge. The rear of the head had a prying tip on it, so the axe could be wedged into the ship's panel gaps, doors, or anything else that needed shifting, and levered free. On the side of it was a magnetic pad, as the titanium itself was only weakly magnetic, allowing Johansson to secure it to her suit's tool pad, on its chest.

Law looked at her and raised an eyebrow.

'Preparing for a close encounter?' she said, confused.

Johansson freed the axe and waved it around experimentally.

'I'd prefer a gun,' she responded, smirking. 'But these are always useful, out here. We almost lost our captain, on the *Terminal Velocity*, to an emergency fire vent; I managed to keep the door ajar for just a few more seconds, so he could get out, thanks to one of these.'

She made a jabbing and twisting motion with the axe and sensed what felt like her limbs becoming heavier. She paused for a moment, extended her arm, and drew it back to her chest. Its motion was normal, but it felt like something was dragging it, slowing its action. She quickly checked everything was where it needed to be, and then called out to Law.

'I think my suit's finally on its way out,' she said, holding her hand over the status lights on its front panel, looking for any illumination in the shade. 'Can you check me over again?'

Law hovered over to her and made her way behind Johansson. Her hands moved slowly and carefully, over the rear of the suit, looking for new issues. At a glance, it appeared not dissimilar to a conventional flight suit, a dull tan fabric outfit with a belt and some metal pieces integrated into it, but a closer inspection would reveal that there was far more to it than initially met the eye.

For starters, although fitted, it was slightly larger than Johansson's frame; the cuffs were what really gave the game away, expanding from thin locking rings and tight elasticated fittings up to a perceptibly larger diameter than the arm beneath. And, up close, folds and creases in the fabric hinted at underlying graphene-titanium structures and pipework: cooling, heating, medical supplies, physical protection, motion assistance, all the things needed to aid a flight crewmember. In places, 3D-printed composite rails and magnetic patches provided secure attachment points for whatever was required.

Law started with the obvious damage, down by the gold-anodised interconnect on Johansson's right side, one of two that tied the upper and lower halves of the suit's structure together. It had taken a heavy blow, which had almost shattered it. The repairs both had made, which were tenuous at best, were just about keeping it together. A slender backup battery was just about visible beneath, and that too had suffered some damage. The interconnect on the other side was dented as well, but was otherwise intact.

'You've been bouncing around a lot since the start of this but, that aside, nothing's changed here,' she said, as she squinted and inspected the damaged components. 'The backup battery on this side, I think that's scrap; your mileage may vary with the other one, as you've been in this suit for so long now.'

Johansson grumbled as Law padded her legs down, all the way to her black-and-tan slender boots. 'Padding and plating are all still basically okay, and it looks like the mags in your soles are still intact. Might need a battery change to use those, though.'

'What about the main battery and medical pouch?'

Law glanced at the inner thigh areas of the suit, which contained two extended pouches, running from crotch to knee. One contained the suit's flexible main battery, which employed recyclable organic compounds, the other a medical pouch consisting of myriad pliable ducts, tubes and cylinders, connected to the suit's intricate pipework.

'Both still look undamaged, but I'd hazard a guess both are depleted, but I'm not going to remove either for inspection until we've replacements,' said Law. 'If there are dregs left, it's best you use them, just in case we can't get new ones in.'

'Getting my money's worth, that's for sure.'

How long has it been now? Five hours? Six?

Law nodded, leaning forward to inspect the suit's front panel. Only one or two status lights, out of some twelve, remained very dimly illuminated. Law leaned closer and could see the ones marked S.PWR1 and S.CPU1 were still glowing, just, like the tip of a match moments after it was extinguished. Another light, with the word DATA underneath, flickered intermittently.

'It's still in there,' she said, 'but only just. All of the primaries are out. Looks like it might still be capturing proceedings, though. Its cameras are still intact, the mics look okay; if we get a chance to break out its black box, it'll probably tell all.'

'It might be watching and listening, but it still hasn't said anything.'

'Well, it's been chewed up, and there's a lot of damaged wiring,' said Law, rotating Johansson slowly. 'If anything, it's probably so low on power that it's nixed most of its features to keep you alive and mobile. Either that or the cores themselves were corrupted or damaged.'

She inspected Johansson's alloy protective collar and neck ring, designed to interface with the suit's helmet, and found the locking surfaces marred and damaged.

'I don't think you can put a helmet back on. The guide ring and latches are all torn up.'

'That's okay, I'll just hold my breath.'

Law let out a short laugh. 'I think anything we might need to do outside would take more than the ten or so minutes you'd last in one of these, anyway.'

'I don't know where my helmet is, anyway,' added Johansson. 'It might be on the bridge, somewhere. I think I was testing it, as the head-up display was glitching after its update.'

'You might want to wash it, too,' said Law, pointing at the patches of blood, vomit, and sweat that mottled the suit's tatty outer fabric. Her gaze shifted to the exposed areas of Johansson's skin; there were myriad scratches, cuts, gouges and burn marks, some peeking out from beneath antiseptic gels and bandages, and areas were heavily inflamed and red.

'This suit has seen some action, hasn't it?' said Law. 'As have you.'

'Yup. It's kept me here, though, so I appreciate that. I think it has done pretty much everything it can, and then some.'

'There are pack replacements in engineering,' said Law. 'I did plan to grab one for you.'

She tailed off, her eyes looking away from Johansson.

'It's okay. You had more pressing concerns. And you've your own issues. You've taken a fair beating, too.'

'There might be spare suits down there,' said Law, nodding slowly, 'but they won't be fitted or calibrated.'

'I'm not sure I want to get out of this one and find out what's underneath. Fresh packs would do me just fine. Its silence aside, as you say, it still appears to be working at some basic level.'

'Mind checking me over, too?' said Law, rotating gently to present her back to Johansson. 'I'm worried that I might have missed something.'

'Sure,' said Johansson, as she cast her eyes over Law.

'I read that you were the one responsible for bailing everyone out in that skirmish over the eye of Jupiter,' said Law.

Johansson baulked for a moment.

Been a long time since someone brought that up in a positive light.

'I was there, yes.'

She moved her hands down from Law's neck to her shoulders, picking at the fabric, looking for wounds that had gone unnoticed.

'That was a good trick with the missiles, again. A neat solution to the standoff. You could have killed a lot of people that day and we'd not have blinked, but you chose not to.'

'I didn't realise you had that kind of access,' said Johansson. 'That's not in my regular files.'

'Well, part of my role here involves studying the psychological and medical condition of the crew; I have to be able to vet everyone, from nose to tail, to avoid any issues. As a result, I have access to a lot of fleet-wide data that others usually don't.'

'What kind of study?' said Johansson, as she worked her way down Law's back.

'Ah, anything really, that might be induced by, or related to, the hardware and flight modes of the ship.'

'Flight modes?'

Law shifted, paused for a moment, and then just nodded. No clarification was forthcoming; Johansson just rotated her and briefly looked over her front.

'You're all good,' said Johansson curtly, completing her checks.

Law made her way back to the centre of the room and resumed taking stock of their equipment and supplies.

'Did you use the emergency generator from here?' she asked.

That was only hours ago, so I should know the answer to that. Maybe? The loader! Yes!

'Yes,' she recalled, finally. 'I used it to power the loader that got me into the munitions lift. Burned that one up completely.'

'We could probably do with another, for convenience's sake, but there will be one near Engineering Access that we can pick up as we go past.'

Johansson swung herself over to Law, touched the table with her index finger, and brought up an overview of the *Prompt Excursion* on the counter's surface. The three-dimensional representation was detailed, its edges glowing white, but the model represented the *Prompt* in its original form. It was cleaner, leaner, and only equipped with a handful of cannon and missile batteries. Unsurprisingly, the mysterious black arrays were absent.

Johansson tapped the Engineering Access section of the ship.

'Has this changed much?'

Law shook her head. 'The main difference, compared to its original configuration, is that there are now two conduit runs and accessways down to the fusion plants, instead of the original one.'

Plants?!

'The *Prompt* has two fusion reactors?' said Johansson, taken aback.

Law bit her bottom lip and hesitated for a moment. 'Yes,' she said, a tinge of regret in her voice. 'Its power demands are far higher, so we stripped the *Ascent or Descent* of its fusion reactor and repurposed the *Prompt*'s fuselage to hold two. It was practi-

161

cally scrap after that run-in with the SFOS near Charon, anyway.'

Johansson's eyes widened.

Those fusion reactors are no joke, she thought, as she stared at the overview. *Whatever this is, it's pretty serious. Even our super cruisers only have one, and those things can suck down the juice. Okay, they might be heavier, but still ...*

Law glanced at her, then pointed at an enclosed unit near the main blast door on the screen. 'This is the main control room, which also functions as the emergency bridge; if you need to, you can operate the entire ship from here. Fly it, fight with it, whatever. This room can also be isolated from engineering, for safety and security reasons, if need be.'

'I've seen it before, but never used it,' said Johansson, head bobbing up and down in acknowledgement. 'What about using the primary or secondary bridge?'

'From what you've said, and the damage throughout the central structure of the ship, which seems to be causing all manner of failures and communications dropouts, the emergency command structure is our best bet.'

The view rotated, showing a cross-section of the structure.

'The primary area is split into two floors. Both are heavily protected, but the first floor is where most of the Main Base Processing hardware is: the ship's core computer, its redundant backups, and its ancillaries.'

'Has much changed at the rear of the ship, otherwise?' said Johansson, trying to get to grips with the revised layout.

'There have been some changes, but the basics are still present and correct. For packaging reasons, during one retrofit, we had to move the old chemical engines to what's now the outer points of the plasma nacelles. We wanted the redundancy but needed a bit more space. That's about it, really.'

'And those new shield arrays, are they safe to be around? You don't need to tell me any more than that,' said Johansson, hesitantly.

'There's no risk to you, provided you're inside their operating area,' said Law.

'I saw one was damaged, what about that?'

'I know. It's accounted for. We got lucky, on that front.'

'And do we know anything more about the state of those fusion reactors?'

'There's been some damage there, too. I can't tell you any more than that, at the moment. I wasn't in engineering for very long and what I need to look at is either unresponsive or reporting something garbled,' she said, a solitary finger tapping her wrist-mounted display.

'I meant to ask you about that,' said Johansson, actively trying not to remember specific details. 'What spooked you so much that you came careering out and collared me?' she asked, frowning slightly.

Law clenched her teeth. 'Some pressure had been building up in the control room, in engineering. Heat, I think, maybe some leaks. When I opened the door ...'

She paused, a distressed look on her face, and then shook her head.

'That's where they were, and that's what pushed them into the main area. I didn't count how many or look to see what might have caused it. The shock froze me, and then I just fled.'

'Better to bail,' said Johansson, rubbing Law's shoulder. 'It won't come as a surprise, this time, and distraction can be fatal out here.'

She rested a hand on the compact axe on her chest plate, its cold metal providing some reassurance.

'Can you tell me about the new fusion plant array?' asked Johansson.

The change of tack seemed to soothe Law a little, her speech speeding up and tone levelling out. 'Both of the tokamaks have been upgraded, and both have their own confinement structure and power hardware, so they can operate independent of damage to the other. You'll easily find your way around them, if need be; there are no tricks or traps. Hopefully, there are no serious issues. I just think the disruption to Main, maybe some kind of older fallback I overlooked, is causing it to try to combine the data from both into one series of subsequently useless numbers.'

'On a scale of one to ten, how badly do we need them?'

'There's no scale. We absolutely must have one, at the very least,' said Law, her voice stern. 'The ship will be a lost cause without.'

'Demanding, is it?'

'Very,' said Law, shutting down the terminal. 'Let's pack up and head back before anything else lets go. We've got to get the *Prompt* moving, and we've got to ensure the safety and serviceability of those reactors.'

Johansson couldn't help but notice that she was shaking.

'Never seen the interior of a ship after a collision or combat?' she asked, cautiously.

Law stopped dead in her tracks and looked at the floor. 'No. I'm not one for combat. I've spent most of my time on the technical and experimental side; our ships just tend to disappear entirely.'

At least some humour remains.

'Just remember that they are dead. You can't help them right now, and they sure as hell won't interfere with you,' said Johansson. 'We'll secure them, get them out of the way, and we can pay tribute to them later.'

Law looked despondent, her eyes fixated on the countertop and the cutaway of Engineering Access. Johansson patted her on the back and gestured in the direction of the platform. They drifted along in silence, making smooth but steady progress through the crew quarters, its light blue-and-white panelling making way for the clean grey interior of the station.

Only two trains remained, the one to the Buffer complex, travelling directly down the centreline of the ship, and the train that traversed the port side of the ship, to the ring. Heat was still coming from its motors and brakes, making a haze, after the mad dash back from Engineering Access.

'What is the Buffer?' said Johansson, swinging from the door rail and coming to a stop. 'I'd forgotten about that.'

'You won't need to use it,' said Law, responding quickly. 'It runs outside of the ship and provides access to those arrays you saw, allowing for inspection and repairs. I'm the only one that has access to it.'

'Meaning you're the only person on the ship who knows about them, and you're also the only person that can maintain and repair them?'

Law nodded. 'It's that confidential.'

'I'm impressed by the breadth and depth of your skills,' said Johansson, approvingly.

A tinge of pink flushed Law's cheeks for a moment.

'Well, then it'll no doubt amuse you to know that I also designed the system and built elements of it.'

Johansson grinned back at her. 'You and it must be pretty serious,' she said, merrily. 'I mean, I've no idea what this all is, but to have justified the investment to put it together ...'

Law smiled, blushing a little, and then snorted. 'Well, we got this far. But we only ever commanded a fraction of the resources and investment we needed to do this properly. What we ended up with just had to suffice.'

'A pretty bare-bones project, then?' said Johansson.

'Too many sceptics, too many concerns, for full-fat investment. But I've made it happen, despite having to rely on the lowest bidder in many a case. But if we can prove its efficacy, it could be the next step we, everyone, needs.'

So, it's not all about her. Okay, I'm in.

The pair floated in peace for a moment, listening to the occasional ticking and pinging from the still-cooling train, its metals and composites contracting as their temperatures dropped.

'I'm guessing that we're going to take the right track,' said Johansson, making a small explosion gesture with her hands, then drawing a finger across her throat.

Law nodded.

'The right it is, then.'

Law broke into a smile, took one final look around, and pushed off towards the train. Johansson hesitated for a moment, and then followed.

CHAPTER THIRTEEN

The train rolled slowly down the port track, its tired motors whining quietly, as Johansson brushed some dried blood off its handrail. She frowned at the rust-coloured splotches, which echoed the myriad on her battered suit, as the train left the station and plunged into the backbone of the ship.

They should make these things dark red, she thought, brushing her gloves off against her suit's fabric sections.

Law, alongside her, was quiet, her eyes flicking back and forth as the train rounded the first corner. Ahead, the tunnel stretched out towards the rear ring and the engineering area, only the blast walls interrupting the view.

'Looks like our high-speed run made the doors lock open,' said Johansson. 'Not seen that before. Mind you, I've never tried that. Or, you know, this.'

Law sniffed in response, and prodded at a few buttons on her computer, as the train proceeded. Pipework and cabling flared out of the steel grey walls, jarring and aggressive, the colours often lurid and attention-grabbing, as the station from the crew quarters gave way to the storage tanks. Small platforms that provided access to the bulk storage tanks, and its infrastructure of pumping stations, valves and safety systems, came and went, the breaks in the railings created by steps and stations being one of the few indicators that the train was moving.

Johansson stared, absentmindedly, at the path in front. The pain in her ribs had subsided significantly, but the burns on her skin were still painful. She sensed puffiness, swelling. Her fingers opened and closed, exercising the joints, still stiff from her nigh-on freezing start to the day and its subsequent exertions. Her stomach still ached, and occasionally caused her to flinch. She suppressed the urge to heave and collated herself, slowly, picking up pieces and putting them back together.

Still upright, still moving. And not alone, now. Engage until expended.

She closed her eyes and the now-familiar mental fog descended, like mist settling into a valley. The day's events, close and tangible, seemed mostly accessible, visible, like the peaks of church towers protruding above the murk. And most of her past, she was conscious of it, able to draw on it, as it rose above the gloom, like surrounding mountains.

But, outside of that, anything about getting here, what happened, almost entirely unreachable, she thought, the gentle push of the train soothing her. *Almost like it's selective. But then that's all much more recent. Maybe that's all it takes.*

The train passed another platform, the expansion of the tunnel into a room causing the noise to change, shaking her mind gently. Johansson chided herself, opening her eyes. It had been a serious event, no doubt a violent and stressful one, and she had been wounded and nearly died.

Who would remember anything after such turmoil? Cut yourself some slack.

Johansson tapped the suit's chest panel unthinkingly as the train passed the dull blue oxygen-handling platforms which, after a few heavy blast walls, were replaced by clay-red fuel tank access areas. Johansson's eyes rolled upwards, following the reinforcing beams for the exterior tank mountings as they traced around the perimeter of the tunnel, and closed her eyes, just listening to and feeling the motion of the train.

'Tell me about yourself,' she said to Law, head resting against the back of the chair. 'I get the feeling I might drop off if you don't, and I'm not sure I'd be inclined to wake up.'

'I generally try not to say too much,' said Law. 'I always figured that was the best approach, in terms of keeping me from inadvertently revealing details about my work. Loose lips, et cetera.'

She rocked her head from side to side for a moment, as if counting, and glanced down at the display on her wrist, watching some of the figures bouncing back and forth.

'And I preferred it that way, working on ships such as this, where I needed to keep tabs on the crew; I always find that people tend to present their true selves if they aren't aware of being watched or studied. We've all been guilty of going to the doctors and then not honestly describing our state.'

Johansson smirked. 'I once reported to the flight ops doctor with two broken metacarpal bones in my hand. Said I'd got it caught in the loading ramp for a missile. A momentary distraction, that was all. Someone in the background dropped something. Truth was that I'd been arm-wrestling with the comms guy and he flat-out beat me. I kept him at bay for a while but eventually relented. My hand hit the top so hard that I broke those two bones, clean breaks, right down the middle. The alcohol took the edge off the pain, but it took a while for my pride to recover.

A smile spread across Law's face. 'Did you get him back?'

'I ended up getting him to sleep with me, and I made sure he provided adequate compensation.'

Law laughed, the smile spreading to a grin, the noise seeming almost alien in the quiet expanse of the tunnel. Her head rolled free for a moment, relaxed, and she tapped the controls lightly, thinking.

'I never really envisioned getting into this line of work. I studied psychology at university. I just wanted to better understand people, to get the best out of them. The healthcare crisis put paid to a decent job in that role, though. I mean, I did subsequently work for some rich well-to-do types, but that got boring pretty swiftly. There were only so many uninteresting and lonely work-from-home types that I could deal with. That's when the RSF caught my eye; it was offering positions at Lunar T1, decent pay, decent package, that kind of thing.'

'Yup. Pave the way to a better future!' said Johansson, musically.

'Pave the way, indeed,' echoed Law. 'I probably spent two, two and a half years there, getting to grips with life in orbit and the conditions that space and off-surface service induced. The RSF seemed appreciative; I pulled some of their best assets back into line after the Perimeter failure and the loss of Coventry and Detroit.'

'Ah, yeah, the first time nuclear warheads had been detonated on civilian targets since, what, the late 2020s? And not even intentionally.'

Law nodded. 'Correct. The only saving grace was that it subsequently pulled the Russian National Alliance and China a little closer to our own interests, in my opinion. A bit more stability. I'd not call it peace, but it was better. And some of the technology that came from the subsequent technical exchanges ultimately let us put this together. China was way ahead of us in some areas, like field manipulation.'

'But we were first past the post with ... this?' said Johansson, a pointed finger tracking around the perimeter of the tunnel.

'Yes. The initial investment required was way beyond what most were comfortable with, and none seemingly had the conviction to push it this far. The budget dried up not long after, admittedly, bu–'

Johansson stuck a finger in the air, silencing her momentarily. 'Why?' she asked. 'Why did they cap you off, if it did hold so much promise?'

A pronounced huff echoed down the tunnel, and Law rocked in her seat. 'We were pushing a lot of unknown envelopes, breaking new ground, and there was a price to pay for that. Both in terms of equipment and people.'

Johansson turned her palms upwards, looking for more.

'Well, there was the first accident above Io, that cost me a lot.'

'But that was before the *Prompt* was dragged into this line?'

Law shook her head instinctively, then glared at Johansson for a moment, her finger tapping on the handrail at the front of the train, annoyed.

'I had a choice. I could either persist, and push through with this, or just leave us to sit around, burning up the remaining resources, until it ends in a bloody war over whatever dwindling essentials are left. I didn't deem the decision as difficult.'

Johansson cocked her head, her eyes narrowing.

'I mean, what's the acceptable cost, for us to get ahead, to avoid a catastrophic collapse, or worse?' continued Law. 'One hundred people? Ten thousand? A million? We've 15 billion people on the sheets now. And if we don't try, we don't push, that number will start getting a lot smaller at a pretty alarming rate.'

'But a few incidents, well, you know how that can cap something off,' said Johansson. 'I mean, planet-based nuclear power. Sure, not without its pitfalls, but, as I understand it, a few failures, a tirade of negative press and misunderstanding, meant we basically drew a line through our one available large-scale source of clean power, for no particular reason, on the grand scheme. And look what happened in the interim. And when fusion finally came around ...'

'The damage had already been done,' said Law, interrupting. 'Exactly. We had a way out, the right voices didn't prevail, and we

171

shot ourselves in the foot. Which is why this must succeed, demonstrably, irrespective of the cost, in my opinion.'

'There must be some limit,' said Johansson, coolly.

'As long as it's less than 15 billion,' said Law, smirking. 'it'll probably be better than the alternative.'

Johansson's eyebrows scaled her forehead.

'I'm joking, I'm joking,' responded Law, rolling her eyes. 'Anyway, I started getting tired of Lunar. I think the comparative isolation of space service exacerbates the need to move on, to change your surroundings. I made the run to Mars at that point, just as we were starting to open it up.'

'I've not been to the ground colonies for a long time.'

'We've almost five million people down there, now,' said Law. 'And we still need space, resources, and roles, for more, many more, and not just there.'

Johansson nodded, glumly.

'Anyway, ships big enough to require dedicated psychologists were few and far between, so I had to broaden my skill set somewhat. The government paid for me to bolster my qualifications with foundation flight and engineering, along with a smattering of medical training, then standalone degrees in physics and space flight.'

'Jesus,' said Johansson. 'You really are a hot ticket, and they evidently thought similar back then.'

'I know, right? That's what I thought of myself too,' she added, eyes bright. 'And with that, they dispatched me on some fairly routine service work; I'd tag along on cargo runs, crew transfers, that kind of thing, building up some experience, presenting papers on aspects I thought interesting. I think that drew some attention from researchers higher up the chain because the next posting was to a military vessel. Just a patrolling corvette, nothing fancy, but a much higher-stress situation and far more complicated.'

'And the leap to this?' said Johansson, as the train rolled slowly towards the undamaged reactor platform.

'Well, two of the facets that had a big impact on psychological conditions in spaceflight were time and distance. I started collaborating with RSF engineers about alternative drive systems as a result, because time, distance and fuel were the real hurdles, in my eyes, to effective space flight. A lot of the technology was already mooted, and elements of it were out there, and I ended up working to combine two separate ideas to deliver a new and functional concept, one unlike anything else.'

'Sounds like you've been at it for a while.'

Law nodded furiously. 'That was, what, twenty years ago. The first test run was eight years ago, thereabouts. And the concept needed a lot more work. But we're here, now.'

'I get the feeling you're going to need a lot of time to report back on this one.'

Law snorted.

'I don't think anyone was expecting this. But, yes, I suppose I've always been more in the background, observing, designing, rolling things out, testing, monitoring; either buried in the engineering spaces, taking readings, seeing how it was bearing up to the loads and emissions that were assaulting it, or digging through the latest crew evaluations and medical reports.'

Johansson dipped into thought for a moment.

'But if this was so secretive, why are you running around using mainline ships, such as the *Hard Target*, to support this? Surely something dedicated would be better, more controllable.'

Law looked upwards for a moment. 'Well, the use of the *Hard* wasn't entirely by the book. The ship just needed the support, as quickly as possible. And the contracts were supposed to secure your secrecy, for one thing, hopefully.'

She hesitated, a look of contemplation appearing on her face for a moment, and then continued. 'But we also figured that cycling through different ships for support would reduce the exposure of those individual crews to the *Prompt* and our activities, minimising the chance of them realising what was going on, or spotting our technologies. Yours, for example: a simple run to a Sark and a station, for a munitions detail. You'd rarely see the ship from the outside, if at all, and you'd not be given access to anything to note from the inside, either.'

'Two Sarks,' said Johansson,' abruptly. 'There were two Sarks at the station. I think I spotted the other on an identification display.'

Law shook her head firmly. 'Just the one. Must have been a worse bump to the head than I realised.'

'And what about the crew of this ship?' said Johansson, feeling confused.

'The *Prompt* was only going from A to B, with seemingly nothing unusual going on, to get the data I needed. A similar story: we'd chop and change crews, pay them to not get too curious, and keep them away from anything they didn't need to be involved with. Minimal crewing, straightforward flights, take the cash, don't ask too many questions. Those who thought about it a bit more seemed to always settle on it being just about integrating more modern weaponry and systems into an older ship. Who would use an ancient ship for anything more involved, anyway?'

'And the automated systems, and repair drones, allowed you to keep it flyable while keeping everyone out of the areas that mattered,' said Johansson, slowly.

'Exactly, although a select few were informed of some changes, for safety's sake, and to support and maintain the essentials, but not to the extent that this would all make sense. And anyone who did clock something different, well, the pay and paperwork clauses made them happily overlook anything. Most weren't allowed past the engineering bulkheads, anyway; we just needed them to keep the rest of the ship safe and in shape. And then there were no unau-thorised overflights, no external cameras with revealing views, only flying in controlled and unmonitored space, docked with repair gantries over key exterior structures, that all kept the *Prompt* out of sight, out of mind. Not that externally it looks terrifically anomalous; the fusion section is different, and then there are the arrays, but most might deem them as some kind of physical shielding system, or anti-detection system. But the ship's only one part of the puzzle, so no one could work it out, even if they stared at it for a long time.'

Johansson pursed her lips, curious.

What is this thing? she thought again, the sight of the large panels looming over the *Prompt*'s superstructure sending a slight chill down her spine.

At least she's warming to me a bit, judging by the chatter.

Law gestured ahead and began slowing the train as it approached the reactor station. She set it to a crawl, unhooked herself, and propelled herself over to the panel by the main reactor access point. Johansson watched her, the screen's display changing and shuffling around, and then she bounded back over to the train, slipping between its rollover bars and neatly back into her seat.

'Port reactor looks fine, but it is still bleeding off some coolant. I think we're going to need it, depending on the state of the fusion plants,' said Law. 'I think both are still up, but we might need the output from this to get any of the engines going. Then we'll set about getting this to its destination.'

'Why do you think that no one has come to our aid yet?' said Johansson. 'It's not like we're unreachable.'

Law squinted briefly as she settled back into her seat. 'You're assuming that anyone has clocked anything amiss yet. And I don't think anyone could get to us, at least not in a meaningful timeframe.'

'But we weren't just out on our own, were we?'

'Any more significant a presence, anything more modern or serious, would have only served to draw more attention, to complicate things, and break the budget. Little would have helped, anyway; you saw the scale of the damage. Telegraphs can only be considered precision munitions if your target never moves unexpectedly. The whole area must have been saturated with them.'

'Were more on their way?'

Law shrugged. 'If we had stayed where we were, someone or something would have caught up to us in no time, I do not doubt that.'

'If we had stayed?' said Johansson, cautiously.

Law paused for a moment, and then nodded aggressively, her hand tapping the computer on her wrist. 'The only good thing I've managed to do so far today was to remotely command a burn before everything went completely south. It wasn't much, but it was enough to at least get us moving, towards some kind of safety.'

'Any idea as to who struck us, or why?' said Johansson, probing.

'Which government or military body doesn't have the power to strike us? The only ones left are the major players, and I'm sure most would like to take this off the board, or capture it, so take your pick. I can't say more than that, to be honest.'

Wouldn't be the first time we've merrily picked off other people's projects and set things back a few years or decades. I've pulled that trigger myself, a few times.

Law went quiet and shrugged. 'But then they won't have a place to inhabit eventually, so the loss will be theirs, and the problems and costs of this project will be justified entirely.'

'I hope we extend friendship, at that point, not firepower,' said Johansson, dully.

'It doesn't matter,' said Law, emphatically. 'We make this work and all the opportunities and successes will be ours, and we'll have a future.'

Johansson sighed heavily, sinking in her seat, as the train entered the final enclosed section of tunnel before the engineering platform.

'It's just down to you and me now,' said Law.

Johansson patted her on the shoulder, lightly. 'Could be worse. You could just have yourself for company.'

Law smirked as the tunnel started to widen, the noise of the train slacking off as the acoustics changed again. Johansson and Law stared stock straight ahead, into the gaping maw of Engineering Access, a coal-black tomb interspersed by only a handful of dull, intermittent lights, barely pinpricks in the dark. The platform itself was well illuminated now, fed by the port reactor, the crisp blue lights throwing odd and uneven shadows on the pale grey decking of the station. The train slowed, shunted against the platform's buffers, and stopped.

Johansson rapped her knuckles lightly against the side of the train, the thin panelling flexing under the pressure, as if testing her sensations. Law looked at her, listening intently. She, too, placed her hand on the side of the train.

A very slight vibration, like the edge of a glass being caressed.

Law glanced at her. 'Do you feel that?' she said, her voice monotone.

Johansson nodded, head tilted, feeling the vibration and listening intently. There was that distant but intense-sounding persistent shriek, interspersed by the odd moment of silence, and then a dull thud; it was like the sound of speeding traffic, from a far-flung roadway, caught occasionally on the wind and lofted to its listener.

'There's a noise coming from engineering,' whispered Johansson. 'A high-pitched screeching or screaming.'

'I think your hearing is better than mine,' said Law, raising her hands, unsure. 'The tokamaks do make a shrill noise, more so when pressed, but we shouldn't be able to hear it from here,' she added, a hint of concern slipping into her voice.

Johansson tipped her head closer to the floor, as if pressing her ear against the wall.

A little louder. Lower in the ship.

'It could just be a pump, perhaps; the fusion plants were showing some hot spots when the missile's thermal camera was cast over them,' said Johansson, voice still low, as if not to break the remaining silence. 'Maybe the ship's queuing up another surprise for us.'

They looked at each other, realising neither had summed up the courage to look elsewhere on the platform. *Are they still in here*, both thought to themselves, fingers clenched against the rail on the leading edge of the train's passenger compartment.

'I'll make a deal with you,' said Johansson, voice rattling a little.

Law nodded, grateful for the momentary distraction, eyes still burrowing into the gloom.

'You exit left, and take the left of the platform, I'll go right. Let's get this out of the way.'

Law shook her head violently, eyes locked on something in front of her. Johansson leaned towards her side of the carriage, looking forward, trying to see what she could see.

A single drop of blood was passing slowly in front of Law's face, her eyes wide and locked on it. She pushed herself back against her seat, knuckles white on the rail.

Don't look up. But, also, you're going to have to.

Johansson put her hand on Law's and squeezed it firmly. Law's gaze turned towards her. 'Come on. We need to do this and move on. They're not going to jump out at you.'

Law looked down at her lap and slowly unhooked herself from the train. Face down, she crawled over the side bars, lowering herself onto the platform, and stood, wavering slightly. Johansson followed her, setting down alongside Law, and touched her hand to her waist.

They both turned, cautiously, to face the back wall of the station.

Law put her hand to her mouth, stifling a scream, and pulled her knees up to her chest.

There they are, thought Johansson, mind afire.

She gagged, her hand finding her forehead and shielding her eyes, the other taking Law by the shoulder. It was a nightmarish scene. The two crew members had suffered heavy blows, stark white broken bones jutting free in places, their suits heavily stained with thick, dank blood. One had entrails spilling from their belly, partially wrapped around their legs and arms; death had not come painlessly for them. Both their faces were contorted, an agonising mixture of fear, surprise and anguish. The air tasted metallic; a fine mist of blood, interspersed with heavy droplets, coasted through the space, accumulating on surfaces like a ghastly dew.

They were no longer moving, at least; when Law had opened the door to the control room in engineering, the slight overpressure had propelled them outwards, into the station, albeit at a crawl. Unattended, they had simply made their way to the back of the platform, and then stopped on contact with the wall, their still-wet blood following them, impacting against the cold metal afterwards.

Johansson covered her face for a moment, breathing heavily. Law doubled over, teeth grinding against each other, and grabbed the edge of the train, its firm, unbroken and clean surface providing a moment's tactile respite from the sensory assault of the dead crew.

Law grunted, heaving. 'What did this?' she stammered, voice rising and falling.

Johansson exhaled heavily and touched her feet to the platform, grounding herself.

That's the worst bit over, she reminded herself. *They're there, we're here, secure and move on.*

'I'm guessing,' she said softly, 'that they were unsecured when the ship was struck.

Combat lighting, she thought idly, *guns in track, hard evasive.*

'Maybe Main snagged the tracks of the Telegraphs at the last moment and was trying to bring its guns to bear, or just trying to avoid them,' said Johansson. 'It would explain why all the gun batteries aren't in their transit positions, and the lighting.'

'Maybe,' said Law. 'I'm not sure. I was pretty busy at the time.'

'If the ship moved in the same direction as the incoming Telegraphs, too, their impacts would only accelerate its roll, pitch or yaw. We're pretty frail things, unfortunately, even in the suits.'

'I think I spotted some loose panels when I went in there,' said Law, finger pointing approximately in the direction of engineering, her eyes still cast unerringly towards the deck. 'And there are a lot of unforgiving edges. But ...'

'That would do it,' said Johansson, nodding. 'Even the lighter panels clock in at 15kg or so. One of those barrelling around, that alone could do this. More, well, that's a bad day all round.'

Law hesitated, but her breathing began to slow, and her eyes came up from the deck. She ran her hands over her face, pushed her hair back, and just shook her head slowly.

You should see what a lightly armoured ship looks like after it's been raked with 40 mike-mike. Dismembered limbs, trails of blood, clouds of composite and steel.

'What a waste,' said Johansson. 'This is a risky business, but I'd not want to get killed by an inanimate slab.'

Law backed away from the train and the wall, towards engineering, but was now focused on the crew, looking, processing the image.

'You okay?' said Johansson, watching her.

She shook her head, but her posture suggested elements of her training breaking through, tackling the situation. Shoulders up and back, hands behind her back, as if being assessed on the line.

That's it. Just fall back on the training.

Johansson made her way over to the emergency panel that had been lowered in the gateway between engineering's two main blast doors and dug through the contents. At the bottom was a large black plastic tub with several warning signs on it. She pulled it free, lowered it to the deck, and popped its lid free. Inside were several tall plastic black bags, with thick secondary linings, heavy-duty rubber gloves, masks, goggles, cleansers, and a small vacuum cleaner.

'Put these on,' she said, beckoning Law over to her. Johansson handed her disposable gloves, a mask and goggles, and donned the same.

'Do we have time for this?' asked Johansson, almost redundantly.

Law looked at the readout on her wrist, but it offered no guidance, aside from an ever-ticking clock.

'Let's set them at peace first, but be quick about it. It'll help,' added Johansson.

Law didn't move, lingering, which Johansson interpreted as agreement. The two moved quickly, collecting the bodies and slipping them into the tall bags, trying not to look too closely. Every time one of the open bags shut tight, the pressure lifted from their shoulders. Gently, they brought both of the crew down to the deck and secured them to the wall.

'See if you can find something to cover them with,' said Johansson, as she switched on the vacuum. Law made her way around the platform while Johansson swept upwards, the powerful vacuum drawing in the floating blood, clearing the air. Its clean white intake reddened rapidly, the coalescing blood ruining its virgin surface.

She looked down to see that Law had found a rough sheet, from a shipping container on the side of the deck, and that she was gently tucking it under the stowed bodies of the crew. It just felt more decent and honourable than leaving them in the cold, ugly black bags, naked and evident, on the deck.

Johansson put the stained vacuum in a disposal chute, trying not to look at the contents of its transparent storage tank.

Who the fuck thought that was a good idea, she mused, angrily.

Law lingered over the bodies of the crew, silent.

'Happy with the costs you're racking up now?' said Johansson, pointedly.

'Screw you,' said Law, anger coursing through her wavering voice, breaking the silence on the platform. 'Now's not the time.'

I might have overstepped the mark a bit there. Got to keep myself a bit more in check. Again.

'I'm sorry. I didn't mean that,' said Johansson, earnestly. 'I just meant that this is the true cost. The price that some are often seemingly happy to pay because they don't face it. They sign the papers, swipe the card, print the dispatches, send the munitions, send the ships, send the people, and this is often the reality.'

Law turned her back on the dead and confronted Johansson.

'And yet you still signed up for service,' she growled. 'You know the requirements and risks. This isn't some righteous game.'

Johansson scoffed. 'No, but we shouldn't just toss lives into the fray unthinkingly and without understanding. Even in the pursuit of scientific endeavours. Take risks, sure, but calculated ones, controlled ones.'

'But that's not your problem. You get your orders, you execute them. Anything else is a matter for those higher up the chain,' shouted Law. 'And we can only work with what's available. There will always be risks because we don't know everything.'

'Spare me the formal line,' huffed Johansson, folding her arms defensively.

Law threw her arms up. 'And what? Is that all you have? Do you think we're going to get ahead without cost, without change? What price do you put on things?' We're talking about fifteen billion people, system-wide, that are ultimately going to be shit out of luck if we don't come up with some way to readily explore, expand, to quell the conflicts, to create a flicker of hope!'

Johansson muttered under her breath, shaking her head aggressively.

'Look, it's a completely different affair when you're on the end of a gun,' she retorted. 'You've told me yourself that you don't have experience of that. The chain doesn't always hold in those situations. It's going to be you, or it's going to be someone else, and you've got to squeeze that trigger for the right reasons. You don't want unjustifiable blood on your hands. It will never wash off.'

Law's fists were still clenched, but no response was forthcoming. The hum from below intensified for a moment, making the loading dock quiver uneasily. Law glanced down, distracted.

'At least I know who I'm dealing with a little better now,' she said, meekly.

A modicum of anger drained from Johansson's face.

'It's a sore point,' she said, relenting. 'I've lost more people close to me than I'd like to recall, and it's been for very little, as far as I can tell.'

'Well, if you don't want to end up in the same boat, I suggest we get on with it.'

Another vibration rippled through the station, the machinery on the decking clattering a little in response.

It's getting more pronounced.

Law noticed the concern on Johansson's face.

'I agree. We should get on with it,' said Johansson, hurriedly.

Law nodded approvingly.

They both cast a final glance around the station and then stepped into Engineering Access together.

CHAPTER FOURTEEN

Machinery stretched upwards and into the depths, Johansson's torch barely illuminating that at the furthest reaches of the main engineering space. Law tapped her on the shoulder, guiding her beam. It clipped the edge of a panel, next to a ladder, and landed on a display.

Another Last Line panel, thought Johansson, recognising the shape of the terminal. *Praise be for redundancy.*

The air was warm, almost uncomfortably so, but the space was unlit, the equipment inert. Only a few intermittent clicks, and the occasional singing noise of a pump spooling up and then back down, indicated any life remained. Johansson leant back a little and touched the wall; there was a very slight tingling sensation, like that of a light static shock. She traced the frame of the door downwards and touched the heavy plating that formed the deck.

There's that vibration. Down there.

'Excuse me,' said Law, curtly.

Johansson had left Law in the dark. She quickly reoriented herself and cast the torch back in her direction, illuminating a slightly peeved-looking face and the sedately flashing display. Law nodded, her hands settling on the now-illuminated keyboard.

'Power from the port reactor has run up a lot of the ancillary systems, including the door, but a load of the breakers are tripped, and some of the Local is completely jacked up,' she said, tapping away.

'Doesn't sound like this end of the ship fared any better than the nose, then,' said Johansson, looking down the main walkway through the room, her voice echoing back from the wall at the far end of the chamber.

Law muttered something, keys clattering. 'Main looks to be all over the place, which explains the erratic behaviour of what's left. We're going to have to purge that if we're to make any headway. It'll probably cause a few problems of its own, but it should help fill in some blanks and get us on the right track.'

'You can access the core systems of the ship?'

'Of course I can. I'm the VFOE,' said Law, snickering, finger tapping the insignia on her shoulder.

VFOE, pondered Johansson, not recognising the rank. *Operations Executive. Very Fastidious? Vain Folk? Vaguely Fuckable? Vastly Frustrating? Best not ask.*

Johansson bit her tongue and moved closer, intrigued, to glance at the insignia. It was a long, thin, elegant silver dart, punching its way through two circles, like an arrow striking paper targets. One half of the patch's background was a dark orange, the other blue; in one corner was the pared-back outline of a ship, which was mirrored in the opposing corner. A little Latin underneath: 'Virtus Per Technologiam'.

'What does "Virtus Per Technologiam" mean?' said Johansson, curious.

Law laughed briefly, fingers still clacking away at the mechanical keys embedded in the display's console.

'It's the motto of my wing. It means "Power Through Technology".'

'That's not a support, tactical or operational wing, is it?' said Johansson, feeling a little restless.

Law hesitated for a moment, head bowing a little. 'No,' she said, definitively. 'It's a research and development wing.'

Johansson nodded once, sensing pressing the matter was inadvisable.

'Sounds like a Skunkworks affair, if there was another,' she said, aiming for a light-hearted tone.

Law laughed quietly in response, then glanced at the corner of the screen as the Last Line updated. 'By the door, the panel. Can you hit the lights? Most of the ancillary equipment in here should be live now.'

To both the left and right of the wide blast door was now an illuminated yellow panel, with a darkened lower section, which gently pulsed, casting an unpleasant glow over the harsh metallic objects looming in the dark. Johansson cast off from the edge of the steps by Law and the display, her body suddenly feeling far heavier, her movements requiring more effort and thought.

'I think my suit's batteries just expended their last,' she said.

Law continued typing, rapidly and incessantly. 'We'll tackle that in a minute or two.'

The lighting panel beside the door was surprisingly intricate. A single touch from Johansson caused it to shift to an overview of the entire room, showing every illumination source available, along with control systems and different types of light, beam and visible alert offered.

'What do you want?' said Johansson, bewildered by the array of options.

'There should be a tab at the top that gives you an "all" option. That'll do,' responded Law, her voice drifting back and forth as she worked at the computer.

There it is, thought Johansson, and pressed the option marked *ALL MAIN. ILL.*

Pow! went every bulb in the room simultaneously, assuming a spherical output of vivid but tolerable clean white illumination.

Johansson turned around, gasped, and moved slowly back towards Law.

'I've found another two crew,' she said, tapping Law on the shoulder as she approached.

'I thought I saw more in here,' Law responded, unwilling to tear her eyes from the screen. 'Are they ...'

'Yes, they're dead.'

One's an arm short. That tallies.

'Could you?' said Law, the sentence unfinished but its meaning intact.

Johansson didn't respond but moved off towards the mutilated bodies. She carefully gathered them up, stowing them with the others on the platform outside, while Law worked frantically at the Last Line terminal. Each trip back and forth took a few minutes, the equipment-packed expanse of Engineering Access taking some time to traverse; at its core, two deep wells plunged towards the fusion reactors in the belly of the ship, thick conduits around the perimeter of each providing cooling and current-carrying capacity. Around them, a metallic jungle of pumps, heat exchangers, blowers, building-sized generators, and heavy-duty electrical systems ensconced in brightly marked cabinets.

The murmur of activity intensified the longer Law was at the keyboard, more systems slowly springing back into life upon her command. Johansson hovered in the portal between the platform and engineering for a moment, listening to the hubbub, cleaning her hands with chemical wipes from the emergency locker. She sluggishly made her way back over to Law, who seemingly hadn't blinked or moved for minutes, her face locked with concentration.

'What's the plan of action?' said Johansson.

Law complained quietly to herself, the display changing

rapidly, over and over again, lots of red and lots of amber visible, even from afar.

'Okay,' she said, pressing both hands against the wall on either side of the display, leaning into the wall. 'Both fusion reactors are still running, although the output of one is fluctuating. But I can't tell more than that, or do much more, with Local, or Main in its current state.'

'Well, you said it needed resetting. Let's do that, get an engine or two lit, and get out of here before someone or something else turns up to punch holes in us. Or this place just falls apart.'

'It won't be too difficult,' said Law, gesturing at some cutaways and diagrams on the screen. 'It's an uncommon process but both the cores and the controls to isolate, restart and reconnect it are all up on the first level.'

'Assuming they're not all toast.'

'If it were that badly damaged, I don't think the ship would still be here,' responded Law. 'It's just scrambled, I think.'

'Something stemming from the attack?'

'Could be,' mused Law. 'Can you head up there? I want to keep tabs on things from here.'

'What do I need to look for?'

'You'll see an armoured series of panels. There should be an emergency hydraulic assistance system next to them, underneath a breakable panel. Pop it, and the panels should lift out of the way.'

I don't want to play with hydraulics again, thought Johansson, her leg twitching unconsciously.

'Alright,' said Johansson, propelling herself off the floor. 'I'll head up there now; I'll still be able to hear you.'

She crept upwards, watching the lower engineering floor roll away from her, marvelling at its scale. It wasn't like the long tunnels, past the tanks; they were just long but narrow, unremarkable. This was a wide, tall space, packed to the nines with hardware.

It's like the turbine halls at Hinkley Point F. And, unlike the rest of the ship, it's not smashed to bits.

Johansson spotted the panelled area as she rose above the gantry that led around the upper floor of the hall. It had the classic core component markings: flat black panels with small blue and white chequered sections around their perimeter, and a single diagonal white stripe across the main body of the panels. To the left, a small shuttered panel. Johansson rolled the shutter across, exposing a fist-sized glass panel, and hit it with her elbow; the plate didn't shatter, but instead dropped into an unnoticed gap in the frame, exposing a grey lever with a black handle. She gripped it and, bracing her feet against the wall, Johansson pulled on the lever firmly. A pronounced hiss from the panel was followed by a fine mist of something, jetting into the air, and the panel climbed slowly upwards, canting away from the wall as it rose.

'There's another set of panels behind,' shouted Johansson. 'Yellow and green ones.'

'That's the isolator wall, for electronic and chemical protection. Behind the panel you just opened, there should be a concealed lever within the frame of the door,' said Law, her voice shifting as she moved around below.

Doors within doors. Story of my life.

She slipped her hand inside the frame and drew level with the original panel on the wall. Her fingertips felt rough textured rubber, cylindrical in shape, caked in grime. She squeezed the object, pulling on it tentatively, and felt it shift inwards. A sharp push and *Psst*, the second set of panels began to retract into the wall itself.

'Four large boxes,' shouted Johansson, staring at the unknown. 'Some pipes and heat sinks.'

'Those are the four separate redundant processors that operate and support Main Base Processing. How do they look?'

'They look intact,' said Johansson, looking for burn marks, shattered silicon, fractured ceramics, or any sign of electrical excursions.

'But only one box seems to have any power, and its display is garbled, most of the status lights are amber or red.'

Law appeared, rolled over the barricade alongside her, landed neatly on her feet, and swung into position in front of the cabinets.

'That needs recycling. Something's scrambled that, and without any of the others up to check against, it won't work properly or sort itself out.'

Johansson nodded. 'Like the comparator processors in the missiles.'

'Right. Processor A says 1, processor B and C say 1, so everything's in line.'

'What do we do?' said Johansson. 'This is outside of my wheelhouse.'

Law beamed, and crouched down, gaining better access to the internals of the core housing. She reached over to the left of the first box, with lights on, flipped up a hand-sized cover alongside it, and grabbed a cast aluminium assembly inside. She pulled it outwards, rotated it 180 degrees to the right, then 180 to the left, and pushed it back inwards.

'Like the door mechanisms,' she said. 'Keep it simple.'

Something inside the panel clunked loudly, and a hissing noise in the distance suggested more afoot.

Law looked at her. 'These,' she said, waving, 'basically serve to hard reset each processor. They halt the core and dump the memory contents to a bin, and then restart it. But if you suspect something more serious is amiss, rotate the control 180 degrees and the system will physically pull the master storage modules and low-level controls, and reinsert fresh and unused components.'

The lights on the working panel began to shift in patterns, running from off, to red, to amber, to green, all flashing, and then settling into a steady state. Some were still amber and red, but the greens began to spread slowly across the board.

The display panel refreshed and text began careening down the page. The lights in the hall flickered briefly as the sole functioning computer began to test and assert its control over the ship.

'We need to get the others on, quickly, just in case,' said Law. 'The breakers have popped for those ones.'

Johansson could see the tripped switches, so she began flipping them upwards, fingers clipping two or three into line at a time. Every time she completed a bank, Law would pull and cycle the processor control, and the panel would start to come to life.

'I think this one's spent,' said Johansson, one breaking obstinate refusing to stay closed. Law glanced at it and shrugged. 'We will make do without. Three is better than none.'

A faint droning noise filled the cavity as pumps and fans began to extricate heat from the ramping-up processors embedded in the hardened cases. Law stepped back, scanning the boards and displays, and nodded.

'Looks good up here. Let's close it up.'

The two clambered down from the first level and Law guided Johansson into a large shielded room which had M.CONT daubed over its open access door in yellow paint. Inside, a series of large semi-circular control boards were positioned behind thick protective glass, providing a view of the engineering space. Their displays were turning off and on, the cycling slowing as Main Base Processing spun up.

There were rusty red spots on the walls, the floor, and on some of the consoles.

Blood.

Law seemingly ignored it, heading straight for the controls.

'Someone had a rough day in here,' said Johansson, noticing that a panel was missing from the rear of the room.

'Looks like your hypothesis might have been right,' said Law. 'Wouldn't take much, in here.'

'Well,' said Johansson, automatically wiping some blotches off the screen in front of her, 'at least these still seem to be working.'

Law muttered something and pointed at a basic illustration of the ship, in profile, at the top of the panel. A series of lights ran along its length, but only those from its tail to the front of engineering were illuminated.

'That's only for emergency diagnostic use, but it basically tells me that Main can't talk to anything forwards of engineering.'

'That'll be because there is a giant hole blown in the conduit,' said Johansson.

'Right,' said Law, cursing under her breath. 'But I didn't expect that to have completely severed the ship's overarching management system in two.'

'The damage could be the same on the other side.'

'Are you implying that it was intentional?' said Law, consternation flashing over her face for a moment.

'It sure didn't look like it originated outside of the ship. And all RSF vessels are equipped with charges designed to incapacitate or destroy them.'

'Maybe they decided it was a lost cause,' said Law. 'But didn't want to take out any survivors.'

'Maybe,' said Johansson, uncertain. She shifted, uneasily. 'But those should guarantee complete failure, for sure, unless they're interfered with.'

'Let's just keep it simple for now and deal with the task at hand,' said Law, in a consolatory tone. 'At least we've got this working, that's good going.'

A four-digit clock on one of the displays ran up to fifteen minutes and then started counting down, chiming quietly every time ten seconds passed.

'It's going to take that long for Main to sort itself out to any meaningful extent,' said Law. 'It's got a lot to unpack.'

'Do we have that much time?' said Johansson, tapping her wrist unconsciously, her eyes glancing restlessly around engineering.

Law looked at the counter on her wrist, which indicated that five hours and twenty-two minutes had elapsed.

'The damage is severe but, if the ship has lasted this long, I'm not sure another fifteen minutes matters. We don't have an alternative, anyway,' said Law. 'But we can do other things while it reinitialises, so we can get on the way quickly.'

'Tell me what you need,' said Johansson, her tone spirited.

'According to Main, the venting on the starboard side, from the tanks, is causing the *Prompt* to spin along its central axis.'

Law brought up the main display of the ship again, showing Johansson a render of the ship and the forces acting on it.

'Stabilisation is going to be a two-part affair; we're going to need to stop the leaks, and then we're going to have to reset and fire up the reaction control system. We're only going to get that back in this section of the ship but, although we might have to burn a lot of fuel, it should be enough to counter the roll and pitch. We won't be able to have the ship travel in the commanded direction, otherwise, without fuss.'

Johansson peered at the diagram. 'You do realise that the starboard tanks are the ones that are damaged and that they're, you know, outside?'

'There are exterior suits back here,' said Law, immediately.

Johansson recoiled a little. 'Fuck that for a game of soldiers. We've no easy way in and out of this thing, and we're talking about step one, for starters. I'm not cashing in all my remaining chips for this first roll of the dice.'

Law glared at her intensely for a second, and then her anger flashed away and she submitted. 'Okay. We jettison the tanks. The explosive bolts won't exacerbate any of our issues that much, and then we'll still have the good tanks on the port side to draw from.'

'That's a much more workable idea. Can we jettison that entire tranche of tanks in one hit?'

'We can, but we can't do it from here now, though, due to the damage. You'll have to go back to the nose of the ship, recall the other train from the shuttered side of engineering, and travel down to the port-side tanks, and just stay away from the reactor,' said Law.

'I'll?'

Law nodded, her attention snapping back to the screen for a moment. 'I need to stay here and continue unpacking and diagnosing the ship's data and systems. From what you've told me, I can't do that from the bridge, and we'll need it done if we're to restart the reaction control system. It's easy to jettison the tanks; pick any platform on that side and use the emergency controls to blow them clear.'

Great. I'm starting to feel like a commuter.

'Alright, then what?'

'Once we've done that, we're going to have to work together to get one, any, or many of the engines lit and burning; I can fly the ship from here.'

'And after that?'

'We'll be on our way to safety,' said Law, immediately looking more relaxed and content. 'And with Main back up, the ship might be able to sort out some of its problems on its own.'

A high-pitched alarm suddenly squealed from the console. Law shrugged quickly at Johansson, turning away, and cursorily checked some readouts. She dismissed the plethora of warning messages, struck some keys, and silenced the alarm. Thirteen minutes and thirty-seven seconds on the clock. More pronounced mechanical noises echoed around the chamber as the ship's systems were checked, corralled, and committed.

Law's toe tapped impatiently against the base of the console as she watched the seconds roll off.

'Clock's ticking,' she said. 'Let's get things in line so we can get out of here quickly.'

'Don't we need to contemplate the "where we are going"

element as well?' said Johansson, pointing forwards. 'Unless you're willing to blindly light the fires and plunge this thing into the nearest star.'

'Trust me,' said Law flatly, 'there's nothing out there to collide with. Getting the ship moving in earnest is imperative, and I know where we need to be. When Main comes up, we should get navigation back, anyway.'

'We're going to be a big, fat target once those engines start burning, you realise?'

'I realise. Don't worry about it,' responded Law, a smug look creeping onto her face.

I sincerely hope you know something I don't, thought Johansson, cocking her head.

'Fine. But you're going to have to help me change the suit battery first. I've not much strength left either, and without the suit I'm not a huge deal of help to anyone,' said Johansson.

Law pushed away from her console for a moment, one thumb outwards and up. 'You just wait here.' She disappeared into the depths of engineering, and Johansson could hear storage bins clattering around.

Johansson hovered, waiting, left with nothing but her thoughts, corpses, and the sensation of the deck vibrating unnervingly underfoot. She closed her eyes for a moment, blocking it out, thinking of the sea and sand again.

'Just a little longer,' she said, comfortingly, in the direction of the suit's chest plate.

The noise of Law making her way back disturbed the moment's peace.

'I've got a fully charged battery,' she said, something resembling a smile appearing on her face. 'I can't find the medical packs yet, though, but I'm sure they're in here somewhere.'

'That's okay for now, I'd just like to be able to move easily and freely,' said Johansson. 'I do feel better than earlier.'

Radiation poisoning will do that to you, she thought, recalling dim and distant medical training. *You'll feel better, for a while, and then the ragged descent begins.*

'Need me to do this for you?' said Law, pointing the packs towards Johansson.

'Please. Bending isn't my forte at the moment.'

Law gently grabbed Johansson's foot and pulled her downwards, putting her waist at head's level. She undid the protective fabric covering of the battery access slip in Johansson's suit, and then unclipped the thin armoured panel beneath. Law slid the old battery out and examined it. Its cells were bulging and scorched in places, and temperature-based monitoring dots, designed to show if the battery had overheated, were all bright red.

'Wow,' she said out loud, 'this thing's toast.'

'I'd prefer it to be a battery,' said Johansson, smiling.

The harness had taken some damage, but the wires were still insulated and the connector was intact. Law unclipped it, separating the old battery from the suit, and a series of pronounced clicks emanated from beneath its exterior.

'Sounds like the other backup still kicks in okay,' said Law, as a new, albeit dim, light appeared on the panel. 'You might have a bit in reserve.'

'I wonder if this'll cheer it up enough to start talking to me,' said Johansson. 'It might fill in some blanks.'

Law nodded slightly as she busied herself reconnecting the new pack, and slipped it back into the pocket. She locked it closed, and sealed it up.

'Should only take a moment.'

More lights began to appear on the suit's front status panel, many red but a handful green, and it made a series of high-pitched whines. Johansson moved her arm tentatively.

'Ah, motion assist is back.'

'Nothing on the front panel or wrist display of use,' said Law, inspecting for any signs of life or imminent failure.

'Looks like previous service has resumed, then,' said Johansson, a little puzzled. 'Most of it working, some of it not.'

'I'll dig up a medical pack when I can,' said Law, working to tidy up some loose cabling. 'The main connector for the medical pack looks damaged, though, I'm afraid. Even if I had a pack, I've not the time to sort it now.'

'Shit. I could really do with that, later, I think.'

'Well, like a lot today, you're going to have to do without.'

'Story of my life.'

Law grinned, a little more warmth in her face.

'We'll try and unpin it carefully later, and then replace the connector, harness and pack at the same time, if it's needed. Otherwise, that's all we can do for now,' said Law, backing off from Johansson and giving her a thumbs-up. 'Anything else I can do?'

'No, I think I'm okay as can be, now; just jettison the tanks, get some engines going, get out of here, save the day,' said Johansson, giving her suit a final once-over. 'That about right?'

Law raised her eyebrows a little, hesitated, then nodded. 'Yes,' she said, the timbre of her voice fluctuating slightly. She turned back to the screen and immersed herself in the data pouring forth.

'Cool. I'm on it.'

Johansson looked around Engineering Access, nodded in Law's direction, and turned towards the nose of the ship.

I'm on my way, she thought, smiling to herself.

CHAPTER FIFTEEN

The pile of heavy black rubber bags were still in the corner, at distinct odds with the light grey flooring and panelling, their ominous shape and weight actively and effortlessly broadcasting their contents. A dull ache seeped through Johansson's body, from head to toe, as she made her way carefully past them, out onto the platform.

Don't let your mind run away. You don't know what happened.

Johansson clambered onto the train and pressed the button for the main station. The train's motors squealed in protest for a moment, and then it smoothly accelerated away from engineering. She could feel weight sloughing off her shoulders as she put distance between herself and the platform; returning to the warm, bright and uncomplicated crew quarters, even in these strange times, was preferable to hanging around in the increasingly complicated and obfuscated engineering area.

Above my pay grade, evidently, she thought, as the train ticked along. *But when hasn't that been the case?*

The train idled past the port reactor station platforms, the displays outside the doors still lit mostly green and positive. The platforms were empty, still, the only signs of life being the illumination and the gently cycling illustration of the reactor operations, in condensed form, on the panels by the door.

Johansson squirmed in her seat, uncomfortable, the exertions of the day creeping back up on her. The medical pouch on her waist still contained a handful of cylinders: two greens, one blue, and one red. She eyed it, contemplating a less aggressive green cylinder, but pushed the thought from her mind.

Save them for when you need them, she thought, as the gentle hum of the train's motors soothed her. Stations for the tanks came and went, each unoccupied and uninteresting, as the train made its way towards the bridge. It rolled into the unchanged main station, clanked against the buffers, and Johansson started transferring over to the starboard-side train. She stuck her head into the crew quarters for a moment, but nothing had changed; Johansson considered grabbing more noodles, but time was against her. She pressed the recall button for the train, which still lingered outside Engineering Access, and watched the coloured interface change from red, to amber, to green, indicating the train was now on its way.

Johansson's mind went blank, seeking a moment's refuge as she rested on the platform, until the train arrived and gently bumped into its stops. She boarded it and pressed the button for the first tank storage station, which was both the closest to her and the furthest station from the damaged starboard reactor.

I do not want to go near that thing again, she thought, unconsciously touching the increasingly inflamed area atop her right hand.

The platform for the first tank storage area was a slender affair; it was more like a gantry that ran alongside the track for ten metres or so, just enough to accommodate the entirety of the train. A lot of the lighting was out, only the dull amber secondaries providing spotty coverage of the dull red grating that lined the platform and its grey tubular structure beneath. The occasional blue, and brighter light, flickered from overhead.

Johansson stepped up from the train to the platform and used the railing to steady herself. Three exits off the platform, leading to three distinct areas: a primary pumping station, a secondary pumping station, and a control room. Each bore a sign above its doorway, smattered with warning labels. Despite it being banned entirely decades prior, a brash NO SMOKING sign was also visible at each end of the platform.

I suspect a cigarette would be one of the things someone could really go for right about now, if such things still existed. A shot or eight would do, instead.

She reached down to her belt, pulled a small bottle of water out of a pouch, and downed its contents. 'I guess we start in the control room, then,' she said out loud, drifting along the platform slowly, boots occasionally snagging on the rough traction-boosting surface of the gantry's flooring.

The control room was secured by a small door with large indentations on its front panel, designed to boost its strength. A small view port offered a peek inside, but only unthreatening operating panels and computers lingered in an unlit room beyond the door. Johansson prodded her code into the touchpad beside the door and, as its control panel cycled from red to green, the door slid slowly to the side, hydraulics hissing softly in the surrounding walls.

Johansson cautiously cast the light from her torch into the centre of the room, revealing it in its entirety. It wasn't large, a single chair surrounded by screens and controls. She sat down and made herself comfortable in the padded chair, its base rotating to allow for easier access, and inspected the consoles surrounding her. There were four large panels, each with their own displays, keyboards and switches: TANK MONITORING, P. STATION 1, P. STATION 2 (SEC), and TANK STRUCTURAL (EMER).

The (EMER) section of text was in white, on a yellow and black hatched background. Johansson smiled.

This might actually be easy, for once.

She tapped on the keyboard and the TANK STRUCTURAL (EMER) display sprung to life. It presented an overview of the ship and then automatically zoomed in on the tanks on the port side. A larger box then appeared, detailing the integrity and status of the tanks themselves. It was littered with warnings; the computer slowly rotated the three-dimensional model of the tank assembly to reveal several markers with flashing red exclamation marks on its upper side, along with venting warnings and ever-shifting percentage bar graphs that indicated substantial per-hour losses. The view then zoomed out, displaying the ship in its entirety, and overlaid it with an axis. Prominent arrows rotated along the X and Y axis, and a smaller one around the Z; the ship was rolling to the right, nosing over and yawing slightly, accelerating at a fractional rate, as pressurised fuel and oxygen bled into space.

Johansson scanned the display and found the large prominent tab marked *JETTISON*. She selected it, using a trackball and buttons mounted in the console, and the display highlighted the eighteen mounting points for each tank, and little indicators popped up alongside each one. Most contained a small icon of a padlock, indicating the mount's clamp to the tank was secure, along with some basic technical information: clamp status, clamp pressure and strain, explosive bolt status, assembly temperature, mount point strain, and the last inspection date for each assembly. Some did not respond, and the black-and-white chequering that appeared over each suggests both were completely unserviceable.

Nothing to be done about that.

She drove the cursor around the screen to the *ALL JETTISON* option and selected it. The display panned out to show the entire ship and a button popped up, with a ten-second counter alongside it.

'Easy,' she said, happy.

She moused over the pop-up button and clicked on it. The on-screen button flashed for a moment and then reset. She blinked, confused, and then, understanding, depressed the button again, but this time held it down. The counter started to run, down from ten seconds. Nine, eight, seven, si–

More haste, less speed, her mind politely reminded her.

Johansson's heart rate soared and, yelping, she released the button, her breathing short, hard and shallow.

Carefully, she drove the cursor back to the *ALL JETTISON* option and selected the *ALL STARBOARD JETTISON* option below it.

'Almost,' she said, giggling to herself.

Why are you here, though, then?

Johansson's hand lifted from the controls.

'Good question,' she muttered, pausing.

Don't trust RCOM.

'This isn't RCOM, though, and not everyone knows the intricacies of these ships,' she said, defensively, rolling her eyes. 'Maybe the port-side controls are out. She's working with more than I am. Or she just plain forgot.'

Hell, I suppose you couldn't even remember your name, earlier. Keep moving. Problem for future you.

Johansson looked back to the screen, checked her selection, and then depressed the jettison button and held it. The timer zeroed out, and something underneath the panel made a quiet grinding noise.

The display was now showing a big pair of red arrows, pointing downwards, flashing. *MASTER RELEASE* blazed away beneath them, flashing in a stroboscopic display of red and white.

Another message popped up, this time on a flashing yellow background.

0046.0I: NO MAIN BASE AVAILABLE. TANK JETTISON WILL CAUSE COURSE DEVIATION.

'That'll be a problem for Law,' said Johansson, closing the warning. 'She can correct that later. About time I gave her something to do.'

Johansson looked under the edge of the console to find that a panel had retracted, revealing two large cylindrical controls. Both had an arrow, pointing outwards, and some upside-down markings; the one on the left was marked FI, the one on the right RE.

I get you, she thought, grinning.

Johansson reached down and grabbed the handle inset into the surface of each cylinder. She rotated the left 180 degrees clockwise, the right 180 degrees counterclockwise: FIRE.

Silence.

Johansson frowned. She grabbed the handl–

It's vibrating.

The staccato vibration intensified, as if drawing nearer, and a hollow and increasingly rapid thudding noise began to permeate the tight space.

Bang-Bang-Bang-BangBangBangBanBanBanBaBaBa-BABABABABABANG.

The noise rumbled on, into eventual silence. The display refreshed, its flashing warnings subsided, and the overview of the ship updated: the starboard tanks had detached and were clear of the ship, propelled by the blasts of the myriad explosive bolts.

Johansson exhaled heavily, rocking herself slightly in the chair, and smiled.

ClickclickclickclickPOP!

The display continued to update, finally showing that additional roll, pitch and yaw were not being added to the *Prompt Excursion*, now that the leaking tanks had been jettisoned. If Law could uphold her part of the bargain, and get the RCS system working, they would be able to level the ship out and get it back under control.

If that's really for the best, thought Johansson, fleetingly.

She sat, for a moment, in the dark and quiet, and closed her eyes. Johansson put her head in her hands, and rubbed her temples; she opened her eyes again but the ship was still there, she was still there, and no fresh recollections sprung forth. Only the dim lights of the panels and displays, and the warmth of the computers operating around her, offered any comfort.

Okay, a bit more speed, she thought, forcing the thought of sleep from her mind. She lifted herself out of the chair and settled her feet back on the deck, hand outstretched to reach the guide rail around the door. Johansson swung slowly around it, out onto the narrow platform, looking towards the train.

A quick ride and we can get on with this show.

But there was something new on the platform. A large shadow, cast from right to left. Johansson recoiled, pushing herself away from the guide rail towards the train, bouncing into the railing on the edge of the platform.

'What the fuck is that!' she shouted, grabbing for the torch on her shoulder mount with one hand, fumbling for the railing with the other.

The shadow did not answer, nor did it move. Whatever was casting it was loitering in the access to the first pumping station, at the far end of the platform from the control room, the lighting behind it flickering intermittently, occasionally ditching the entire area into blackness.

Johansson managed to unhook the torch and pointed it directly at the shadow. Nothing. Whatever it was lay beyond the corner, obscured by the wall.

It might be another member of the crew.

'Hello?' she called, tentatively.

The shadow spasmed, as if in pain.

Johansson pushed off from the platform wall, using the railing as a guide, and tore down the platform.

'I'm coming!' she shouted, twisting to keep her feet from snagging in the platform's vertical railings.

She passed the secondary pumping station; it was shut and clear. Her fingers closed a little around the railing, acting as a brake, slowing her as she approached the corner. She squeezed tightly as it drew closer, and pivoted, swinging her feet down to the deck.

Johansson braced herself against the wall, head cocked towards the corner, and listened. Nothing but silence reached out to her. She drew a deep breath, slowly wrapped her fingers around the guide rail at the junction of the corridor and platform, and jutted her head around the corner.

Holyshithol–

A figure, slouched, was facing the door of the pump room.

Johansson composed herself and slowly looked around the corner again. The figure was still stationary. Nothing else was floating in the corridor. Johansson cautiously drew her torch upwards, tracking it along the floor, until it reac–

It's a repair droid, she thought, fear and concern evaporating in a flash.

She swept the torch's beam over it. The droid appeared undamaged, and it seemed to have been working on something inside the main pump room for the starboard oxygen tanks.

It was the first Johansson had seen all day. A Sark would usually have a complement of five, alongside ten smaller flying drones designed for remote and external repairs, most of which predominantly spent their time in the less human-hospitable ring and engineering spaces. Keeping them separate was also a sensible safety move; the six-feet-tall droids, painted orange and white for visibility, were powerful and weighed almost 100 kilograms. It was unlikely that one would lose its footing, and that its thrusters would fail and allow it to drift free, but if crew collided with one, it was going to smart.

'I bet some of your friends ended up taking an unexpected spacewalk,' said Johansson, in its direction, recalling the craters blown in the ring and engineering areas. 'Main got you back up and out, eh?'

The droid remained idle. Its arms were in a neutral position, by its side, and, on each hand, its four fingers and thumbs were outstretched. Its antenna arrays, slightly creased and dinged, jutted upwards, and its shielded optics section was dark, only a slight tint of welding arc-protecting purple visible in the torchlight. Not a single light was illuminated on its body and its static work-worn limbs, protected by composite panels, showed no signs of life.

Johansson shrugged at it. It probably hadn't been able to return for charging, after engineering closed off, so it had instead worked on repairing the systems of the now-jettisoned tanks until its primary battery was discharged entirely.

'I might come back for you later, get you charged up,' said Johansson, contemplating the droid. 'You might be able to calm down some of that chaos in the starboard reactor.'

She turned back to the platform and drifted around the corner. The silver train lay in wait, ready to travel back to the crew quarters area.

That thing's probably pretty hot. But, oh well. So am I.

She smiled, and something graunched behind her. Johansson spun around, torch outstretched and pointing.

The droid had moved. It was now standing upright, facing the platform, facing her, Johansson's torch casting its imposing shadow over the door behind it. It filled the corridor, looming, but did not move further, its head still bowed into its chest.

'What?!' said Johansson, angrily, annoyed by its irregular action.

A faint mechanical *clickclickclick* filled the corridor, followed by a low-pitched whine. The droid's head climbed upwards, slowly, until level, its optics and status lights still dark and unilluminated.

It took a step forward, lurching unevenly.

'All stop,' said Johansson, pointing at it. 'Now.'

The droid's head rolled unevenly, and its chest section rose as it seemed to gain full control of its legs.

'All stop,' shouted Johansson, frustration and concern flooding her voice.

The droid extended an arm, as if pointing at her, and it put another foot forward, the deck reverberating as the droid's magnets energised and coupled its foot to the floor, the loud *bang!* echoing down the tunnel.

It's not stopping, her mind shrieked. *Go!*

'Fuck this,' yelped Johansson, pushing off towards the train, looking back over her shoulder as every metre passed. The clicking intensified, and the low-pitched whine began to rise to a hissing, slowly shifting towards a high-pitched scream.

'Nope!' she shouted, boarding the train and clipping herself in. 'Nope!'

Johansson reached under the control panel, remembering Law's action, and yanked the lever. The train shuddered, responding to the sudden command for maximum power, and heaved forwards.

The droid appeared at the end of the platform, its body still unlit and seemingly unpowered.

What the fuck! screamed Johansson's mind, as the train shot past the droid, heading through the tunnel towards the crew quarters and bridge.

The droid's thrusters fired briefly, propelling it up and over the rail at the edge of the platform, and it settled awkwardly on the train's track for a moment, crouching like a sprinter at a starting line. It looked up, studied the receding train and its terrified occupant for a moment, and then took off in hot pursuit.

It's going to catch you! she thought, as the train barrelled along the track, the droid careening along behind it. Its thrusters were venting hard, practically locked open, a thin trail of white mist emanating from each one, propelling it along behind the train. The gap was closing.

Johansson glanced back at it as she affixed the torch to her suit. There were still no lights on its front panel, and it didn't appear to be powered. The droid ploughed onwards, its thrusters hissing, the screaming continuing unabated.

Some kind of chemical backup power. Maybe an auxiliary power unit.

'Well, it's not being willed along by the sheer power of fucking thought,' she screamed. The nose of the train dipped, Johansson dabbing the brakes for a moment, as the crew quarters and bridge station approached. She reached down and unclipped her harness, and squatted on the seat, primed to bail from the train and dodge the trailing droid.

Just got to get away from it! Keep moving!

Johansson didn't wait for the train to come to a stop. As it exited the tunnel, onto the crew quarters' platform, she threw herself clear and towards the train leading safely back to engineering. The train, its accelerator still engaged, smashed into the buffers at the end of the platform; its nose pitched down hard, it tore free from the rails, leaving its motor section straddling the rails, sparking, and the body slammed into the floor, sending a tremendous crash and shudder through the station.

Dust erupted from long-untouched seams and ledges, creating a faint fog, as the droid piled into the station behind it, thrusters still shrieking. It did not have the time to slow, nor the space to stop, so it simply ploughed through the wreckage of the train and embedded itself in the far composite wall, the panel cracking and splintering as it absorbed the blow.

It is overspeeding, she realised. *It is unrestricted, rogue.*

The droid had sunk itself several inches into the panel. Johansson glimpsed at it as she slammed herself down in the seat for the return train, back down the safe side of the ship; the droid reached out with its free arm, pressed it against the wall, and pushed. The composite panel made a sickly grating noise as the droid freed its torso and shoulder free from the wall. It turned, slowly, to face Johansson again, its movements uneven and awkward.

'What the fuck is wrong with that thing,' shouted Johansson, as she smashed the button for engineering and clipped her harness into place.

It should not be able to do this, shouted her mind, as she fumbled with the controls of the train. She grabbed the emergency lever for acceleration and pinned it against its stop, bending it.

Johansson's train tore past the first of the tank platforms, towards the reactor assembly and engineering, the bearings in its motors and gearboxes howling in protest as it sped along. The droid was flying again, accelerating towards the rear of the train, unimpeded.

It's going to catch you! she thought, pushing the control lever forwards even harder.

Johansson tapped the brakes experimentally, and the nose of the train dipped, and she flew forwards, only to be retained by her clipped harness. She pulled the accelerator lever back a little, and the train slackened off fractionally, its speed ebbing for a moment. The droid closed, still accelerating.

It's going to catch you! But not if I trash it first!

The droid was metres away. It had one arm outstretched to its side, to catch anything suitable for reorienting itself, and the other was stretched towards the train, its fingers open and ready to clamp. Johansson could glimpse intermittent puffs from its propulsion pack; it was running low on propellant, and dialling back on thruster action. The droids didn't carry the propellant required to run at full throttle for extended periods. Still no visible lights, but Johansson swore she saw the droid's lenses shifting and focusing behind its vision shield, a momentary detail glimpsed in the chaos.

Going to get a real good look at that in a moment.

Johansson looked over her shoulder, cut the motor power, and stabbed the brakes. The train's brakes and motors erupted into firestorms as they converted its kinetic energy into heat and light; it nosed over hard, tail riding high, and the still-accelerating drone hurtled into the back of the carriage, the plexiglass shield exploding into a thousand fragments as the drone's extended armoured arm smashed through it. Johansson immediately released the brakes and threw the accelerator forwards, and the train began to pull away from the decelerated drone.

The arms of the drone flailed as the train began to move away from it, seeking any kind of purchase, its thrusters spluttering. A fingertip wedged in the corner of a panel at the rear of the train but, as the droid accelerated and reached forward with its other arm to secure its grip, the panel gave way, clattering into the droid's face, sending it off course momentarily.

Johansson looked over her shoulder and screamed at the droid.

'Fuck off, you inanimate piece of shit,' she shouted.

The train rushed past the reactor station and towards engineering. Ahead were the blast walls, staggered left and right, the track wrapping around them at sharp angles. The droid was still struggling to free itself from the panel embedded in its chest, its thrusters intermittently firing as it bolted down the tunnel.

It's struggling to catch me, thought Johansson, fleeing.

She barely touched the brakes as the first blast wall approached, and the train heaved sideways as it tried to remain coupled to the rails. The corners of the carriage ground against the walls, sending showers of sparks outwards, but then the track's direction reversed, causing the train to tip precariously in the other direction. An under-rail drive wheel sheared off as the loads grew too high, and rocketed off into the tunnel, a trail of glowing orange steel shards following it.

The track reversed its turn again, around the final wall, and the carriage protested as its grip on the rails grew weak. The train clashed hard against the wall, its windows shattering and roof deforming, and components spewed from its drive modules, bright blue arcs of electricity jumping from train, to rail, to drive section, back to the rail.

A deafening *CLANG* ripped through the ship as the trailing droid slammed into the first of the blast walls, the almighty impact crushing most of its frontal structure, yet only leaving a series of negligible scratches on the blast wall.

It won't do that again, thought Johansson, as she preemptively unbuckled her harness.

But the droid kept coming, its thrusters flaring, its emergency chemical power source whistling, red-hot, scorching its casing. An uneven clattering noise reached forth from the tunnel, its pace increasing.

I've got to get away from this, thought Johansson. *I cannot fight this.*

Her train blazed towards the tunnel exit, into the Engineering Access station, entirely out of control. She hunkered down, crouching on its floor, arms outstretched and gripping the frame of the door, and she propelled herself upwards with all her might as it entered the platform.

She flew, diagonally, clear of the train, towards the ceiling of the station, at a neck-breaking speed. But, like the lifts to the ring, the top of the station was lined with a heavy-duty crash- and impact-absorbing netting, designed to catch loose cargo or crew. Johansson blasted into the netting, sinking feet into it, and the train crashed clean into the end of the platform. Its speed carried it straight over the buffer, its motor sections shearing from the carriage, and it careered into a parked loader, both scattering parts and panels across the platform as they partook in a deadly dance of destruction.

It's still going to catch you!

Johansson pitched into the netting, hard, and yelped as pain stabbed through her chest. Shrapnel from the train and loader peppered her, some puncturing the suit's outer liner, some tearing into her exposed skin, and then it was over. She blacked out for a moment, the tremendous din of the crashing train and collapsing loader fading as quickly as it had arisen, smoke and sparks erupting across the station.

She wiped the blood from her forehead, and flicked her left hand away, blood sheeting freely from it towards the station's platforms. She grabbed a patch from the pouch on her belt and, having peeled its contact surface clear of its protective layer, Johansson shoved it down on her arm where she thought the blood was coming from.

Must resist the temptation to shout, she thought, fleetingly, *but there's no way Law could have missed that.*

The dull clanking from deep within the tunnel intensified, its pace increasing further still.

Fuck! That thing's still going! Observe, orient, decide, act!

There wasn't much of use left on the platform. The train had disintegrated into a pile of metals and composites, and the loader had been obliterated in the impact. Johansson instead reached out and grabbed the next section of netting, and pulled herself along the roof until she reached the wall the tunnel exited from.

Don't look up.

Below her, the droid stormed out onto the platform, its exterior casing battered, sparking, a little smoke drifting from one of the lower panels on its back. It looked left, it looked right, and then it stepped forwards.

Johansson's muscles relaxed a little.

And then it looked directly upwards.

'Fuck!' shouted Johansson. 'Just fuck off!'

The droid's head rotated, and it prepared to leap upwards. As it jumped, Johansson grabbed the netting and fired herself towards the far wall, above the Engineering Access doors, trying to put fresh distance between herself and the droid. Its thrusters were now completely depleted so it sailed upwards, past her, and entangled itself in the webbing on the ceiling.

Johansson crashed into the wall, her ankles and the suit absorbing most of the blow, and turned to face the droid. One of its arms and a foot had penetrated through several layers of the netting, snaring it. It was struggling violently, and Johansson could see the attachment pins for the webbing vibrating and pulling, the fabrics fretting and stretching.

'Where the fuck are you!' screamed Johansson, as she pushed off again towards the floor, wincing as she touched down.

Definitely sprained that, she thought, wincing. *Not that it's going to matter much soon, at this rate.*

The droid produced an unpleasant mechanical noise as its arm suddenly came free from the netting, tearing clean through the remaining webbing. It stopped for a moment, looked directly at Johansson, struggled again, and then reached slowly down towards its foot.

Maybe I can slow it down, she thought, eyes darting around the platform again. A bright yellow cabinet, behind the wreck of the train, grabbed her attention: Fire and Spill Kits. Johansson limped towards it, pushing off from the floor with her good foot when she was close enough, and grabbed the access lever as she sailed up to it. She ripped the door open, revealing two large conventional water-based extinguishers, two large chemical extinguishers, medical kits, torches, fire-fighting gear and a large sealed bucket with A.I.M. written on it. Johansson strapped one of the chemical extinguishers to her back, and then grabbed the bucket firmly by its handle.

The droid's hydraulic system shrilled angrily as its foot tore clear of the webbing, freeing the machine. It was moving down towards the platform, but only slowly, its body contorting as it tried to rotate towards Johansson. Smoke plumed angrily from vents on its back as it fruitlessly flailed mid-air.

Johansson grabbed the guide rail around the Engineering

Access door, lifted herself away from the floor, released the bucket, and pointed the chemical extinguisher towards the droid. It drifted closer, its path taking it slightly under her, its rubber-coated, titanium-cored fingers stretching out towards her. She leaned towards it, one foot tucked into the guide rail, pointed the extinguisher at it, and unloaded its contents in its face.

To her surprise, the droid did not respond. It simply remained reaching out for her, crawling through the air, a thick layer of chemical foam saturating it from head to toe. Smoke and heat waves plumed from its exhaust and panel gaps, and Johansson swore she could see elements of it glowing, causing some of the extinguishing foam to blacken and burn.

Johansson swung along the rail at the top of the door, putting some distance back between her and the droid. It did not seem to recognise that she had moved.

I blinded it, she realised, one fist clenched, as the droid drifted into the lower edge of the door frame.

The droid stopped, jamming its feet against the solid metal bulkhead, and stood still, its hands clawing at its face. The rubberised coating on its fingertips served only to smear the chemical suppressant all over its optics, blurring its view modes. It took a step back, buzzing angrily, turned back to face the station, and set about slowly scanning the platforms.

And now it's just listening for me instead, realised Johansson. *Great.*

Johansson crept back towards the droid, inching along the rail, pulling herself along with her fingertips, keeping every section of her suit, every inch of her body, away from the wall.

Easy does it, she thought, approaching the droid from above, *quietly does it.*

The droid was now directly below her, its sensor and optical arrays facing into the station, seeking her out. Johansson reached for the floating bucket's handle and tried to gently pull it towards herself without making a sound. The handle shifted in the bucket's plastic frame, graunching a little, but the droid remained motionless.

Maybe I've deafened it a bit, too, she thought, as she carefully and quietly pried the lid off the A.I.M. bucket. She left the lid drifting beside her and checked the contents of the large pail; it was filled with a gently swilling, but very thick, pinkish-coloured substance.

Johansson inverted the bucket, pointed it at the head of the droid beneath her, and pushed it straight towards it. The opening of the bucket neatly slipped around the head of the droid, and a sickening *squelch* followed as the material made contact with metal. The bucket came to a halt, but the material within continued on its downward trajectory, slowly falling down the droid in long, pendulous drips, until it came into contact with the floor. The droid moved uneasily, staggering a little this way and that, the thick layer of slurry seeping into its hissing grills and vents.

It stopped moving but remained upright. The chemicals in the pail continued to wick down the length of the machine, thickening and expanding slightly, encasing the droid. Johansson stared at it, watching for any hint of movement. One minute became two, and then three, but the droid remained still.

'That stuff works pretty well,' she said out loud, a dry laugh escaping her throat, her heart rate dropping a little. 'Thank fuck.'

Johansson shed the dispensed extinguisher from her back, and slumped against the entrance to Engineering Access, eyes still locked on the droid. The Anti-Incendiary Mud continued to drag and drip slowly down the droid, blistering in places, but the droid remained immobile.

Something touched her and she leapt what felt like a mile, every limb going in a different direction at once.

'It's just me!' shouted Law, brandishing a compact and slender pistol.

215

Johansson clutched at her chest, half-jokingly, half in pain, as she drifted away from Law.

She bobbed after her, snagged a loop in Johansson's boot, and pulled her back down onto the deck. Johansson's chest was pounding, and sweat poured from her brow.

'Jesus, Law,' she said, voice trembling, 'where the fuck were you!?'

Law moved past Johansson, her eyes flicking up and down the vaguely droid-shaped pink pile, which occasionally smoked intensely.

'That's the first time you've addressed me by name,' she said, smiling. 'And that's one way of doing it,' she said, pointing at the droid, eyebrows high on her forehead.

'Where the fuck were you?!'

Law turned towards Johansson, pistol pointed at the decking, its brilliant orange holographic sight bobbing in and out of view. 'I've been working on the second fusion plant, trying to see if I could find out what that noise is, and if I can stabilise it and bring the power output up. It's loud down there, behind the barriers.'

She gestured at her ears, which had little yellow plugs protruding from them. 'I turned around and saw on a console what was going on. It just took me some time to get back up here.'

Johansson dragged her hands across her face, clearing some of the sweat and blood from it. 'Fucking hell,' she said, dragging each word out. 'That thing just went nuts, chased me the length of the ship. It tried to kill me.'

Law eyed it, cautiously, watching the smoke trailing outwards from it. 'Good thing it didn't,' she said. 'I still need your help.'

Johansson waved her hand over some of her wounds, pointed in the direction of the train, and then at the congealing pile of chemicals and droid. 'Water, please,' she added. Law passed her a bottle and then handed over some more pills; Johansson necked the bottle almost instantly, downed the pills quickly, and sighed noisily.

'There was definitely something amiss with it,' said Johansson. 'No status lights, no audible alerts, nothing. Almost like it had been compromised to its absolute core, which might explain all this.' She waved again, arm flitting across the station and her now more-ruined suit and bloodied body.

'What was that stuff,' said Law, pointing at the gel coagulating around the droid, the occasional bubble rising to its surface and popping.

'It's a chemical agent for tackling incendiary munitions, for use if something gets triggered inadvertently or damaged in the bay. You just chuck it on and it travels and swells, starving the fire of oxygen,' said Johansson, glancing at the droid, the bucket now adhered firmly to its head. 'I used it on the *Terminal* once, on a missile that lit up during loading. Duff weld, fuel leak.'

Law nodded as she checked that the safety catch on her pistol was in the on position. She pulled back on the pistol's slide and Johansson saw the elevator inside present a tan-coloured cartridge, with a thin green tip, in front of the bolt. Johansson froze as Law released the slide, the bolt picking up the round and guiding it into the chamber.

Striker fired, thought Johansson, curious. *No electronics to interfere with.*

Law swung the gun towards the droid, flicked the safety off, aimed squarely at the visible remnants of the bucket, and squeezed the trigger. The gun barked and a violent mist of silicon, composites, glass and shrapnel erupted from the back of the droid's head.

She lowered the pistol, a few embers of still-burning propellant drifting from its barrel slowly. 'What?' she said. 'You think I was going to take chances with that thing?'

Johansson shook her head wearily. 'Looks like VFOEs get better kit than us, at any rate.'

'Heh,' snorted Law. 'Try not to be on the receiving end of this. The green tips are armour-piercing.'

Not to be fucked with, thought Johansson, again.

'Thanks,' said Johansson, nodding.

'You're welcome.'

The pair just stood for a moment, looking at the wreckage in the station, and the remains of the droid, fragments of its head now spiralling around the platforms.

'I punched the tanks off,' said Johansson. 'I could have done it from this side, though, and avoided all of this.'

'I didn't know,' said Law, shrugging softly, her voice suddenly sounding warm. 'But I saw the tanks go. Flight reported that the persisting pitch, yaw and roll went almost immediately. There's only a little correction required to account for jettisoning the tanks. I'm ready to fire up the reaction control system now, if you're up for tagging along.'

'Can you help me with some of this,' said Johansson, faltering a little. She gestured to the blood seeping from below her cuff on her left arm, and rotated her hand in front of her face slowly, head sagging a little.

Law nodded, and made her way over to the emergency cabinet, quickly returning with a green box full of medical supplies. 'I'm surprised you're still going,' she quipped.

'So am I,' retorted Johansson, woozily, adrenaline fading away yet again, as Law wiped the blood, ash and debris from her face. 'I just want to see my daughter again,' she mumbled, her eyes dimming.

Law paused for a moment and then reached for a clean wipe. 'Stay awake, you fool,' she said, firmly. 'Tell me about her.'

Johansson's expression lifted for a moment. 'She's ... remarkable. She's doing so much more ... more than I ever could.'

Tweezers firmly gripped and extricated some larger chunks of metal in Johansson's neck, and forehead, and then Law applied a thin smear of sealing and healing agent to the exposed wounds.

'When did you last see her,' said Law, loudly, poking Johansson's shoulder before reaching for some medical tape.

Johansson's face went blank for a moment. 'Maybe ... three or four years ago.'

'That's a long time.'

'I was ... holding her back,' she responded, a despondent look on her face.

Law nodded as she taped up some of Johansson's larger and more obvious gashes, and then turned her attention to her bleeding arm. A sharp piece of metal had cut clean through the suit, deep into Johansson's forearm. A little white bone was visible at the base of the cut, causing Law to gag a little.

'It's worse than it looks,' said Johansson, wryly, drifting in and out.

'Just a flesh wound,' murmured Law, as she poured cleaner into the gaping cut. Johansson writhed, weakly at first, then more firmly.

'Stop it,' commanded Law, as she dabbed adhesive and healing agents against the exposed flesh and muscle while doing her best to suppress her inclination to vomit all over Johansson. 'Just a few more moments.'

Law slipped an elasticated strap, loaded with fabric impregnated with more clotting and healing agents, through the gash in Johansson's suit and around her arm. She tapped the strap and it sprung close, tightening around the wound, causing Johansson to groan. Law unconsciously squeezed her, pulling her tight.

'That's it,' she said. 'Think you can handle a green?'

Johansson shook her head. 'I'll live without, for now,' she said groggily. 'Rest, water.'

'Well, you're in luck,' said Law. 'Main's still got some unpacking to do, and it's going to take me a little while to straighten the ship out before we start looking at propulsion. There are plenty of drinks and edibles back in engineering, too.

'If I can just sit, eat, drink and snooze, that'll do,' mumbled Johansson.

'Sure. And, while we're there, we can start checking through some other things, too.'

Johansson nodded sleepily as Law started dragging her back to engineering.

'And, if you keep on ticking, I'll see about getting you to your daughter.'

Pure delight beamed from Johansson's eyes momentarily, and then slowly faded away with her consciousness.

CHAPTER SIXTEEN

Johansson stirred, the suit's self-test procedure disturbing her. It was flexing her gloved fingers through their range of movement, back and forth, checking the motion and range calibration.

She opened one eye lazily; Law had pulled her back into engineering, into the control room, and set Johansson down in a corner. She was now busying herself at her console again, tearing through reams of data, diagrams and text, status alerts coming and going, the ship slowly returning to her control.

At least I'm safe here. At least, as safe as I can be on the Prompt.

The urge to doze off again was almost inescapable, but the suit's motions caught Law's eye. She floated over, inspected the suit, and realised Johansson was in the realm of the living.

'Kind of creepy when they do that, isn't it?' she said. 'I try to avoid having one of those, these days. I prefer to be in complete control.'

Johansson nodded weakly and set about trying to sit up.

'Just give me a minute.'

Law moved back to her console. Johansson watched as the display changed to show the in-flight status of the *Prompt Excursion*. It showed a three-dimensional representation of the ship, looking from tail to nose, against a pure black background. Overlaid on the ship were arrows, indicators and percentage readouts that displayed which way the ship was moving, how fast it was going in that direction, and how quickly that velocity was being slowed or increased.

The data being projected on the large transparent display showed that the ship was still slowly rolling, yawing and nosing over. But, now that Johansson had successfully ejected the leaking tanks, it was no longer accelerating in any of those axes. Instead, its gentle corkscrew was just continuing, uninterrupted by any force. A small arrow indicated that the ship was travelling forwards, too, but at a fractional rate. So much so, Johansson noted, that the display was having trouble even registering anything, the readout continually bouncing from zero metres per second to one.

Law called up two display panels, which materialised on the main display and slid into place alongside the ship. The first was for the main propulsion systems. A small circle appeared above each key component, then counted down from 100 per cent, then back up to whatever the status of that particular element was. A grim number of them remained at zero, then flashed red momentarily, and then were overlaid with a plain black-and-white stripe.

'No painless way out of this mess,' said Law quietly.

The second panel showed the intricate arrays of thrusters dotted around the *Prompt Excursion*, which were responsible for low-speed manoeuvring and attitude control. The same percentage assessment appeared, overlaid on the technical layout of the thrusters, and ran through its checks. Those at the front of the ship didn't report in, as predicted, but many in the ring and around the engineering and drive sections reported in green.

Johansson watched on, impressed by the speed and efficacy of Law's inputs and commands.

A large warning message popped up, cataloguing the litany of communications and Local and Main system failures that had eventually led to the reaction control system shutting down, after it received so many spurious and real errors that doing nothing was deemed better than doing anything. Without it, the ship couldn't maintain the desired orientation and, if a force acted on it, nothing would work to hold it in place.

Law looked back towards Johansson, her fingers hovering over the board for a moment.

'You alright to handle a little manoeuvring? I still need you in some usable shape later on.'

Johansson braced herself against the wall, her legs outstretched, feet pressed against the base of the console, and nodded. She put out her hand and grabbed a guide rail next to her, just in case.

Should be pretty gentle, though. But, hey, we're getting somewhere!

'Main's still coming up across the board but the priority RCS elements are up,' said Law. 'Let's see if we can stabilise the ship.'

She deftly navigated through a torrent of menus, and the screen showed remotely cycling valves, breakers, gimbal and ignition systems springing to life. Pipes rumbled and machinery grumbled, then settled into a hum, in the depths of Engineering Access, as hydroxylammonium nitrate and methanol worked their way out to the thruster stations at the rear of the ship.

Both sensed the deck shifting a little beneath their feet, very gently, and the numbers on the flight screen started rolling back, slowly. A loud grating noise rumbled through the room, pursued by a series of long, drawn-out screeches, and some discordant pops. Instrumentation flashed red briefly, and Law glowered at the displays.

'We've still got little to no RCS control up front, due to the damage,' said Law, watching the screen intently. 'The rear ones are going to have to work overtime to counter this spin, so I'm setting them to low but long thrust.'

'Better to err on the side of caution,' said Johansson, piping up, echoes of the ship's protests still jittering through her body.

'Exactly,' said Law, smiling in Johansson's direction. 'And once it's done, we can see which of the main engines will fire up, and get on the road. The self-tests are starting to run now.'

Law pulled up another large display, which showed something resembling a tunnel, and quickly closed it. Johansson could see her muttering something under her breath, her head shaking a little.

I'm starving, Johansson suddenly realised.

'Food,' she said.

Law glanced back, then at the screen again. 'You stay put,' she said. A minute passed, then Law returned with two packets of food, and more self-heating cans of drink. She opened up the silver package of Mexican rice and tuna, pulled its integrated bamboo spork out, primed the heating element of the can, opened it, and proffered both to Johansson. She then set her own down on the console, resting for a moment, and sipped on the drink.

Johansson just stared at the food and drink for a minute, her brain slowly creeping into action. Eventually, she summed up the energy to dig the spork into the rice, and guided it into her mouth, at a pedestrian rate. She chewed, steadily, eyeing Law and the display.

'You seem a bit more relaxed,' said Johansson, through a mouthful of rice.

'Well, we're not out of the woods yet, but the woods are no longer on fire,' said Law. 'The pumps on the second fusion reactor are still a concern, though. I think the bearings or impellers are damaged on some of them.'

'Is that what that juddering and noise was, down there?'

'Possibly,' said Law. 'But it's pretty inhospitable at the moment, so I couldn't inspect them properly. And some of the equipment is still glitched to hell, so I've no vibration or acoustic sensors in the containment areas.'

Johansson looked in the direction of the fusion wells. The view above one was distorted slightly, shimmering.

Overtemp.

'There was damage to the exterior. Maybe shrapnel or a projectile wiped out some of the monitoring systems.'

Law nodded, chomping down on another sporkful of rice.

'Tell me,' she said.

Oh, here comes the heat, thought Johansson, wearily.

'Why didn't you kill everyone over Jupiter?' said Law. 'It's always puzzled me. You could have wasted that super cruiser, in the blink of an eye, and the RSF would have made you a hero.'

Johansson baulked, the question catching her off guard.

'It's been a while since anyone asked "why?",' said Johansson, flatly. 'Most tend to tell me that "You should have".'

Law sporked another mouthful of rice into her mouth, nodding, and washed it down.

'Unnecessary force just isn't my thing,' said Johansson, slowly coming around to the conversation, her head shaking defensively. 'I signed up to serve, yes, but to serve as a defender, not an aggressor. So that the nations in the system could go about their business, their expansion, and their development, hopefully, safely and sensibly. So that we might do better.'

'Ah, the honourable and pragmatic type,' said Law.

Johansson scoffed.

'No, I just prefer to do right by myself and others. It's not that complicated. No bloodlust here.'

'And how's that been working out for you?'

Johansson just laughed, winced, and then waved the tip of the spork around the room.

'I find it makes living with myself easier, at least. That's why so much of the Jupiter report is redacted. I launched missiles, but didn't arm them; I just parked them around the mission- and mobility-killed ships, despite the initial orders. We were still a risk to each other, but the captains saw sense and ended up agreeing to go their separate ways. Three ships and a few hundred people lived to see the next hour, and neither side lost anything in particular.'

'There was more than that to it, though?'

'Oh, RCOM was mad at me for simply not turning the crippled ships into dust, when we had the chance, but the reduction in damage to our ships, and the reduced losses, meant they chose not to turn me out for that humanitarian act. It just put me on a bad footing.'

'And,' said Law, knowingly.

'Okay, yes, so those same ships returned five weeks later, fresh out of the docks, and successfully assaulted the same station again. And the captain even proclaimed that it was our weakness and failure that led to it occurring, all because I let them get away. But even if I had destroyed it, others would have simply taken their place.'

She squinted at Law, a flash of anger in her eyes, and waved a finger. 'Don't try and pull that one on me.'

'Valid, I suppose,' conceded Law, making a spinning gesture with her spork.

'I bounced around a bit after that. I spent some time on the military fuelling station above Saturn, taking pot-shots at incoming rocks and getting to grips with some of the more menial tasks required to survive in space. The attacks on the same platform above Uranus, as the demand for hydrogen and helium increased, cost us a lot. The RSF found itself in need of weapons officers again, so I ended up back on corvettes. I made a few more problematic calls and got myself shuttered again.'

'The standoff over Despina.'

'Congratulations, you read my file. Yes, that and a few other things. Firing on friendly ships? Good one,' spat Johansson. 'There was no way I was going to advance, and if those were the kind of decisions they expected me to make, then I sure as hell wasn't going to.'

She paused for a moment, reflecting.

'Your daughter,' said Law, interjecting.

She did some digging, thought Johansson, starkly.

'She was following in my footsteps, yes. And she was much smarter than I. She could create the illusion of toeing the line while still acting in a way that was true to her. I could never manage the former.'

'So you cut and run on your own career.'

'If I stayed, persisted, kept on pushing and making noise, I–'

'Might have kicked problems down the road to her.'

'There wasn't enough room for two Johanssons in that town. I just couldn't handle it, amid everything else. She deserved the best chance; I didn't have any doubt about her potential, so, yes, I removed myself from the equation.'

Johansson looked at her feet for a moment, the corner of her mouth twitching up and down restlessly.

'It sounds like you cut yourself out of her life completely.'

'I didn't want to but it felt like the path of least resistance. She has tried to contact me. But, I–'

She tailed off, letting silence fill the room, and a rueful look flooded her face.

'It's not easy, in this line of work, to maintain sense and perspective, doubly so when it comes to family relationships,' said Law, her tone comforting. 'The distance and time frames alone, and the stresses and strains.'

'I couldn't hack it,' said Johansson, bluntly. 'I couldn't leave, but I just needed something different for a while, like yourself. So I took rearguard and supporting roles, quieter stuff, and just tried to do my job. I figured there was a demand for competent crew, and it could be constructive and helpful, but with less action and fewer hard calls, less chance to get caught in the spotlight.'

'Whoops.'

'Quite,' said Johansson, regretfully. 'But it was interesting work, and there was always another ship in need of crew. I kept on working my way, from vessel to vessel, trying to forge something of a meaningful retirement fund, until I ended up on the *Hard Target*.'

'I saw that was a new posting,' said Law, a curious tone to her voice, 'one you'd only just accepted.'

'Yeah, an associate sent up a flare about it. I'd seen the listing but they'd said there was a last-minute call for a WSO, and they nudged me towards it; here, have this drink, this is a regular posting but the first loop might be a quiet one, don't ask, don't tell, simple in-and-out affair, take this big stack of cash, handle the munitions side of things, don't look at anything unless someone says to, here's a document with what you need to know, you know the routine.'

The corner of Law's mouth lifted a little.

'They made it sound like it was worth my time, and not just financially.' said Johansson, huffing slightly. 'I mean, I think I got the impression that our initial objectives were a bit hazy, and there were some question marks as to what we were doing, and, yeah, maybe it should have rung a bigger bell, but, afterwards, it was otherwise just a boggo six-month stint on a Sark, and I guess the payoff made me clean overlook any other foibles with the specifics, among other things.

'That I don't blame you for,' said Law, nodding affirmatively. 'Without funding, or a formal retirement agreement, you might as well just walk out of an airlock, these days. And where's the fun in the safe options? Not everyone gets to fire missiles, take down droids and punch off tanks every day.'

'I'm all for firsts and trying new things but this caper takes the biscuit,' said Johansson, staring back into the depths of engineering. 'But you're right about retirement. I would like to stop doing this, and the only way I can do that is if I keep my sheet clean and keep my cashflow up. Otherwise, I'll be scrubbing sheets and sweeping streets until my heart beats its last.'

'No help from a partner?'

'Don't ask.'

Law fell quiet, and then turned her attention back to her display.

'Three minutes, then we'll start looking at the main drives in earnest,' said Law.

'Can you bring up a WEPS panel on one of these,' said Johansson, pointing at an unoccupied and dark console.

'What for? There's nothing to shoot at out here,' said Law.

'Have you ever seen a ship with this widespread, erratic and seemingly unrelated series of failures?'

Law shrugged. 'I can think of at least six or seven governments, agencies or official bodies that could and might employ force against the *Prompt*.'

'But the drone, the unlit emergency stations and illumination, the conduit damage, the way Main was behaving, that's not normal.'

'Your point being?'

'I'm wondering how widespread the attack was on the ship, because I'm guessing that a lot of it wasn't physical, something we haven't and can't see.'

'And the WEPS logs will reveal that?'

'Sure will,' said Johansson, nodding. 'At least, that is, it'll give us some idea of what else might have been done.'

Law's head tipped to the side.

'Come on, it's not like there's anything else I can do at the moment,' said Johansson.

Law nodded, tapped several keys, and swiped her hand to the side. The large display on her left flickered for a moment, then presented a digital duplicate of Johansson's console and display panels on the bridge.

'Neat,' said Johansson, getting to her feet, 'but physical buttons for me, any day.'

Law waved her hand about. 'Main is still decompiling a lot of materials, and a lot of systems are still in self-test mode, so you might not be able to access everything just yet.'

'That's okay, offensive and defensive hardware is a priority system, like RCS, so that should have been gone through already.'

Johansson listened to Law's typing, which seemed to be speeding up, as she settled at her new station. Torrents of data began pouring across Johansson's screens, hours and hours of back-logged reports, updates, notifications, issues, alarms and alerts, spooling almost unceasingly, quicker than she could acknowledge or clear them, and interruptions about current issues and faults stacked up at an almost comical rate alongside them. Some flashed up just momentarily, then appeared to corrupt, disappearing off the display before she could read them.

'Set me up a secondary, please,' said Johansson. The display to her left cleared and a less complicated version of her interface appeared, uninterrupted by updates.

She moved the pointer to the first tab in the alphabetical list-ings, marked ECM, and selected it. Johansson scrolled back through its logs, just before the first impacts.

'Jesus,' she said out loud, 'would you look at that.'

Law peered over her shoulder, her fingertips still rattling away at her keyboard.

'Didn't want this thing going anywhere, or making as much as a peep, did they?' said Johansson, pounding the console softly. 'I haven't seen this many countermeasures, blind jamming attempts and data injection attempts since we parked those corvettes over the CSP munitions depot at Sinus Meridiani.'

'Were they local, or?' said Law, stopping mid-sentence, focusing back on her own inputs.

'Can't tell,' said Johansson, gruffly. 'Whatever it was, it practically blinded the ship. Most of the external inputs are down; they're either simply gone, or scrambled by the electromagnetic attacks.'

Johansson clicked on one of the logs, each of which catalogued the individual electronic warfare attacks, experimentally. The system froze, refusing to respond to her commands, and then reset. It dumped her back to the main menu so she tried another, and the system locked up again.

'I think they might have spiked some of the storage somehow. I can't access any of these.'

'It might still be unpacking and defragmenting. Main isn't at its best.'

Johansson shook her head. She pulled up the weaponry logs and external camera views; the data was just as incomplete, the logs erratic, with giant gaps in the timeframes. There was nothing useful to be seen.

'A lot of information is miss–'

Law held up a finger, butting in. 'In-ship comms are coming up, and I've managed to get one of the external communications relays up.'

'Don't waste your time,' said Johansson. 'It might power up, but the antennas were smashed to bits when I last looked outside.'

'Which of them?'

'All of them,' muttered Johansson, a chime and a chirrup only audible to her announcing that her personal communicator was broadcasting externally now, as well as internally. 'The long-range ones, in any case.'

'Well, they'll know when we get back, regardless,' said Law, her display changing to present other sections of the ship. 'I've set them to broadcast automatically to and from our personal microphones and headphones, anyway, in case contact arises.'

Standard procedure. There's something we haven't seen for a bit.

The lights in the engineering section dimmed a little, and breakers in the distance popped, closed, popped again, and fell silent. The pitch of the vibration of the decking seemed to change a little, and an acrid haze drifted out of the panels near the rear of the section. A heavy smell of ozone flooded the compartment.

Johansson raised an eyebrow and tapped Law on the shoulder. 'I'm working on it,' she responded, remaining focused on her display. The underlying vibration ceased for a moment and then intensified, becoming more of a prominent and continual knocking. Johansson lifted herself off the deck, nervously, isolating herself from the sensation.

I'd rather not know.

'What's the game plan here?' said Johansson, frustrated.

'I'm going to need a minute.'

A pungent smell filled the air, and a harsh crackling noise erupted from below the decking.

Something electrical is having a day as good as mine.

Law bashed her console, a yell of frustration breaking the silence. She cursed, under her breath, fingers clenching the edge of the panel, and pushed herself away from it. Johansson stared at her, waiting. Law tipped her head back, grimaced, and then moved back to the console, its displays starting to cycle and change again.

'The cooling system for the second fusion reactor is starting to struggle,' said Law, her voice riddled with angst.

'Do we need it?' said Johansson. 'There's a reason we have two.'

'In its original configuration, that would have been fine,' said Law, her jaw clenched.

'You mean the ship's original configuration.'

'Yes.'

'And the problem this presents us is?'

Law craned her head back, eyes rolling in their sockets. 'Sure, the ship could originally fly on one fusion plant, loaded to the nines, and it could even get by on just the reactor sponsons; it had to, right, to even get signed off.'

'But the *Prompt*?'

'It needs one fusion reactor to just get by, in this situation. The second is there for redundancy, but it's already taking some load.'

'This ship can draw that much power?'

'Yes,' said Law, emphatically. 'And all the time.'

'And the problem this presents us is?' repeated Johansson, frustration coursing through her voice and across her brow. 'Can't you just shut down whatever those panels are and presumably alleviate that load?'

Law hesitated for a moment.

'No. We would lose the ship.'

Her eyes darted around the room.

'They are maintaining the integrity of the ship, protecting us,' she added.

'Protecting us from what?' said Johansson, moving towards Law. 'You said it yourself: there's nothing out there.'

Johansson realised that one of Law's hands was no longer on her console. It was on her hip, resting atop the compact grip of her pistol.

'We are operating outside of conventional bounds,' said Law, coldly. 'And you're providing sterling service, so don't change that. It would be a shame to preemptively end your career, just when you're potentially on the cusp of something great.'

'I'm guessing that means that you still need my help,' said Johansson, belligerently.

'I still need your help, yes,' admitted Law, her sudden ice-cold demeanour sending chills down Johansson's spine.

'Fantastic,' she said, coughing, slumping to the deck. 'And what exactly is in it for me?'

Law took her hand from her gun and crossed her arms.

'You help me do this and I will ensure that you get a commission of your choice, plus whatever benefits you want. Maybe you can correct some of the wrongs of the RSF, with a good enough rank. Wipe the slate clean, start anew, and maybe even patch things up with your daughter. There's always time.'

Johansson hacked, her shoulders slumping. 'You're assuming I'm going to make it, for one thing.'

'We'll make it back,' said Law, pointing towards the screens. 'We don't have far to go.'

Johansson stood up, slowly, hands out, pushing herself up the wall with her legs.

'Are you serious about all of this?' she uttered, hope infusing her eyes with a glimmer.

'As certain of anything as I've ever been,' said Law. 'If I prove this works, we'll get anything we want.'

Johansson pulled herself over to her console and sat down.

'And this isn't a weapon?'

'This technology is not designed to be used offensively, no. But it can change everything, for the better, including our futures.'

Johansson slumped in her chair, the rumble from the wounded fusion plants below creeping into her ears.

'Alright.'

Law nodded at her, a satisfied look on her face, and returned to her console. She immediately drew up the reactor display screen, and her fingers were soon stabbing keys again.

'Trust me, it'll be okay,' she said, her voice more neutral, her attention entirely focused on the screen.

Trust me. Good one. But I don't have much choice.

Johansson's fingertips hovered over the keyboard for a moment.

Trust me, there's nothing out there to collide with. We are operating outside of conventional bounds.

Johansson pressed a few buttons and selected the data link from the remote weapons station in the ring. It was still transmitting the live feed from the missile, which was keeping the launcher in view, holding its position relative to the ship.

Best not fiddle with that right now, she thought, envisioning it spearing into an essential structure inadvertently. *Not in the state to fly.*

The remote weapons station's archive, operating independently, contained standalone captures from the missiles she had attempted to launch beforehand. Johansson clicked on the first video file; its playback showed nothing from the conventional nose camera, and then the missile shut down. The second did similar.

She clicked on the third. This time, the instrumentation embedded in the video suggested the missile had left the launcher, but the view was just black, as it had been at the time. And then the missile failed, and the instrumentation went black as well.

But it looks like it was working.

Johansson spooled the footage back to the start and set the playback speed to half. The instrumentation sprang up, bright and vivid, an–

There's something there, she thought, rewinding the footage. Johansson advanced through it, frame by frame. Black, black, black, a dim grey shadow, perhaps a hint of red, and then nothing. No ship illumination, no marker lights, no emergency lights, nothing.

And no stars. Nothing.

Johansson advanced back through the frames again, peering at the imagery. A grey shadow, a hint of a red marking.

That's part of the launcher, the ring, she realised, *being illuminated by the rocket motor.*

Johansson stared at the subsequent frames, uncomprehending.

Its camera was working, but there was nothing to see.

'Is the ship's exterior illumination or camera network up,' she asked, trying to keep her voice steady.

Law's hair made the S-shape again as she shook her head. 'No, it was all out when I was out there earlier. Same with the cameras, and the archived footage. Maybe that'll come back later.'

Trust me, there's nothing out there to collide with, sang Johansson's mind. *We are operating outside of conventional bounds.*

Johansson spun through the frames again, watching each one even more closely, her eyes obsessing over every pixel. No ship illumination, no marker lights, no emergency lights, nothing.

She swallowed dryly and lifted her fingers from the keyboard, a slight tremble coursing up and down her arms.

No ship illumination, no marker lights, no emergency lights, nothing.

Johansson stared into the abyss presented by the image and felt her soul sinking into it.

No stars. No planets. No ships. No stations. Nothing else.

'What the fuck,' she said to herself, quietly.

CHAPTER SEVENTEEN

The *Prompt*'s roll slowed, its reaction control thrusters winking out one by one, and then stopped entirely. Debris continued to spin slowly around the ship, clouds of shattered armour plating, unexpended munitions, and fine clouds of vital fluids, spiralling around it like a vortex; it looked like a freeze-frame image of an airliner striking the ground, still recognisable, but a fraction of a second from destruction. A dull orange light peeked through the holes punched in one of the fusion reactors, and gases pulsed forwards from the openings, dissipating quickly into nothingness.

The thrusters sprang back to life, the glare violent against the darkness of the *Prompt*'s unlit hull, pushing the ship towards a commanded orientation. One coughed briefly, then detonated, a sickly flash of white and blue casting harsh shadows across the *Prompt*, the fleeting light scattering erratically through the detritus and mist around it.

A series of dull thuds cascaded through the floor of engineering, closely followed by a lazy *whoomph*.

'I can compensate for that,' barked Law, fingers jutting firmly into the console's keys.

The other thrusters continued to burn smoothly, then cut out sequentially, spooling down, a thin cloud of unburnt propellant drifting lazily from each one. Law tapped at her console again, a handful of the still-hot thrusters popping back into life, burning more vigorously. The ship shuddered, its structure creaking, as the thrusters slowly reoriented it, pointing its nose towards Law's inputted target.

'Dead ahead,' said Law, shutting everything down again. 'Good.'

Johansson's eyes were still locked on her screen.

I saw something on the camera, and still nothing else.

Johansson was conscious of Law moving towards her. She looked up and stared, unblinking, at Law.

'Where are we, Law?' she said, icily.

Law's face remained expressionless but brittle. A single snort, a slight roll of her eyes towards the ceiling.

'I have looked outside and there is nothing out there,' said Johansson. 'And I'm not convinced it's an imaging issue.'

A warning message popped up on Law's console and she turned back towards it, studying it. Johansson squinted at it, catching the words *pellet injection* and *cooling* before the message disappeared.

Law glanced back at Johansson, then back at the display. Johansson lifted herself from the deck by an inch, fingers tight around the edge of the console. The message popped up again, this time with a flashing red border around it. An indicator of some kind, climbing a graph, erratically, triggering more warnings.

'Law,' said Johansson, imposingly. 'What is the *Prompt*? What is going on?'

A pained expression poured down Law's face, followed by a flash of panic, her face hot. She shook her head defensively and made a beeline for her console. An audible warning rang out, a single attention-grabbing tone.

Fuck this.

Johansson paused for a moment, breathed in as deeply as she could, and carefully threw herself around the console, silently launching in the direction of Law. The audible alert intensified as Johansson ploughed into Law, pushing her sideways away from her station, a loud *Erk!* jumping from her lips.

'What the he–'

Johansson grabbed Law's arms, her suit pulling them behind her back powerfully, crossing them over, and put a boot against her back, levering against her. Law yelped, Johansson's suit-assisted strength surprising her. The audible alert continued to grow more intense, banging away in the background.

'Get off me, you bitch!' shouted Law, as the pair drifted into the wall, Law's face taking the brunt of the impact.

'Tell me what is going on, and tell me now,' said Johansson, firmly, applying more force to Law's back, her arms stretching.

'Now is not the fucking time, you moron. Get off me!'

A series of amber rotating lights sprang to life, casting jittering shadows throughout engineering. The entirety of Law's console flashed to red, and the haze over the accessway to one of the fusion reactors shimmered menacingly, heat pouring from the containment structure.

Law squirmed, trying to free herself, to no avail. A timer appeared on the screen, displaying 325 seconds, and then started counting downwards.

'It's on you if that times out and this ship bites the dust,' said Johansson. 'Your call. I've got all day.'

Law whipped her head around and fruitlessly kicked her legs, frustration tearing through her. The pair continued to bounce slowly around the room, Law's arms straining at their sockets as Johansson forcefully kept her foot in the small of her back.

I've got you, dumbass. Thanks, suit.

The audible alert became a full-on alarm, screaming up and

down Engineering Access, the amber lights changing to red, their pattern now more frantic.

Law suddenly slumped, her body becoming loose and pliable.

'Alright, alright, alright,' she snarled, agitated. 'Just let me at my console, first, please.'

Johansson squeezed Law's wrists. 'And you'll tell me what's going on?'

'And I'll tell you what's going on.'

'Okay,' she said, the aggression trickling out of her voice. 'But first, this.'

Johansson took her foot from Law's back and then pulled her closer. She kept one hand firmly around the wrist of Law's dominant hand, the side her firearm was holstered, and used her other to extricate Law's pistol from its holster. Johansson then pushed Law away, into the corner of the room, the pistol trained in her general direction, its safety on.

'Keep your movements slow and steady,' she said, her voice getting quieter as her muscles and stance softened.

Law looked at her, face a seething mass of anger, and then scurried over to her console, her fingers moving more quickly than Johansson could believe. The screen ripped back and forth, diagrams and menus coming and going. Heat swelled from the fusion accessways, followed by the odour and taste of burning exotic metals. An uninterrupted stream of curse words poured forth from Law at her console as she hammered away, tackling the unseen below.

Johansson watched the display closely. She could see images of the magnetic cooling loops coming and going, coolant and pellet injection system warnings, a model of the two tokamaks side-by-side in their standalone containment units, more errors, some complete fail–

The screeching alarm stopped and the rotating red lights switched back to less aggressive amber. Law spun towards her, face dripping with displeasure. 'You might have just cost us this whole fucking ship.'

'We've still got the other plant.'

Law clenched her fists. 'Did you not fucking listen? The first is already practically topped out, the second already taking up some load. If it goes out, that's game over. And it's not like its condition just improved, is it, you fuck. The demands are rising, not falling!'

Johansson pulled the slide of the pistol back, saw nothing, ejected the magazine, glanced at the ammunition, and reinserted the magazine. She then racked the slide, the *snick* of it running forwards making Law jolt.

'Green tips, still,' she said, waving the gun in Law's direction, her thumb hovering over the safety catch. 'Play nice and fill me in. And we'll go from there.'

Law glared back at her, seething, anger radiating from her more intensely than the heat from the struggling reactor.

'God!' she barked, pounding her fists on the console. 'Alright! Just don't point that thing at me.'

The nose of the pistol dropped, towards the floor, and Johansson opened her arms slightly, a less aggressive stance.

'Alright, alright,' said Law, voice quieting, her eyes skipping from Johansson to the display and back repeatedly. 'But if I tell you this, you have to promise to help me, and quickly.'

'What you tell me will decide whether I promise to help you or not.'

Law nodded, her eyes settling on the screen in front of her. Her fingers began to move again, slowly, characters and readouts on the screen changing.

'I ...'

'You can start from scratch, if you like,' said Johansson, lowering the pistol to her side, 'if that makes things easier.'

Get that tongue rolling a bit, she thought, resting against a computer.

'Okay,' said Law, hunkering down at her console, attentively. 'You know as well as I that travelling meaningful distances in space is difficult. The first time we pointed a ship at Mars, it took, what, seven months? And that was just some thirty-four million miles, which is effectively just around the corner from Earth, in space terms.'

Johansson nodded. 'And the fuel, shielding, serviceability, those were all major hurdles. The flights were pretty moot, given that most of the ships' weight was just fuel and protection.'

'Right, which is why NASA, before it was disbanded, initiated another Breakthrough Propulsion Physics project. It was decided that we needed to start pushing outwards, and find ways to travel longer distances more quickly, before climate, overpopulation, water, food, wealth imbalance, a dismally underperforming education sector, the whole sordid clusterfuck we'd just willingly walked into, started making any such efforts unfeasible.'

The amber lights stopped rotating and settled into a less alarming pulsing pattern. The red faded from Law's console, too, and the temperature dropped by a few degrees. Johansson looked around, cautiously.

'Anyway, a lot of it focused on experimenting with the Alcubierre drive. Field manipulators would alter space to form a protective bubble around the ship, then compress the space in front of the bubble and expand that behind it. It effectively moved space around the ship until it arrived at its destination, and allowed for faster-than-light travel.'

'I thought that idea got scrapped a long time ago,' said Johansson.

'And it did. It needed too much power, and it transpired that the particles and energies that accumulated on the ship's protective bubble during flight were released on arrival, potentially obliterating everything in front of it. We tried it a few times, using sun-orbiting solar arrays, nuclear-pulsed generation and lasers to remotely power ships, but ...'

'It didn't pan out.'

'There were complications. The first RSF prototype didn't work as expected and then there were incidents of, uh, collateral damage.'

'Did someone misconvert from metric to imperial by mistake again? I'd have thought you'd be wise to that by now,' said Johansson, making circles with the barrel of the gun. 'Expand.'

Law frowned and hesitated briefly. 'Well, we subsequently got one ship to fly, and fly true. When it arrived at its destination, Io, the energy released destroyed a station, three corvettes and a super cruiser. And that test ship itself was damaged in the ensuing mess.'

'I bet that went down brilliantly.'

'Exactly. We might have been able to make it safe but that whole avenue was shut off, and the officials drew a line through any other such technologies that were being proposed. Too much risk, like working with chlorine trifluoride.'

'Chlorine trifluoride?'

'It was a compound discovered by a pair of German scientists in the early twentieth. Some looked at it for a long time as a potential oxidising agent for space flight. The problem was that it basically wanted to cease the existence of everything else around it, immediately. Even stuff that you'd not perceive as combustible will burn on contact.'

She made an explosion gesture with her hands again.

'We played with it a bit, just to see, as sometimes there's something someone overlooked,' she said, tapping the crest on her shoulder. 'We had a tank rupture on Pluto, which released about a tonne of it. It ignited on contact with the exterior of the tank and burned through half a metre of concrete, and then three metres of the stabilising pad beneath, without any oxygen around.'

Johansson raised an eyebrow.

'Yeah, quite. Back in the NASA days, one of the scientists said that it would ignite spontaneously with absolutely everything, from other fuels through to asbestos, sand, water, wood, and test engineers. The only advice he had was to keep a good pair of running shoes to hand. He wasn't wrong.'

The amber lights went out, and a steady and reassuring hum of machinery permeated the engineering space.

'So what's this, then?' said Johansson, the barrel of the gun sweeping upwards, around the *Prompt*. 'It certainly seems to have riled people up to a more significant extent.'

'With that research shuttered and the RSF prototypes mothballed, we had to look more closely at solutions that could perhaps offer a shortcut through our own space without endangering that within it. Solutions using both natural and artificial wormholes, and other space-bending techniques, from wild but tangible to the purely conceptual, that could allow us to travel vast distances, in the blink of an eye, using little to no fuel.'

'But this has no advanced drive system,' said Johansson, adamantly.

'The *Prompt* isn't that important,' said Law, tapping her console once, a look of concentration on her face. 'The heavy lifting is done by the Transit Stations. The *Prompt* is just the train in their tunnel.'

Johansson's eyes bulged.

The Transit Station, she thought, eyebrows doing a passable impression of climbing up and off her forehead.

'The Transit Stations,' said Johansson, mouthing the words slowly.

'Correct. The intent was to test the feasibility of creating a wormhole between two known points, with the aim being to fly a ship in at one end and have it arrive almost instantly at the other, travelling through the short void in between, making longer-distance flights quicker, safer and easier.'

'*Of course I can. I'm the VFOE,*' chanted her mind. *Void Flight!*

Johansson shook her head, slowly, disbelievingly.

Law smiled, the mere thought of the concept energising her. 'At the core of each station is a hollow cylindrical structure, extending into space at both ends, in which we established a wormhole by distorting space-time and curving it, collapsing it inwards on itself. It took a lot of power to manipulate gravity and excite the vacuum of space enough, but it did work.'

'But that's just one point. What's the use of that if it doesn't go anywhere?' said Johansson, mind spinning.

'Well, the result was a stable wormhole, with two sides, which could be crossed in both directions, unlike a black hole-based one. We'd create one at the union between two stations, and, once stable, we effectively just moved the stations apart, separating the sides of the wormhole.'

'So you could transit between two known points,' said Johansson, dryly.

'Exactly. We refer to them as void gates, given where they go and how they work,' said Law, nodding. 'That and it sounded better; it made the project easier to sell and get signed off.'

'And we're currently in the space between those two ... gates.'

'Exactly,' said Law, nodding. 'And we've been creeping along in it for a while, drifting towards the exit.'

She didn't take us away from the station, realised Johansson, her muscles going limp. *She took us into it.*

'So your initial remotely commanded emergency burn ...'

'Took us through the station's gate, into void space, yes,' said Law, beaming. 'It was a risky move, but it was either that or lose everything, and once in flight all we would have to do is reach the exit gate.'

'Which is?'

'We left one gate at L3, Transit Station T1, from which we departed; the other, our destination, T2, we towed to the Mars-Phobos L1 Lagrange point. Both require minimal propellant to maintain position, due to the gravitational forces in those areas balancing out.'

Numbers on Law's screen continued to drop, their colour changing from red to amber, a handful dipping into the green, as the heat ebbed away from engineering.

Johansson shook her head again. 'But, surely, it's of little use if you have to move the gate to wherever you want to go in the first place, really?'

'That's an astute point, but all we had to prove was that it worked. If a ship travelled from T1 to T2, in a significantly shorter time than flying directly, then we'd get all the funding and support we needed. After that, we hoped that additional research, focused on quantum entanglement, might enable us to alter the destination of an existing gate to that of another, or that of a preexisting wormhole. We even penned a system that could be flung into black holes, perhaps emerging on the other side, to then remotely establish a traversable void gate in a new region.'

'And the flight times?'

She beamed, her eyes sparkling. 'At speed, we're talking seconds, minutes, hours, not days, weeks, months, years, depending on where you're going.'

Fleets of ships, exploring new lands, a new gold rush in space. All for the taking.

Johansson's shoulders slumped. She cleared the pistol's chamber, made sure it was safe, and sighed.

'And this is why they attacked the ship,' said Johansson. 'Or, at least, tried to immobilise it, to incapacitate its crew.'

'It's the cusp of a revolution, and everything will go to those willing to make it work, so that's my working assumption, yes,' said Law. 'Destroy the ship, capture the ship, immobilise the ship, any would probably have done. Or maybe they were just sweeping the area, to make a clear path through which they could take the station. If they could capture an already-outfitted ship, like the

Prompt, though, it would make it quicker to duplicate and employ the technology.'

'The shielding system?'

'The shielding system, yes. That's the one thing that distinguishes this ship, the one thing that makes flight, in what we call the void, safe. But it is not new technology, in itself, and someone, who applied themselves, would soon work out what was required.'

And someone would.

'If they had given me the budget and support from the outset, we wouldn't have ended up in this mess,' said Law, aggrieved. 'But no. "We deem the project unviable and ..."'

She went quiet, one fist clenching firmly, body tense.

Johansson put her hands up, slowly. 'We've come this far,' she said, weakly. 'And I promised to help you, and I will. This, from what you've said, sounds like a shot at a better future than anything else on the books.'

'Pave the way to a better future!' said Law, mustering a smile and extending her hand.

Johansson snorted and put her hands down on the console in front of her. 'By simply flying this thing out of here?'

'That's it,' said Law, nodding. 'I've oriented the ship, thanks to your help, the reactors are holding up, for now, and it's just a case of getting down the pipe to home.'

She pressed some buttons and a new illustration appeared on her display. It showed the *Prompt*, in what looked like part of an hourglass; ahead, in the distance, was a single circle, flat and facing the ship. 'That's where we need to get to.'

'What are our options?'

'There's not enough power overhead to safely run the plasma drives, so we're going to have to rely on the chemical rockets. The only consolation is that we just need a small push to set us on our way.'

'And that won't close before we get there?' said Johansson, tapping the circle on the screen, her motion slowing.

'No. The stations are unmanned, automated and will keep the gate open, at least until whatever ingressed on one side egresses on the other, for safety reasons.'

'To make sure the ship doesn't get stuck in void space?'

'Well, yes, but, more pressingly, we're not entirely sure if a ship would drop out of void space into conventional space, if a gate were to be closed, somewhere along its potential flightpath. Or, well, we don't know.'

'So it might just reappear, say, in a plan–'

'The chances are so small as to be impossible, and the risk worth taking,' retorted Law, stridently. 'But, more crucially, the stations and their redundancies must keep their respective gates open, because if that connection is broken then the stations currently become useless until you move them back together and form a new void gate.'

'And because we're still in void space, and that gate's still there, that means the stations should still be there and be operating,' said Johansson, gesturing at the screen, her speech slurring slightly. 'And the return will be safe.'

'That's right. They are heavily armoured, for one thing. That strike wouldn't have so much as scratched them,' said Law, confidently. 'And wiping them out wouldn't help their cause, either, anyway.'

Johansson weakened suddenly, slumping over the console, her bouncing arm kicking the pistol free from her grasp. It spiralled towards Law, slowly, its barrel pointing at her, then Johansson, and back again, as it spun.

Neither moved. Johansson's head now rested on the console itself, her breathing heavy, her eyes tracking the still-spinning pistol. Law put her hands above her head and moved cautiously towards the pistol, drifting slowly through space. She grabbed it by the slide, barrel towards her, immediately slipped it into her holster, and then raised her hands again.

Johansson managed a nod, her eyes closing, as Law swept over to her. She freed a green cylinder from the pouch on Johansson's waist, pressed it to her neck, and hit the button. It hissed, and then Law tossed it over her shoulder.

'Not yet,' she said, pulling Johansson off the console. 'I still need your help to get the ship out of here.'

'Suit,' uttered Johansson, almost dreamily, one hand reaching down towards the medical pack on her inner thigh.

'That might help, yes, in the longer term. Don't go anywhere.'

Law disappeared, deep into Engineering Access. The sound of drawers being opened and slammed closed, and cupboards being rummaged through, rang throughout the engineering space. She reappeared, clutching some cabling and a small box, teal in colour with red medical markings on it.

'Someone had put these in the wrong place,' she muttered, waving the box around. 'Old markings, not current ones. The budget obviously didn't extend to new labels.'

Law pushed Johansson's left knee to the side, popped open the pouch and lock plate on her inner thigh, and extricated the medical pack from her suit, snipping some of its damaged connectors free.

'Jesus,' said Law, shoulders dropping, as she studied the pack. She held it in front of Johansson; its myriad enclosed cylinders and voids were mostly empty, but there were three that still contained fluids. The first was one marked N.SUPP, which was about three-quarters full. The next was N.MOD, of which half remained. The last was M.REL, down to just an eighth of its original amount.

Law craned her head ceiling-wards for a moment, muttering to herself, then held the pack closer to her face, inspecting its every detail.

'You've burned through almost all of the stimulants, and some of the oxygenator, which is understandable,' said Law. 'You've got through a fair chunk of the muscle relaxants as well, which have no doubt been taking the edge off and reducing strain during the less stressful periods. The painkillers are drained; I think your suit might have resorted to using the relaxants as a stand-in.'

She paused for a moment, turning the pack slowly, looking at it through the lighting from above.

'These neurosuppressants and modifiers, there's less call for these, even in arduous conditions,' said Law, categorically. She tapped the N.SUPP and N.MOD tubes. 'But there's no way, even on a job like this, that you would have been dosed with anywhere near these amounts.

Johansson shrugged, slowly. 'On a job like this?' she stuttered, becoming more alert, but uncomprehending. 'A leak?'

'Maybe,' said Law. 'It might explain why you're having trouble recalling some of the more recent history. If the dispenser was damaged in the initial smash, it could have flooded you out with suppressants and modifiers, decimating your short-term memory and making everything else a mess.'

Law looked over the pack again, frowning. 'I'm not sure what happens with that kind of dose, and that combination of medication. You'd usually only get a few hits doled out automatically, if you were on this ship, to help avert direct recollection of anything important.'

She set about repairing the fittings and slipped the new pack into its receiving pouch, and then tapped Johansson on the waist, letting her know it was finished. Johansson grumbled as she dragged herself back to the vertical, the suit doing its best to steady her motion.

'Your memory of what happened might come back in time,' said Law, shrugging. 'I can't say what other symptoms may or may not persist.'

Great, thought Johansson, woozily. *Fucking great.*

CHAPTER EIGHTEEN

The sound of Law's holster being snapped closed echoed through engineering. She passed Johansson some water, shook herself down, and lingered by her console.

'Ready for the next hurdle?' she asked enthusiastically. 'We need to get underway before any other oddities materialise, or something gives way back there.' Law was gesturing rearwards, to the fusion plants.

Johansson nodded wearily. 'Burn, home, a world-changing welcome.'

'Something like that,' said Law, tapping away at her keyboard again. 'I put the engines through their self-test process already, when the reaction control system came online. Three are reporting in as serviceable, the gimbal's out on another, and two are just unresponsive. Two, four and six are green, but we're going to need two and at least one of the others.'

'Not enough gimballing?' said Johansson.

'Yup. Because they're outboard clusters, if number two doesn't light then we'll end up with uncorrectable asymmetric thrust and the ship will end up going in circles. I doubt any of the front reaction controls will work, so we won't be able to control that degree of yaw.'

'How long do you think we need to burn for?' said Johansson. 'I'm hoping it's a brief one, given the state of the ship.'

'I'm solidly with you there. I reckon thirty seconds, just to get us moving onwards in earnest, and then we can just coast the rest of the way.'

'How long will it take to get out, afterwards?'

'I'm going to keep the throttles set low, to preserve the engines, so we'll only be moving at a crawl. It's going to take us about fifty minutes to make the remaining transit at that pace,' said Law. 'Even if we have to push this thing, we have to get it out of the void space.'

Johansson made her way over to the console Law was working at and looked at the display. It was a close-up technical diagram of the *Prompt*'s chemical rocket assemblies, its readouts flitting back and forth, component animations coming and going.

'What's the story?' said Johansson, watching the almost incomprehensible mess drift across the screen. 'I've never been much involved with full-scale flight.'

'We're going to take it real slow, and we're going to try and light number two off from here,' said Law. 'If that one doesn't start then, well, we might as well not bother with anything else.'

'Do these still burn liquid oxygen and hydrogen?' said Johansson, pointing at the rocket assemblies. 'I've not dealt with a Sark like this for a while.'

'Very early on, yes, but we're on a greener mix, these days,' said Law, nodding. 'Even so, it's old but pretty reliable. And I'm going to get your help to start it. The auto-sequencing is up for four and six, but two is manual operation only.'

'What happened to it?'

'It's got part of a Telegraph wedged in it, so I think it's safe to assume that it's damaged,' said Law, deadpan.

'Is it even advisable to try starting it? It's only going to take a sheared line, a broken igniter, or any multitude of things, and that whole assembly will blow up, and that'll probably be the final straw.'

Law dipped her head for a second and then stopped typing. 'It's all we can do, right now, to try and get this ship back. If the RSF doesn't know this ship survived, if I don't survive, this technology will die, on the spot, and no one will touch it. I'll lose everything, and we'll be set back decades, if not more, and then that'll be all we wrote.'

'So you're willing to gamble,' said Johansson, unquestioning.

'I have no choice but to gamble,' responded Law, adamantly. 'I'm not a fan of the option, and I know the risk, but we simply must. This ship must get home.'

'Well, let's make it happen,' asserted Johansson, her posture smartening, stiffening. 'What do you need me to do?'

Law nodded, appreciatively. 'The real problem we face is that the tank pressures are fluctuating, either because that port tank's damaged somewhere as well, or heat is transferring from elsewhere in the ship into them.'

'Figures,' said Johansson, grimly.

'What I need you to do is watch these two pressure gauges, one for the fuel, one for oxidiser, like a hawk. The pressures have to stay high enough to allow us to get the fuel preburner in the engine wound up, so it has enough power to drive the turbopumps that supply the main combustion chamber. If the fuel pressure falls below this marker, or if the oxidiser pressure runs outside of these limits, shout and I'll abort the start-up.'

'Low fuel pressure is a problem?'

'In these, yes. If the oxidiser doesn't have anything to burn with, it goes after the internal components of the rocket motor. The temperatures spike, and the engine can't handle sustained spikes.'

'And then you get an unscheduled rapid disassembly,' said Johansson, shaking her head.

Law laughed. 'Look, I know it's another hurdle, but if we get this done then we'll be on our way and out of the ashes of the woods.'

'And then?'

'We'll cross that bridge when we come to it,' said Law, unconvincingly, tapping the clock on her wrist. 'Let's get on with this: you monitor those gauges, and I'm going to run the start-up sequence.'

'Alright. Needles up, gauges in the green,' said Johansson, crossing her fingers under the console.

'Go for start-up on two,' said Law, authoritatively, settling into her seat. 'Pipe and pump chilling complete. Fuel valve one open. Oxidiser valve one open. Throttle set. Go for turbine spin, ignition.'

Johansson could see her counting under her breath, two, three, four, and an audible whine arose in the distance.

'Pump torque coming up,' continued Law. 'Priming fuel and oxygen preburner, priming main combustion ignition.'

The whine continued to increase in volume, and a hollow *whoomph* echoed through the bay.

'Turbopump at speed, check, preburning, check.'

Johansson noticed that Law's foot was rapping on the floor, her leg bouncing slightly, ticking away. Her eyes flicked back to her gauges. 'Gauges green,' she shouted.

Come on, you old hound.

'Main combustion prime, set. Ah–'

'What?'

'Don't worry about it!'

A series of dull thuds echoed through Engineering Access, like an engine sputtering on a handful of cylinders.

'Oxygen flow set, fuel flow set, prime set, star–'

The floor vibrated aggressively, loose panelling rattling. Johansson noticed the floor rotating, slowly, and rising towards her.

'Two seconds, sequencing, ramping up t–'

The ship bucked, the deck plates rattling.

Law grinned. 'Oh, yeah, it's going.'

One, two, three, under her breath again, thought Johansson, distracted from the gauges momentarily.

'Go for throttle up, twenty per cent max.'

The ship felt like it was heaving. So did Johansson's stomach.

'Gauges are still green,' shouted Johansson.

'It's in closed loop; two's up and in the clear!' cheered Law, giving a thumbs-up to the ship.

'Auto-cycle set for four,' she added, tapping the screen, thumbing the large buttons marked RUN. The functioning computers in the nacelle took over, operating the entire process from start to finish automatically.

'Fuel pressure is flailing a bit,' cautioned Johansson. Something banged unhappily in the distance, and the ship's acceleration ebbed for a moment.

Law cursed and hit a button marked ABORT. 'Pump on four is struggling; there must be a leak somewhere. I don't think we can start that one.'

The ship continued pitching up, the reaction thrusters at the rear having little ability to counter the off-centre thrust being provided by the powerful rocket engine. Johansson's feet touched the floor.

Law cycled the selector switch through to six and stabbed RUN again. The computers stepped in again and set about bringing the engine to life.

'Gauges wavering but green,' shouted Johansson.

She sensed the floor exerting less pressure on her as the mechanical noises in the background settled, soothed, the clanging of rapidly contracting then expanding metals becoming intermittent, then quiet, as the engines came up to temperature.

'Two and six are lit and burning happily,' said Law, whistling through her teeth, 'and the gimbals and reaction control system are bringing the ship back on an even keel. Course and speed are programmed.'

The display updated to reflect the *Prompt*'s course, a straight line through void space, its speed slowly climbing. It was crawling, by space standards, but mobile.

Law patted Johansson on the back. 'See, it's not all bad. We're on the cusp of making history.'

Johansson reached up and reset a mission-counter clock, setting it for fifty minutes. The *Prompt* continued to burn, into the void, its two lit engines casting brilliant blue spires behind it. Spent gases, particulate matter and debris trailed it briefly, and then were gone.

The engines completed their burn and, as commanded, throttled back and shut down, leaving the *Prompt* cruising towards its destination. Law checked her display, intently, nodding to herself, and then disappeared into the depths of engineering, returning a moment later with two full hot cups of tea and coffee.

'That'll do,' she said. 'Gambled and won. We won't push our luck, or the engines, any more.'

Johansson took one of the cups, grateful for the warmth, and grateful for something to flush the faint aftertaste of medicines and copper out of her mouth. They both hovered by their consoles, listening to the machinery at work, sipping on their drinks, as the ship slipped otherwise silently through the void.

'So, what's actually out there?' said Johansson. 'Not regular space?'

Law blew steam from the top of her coffee cup. 'The void between the gates is, to be frank, still somewhat of an unknown. Our experience of it is limited, in the extreme.'

'But is it just empty, or ...'

Law tipped her head, understanding. 'No, no, it's not conventional space, that much we have established. It's one of some eleven higher-dimensional planes, a concept called "the bulk", and what we've so far accessed is rife with exotic energies, particles and processes that we've not even begun to catalogue. The one thing they have in common is that, in some way, they underpin the four tangible dimensions of our universe.'

'I always remember one of my lecturers saying that one of those dimensions might contain a much stronger form of gravity, or something along those lines, which would explain its comparatively weak presence in our own universe,' said Johansson.

'It's exactly that. Home to things that we've yet been able to document or explain, spread across different planes of existence.'

'And a lot of money to be made, and power to be wielded,' said Johansson.

'Definitely,' said Law, quietly, casting her eyes back to the readouts.

Forty-six minutes and three seconds.

'At least we're not just going to cease to be,' she said, out loud.

'What?!' said Law, alarmed but inquisitive.

'It's always been one of my pet fears,' said Johansson, gulping down more tea. 'A ship disappearing, no reports, no one ever knowing what happened. I'd hate to put that on someone, that lack of closure.'

'Sounds like you're speaking from personal experience,' said Law, glancing in Johansson's direction for a moment. 'You probably didn't pick the best career for minimising that possibility.'

'I wasn't the first of my family in the RSF,' said Johansson. 'Several others had joined up, long before I arrived on the scene. I suppose you might say it's tradition, so here I am.'

'How many others, in total?'

'Five, my mother being the last before I joined up,' said Johansson. 'She crewed one superb corvette. A tight-knit crew, long-serving, upstanding. And then they ended up tasked with an escort mission, and that was that. That was the last I ever heard of them. My home fell apart after that, and only the efforts of my uncle kept me together for long enough to enlist and get into the service.'

Law stopped typing and looked over her shoulder at Johansson.

'They wouldn't tell me what had happened, even after years in the service. Everything was redacted, quelled, obliterated. All I know, from a few words uttered by those on the fringes, is that no one was sent to help. There was a window, an opportunity to save them. But they instead chose to do nothing. All those years of service, all those achievements, all that good done, was wiped away, and for what? To what end? And then it just left me, picking up invisible piece after invisible piece, never knowing.'

Johansson shifted, uncomfortable, heat coursing through her veins.

'Shit just never leaves you, you know. It makes you restless, for life.'

Law's eyes crept away from Johansson's, a hint of shame creeping in at their corners.

'It wasn't the only instance, either, but I felt that one the hardest. People just gone, snuffed out, eliminated from the files with a casual press of a button. And then that's it, the world rolls on. I don't want to put anyone in that position, and I don't want to end up like that.'

'I'm sorry, I didn't know,' said Law.

'Yeah, well. I'd say it was in my files, but those elements of it are redacted to the point of being illegible. I think they've written off my angst a long time ago. I've just kept my head down and kept on,' muttered Johansson. 'And it's not like they have the people with appropriate qualifications lining up for gigs like this,' she added, wryly. 'A good hand, in the wrong place at the right time, can make a difference. They didn't object to me continuing on, in the background, at least.'

'And you cleared the way for your daughter by doing so,' added

Law. 'You did a good thing there. I don't think anyone would fault you for that.'

'That's kind,' said Johansson, smiling gently. 'But, really, I think the reality is that I was just scared. I was scared about standing my ground again, scared about what might happen to her, and scared that I might expose her to the same loss that I experienced. I'm not sure I have that willpower, that drive, like yourself, or her, to overcome that.'

'There's nothing wrong with being afraid. We'd lose a lot more ships, out here, if people didn't let fear and concern temper their actions.'

'Oh, we still occasionally push the envelope, I know that much,' said Johansson, snorting. 'Stick a load of people in something fast and heavily armed and one of them will do something stupid eventually. Comes with the territory.'

'Stupid, or brave?'

'Depends on who survives,' she responded, sneering a little. 'Can't say I've done anything resembling the latter for a while. I can't even sum up the courage to send my child a message.'

'Why?'

'Well, time, for starters. I couldn't, didn't make the time, to see, and then talk, to her. And, before I knew it, a year had gone by. And speaking to her just got more intimidating with every passing day. Eventually, I decided it was just easier to leave it be.'

'You don't strike me as someone easily intimidated.'

'When it comes to work, sure. Family? That's something a few good miles out of my comfort zone,' said Johansson, sniffing. 'But I figured that, well, I didn't want her to experience what I did. I figured if I stayed out of sight, out of mind, then it would be less painful if the worst happened. I just didn't want her to get that ping from RCOM, with no details, and for it to tear something tangible away from her, leaving her feeling like I do.'

'You know full well you're capable of it,' said Law, snappily.

'Look at what you've done in the past, look at what you've done today, on this flight alone. That takes some real guts. Forget about the should-have-could-haves; muscle up when you get back and speak to her.'

Johansson's brow furrowed, the creases on her forehead deepening by the minute.

'Are you okay?' asked Law, studying her intensely.

'I think that was one of the reasons I stepped foot on the *Hard Target*,' she said, shakily. 'I think I took it because I was told its run would terminate at Mars.'

'Rings a bell. And?'

'And that's where the ship she's on is stationed at the moment. I guess I thought maybe it would be easier to see her in person, that being in proximity might force me to act.'

'Your bold streak again,' said Law, laughing dryly. 'Nothing by halves, hey? See, you're getting there.'

Johansson blushed, and her brow settled. 'I'm just taken aback a bit by the recollection. That was all muddy earlier,' she muttered, as her mental train slowly put more of its wheels back on the track.

'I told you that you could trust me. Maybe something in the greens helps reinstate a bit of edge, or flush something out,' said Law, watching a measured distance ticking downwards.

'I'd show you a picture, but you know what it's like on these things. Impersonal. Interactions to a minimum, strictly professional relationships, no identifying objects that could be easily employed against us, should the ship and its crew fall into enemy hands,' said Johansson, her voice imitating the flat tone of the RSF training videos.

The corvette!

'That's why I only carry a picture of my mother's corvette,' she said, a warm glow settling on her face, a spark in her mind. 'I guess it serves to remind me of family, past and present.'

'What was the name of the ship?' said Law, seeking something less charged to talk about.

'The corvette? The *Not Your Problem*. It was a beautiful ship, the first of the Gloster Juno line. A real heavy-hitter, one of the first with rod-slinging railguns. Open-cycle nuclear propulsion, though, which was a bit troublesome. Still. Ancient history. There one day, gone the next.'

She tailed off. Law had looked away, back to her screen, a new pop-up wrenching her attention back to the land of the digital.

'Looks like Main is now in full effect,' said Law. 'There are still outages and systems behaving erratically, across the board, but that might settle as the new cores continue to straighten things out.'

'Any updates on what happened, or the whereabouts of the rest of the crew?' said Johansson, hopefully.

Law's screen shifted slightly. 'Internal communications are working, but there are no new counters. Just four markers.'

'And I'm guessing that's not the full complement. What about the others?'

Law looked slightly puzzled for a moment, her body freezing, and then resumed typing. 'Maybe they were in the rear ring when the attack took place. Probably preparing the caches for your inspection and help.'

'All of them?' said Johansson, doubtfully. 'This thing would have been like a museum piece, in that case; practically everything would have been shut down and secure.'

'There were issues with the airlocks throughout the ship, too, don't forget,' said Law. 'Maybe the attackers compromised those systems and vented the ship as part of their efforts to take it over.'

That might explain the disarray in the crew quarters. If not caused by manoeuvring, or whatever the hell has gone on here.

'How fast was the ship going when it entered the station?' said Johansson, her muscles tightening slightly.

Law looked back at her, another confused look on her face.

'I only got a short burst out of the thrusters before the systems started going down,' said Law, quickly. 'But it was just enough to get the *Prompt* creeping forwards, into the station's tunnel, and into the open gate. Just enough so we didn't soak up any more damage.'

Hovering around a metre per second, if that, remembered Johansson.

'There wasn't enough time to get anything else spooled up, I can tell you that much,' said Law, continuing, a proud look flashing over her face. 'The ship was cold, and not due to fly.'

So it was inactive, thought Johansson, ignoring her aches and getting to her feet. *Less of this is adding up*.

'Law,' said Johansson, hesitantly, her fingers wrapping around the shaft of the axe on her chest plate.

The typing stopped again.

'You're telling me that there was no evasive manoeuvring, no main thrust, before the ship transited to void space.'

A few seconds passed. Law's head bowed.

'That's right. That's probably why we took so many hits,' said Law.

'If that's the case,' said Johansson, 'then how the hell did those four end up dead?!'

CHAPTER NINETEEN

The two faced each other, their breath held. Johansson's hand tugged at the shaft of the axe, pulling it free from the magnetic pad; Law's hand slipped down to her waist, onto the beavertailed backstrap of her pistol.

'That wasn't anything to do with me,' hissed Law, her speech sharp, insistent. 'Do you think you'd still be alive if I had killed the rest of the crew? What would I gain from that?'

Johansson shook her head, her hair brushing against the wall behind her. 'I'm not sure. But I'm starting to wonder if I'm only still here because I'm useful to you.'

'And that doesn't need to change,' said Law, raising her hand from her pistol a fraction, her eyes softening. 'Look, Main is up and everything should be accessible now. If you need proof, let's just decompress the footage from the cameras in that area. That'll tell us the full story.'

Johansson felt a stabbing pain in her waist as Law brought up the internal camera archives.

The suit trying to stave off whatever's trying to do me in now. Thanks.

She squinted, her vision blurring for a moment, the hours in action on the ship now feeling like days without a break. Johansson rubbed her eyes, the gloves digging into her sockets.

Law waved Johansson over to her console. She approached, slowly, but kept a good few feet between the two of them, and positioned herself on the far side from Law's holster. She didn't object, or even acknowledge the movement, and continued to prod away at the console.

An unbroken timeline of video feeds appeared on the screen, showing footage from the countless cameras dotted around the *Prompt*. A vast number of them, most of the external ones, had failed, their timelines blank, a harsh blue colour occupying the space where footage previews would otherwise appear.

Johansson recognised one of the internal cameras and pointed at it. Law moved the cursor over it, clicked, and a view of one of the starboard oxygen tank platforms zoomed into view. Johansson was moving around on the platform, her eyes flitting about, and then disappeared into a control room.

'This might be one for the archives,' said Law, watching the footage intently. Johansson nodded, her eyes locked on the screen as well.

Just don't watch the bit where I almost ejected all of the tanks.

The footage played on, showing the droid screeching back to life, pursuing Johansson from the tanks, it careening into the blast walls, the station, and eventually crawling to a halt after being doused. All of it exposed in high-framerate, high-definition, high-visibility capture. Law spooled back and forth through it a few times, watching, seemingly fascinated by the droid's actions.

Johansson pushed back to her console, shaking her head, and pulled up her electronic countermeasures panel while Law continued to scan through the footage.

I don't need to see that again.

She quickly copied the timecode from the footage and scrolled through the countermeasure system's logs, looking for anything that was broadcasted or received at the same time, anything that could be perceived as some kind of hacking or override attempt. There was nothing, just blank holding pages; moments after the initial attack, the ship had simply stopped receiving or transmitting anything. And, with Main out, any records would be patchy, at best.

I'm not sure what I'm looking for. But there will be something.

'Maybe it was cued up earlier,' said Johansson, out loud, digging through the previous entries in the system.

'Mmmmm,' went Law, watching footage of herself and Johansson restarting the port reactor.

Johansson closed the countermeasures tab. There was too much clutter to discern any specific focus; the *Prompt* had been saturated with all manner of electronic attacks, sending its defensive electronic systems into overdrive, report after report piling into its logs.

'Credit where it's due, even though this isn't a fully hardened and current ship, it held up pretty well,' said Johansson.

'We might have cut lots of corners elsewhere, but they were pretty set on making sure that someone unfamiliar didn't simply walk away with anything we came up with,' said Law, her screens now showing the pair of them riding around on the trains.

Law huffed, her eyes scanning the small footage preview window carefully, and clicked further back in the timeline, the footage jumping back several hours in one hit.

'There I am,' she muttered, head shifting towards the display a little.

She maximised the view from one camera, which showed her traversing space, drifting from the rear of Engineering Access towards the starboard reactor station. Law watched as she scrambled onto its radiator array, and set about working. The camera showed her free hand tapping busily away at her wrist-mounted computer, the pace of her typing quickening, as access panels on the reactor began to open. Law bumped the footage forward ten seconds, and then another ten, watching.

'Feels like a lifetime ago, doesn't it,' said Johansson, looking over her shoulder.

Something flashed, for a solitary frame, across the view of the camera. Then, dazzling white light. The *Prompt Excursion* looked like it was leaning, staggering; the *Hard Target* was visible in the background, briefly, at a wildly different angle to the *Prompt*, and then disappeared, bright flashes all that remained at the edges of the screen, debris scattering wildly and rapidly across the camera's view. The weapons of the *Prompt* began to turn, and autocannon began to blaze away.

'Jesus,' murmured Johansson, steadying herself against the edge of the console. The weapons fire intensified, and countermeasures and missiles began to fly past the camera. And then nothing; the footage cut out, the camera destroyed or its systems failing, and pitch black filled the screen.

'What about a view of the station?' she said.

'I think we need to find out what took place here, first, but I've not had a chance to review the footage yet,' said Law, returning to the security system's main menu and selecting a view showing the Engineering Access control room. She idly spooled through the footage, watching people come and go until the attack started. The internal camera did not cut out, though, unlike those outside the ship.

Law placed her chin in her hands, elbows on the console, and watched, eyes glued to the screen. The camera was mounted high up; beneath it were the semicircular control panels, surrounded by other displays and switchboards on the walls. The floor underneath was a light grey, but darker where people regularly traversed from the doorway to commonly used controls, the scuffs of socks footwear transferring dirt to the panelling underfoot. A thin wisp of smoke occasionally drifted past the lens, and odd patterns were being cast over the wall by a rotating amber emergency light.

Much on the boards was red and pronounced alert messages kept appearing on the screens. Outside, at the edge of the view, smoke and steam could be seen pouring from the panelling and machines, and bright blue arcs tore along the walls, from shattered gaps in major conduits. Flames licked from underneath the floor, scorching and melting composites, occasionally drifting free, small orbs of brightly burning materials and fire floating across the deck.

Four crew were pounding away at the consoles, trying to stave off the worst of the immediate failures: doors were being closed and secured, power was rerouted, crippled systems were isolated and shut down, valves closed, damaged munitions ejected. The power output readout from one fusion plant bounced up and down like a yo-yo, flitting between critical excess and nothing, but every moment at the boards seemed to reduce the severity of its oscillation. The ship was in a bad way but they were striving to save it.

Two left the room, rolling out fire suppression equipment and opening breakers, a hectic but carefully drilled and focused attempt to get everything under control and in order. Their high-visibility orange suits were neat and crisp, but foam, charred electronics and ash soon blemished them.

Just overalls, not suits, like Law, thought Johansson, fleetingly. *Engineering staff, perhaps those in the know.*

One of them was shouting something frantically as they returned to the room, but their voice was inaudible given the racket. They were repeating the same thing over and over again, a confused look on their face. Johansson watched, carefully.

Aye see bee hurrays. Aye see bee hurrays? That's what it looks like he's saying.

She shrugged, the hubbub on the screen subsiding as patches were fitted, panels were removed, valves opened again, pipework clamped and sealed, fires extinguished, and breakers thrown. The ventilation system quickly pulled most of the smoke out of the room as red lights began to turn amber, then green; a few high-fives were exchanged.

The crewmember who had been shouting reappeared again, gesticulating wildly toward the front of the ship, the other engineers shaking their heads in response, the state of confusion shifting from the attack to the present.

Hurrays powered, glimpsed Johansson, watching their lips again. *Arrays powered?*

The four regrouped in the control room, heads gathering around the main console and display, as the display brought up an overview of the *Prompt*, showing the ship moving away from what looked like a circle. The thin wisps of smoke still lingering in the room moved outwards suddenly, causing heads to spi–

And then Johansson marched into view on the screen, a compact axe in hand. She drove its blade deep into the back of the closest crewmember, pulled it free and then hacked at the neck of the one standing next to them. The two convulsed, losing their footing, blood slowly arcing into the atmosphere from their wounds. The remaining crew in the room turned, to face the source of the commotion, and threw themselves backwards, partly in shock, partly trying to create some distance. One grabbed a pry bar from the panel to their left and swung it at Johansson, slamming it into her helmet. The impact smashed her visor into her face and then the helmet broke free, spinning wildly off into engineering. But she kept coming; the crewmember grabbed a rail, braced, and put their entire force into the bar, catching Johansson square in the side as she advanced, axe raised. She didn't flinch, but the impact pushed her sideways, her suit sparking furiously, and her downward blow scythed past the head of the striking crewmember, the head of the axe burying itself deep into their arm, cleaving it off. Blood splattered across the console and the remaining unwounded crewmember, who was scrambling around the edge of the room, trying to make it to the exit.

Johansson's foot shot out, neatly catching the edge of a console, and she powered towards the fleeing crewmember, crossing the distance in a flash. She slammed into the wall in front of them, blocking their path, and thrust the head of the axe into their stomach, causing them to double over instantly. Johansson pushed them back against the wall with it, tipped the blade into their belly, and wrenched the axe lengthways across them, spilling their intestines into the air.

She then proceeded to each of the crew, some still struggling, hands clamping their wounds, and struck them repeatedly with the short, dull-grey titanium axe. Its head sparked occasionally as it cut clean through flesh and into the steel of panels and consoles behind, the blows hard and unrelenting until all were unquestionably dead.

Johansson lingered for a moment, and then turned, seemingly unfazed, and was gone as quickly as she had arrived, leaving nothing but floating, partially dismembered corpses, and clouds of blood, all drifting slowly towards the door, like the last drinkers leaving a bar at closing time.

Twenty seconds, and it was over. All of them were dead.

Ohmyg–

Law went for her gun.

CHAPTER TWENTY

Red tinges of flaring pain crept into the blackness of Johansson's vision, intensifying every time her head pounded. She couldn't see anything, apart from the odd flash of blinding agony that shot through her mind. Her wrists were bound tightly, behind her back, pulling her arms from her sockets, and her ankles were roughly tied in a cross beneath a chair. Sweat sluiced off her brow and soaked into fabric wrapped around her head, covering her eyes.

'Who the fuck are you?' screamed Law, her voice muffled by the blind. Johansson's jaw crashed into her shoulder, making her teeth rattle, as she was struck by something. Her eyebrows pumped up and down, her eyes widening, the blind shifting up and down, light creeping in, as Law's open palm battered into her face.

'What is your allegiance?' shouted Law, her breath hot on Johansson's exposed neck and forehead. Something sharp jammed into her waist, and she bawled as her body tried to contort, rolling into a ball, away from the anguish.

Johansson sensed Law moving away, and silence descended. It was more disconcerting than having her in her face. *Whatthefuckwasthathelp!* screamed her mind, as she writhed against her restraints.

That's something really strong, she thought, hastily. *Tigercord or similar.*

She coughed, a little blood trickling down onto her chin.

'Have you gone fucking mad,' spat Johansson, head rolling freely around.

'You're the one that's gone mad,' yelled Law, batting the back of her hand across Johansson's temple. 'You deceitful bitch!'

Johansson's mind boggled, her muscles tightened, bracing for pain.

Whatthefuckwasthathelp!

'I don't know what that was,' pleaded Johansson. 'You're the one with the files and firearm, why don't you tell me!' she screamed. 'You're the one responsible for this nightmare!'

Law ripped the blind from Johansson's head, the light in the control room blinding her momentarily. She looked warily in the direction of Law; she was floating by a console, hands on her hips, chest rising and falling heavily, her face contorted and red, a few feet away.

'I trusted you, but I clearly cannot reciprocate,' said Law frigidly, pulling her pistol from its holster. She pulled back its slide, locking it open, and slipped a magazine out of a pouch on her waist-band. Law ejected one of the rounds from the magazine, thumbed it into the breech of the pistol, and reinserted the magazine into its pouch. Her thumb brushed the slide release on the gun and it sprung forward, the bolt chambering the carefully selected round. The light metallic noise of the slide running forward echoed around the room for a moment.

Jacketed hollow point. That'll do it for me. Won't hurt the ship, though. Of course.

'I don't know what you're talking about, you clandestine cunt,' barked Johansson through gritted teeth, desperately writhing against her restraints.

Law pressed the pistol against Johansson's temple, its cold

muzzle squashing skin against bone, the sharp edges of its accessory rail digging tiny chunks of flesh out of her forehead.

Not now.

'Who paid you?' said Law. 'Who's trying to take this from me?'

Johansson remained silent.

'Which government–'

Law braced herself against the console, leant into the gun, and pushed harder, forcing Johansson's head against her shoulder.

'– paid you?'

Johansson glared at Law's shoulder, the only thing she could really see, and spat blood into the air.

'Paid me for what, you lunatic?!'

A hollow click rang out, louder than anything Johansson had heard in her life.

Safety's off. Be seeing you.

Law loomed over her, moving from Johansson's side to stare directly at her. Law's eyes were ablaze, face flustered, pulse racing. She reached out with her free hand to grab a floating display tablet behind her, the security footage bright and ugly on its screen, and then rammed it into Johansson's face.

'How could you do this, you malicious lying bitch,' shrieked Law. 'You put my project at risk!'

Johansson tried to focus on the tablet's display but it was too close, its protective edge jarring against her teeth, the panel crushing her nose.

'I can't fucking see it, you moron,' protested Johansson, squirming, trying to pull her head back, to put some distance between herself and Law.

Law backed off, pistol pointed squarely at Johansson's forehead, and held the panel up, front and centre.

Johansson looked at it, but she knew what would be on the display already. It was a looped piece of footage, running over and over again, showing her marching into engin–

She closed her eyes, not wanting to see it again. Johansson heaved, spewing a thin sickly fluid in Law's direction, and blacked out for a moment. Her heart hammered away like a piston in an engine, running into the red, and confusion coursed through her veins.

'I swear to go–' she stammered.

'Say it in person, bitch,' said Law, placing her feet firmly on the decking, one toe tucked under a grip ring. She released the tablet, put both hands on the grip of the pistol, and pointed it directly at Johansson's head.

'No!' shouted Johansson. 'No!'

Law leant forward, into the shot, and exhaled, taking her time. Her finger tensed on the trigger, its cool metal sinking into the tip of her index finger.

Johansson jerked this way and that, flailing her head around, rocking.

'Fuck!' she screamed. 'Fuck! Okay!'

'Okay, what?' snapped Law, finger still squeezing ever so slightly on the trigger, its pawl barely engaging with the sear, striker primed to spring forward.

WhatthefuckamIdoing?! thought Johansson, panicked.

'Can I see the footage again?' she pleaded, clutching at straws.

Law squinted, taken aback slightly.

'You'd willingly watch that again, you sick bitch? No, you don't get to gloat.'

Help.

'Any last words before I wipe the slate clean of you, for good?'

Her mind raced.

'Show me before,' she stammered.

'What?' said Law, confused.

'Show me before that happened,' Johansson repeated. 'I'd never do that, not to crew, to family, to put the ship at risk!'

WhatthefuckamIdoing?!

Law eyed Johansson cautiously and retrieved the tablet. She tapped its display, calling up new cameras and footage timeframes, and played it back to herself, watching.

'It shows me all I need to know,' said Law, flatly, fingertips brushing the side of the pistol again. 'You're on the bridge, you go down to engineering, you murder everyone, you secure it, and then you head back to the bridge.'

'I swear on my life that it wasn't me.'

'That doesn't command much weight when your life's about to last for just ten more seconds.'

'I implore you. Let me see. Please. For my sake.'

WhatthefuckamIdoing?!

Law stuck the tablet in front of her face, showing Johansson the same loop. Johansson was on the bridge, at the weapons station, and then it cut to showing her boarding a train and riding it to engineering. And then she murdered everyone, left engineering, closed the blast doors, and then reappeared on the bridge. Her head lolled, freely, as she collapsed onto the floor.

No muscles, thought Johansson, mind racing, *and I can't remember any of this.*

The footage looped. Johansson was on the bridge, at the weapons station, and then her head rolled forwards in her helmet. She turned and her head swung weakly around, as if her neck muscles had ceased to be. The lights on her suit were out.

Howthefuckarethelightsout?!

She got on the train and rode it to engineering, her head lolling around the inside of her helmet, her stance conflictingly powerful and fixed. She remained steady and unflinching, even when the cameras shook as weapons struck the ship. She murdered the crew, her head lolling merrily, body moving authoritatively and powerful, axe cleaving skin from bone without effort, and metal from panels without care. The lights on her suit were still out.

'Please, look at this, I beg you,' said Johansson, nodding frantically at the tablet.

Law turned the tablet around, watching the loop again.

'Look at my head, follow it,' said Johansson.

Law watched, eyes snapping over the tablet's edge occasionally, locking onto Johansson's briefly, then back to the footage. Law set the tablet down on the edge of a console, her other hand still wrapped around the pistol, and made a pinching gesture on the screen.

Law watched, stock still, silent.

'Your eyes are closed,' she said, sombrely, tone dropping further as the realisation sank in.

Johansson didn't move.

Law placed the tablet in front of her and played the loop again. She'd zoomed into the footage, enlarging Johansson's head and shoulders in each shot. The camera tracked her face, lifeless, eyes closed. Leaving, eyes closed. On the train, eyes closed. In engineering, eyes closed. Returning, eyes closed. On the bridge, eyes closed, collapsing. In the lower edge of the frame, the few visible lights on her suit flickered for a moment.

Law backed away from her, pistol still in hand but pointed at the floor.

'What the fuck is happening?!' yelled Johansson, writhing against her restraints.

Law watched the footage again. Johansson's movements were strong, precise, almost mech–

'It was your suit,' shouted Law, her eyes boggling. 'It's your fucking suit!'

Johansson's skin tried to jump ten feet to the left, her panicked yelping echoing around the close quarters of the control room. Law backed off, hurriedly, the barrel of the pistol trained on Johansson, or at least her suit. She snapped the slide back, ejecting the hollow-point round, the elevator serving up an armour-piercing round, and released it, keeping the gun pointed directly at Johansson's chest plate.

'Get this fucking thing off me!' she screamed, bouncing around in the chair, restraints unrelenting. 'Get it off me now!'

'What the fuck!' screamed Law, unhelpfully.

Johansson collapsed in the chair, unable to free herself. The lights on the front of the suit merely blinked, in their usual patterns, as if all were normal. Johansson rocked back and forth, one more time, then stopped, chest heaving.

'That wasn't you!' shouted Law, still brandishing the pistol. 'You were completely out. All of that was the suit!'

'No shit,' growled Johansson, 'and need I remind you that I'm still wearing it!'

'But it's not doing anything now,' said Law, the barrel of the pistol tracing increasingly lower arcs, moving towards the floor.

'But that doesn't mean it won't!'

Law shook her head, her pulse subsiding but her eyes blazing. She scanned the room, hurriedly, looking for anything out of sorts, her index finger massaging the side of her pistol nervously. She reached out with her other hand and grabbed the drifting tablet, the horror show still unwinding on its screen.

Her eyes flicked to the screen, and then back to the room, taking everything in. Johansson moaned, quietly, weakly rocking against her restraints. Law remained motionless, eyes still scanning back and forth furiously, the tablet inching closer to her face.

She let out a long, unbroken huff, her head still waving back and forth angrily, her fingers digging into the edge of the tablet. 'See its status lights?' she said, slipping the tablet back in front of Johansson. 'They're all off, just like they were on the drone.'

Johansson looked back, face blank. 'The drone, I could perhaps get behind that,' she said. 'But the suit, the suit is military. Tough.'

'Someone must have come up with a way to circumvent the other systems, to assume control of its functions and power without tripping any of the interlocks. It must be a real low-level attack, right at its core.'

The pistol dropped to Law's side, snug against her holster.

'Why didn't it just kill me?' said Johansson, her voice wobbling.

Law looked at her, suspicion draining slowly from her face. 'The suit has multiple layers of computers, but the one designed to protect you, to make sure you don't die at all costs, through physical or medical means, it's protected, powered independently and physically encoded.'

'Meaning?' said Johansson, tilting her head back, trying to breathe more freely.

'It couldn't kill you, not intentionally. Perhaps that's practically all that's left running, and has been since you woke up.'

'But then why did it stop?' stuttered Johansson, the restraints cutting into her.

Law stepped back slightly, her brow arching downwards.

'Either the damage was enough to knock whatever was doing it out of the loop,' she said, uncertainly, 'or whatever was broadcasting to it was cut off as you reached the bridge.'

'Were we through the gate by that point?'

Law tipped her head a fraction. 'They must have spiked your suit somehow, perhaps by slipping something into a core update, and then triggered it or taken it over as the attack started, with the aim of taking control of the ship at any cost.'

'But whatever was broadcasting couldn't communicate with or control it beyond the gate,' stuttered Johansson, her skin crawling.

Law nodded. 'Possibly, but we're just guessing now. And when you woke up, that disconnect, or the damage, meant the suit's base processing was all that was available, just to keep you alive and going. That might also have been what led it back to the bridge, after the attack; it might have deemed it the safest spot for you.'

She swore under her breath, muttering to herself, her tone angry and hateful. Johansson strained, trying to hear her.

'—ew it was a bad idea to bring another ship into this,' said Law, spitefully. 'Should have stuck with our regulars. Too many variables. But we needed the loadout. Someone must have spotted the change, a vuln–'

Johansson's head slumped forwards, then shot back up, her chin touching metal, her mind spearing back to the suit. 'Can you get me out of this thing?' she pleaded.

Law looked at the mission clock, distracted. 'Thirty minutes.'

'I just get the feeling this thing might jump up and kill me at any moment now.'

'You're not the one that has to worry about that,' said Law, ruefully, holstering her pistol and undoing Johansson's restraints. 'At least I know it wasn't you.'

'Not much relief,' said Johansson, wiping the blood from her chin, catching the repeating security camera footage in the corner of her eye. 'What a fucking mess.'

'At least we're getting somewhere,' said Law, turning her attention back to the consoles. 'And if it goes dark again, just scream.'

Johansson put her hands on her knees, bent over, and took a series of long, hard breaths, then slumped against the floor, stretching her legs out across the floor.

'You alright?' muttered Law.

'I've been better,' she responded, curtly, fresh blood weeping from one of the unions between her suit's arm and her wrist.

But that radiation is going to get me, I guess, if the suit or the ship doesn't.

Johansson slipped off her gloves and looked at the redness on the back of her hands. It was intense, burning, and unforgiving.

But not yet, she thought, as the *Prompt* slipped through the void.

CHAPTER TWENTY-ONE

The leading digits of the timer shifted from a three to a two. Johansson rubbed the tops of her hands, agitated. She applied some gel from her medical pouch, then put the gloves back on, the locking rings sticking slightly, drying blood interfering with the mechanisms.

Law's attention was split between watching the rate of closure and distance to T2 and the display showing the diminishing status of the second fusion reactor. Its output was starting to falter again, its temperature increasing.

'You took out the droid without thinking about it for too long; are you sure this thing's not going to snap and take you out?' said Johansson quietly, swaying a little.

'You might need to keep that on, and go down there,' said Law, assertively. 'It's hot but tolerable.'

Johansson looked down at the suit, unconvinced, lights dancing across its front panel. She laughed grittily, the movement sending a torrent of stabbing pains from her neck to her waist. Something in the suit jabbed her again, and a chill joined the pains. She looked around, trying to ignore the dull red smears and patches on the wall and floor. Something was still pummelling the inside of her head, like a jackhammer trying to break out from a concrete enclosure.

'I'm glad to continue to be of use,' she said, fumbling for words momentarily. 'But good one.'

She rubbed her temples and collapsed into a seat in front of a console, perspiration seeping from her brow, and frowned at the sensation of the suit's servos operating in tandem with her. Law drifted over to her and pulled the red syringe from Johansson's waist.

'No,' she said, firmly, pushing Law's hand away. 'Not yet. Best save that for if things get desperate.'

Law nodded as the *Prompt* continued to close on the void exit at Transit Station T2. Outside, a dim amber glow seeped from sections of its fusion reactor station, and gases and coolant continued to weep from its panels and pipework, tainting its environment.

'We're going to make it. Just stay with me for a little longer, just in case,' said Law.

Johansson let her chin rest on her chest plate, and her eyes closed. Law was silent, alongside her, crouched, fixated on the screens, the metres to target shrinking at a rapid rate. She put her hand on Johansson's shoulder, squeezed it, and moved back to the console.

'Why don't you tell me more about your daughter?' said Law, the volume of her voice rising and falling as she glanced up and down the displays in front of her. 'What's her first name?'

'One of the best things that I'm responsible for,' said Johansson, sighing. 'She's call–'

The ship rumbled and a harsh metallic clatter rang out. Visions of the axe blade carving through the air and striking unyielding metal swept sharply into Johansson's mind. She forced her eyes to open, seeking a distraction.

The aye see bee hurrays are powered popped into her head,

along with the face of the crewmember, before the leading edge of the axe changed its shape. *The ACB arrays are powered.*

The ACB arrays were powered, and that was a surprise to the engineer.

'What are the ACB arrays, Law,' said Johansson.

They are the panels outside the ship, she thought, preempting Law's answer.

Law froze again, even her hair refusing to move in the zero-gravity environment.

'They are the panels you have seen outside the ship,' said Law, body starting to shift a little. 'They are what protects the ship in void space.'

'And they're linked directly to the fusion plants, like conventional shield grid arrays?'

'Yes. They're what draws so much power,' responded Law, voice fluctuating. 'It's about the only major modification required for successful void flight, and they're hardwired to the fusion reactors.'

'What do they do, Law?' said Johansson, voice stony, her eyes narrowing. There are no laser matrices, no plasma emitters, nothing conventional visible out there.'

Law had a hand over her mouth, an elbow resting on the console. She huffed through it, noisily.

She looks like she's going to explode again.

'It always comes down to that, doesn't it,' said Law, her voice rising, harshening, with each word. 'Every single time.'

Law pirouetted, launching herself from the console, and loomed over Johansson, the display behind her bracketing her, each end of the *Prompt* visible on her left and right.

'Every single hurdle I have crossed, every single facet of my life and career I have binned to get us out here, and it always comes back to that fucking concept,' she shrieked. 'It's not even mine!'

Johansson upturned her palms, utterly confused, an undercurrent of fear ebbing through her. Law's head was bobbing, agitated, her face reddening.

'And to think that they were convinced it would never work, that it would never make it through void space!' shouted Law, her arms stretching out, spiralling around the room as she rotated. 'Just look at it now, you bastards!'

Oh fuck! thought Johansson, worry growing. *Oh, fuck!*

She could barely bring herself to speak.

'This has never been tested?' said Johansson, finally drumming up the courage to spit the words out, towards the still-spinning Law.

'Oh, we did some small-scale tests, but the results, the results weren't what I hoped,' she shouted, spiralling intensifying. 'The only way to get where we needed was full-scale flight, but after all that work, all that effort, they wouldn't let those trials start! They wouldn't let us fly! But here we are, in the void, and still! Ha!'

The laugh was sharp, cutting. Johansson pushed herself back against the wall.

I don't know what to do, she thought. *Observ–*

The numbers on the mission clock continued to decrease.

Twenty-five minutes, thought Johansson, an unstoppable feeling of panic rising from the pit of her stomach.

'Law,' she said, trying her best to sound straightforward, to ground the conversation, 'why would they not let you test this?'

Law grabbed the edge of her console, stopping her spin, her hair continuing merrily on its way.

'Because every time we sent something into the void, it never came back. There was something in there,' she said, stabbing incessantly at the console, 'something in there, something we didn't comprehend. Drones, missiles, junk ships, remotely operated ships, crewed ships, all just, poof, gone.'

She clicked her fingers, once, the *crack* harsh to Johansson's ears.

But we're here, thought Johansson, confused.

'But you made it work,' she said, hoping she sounded impressed, positive.

'Ah, but the cost, that was always the problem,' said Law, flustered. 'That was what they always asked me about, always challenged about, always, over and over, until it ground everything to a crashing halt.'

'I don't understand,' said Johansson, pleadingly. 'What is the cost of travelling in the void?'

'What limited information we scraped together from our trials suggested that there were energies, forces at play, in the void, that we didn't, couldn't understand,' said Law, irate. 'They almost binned my project just because of that. Like any of this comes easily.'

'And that's what was preventing anything from making it through the void,' said Johansson, unsure.

'Yes. But I solved that problem, using the ACB arrays, and here we are.'

'And they are?' said Johansson, her eyes wide, her head waving from side to side, seeking answers.

'I took the experimental Alcubierre system that was being trialled and applied its technology to create a protective buffer for my ship, a shield of sorts, that would allow it to travel safely at sub-light speeds in the void,' said Law, proudly. 'And it worked!'

'But I thought that the Alcubierre system was underdeveloped, dangerous, and that everyone was against it being used?'

'It is,' snapped Law. 'That's how we damaged the sister ship to the *Prompt*, among others.'

Clock's ticking, thought Johansson, feeling unhappier by the second.

'And how do those issues translate to here, to the *Prompt*, in the void?' said Johansson, her voice quietening, speech slowing. 'What happens when we come out at the other end?'

Law cackled and brought up an image on her console's display.

It showed a sectional view of the leading Alcubierre buffer, at the nose of the ship.

Field-manipulating panels, power control systems, large redundant power sources, thought Johansson, trying to take it in quickly. *Heavily protected.*

'These arrays work to keep whatever the exotic energies and particulates, or whatever else is in here, a safe distance away from the ship,' said Law, finger tracing a line around an adjacent outline of the *Prompt*. 'The only pitfall is that they accumulate in front of its protective bubble like snow on a plough blade, and they also stick to it, and slip into its wake, trailing along behind.'

Like a magnet on a workshop floor, gathering filings, thought Johansson, a hint of bile touching the back of her throat, as the display switched back to the in-flight screen, showing the systems of the *Prompt*, its speed, course, and current timers.

'That explains why I lost my first missile,' said Johansson. 'It must have drifted outside the bounds of this bubble. But wasn't the problem ...'

Law smiled at the ever-decreasing counter, the seconds sleeting away from the screen. 'Yes, those energies, and anything else the ship's shielding has picked up, will be cast outwards on arrival, just like the original Alcubierre prototypes for space flight, and just like the small prototypes for void flight that followed.'

'So this ship is going to obliterate everything that's at the station when it arrives.'

Just great. Fucking great.

'Oh, it'll probably be a bit more dramatic than the original failures,' said Law, smirking. 'These energies are unlike anything we've encountered, and the prototype void flights were only seconds long, with tiny, by comparison, vessels. The original runs for this were only supposed to be seconds long, too, perhaps minutes at a stretch, only requiring a fraction of the reactors' outputs, to prevent the ship and shielding from accumulating too much destructive energy.'

Johansson's heart dropped through her stomach, into the void.

'We've been in here for hours, Law,' she said, quietly.

'Yes,' responded Law. 'The station will only be able to absorb a tiny proportion of these energies. The rest will go onwards, outwards; it wouldn't surprise me if there's enough to ...'

The station is at Mars! screamed Johansson's mind. *And so is your daughter!*

'To what, Law? To what?' she said, incredulous.

And millions of people on the surface! screamed Johansson's mind, the volume of the thought almost deafening.

'It's going to be a hell of a light show, that much I'm sure of,' she said, wildly. 'But we'll find out in about twenty minutes!'

Law's face was wild, her eyes erratic, intense. Johansson dragged herself to her feet, arms outstretched, palms up and open, her back pressed against the wall, supporting her, the suit's motors taking up some of the slack.

'We can't do this, Law,' said Johansson, firmly.

'That's what they said,' she responded, smiling, flinging her head backwards. 'No flights allowed, ever. Park it and forget it! So, I set up a little snatch-and-grab!'

'You stole thi–'

Johansson didn't finish the sentence.

They weren't trying to steal the ship, she realised, stomach plunging further. *They just wanted to stop it.*

The jackhammer in Johansson's head started up again. She was conscious of Law moving, but her mind was slipping, her vision hazing over.

Was the droid an attack or a failsafe?! she thought, panicking. *Was the suit an attack or a failsafe?! Was anyone else actually trying to steal this?!*

'I have to prove that it works, at any and all cost,' said Law, her voice quietening, moving relative to Johansson.

Why was the Hard there? Were we actually aiding? Intercepting? I don't–fuck!

She squeezed a gloved hand closed sharply and ramped up her breathing, hoping the suit might interpret it as panic, and respond.

A little help would be great, right about now.

'If they wanted it to have been safe, they should have supported the project properly from the beginning,' she added. 'This ship will make it to the station, and a new era will await us all.'

Or a scorched one, thought Johansson, trying to move sideways, along the wall, away from Law, her responses slowing and stuttering. *I can't let that happen.*

'I will get this ship to the Transit station. The price of arrival will be costly, I have no doubt, but I will have proved it, demonstrated it, and it will all be worthwhile,' said Law, assuredly. 'I'm willing to pay the price. This cannot be this century's Concorde moment.'

'How do you know that we'll even make it,' said Johansson, gripping the next rail along, her vision fading, muscles weakening.

Not sure I can get to that last red cylinder quickly enough.

'That doesn't matter either,' said Law, jubilantly. 'Even if the ship is obliterated on arrival, that alone will be proof of concept, and I am sure my name will find its place, eventually.'

Yeah, as a lunatic, thought Johansson, as she made her way towards Law's console, circling around the room. *But, fuck, she's got the bases covered!*

She glanced at the screen, as she passed behind it, the console and display obscuring her, hoping for inspiration.

'And if you try and stop it now,' shouted Law, 'you'll throw the final faint chance of ever seeing your daughter clean out of the window!'

Johansson grabbed the edge of a damaged panel, steadying herself, and squeezed it, the sharp edge biting into her, the fresh pain enlivening her.

'And no one will ever know what happened,' screamed Law, sweat beading furiously on her forehead. 'You'll be wiped from existence, just like your mother, and the RSF and my arrangements will see to the rest.'

Slow it down! shouted her mind. *Stop!*

'Another Johansson line, neatly terminated, written out of existence,' added Law casually, laughing. 'Just like the remaining crew of the *Prompt*, blown out of the airlocks, on my command.'

She tapped her wrist-mounted computer enthusiastically as Johansson's jaw dropped.

'The engineering team were too quick to fall foul of that, though' said Law, grinning. 'And you had your helmet on, by sheer chance, but that ended up panning out well for me, too!'

Oh my god!

'And you can forget about the *Hard Target*. Someone seems to have got a bead on what I was doing, so I turned it to scrap the moment the first Telegraph fell, just in case. It's shrapnel, turned to dust, just like you soon will be!'

And fuck you!

Johansson slipped her hand down to her waist, twisted the red cylinder so it was pointing into her thigh, and thumbed the end of it. Pain ripped through her, a scream rising from the very depths, pouring into the room, catching Law off guard; she shrieked, surprised, and dived towards the exit.

Engage until expended!

Johansson clenched her teeth, placed one foot firmly against the wall, one on the deck, and flung herself over Law's console, gripping its edge, landing solidly on her feet on the other side. She tore the protective cover on the emergency CRASH STOP control clean off its mounts, grabbed the rotary dial, spun it hard, and then yanked it upwards.

Here goes noth–

An alarm ripped through Engineering Access and bright

pulsing rotating white lights filled the space. The main reaction control system thrusters sprang to life, burning hard; they weren't trying to slow the ship, they were trying to rotate it, to get its engines facing towards the approaching void exit, so the *Prompt* could light its powerful rockets again and bring itself to a halt.

The tail of the ship started to move, the ship's structure groaning and protesting. Law's head ripped up from behind the console, her eyes mainlining towards her station, its display now flashing red violently.

'No!' she screamed, propelling herself from the deck. 'You bitch!'

Law careened into Johansson, grabbing her by her suit's collar, shaking her violently.

'What have you done?!' shouted Law, spittle splashing across Johansson's face.

'Fucked it up, hopefully,' said Johansson, leering at Law.

Law threw her to the ground, yelling incoherently, and dashed towards her console, her fingers already poised to strike the keys. The *Prompt* had barely started to turn, but any deviation was going to be hell to correct.

Just blow up, wished Johansson, as she bounced off the deck. *Do us all a fucking favour!*

She stood up, ragged, fresh blood dripping from her nose, her senses on fire, chemicals rippling through her, and stumbled towards Law, her footsteps becoming more confident as the stimulants eked every remaining ounce of power from her tattered muscles, the suit bolstering her movements. Her hand fell on the axe stowed on her chest plate and she pulled it free, rotating it so the butt of the head faced forwards.

Law was still absorbed entirely by the cascade of alarms from the console, her gaze fixated on the shifting indicators around the illustration of the *Prompt*, new commands flying from her fingertips. Johansson advanced, her boots making a scraping noise on the

288

composite decking as she closed on Law; her head cocked slightly and she suddenly started to turn, gasping, one hand going instinctively for the pistol at her waist.

No you fucking don't, thought Johansson, preempting the move. She swung the axe towards Law, its blunt butt carving an arc through where she would bring the pistol up. But the axe didn't connect with anything; it sailed through the air until it ploughed into the edge of the console, embedding itself in the metal, the harsh vibration making Johansson's vision blur for a moment.

What the f–

Law's pistol was pointing straight at her, flipped out from its holster; her draw had kept it close to her waist, shooting from retention.

Sneaky bitc–

The report was deafening but the round sailed clean past Johansson's waist, ploughing harmlessly into the wall behind her. Johansson suddenly came to a jarring stop, her fist clenched around the stuck axe, and she grabbed wildly for Law's pistol, her fingers desperately trying to get a hold of it, pushing it aside. Law's free hand grabbed at Johansson's suit, pulling, seeking a handhold, tearing the torch from its anchor point and tossing it away.

Johansson felt something give under her fingers as she squeezed, but then the gun went off again, cracking violently, the shot careening off to the right as Law tried to pull away, her legs pedalling wildly. The two closed on the rear wall as they wrestled, Law's legs making contact first. She pushed, with all her force, flinging herself over Johansson, dragging the gun with her, tearing away to safety on the far side of the room.

Johansson turned, pivoting against the axe, its head ripping free from the console. Something clipped the side of her head as she turned, and spun away from her.

Fuck, she's qui–

Law was braced firmly against a guide rail, by the door, her arm outstretched, the pistol pointed cleanly and calmy at Johansson.

Click!

Click!

Law looked at the gun, her eyes wide. Its slide was locked back, its chamber empty, the magazine gone. She shrieked again, one hand darting towards the ammunition pouch on her bel–

Tink! went the ejected magazine as it bounced into the corner of the room, past Johansson's floating torch.

The torch!

'Torch!'

Bing!

Law turned towards the jarring alien flash and noise, startled. Johansson leapt off the deck, springing forwards, closing on Law quickly. The pistol was empty but Law instinctively started bringing it back to bear, its muzzle swinging around quickly, her free hand still desperately seeking a new magazine.

Johansson swung the axe downwards, hard, its head cleaving through Law's extended forearm, shattering it. She screamed, shocked, as Johansson slammed into her, crushing her against the wall before bouncing away.

'I'll ki–' she shouted, her body spinning, dashing against a console, as Johansson drew the axe to her side, feet planted solidly on the deck, ready to swing again.

Law fell silent, blinking rapidly, as she tumbled through space, her hand still clawing at her waistband, a black curtain descending over her.

She's passing out, thought Johansson, as her heart rate sunk below 160 beats per minute. *Not familiar with the pain.*

Johansson laughed, louder and louder, until her vision began to swim, straight lines becoming curved, and greyness crept into the corner of her sight. She steadied herself against the console, trying desperately to bring her breathing and body back into line.

'Don't you fucking dare,' she said out loud, trying to stay awake.

Johansson glimpsed Law's shoulder patch as she slowly drifted past her, unconscious body bouncing slowly around the room, fist clenched in a last and defiant angry gesture.

Intricate stitching, thought Johansson, absentmindedly, her consciousness seeking something sane and unremarkable to focus on. *They even got the identifier right on the ship.*

Her eyes flicked from the detailed outline of the ship on the patch to its mirrored counterpart, tracing along the stitchwork and soaking up the details.

'Sloppy stitching on the second,' she mumbled, the room unresponsive. 'That should be a six, not a seven. It's all in the details.'

Johansson rolled lazily, her mind fighting against the dark, as Law's body thudded against her console, its tumble slowing.

Law's fist spread slowly as her muscles relaxed, revealing a small metallic object, painted a satin green. A lever covering it, now unsecured, popped free, as her body lazily rotated in front of her screen.

Ping! went the metal lever quietly, as it sprung into space.

Oh, great, thought Johansson, as the *Prompt Excursion* careened towards its destination, thrusters afire.

CHAPTER TWENTY-TWO

A sole droplet of blood trickled inexorably down the head of the axe, leaving a thin trail on its dull grey surface, the red appearing almost luminous against the metal's subdued finish. It trickled slowly over the handguard at the top of the axe's shaft, collecting another drop along its way, forming an orb. It then rolled ponderously down the handle, a thicker red band in its wake, the textured grip proving more difficult for it to traverse.

It lingered at the toe of the axe, swilling fore and aft gently, becoming almost teardrop shaped, the soft rocking motion of the axe stretching it, testing its grip. The axe shifted, sharply, and the orb detached, free from its constraints, joining those already floating freely in the space around it.

In the distance, a brilliant spherical shower of sparks erupted from the wreckage of the train, its twisted metal jutting awkwardly upwards and outwards, defying the clean, straight lines of the platform. Scorch marks and friction material marred its unpainted surfaces, and torn cables reached vainly for components that were no longer there.

The droid, its head shattered, stood tall, inert, its now-defunct fuel cell ticking noisily as it cooled, metals contracting and wrenching. A thin plume of smoke still seeped from its exposed housing, from within its cladding of toxic chemicals, the nose-wrinkling smell of burning rubber and electronics drifting across the platform.

Beyond, the reaction control thrusters of the *Prompt* continued to blaze away into the void, the ship lazily rolling from nose to tail, reversing its orientation. Main was working overtime, calculating gimbal angles, trying to establish if it could even use any of its remaining engines for braking thrust. Turbopumps began to spin, just in case, priming the engines for action.

Five dead bodies, one live one. The overhead lights flickered for a moment, and then brightened. An alarm sounded, its slow, doleful tone routinely fracturing the stillness, like the bark of a deer on a quiet winter's night. In the distance, something of great significance sluggishly gave way. A terrible yawning noise, metal rending from metal, reached the platform, followed by a series of staccato pops, each vibrating the floor. The bodies rolled sideways, piling up against the wall, as the ship shifted.

The alarm halted, and then the lights went out. Silence resumed its place on the platform, momentarily, only to be broken by the quiet metallic *ting* of emergency lighting in the floor and ceiling springing to life. The green light was soft, its mellow glow simultaneously softening and shadowing the grim presence of the now-ruined station.

An arm swung slowly through the cloud of droplets, dashing them towards the floor. Some collided with the gloved hand, flattening and spreading out, rolling along the warm surface until they found freedom, careening from the webbing between the fingers into the void beyond.

The hand twitched, the fingers trembled. A guttural, baying scream peeled across the platform, as consciousness wrenchingly and unpleasantly permeated Johansson's mind. She bucked, jerking in mid-air, as every nerve ending in her body shouted in anger and agony. Her body contorted, and then its motions diminished as blackness descended again. The silence resumed as almost as quickly as it had been broken.

The suit stabbed at her again as it continued to pump adrenaline, and countless other chemicals, into her system. Debris lifted from the deck as the ship shook more violently, the composites and metals bouncing softly against Johansson's body, pattering off the axe embedded in her and the suit's waist, the smaller particles sticking to the blood still trickling down the handle.

A kick, another deep groan, a spark. Her hand resting on the head of the axe now, exerting a little pressure. Another scream. The hand wrenched the axe, its cutting edge squealing as it pulled back through the suit's interconnect, flaying more cabling, the tips prying at more exposed flesh. Johansson flung it away from her, a thin trail of blood following it like a contrail, and sobbed.

'Fuck,' she bawled, into the room. 'Fuck!'

The suit's interconnect fizzed, ominously, and acrid smoke plumed up from her waist. She felt uncommanded motion for a moment, a spasm, like a rabbit trapped in a snare kicking for the final time. Something clicked and a few faint lights flickered on and off on its display panel, intensifying slowly. The sensation of something pricking her again, once, her muscles easing a little, then one or two steady lights on its front panel, control and normality resuming.

She breathed out, completely emptying her lungs, for the first time in what felt like hours. The suit did not impede her. Johansson placed a hand on the wall and rolled, listlessly, to place her feet on the still-shaking deck, her eyes locked on the floor.

'Just us three now, then,' she murmured, eyes adjusting to the gloom.

Another shudder ran through the deck, intensifying, like a volcano cresting to eruption point. The ship swirled slowly beneath her feet, Main struggling to keep it in check.

Law's corpse twisted in front of her, echoing the revolutions of the *Prompt*, spilling viscera into the room. Blood seeped from countless shrapnel wounds, and her arm was peeled from wrist to elbow, flesh floating freely alongside it. She had taken the brunt of the blast, inadvertently shielding Johansson as she unconsciously spun, but the axe had been turned into a projectile, bouncing around the room until it found something to embed itself in.

Me, thought Johansson, staring at Law.

A wave of sadness crested and spilled over her, but it dispersed as soon as she saw the mission counter: it was blank, the display flickering, damaged.

Not your problem, she thought, hastily, *but mine.*

The consoles were fragged, inoperable.

Can't be more than twenty minutes left.

The turbopumps rumbled into life as one, then two, of the engines caught; Johansson felt the yaw, the uncorrectable yaw, as the thrust pushed the ship off axis.

Main must figure it'll at least slow it, she hoped, dragging herself along the wall to the exit. She pushed off from the console, out of the doorway, out of Engineering Access, grabbing a rail protruding from the wreckage of the train.

The engines thundered behind her, valiantly trying to slow the ship, the drive cones melting in the intense heat as the throttles ran wide, beyond their limits, but the *Prompt* was starting to spiral, still slipping towards the Transit Station and whatever lay beyond. The engines cut as the ship rotated in the void, Main not wanting to instead accelerate the ship towards the gate.

Might have been enough. Might not. Can't take that chance.

She pushed off from the train, into the passageway next to the platform, catching a glimpse of stoved-in panels, damage from the runaway drone. She slowed, her suit's motors cogging and its hydraulics ebbing away.

'Just a bit more, please,' she said, softly, eyes damp, as she reached the crew lift to the lower ring, her hand unconsciously reaching for a cylinder at her waist that was no longer there.

For her, if anything.

She paused, the lift humming peacefully to its stop, and then started inching her way along the ring's main corridor, hand over hand on the guide rail, working her way towards the weapons control station. The corridor was dark, and slowly filling with smoke, but the still-active emergency terminal was emitting a feeble phosphorescent blue glow, casting a distorted rectangle of light into the walkway.

The suit's motions became more sluggish by the inch, its battery damaged, its reserve power fading. Johansson paused, looking down, as a strange fluttering sensation rippled from her neck to her toes. The lights on the suit's panel went out entirely for a second, as if it was merely hanging on by its fingertips. She watched the lights come back on, then go out again, cycling frantically as if some kind of internal conflict was taking place, an occasional flicker of movement striking when a light went out. The droid sprang back into her mind: all black, all off, definitely not inert.

I'm not sure it's in there any more, she thought, her hackles standing up slowly. *Don't gamble. Not now.*

She wrenched off her gloves, unclipped the interconnects, and pulled the top half of the suit off, as if removing a bulky and unco-operative jumper, its lower assembly snagging on her personal communicator for a moment. Awkwardly, she kicked the boots and leg sections away, leaving her in just a light cotton jumpsuit. It had been pristine at the start of the day; it was now riddled with patches of red, yellow, brown, and black, and it was torn, shredded, stiff and unyielding.

Johansson watched the interplay of lights on the front of the suit's panel, it still occasionally twitching and sparking. She drifted across the room, opened an emergency bin, and placed the suit inside. She carefully folded its still-shifting limbs as best she could, stared at it for a moment, nodded, and then locked the hatch and ejected the suit into the void.

'Thank you,' she stammered, as the disposal system hummed for a moment, cycled, and then reset.

Johansson made her way back to the corridor and resumed her climb, cotton-clad feet dragging loosely on the floor below. 'I hope,' said Johansson feebly, trailing off, as she wrestled along the last few feet to the door, to the console, and collapsed in front of it.

It was. The screen was still lit. The missile was still there. It had been clipped by the edge of the launcher when the *Prompt* accelerated and had nosed over into a damaged section of the ring, near one of the munitions caches, as it tried to correct its position. Its warhead was wedged in the ruined structure, and its camera revealed a view of the ring's interior, faint warning lights glowing in the distance.

Great, thought Johansson, chest lifting a fraction. *And I mean it.*

She pulled the console into her lap, trying to focus on its screen, and poked the controls for the missile's thrusters.

The day flashed through her mind, and she stopped.

More haste. Lost a missile, must have gone outside that shield, gone.

'Can't risk losing this,' she mumbled. 'Ring will have to do.'

She hesitated for a moment as the *Prompt* flew out of control around her, only the one engine now trying valiantly to relight, the ship's reaction control thrusters glowing a blinding white, sputtering wildly as the ship's roll rate increased.

'No one's going to know about this mess,' said Johansson, under her short, harsh breaths, as the ship thundered around her. 'But at least they'll have a chance.'

At least she'll have a chance.

The tail of the ship pointed straight towards the approaching gate for a moment, and the remaining engine exploded into life, its exhaust brilliant in the void, elegant blue shimmers roaming outwards from its hot orange core, Main still fighting to bring the battered ship to a halt.

Observe.

'Crew KIA by VFOE, control lost,' she said out loud, automatically.

Orient.

'On approach to T2, arrival is imminent.'

Decide.

'Arrays powered. Hours in transit. Can't let this return.'

Act.

The *Prompt* continued to tumble through the void, decelerating, the gate drawing closer still. Tears streamed from Johansson's face, pooling on the headrest of the seat, and heat flooded the room as the fusion plants redoubled their efforts.

At least it's me here, and not my daughter, she thought again, a bittersweet smile spreading across her face.

She armed the missile, its information display changing colour from green to red, and selected the flashing *Remote trigger* icon. A small panel on the console clicked, slid aside, and presented her with a covered toggle switch and a red button. She weakly flipped the cover up, pushed the switch forwards, and rested her finger on the button.

Last orders, please.

The console beeped, confirming that the missile was ready to detonate.

Johansson felt the sand between her toes, smelt the salt in the air, and saw someone walking towards her, smiling.

'I love you, sweetheart.'

She pressed the button.

EPILOGUE

The *Terminal Velocity* sprang forwards, accelerating towards its target, burning every engine as hard as it could. Everything the corvette had was trained squarely dead ahead, locked firmly on the solitary bogey on its scopes: shield emitters, imaging equipment, sensor batteries, and weaponry. It hammered past the *Improbable Actions*, its sister ship, its shadow momentarily concealing the ugly scars that riddled the armour plating of its counterpart.

'Jesus,' said Hubbard, the *Improbable*'s captain, irritated. 'They know something we don't?'

'No updates on the last emergency dispatch,' responded O'Brien, the ship's communications officer. 'And there are definitely no cash prizes for being there first, unfortunately.'

Hubbard snorted and shook his head at her. 'Berks. Probably attempting to win back a bit of favour with RCOM after we took the brunt of all that incoming for them last week.'

O'Brien smiled at him, winked, and turned back to her screen. He watched her out of the corner of his eye for a moment, shook his head almost unnoticeably, and then settled his gaze back on his display. He zoomed in on the *Terminal* and the computer automatically brought up a small window showing a live feed of it, cropped from one of the *Improbable*'s external cameras. The exhaust plumes from the *Terminal* were uneven, the trailing edges of its engine assemblies white hot. Hubbard could see the reaction control systems working overtime, trying to keep the ship straight and level as the output of its four engines wavered, nudging the *Terminal* in different directions.

Jesus, Nangolo, don't push it that hard, he thought, shaking his head again.

'Comms,' he said, authoritatively, 'ping the *Terminal*, knock it off, speed two five triple zero, rejoin. This isn't the time.'

'Comms, copies. Message to *Terminal*, KIO, speed two five triple zero, rejoin, immediately. Message relayed.'

We don't even know what we're dealing with, he thought, tapping the edge of his console. He found himself looking at the back of O'Brien's head again, his mind wandering, as the nose of the *Improbable* shifted, the pilot adjusting its path. He pinched the top of his thumb and reprimanded himself quietly.

He noticed the exhaust plumes from the *Terminal* shrinking, their shape becoming more uniform and steady, as the ship cut its thrust. Hubbard enlarged the view of the ship, the space around it black and devoid of detail, and cycled into an infrared view. The blackness disappeared entirely, replaced by a dim, almost uniform purple.

So, that must be Transit Station T2, he thought, zooming out, causing more and more purple to fill his screen. *And what do you want us to do now we're here?*

Hubbard noted the drives on the *Terminal* cooling off, shifting from a brilliant white to a more tolerable yellow on his display. He switched back to conventional imaging for a moment, and the station all but disappeared.

They really don't want people looking too close–

'Captain, front sensor grid just went absolu–'

The *Terminal Velocity* exploded, scattering hundreds of tonnes of materials, and all of its crew, immediately into space. The debris sprung away from where the ship had been, at a terrific speed, a giant billowing fireball following and slowly engulfing it; a mix of burning propellants, oxygen, munitions, reactive armour, drive elements and reactor materials, all spiralling, mixing and flaming. It looked like the creation of a new star, albeit on an infinitesimal scale. Hubbard's display dimmed rapidly, protecting his eyes, and then locked up, unable to interpret or display the havoc outside.

'Brace!' he roared, as the *Improbable Actions* thrust forward into the chaos, its shield grids springing to life, their deep teal signatures flashing across the ship's hull. 'Go around!' shouted Hubbard, instructing the pilot to abandon their approach to the station. 'Back off, now; pilot, Defensive D2!'

The *Improbable* started to accelerate and its nose ascended sharply, the ship's thrusters pushing it into a tight turn. Hubbard felt the deck shudder slightly as the main fuel pumps responded to the sudden demand for more thrust. Behind that judder, he also sensed the smoother, reassuring hum of the shield grid emitters rotating to meet the threat.

Didn't help the Terminal, but thanks, Main.

His fingers were pressed to the side of his console, its cool titanium settling his nerves a little. His right foot, regardless, continued to bounce up and down, drumming against the deck. The ship's LIDAR and radar screens suddenly lit up again, as more threats jumped onto its scopes from seemingly nowhere, and myriad readings suddenly jumped to their maximums.

'Incoming, unknown,' yelled Nikitovich, the Weapons System Officer.

'Peg the needles, engineering,' bellowed Hubbard. 'Everything we've got!'

'More on the way, I think,' shouted Nikitovich, as the lighting in the bridge switched from white to blue. 'Unknown classification, everything's going off scale.'

'Going to need something more concrete, WEPS,' responded Hubbard. 'Engineering, priority shielding, Comms, call for backup.'

'Comms, relaying QRA to RCOM now.'

The *Improbable*'s tracking computers rapidly imaged a huge area of the space from which the incoming was originating, analysed each frame, correlated it with radar data, light detection and ranging imagery, and forwarded their conclusion to Nikitovich.

'QRA, one ship's responding,' shouted O'Brien, 'It's–'

'Computer says there's nothing else out there, sir,' said Nikitovich, interrupting, just as her display lit up again. Her pulse went through the roof. 'Looks like more incoming, bigger, much bigger! Unknown, source unknown!'

Her hands flew across her keyboard, relaying what looked like the safest path to the pilot. The bridge suddenly plunged into darkness and a sickening *crack* erupted from behind the bulkhead. Someone yelped; dull blue emergency lighting slowly replaced the blackness, and the consoles flashed back to life, their imagery tearing and warping. Smoke plumed from the floor, and the harnesses in every seat suddenly clenched their occupants with terrific force.

Hubbard grunted as the straps dug deeply into his shoulders. He was conscious of the station suddenly disappearing from view, jumping off the left of the screen.

'WEPS!'

'It's like we've been dumped into a solar flare,' she shouted. 'We're getting hammered across the board!'

'Departure,' barked the pilot, Evans, from somewhere up front, his voice strained. 'Dead pole!'

Damn, thought Hubbard, as the station spiralled past on his display. *We're tumbling*.

'Fire in stat–' went one voice.

'I got nothing on bus A,' yelped another.

'Hull, top, Local's gon–' came the response.

'–xpedite resets,' screamed another, over the din. 'Get it together!'

The ship felt like it was ploughing over speed bumps and then through walls, its structure hammering and grating as the forces acting on it rose and fell erratically. An intense smell of burning permeated the bridge.

Ride it out, thought Hubbard, fleetingly.

'Just hang on,' he barked, as the *Improbable*'s tail overtook its nose again. 'Engineering, alternates, now!'

'Switchover, aye,' yelled one of the voices.

A loud *pop!* tore through the bridge, momentarily deafening everyone, followed by an abrupt clanking noise from behind the bulkhead. The bridge lights flicked back on, intensified for a moment, and then settled. The nose of the ship abruptly heaved around, and Hubbard felt the *Improbable* rolling hard to the right.

'Stick's alive,' Evans cried out. 'RCS is up, needles are climbing.'

The ship shuddered but the blows were lessening as the maelstrom swirled around and past it.

'WEPS, we out of the worst?' said Hubbard, clocking indicators changing from red to amber on his screen. The ship's course shifted and it started to accelerate again, away from the station.

'It's weakening,' said Nikitovich, her voice vibrating with the ship. 'Both semi-spherical and projectile-like emissions, unknown, still tracking.'

'Whoever's in the way of any of that is going to have a real bad day,' he responded. 'Nav, comms, plot and relay those contacts, get on the line to Mars, anyone in the path of those things, and let them know as soon as you can. Priority!'

'They came from the station, sir,' added Nikitovich.

'What?' he responded, pivoting towards her, his harnesses relaxing.

'Whatever those were, they originated from the station. From the very end of that gantry structure. But there's nothing there.'

'Engineering, mid power mix,' said Hubbard, 'Pilot, orbit, one hundred clicks, but make it off axis from whatever that gantry is.'

'I've got nothing else, sir,' said Nikitovich. 'And the *Terminal* ... it's gone.'

No shit, he thought, soberly.

'Status on the station?'

'It's taken a beating, and it's drifting, but whatever that was looks like it emanated away from the station, outwards from it, not into it.'

'Engineering, status?' asked Hubbard, his eyes locked on his screen's view of the station.

'VSF, but operable,' responded a voice from over his shoulder.

Shit.

'Pilot, cancel orbit; current range, all stop,' commanded Hubbard. 'Let's not chance our luck. Engineering, hop to it. Everyone else, eyes and ears open.'

'Aye, sir,' said several people simultaneously.

'It'll take us about ten minutes,' added another, the voice moving away.

No rush now, guessed Hubbard, nodding in his seat. *I think that was it, whatever 'it' was.*

He stared at the external camera feeds as the crew bustled around him. From afar, T2 resembled a giant tower block with a dull black surface finish, but at what could be construed as its top, a vast arm stretched out into space. At its extreme was a hexagonal tunnel, open at both ends. It was empty, and, at a glance, appeared to show an unobstructed view of the space beyond. To say it could easily accommodate the *Improbable Actions* was an understatement; the seemingly featureless black tunnel looked to be getting on for a mile long.

'WEPS, comms, any updates as to what we're looking for?' he

said. 'We could be a flea compared to whatever lingers around these places.'

I've heard the hearsay, he thought. *Ships that simply didn't exist most of the time.*

Nikitovich stuck a finger up. 'Nothing new, but the station's been pushed out from its stable anchorage. It's moving away from us, and it's not correcting.'

He inspected his display, looking for any signs of thruster activity.

Like a cannon recoiling, he mused. *Is this thing a weapon?*

Hubbard dialled up the camera's zoom again, the imaging sharp and stable now the *Improbable* had come to a halt. The station had the air of a structure that had been in service for a long time; its protective armour was pockmarked, with lengthy and fresh-looking scars in places, while docking ports and other moveable parts exhibited shiny, polished surfaces from continual and repetitive use.

Definitely been around for a bit. Looks like it might have been a munitions dump at some point.

'Comms, any routine patrols for this area?' said Hubbard, studying the station's thick ablative armour, spying partially concealed and protective shield generators. 'Not that it looks like anything could make much of a dent in it.'

'I've got no logs that show any kind of active patrol,' said O'Brien. 'Perhaps whatever protects it, ships or defences otherwise, aren't catalogued. Or visible.'

Nothing to see here, we're just out here drifting around on our own, don't mind us. No wonder all manner of wild rumours exist about these places.

He cast the functioning remains of the *Improbable Action*'s sensor array over the featureless dark station again, and then over its suspended tunnel. Nothing appeared significantly damaged but, nevertheless, something did appear to be amiss; most of the station's orientation lights were cold and out, the docks were darkened, and few of its antennae, beacons or arrays showed any signs of life.

But that might just be par for the course with one of these.

'Nikitovich, anything?' said Hubbard.

'Nothing anomalous on the short- or long-range arrays.'

'Okay. Anything from the station?'

Silence flooded the bridge. Nikitovich unconsciously leaned into her headset again, fingers drifting across her keyboards as she switched frequencies, sent out interrogation messages, and listened for any replies.

'Nothing on the main channels, nothing on the emergencies. Aside from a position marker, the station is silent.'

She scanned through the frequencies again, lines scrolling past at a terrific rate. One blip, one minor blip on one channel, something relayed, automatically recorded, boosted, filtered. Nikitovich spooled it back quickly, glancing at the waveform, and replayed it.

'I had something else for a moment,' she added, leaning closer to her display, and then shook her head. 'No, it's gone.'

Hubbard's index finger started its familiar tap-tap-tap again.

'I can tell you that the station's marker is still broadcasting. But it's relatively weak, even though we're almost on top of it,' said Nikitovich.

'Power outages, perhaps?'

'On a station of this size, sir? It must have redundancies atop redundancies atop redundancies.'

Evans chimed in from the front of the bridge. 'She's not wrong; my first post was on a small station and that had two standalone reactors, at opposing ends, along with battery backups. No way one of those would go quiet without a catastrophic failure.'

Hubbard nodded. 'Agreed. But you'd expect some noise from something as substantial as this.'

They might be juniors, but they're clued in and paying attention, he noted.

Nikitovich swept space with her instruments for a moment. 'Are these stations manned?'

'That's a good question,' said Hubbard. 'The short answer is that I don't know. This was a priority redirect for both ourselves and the *Terminal*, as we were the only vessels within striking distance.'

The *Improbable Actions* remained motionless, its arrays sweeping back and forth across the station, but its barrage of electronic interrogation, cameras and sensors revealed little of interest.

'Nikitovich, the computers got any useful information about whatever those flares or barrages were?' asked Hubbard.

'Still processing. But I don't think they were missiles. The *Terminal* took one ... wave ... square on, dead centre, we got lucky and just clipped an edge.'

She tailed off as numbers flashed past on her screen.

'In your own time,' said Hubbard.

Nikitovich swallowed and leant forward in her harness so she could see Hubbard. 'I can't get any meaningful reading on the energy sources. But there was a comparatively tiny quantity of metals and composites in the mix, some radioactive elements. The computer says there were some geometric structures, in places.'

'Maybe we should take a closer look,' said someone behind him, offhand.

Hubbard hesitated. They were still some way out from the station, but he preferred the degree of safe distance from the unknown. He brought up the original mission package from Base T1 on his screen again.

'Proceed to T2 for "function check", whatever that is, at all possible speed,' he muttered. Evans and Nikitovich glanced at him, then shrugged at each other.

'No details, no insight,' muttered Hubbard. 'Alright, whatever this is from RCOM was copied and dispatched in a hurry, and sent to us without further ado. Looks like we'll have to figure it out for ourselves.'

He scrolled through the message again and again, vainly picking through every keystroke and word, seeking anything that might help further. In fifteen years' service he'd seen all manner of madness, but this outright lack of information was a new one, and concerning. No routing, no manifests, no coding, nada. Reluctantly, he acknowledged that the message only really said one thing: *We don't know!*

'Engineering, operable?' said Hubbard.

'Affirmative, we can work around the hot stuff, but we'll need to be dead in the water in thirty minutes,' said a voice in his earphone. 'A tow wouldn't go amiss.'

'Understood,' said Hubbard. 'O'Brien, status on the QRA.'

'One local response. It's the *Lucky Breeze*,' she said. 'They're en route at speed. Should I tell them to stand down?'

'No,' responded Hubbard slowly, tapping his screen. 'We're going to need help getting back and, with the *Terminal* gone, we could do with the support. Just tell Johansson not to burn everything out trying to get here.'

'On it.'

'Evans, close to fifty kilometres,' said Hubbard.

The *Improbable* canted towards the station, and its main engines belched into life. Slowly, the station filled the ship's scopes, stretching this way and that, eclipsing the sun behind it as their orbit shifted closer.

'Anything left behind from that melee?' said Hubbard, the ship matching the orientation of the station, its speed slowing.

'Uh, getting into it now,' said Nikitovich, hurriedly, tearing her eyes away from a feed showing the station. 'A few weak contacts, doing around fifty metres per second.'

'Where and constitution, WEPS.'

Nikitovich stammered for a moment.

Still a little way to go.

'Some small debris fields,' she responded, clearing her throat, 'by the ... entrance, or exit, to the tunnel system. Imaging now.'

'Evans, shift the nose onto that target, and cut our speed.' said Hubbard.

The *Improbable Actions* dropped out of its automatic flight profile, allowing the ship to continue travelling along its current vector while orienting itself in any direction. Its thrusters puffed once, slowing it, and then again, the nose swinging to orient with Nikitovich's contact marker. Most of the *Improbable*'s most powerful sensors were in fixed arrays, shielded from the hardships of space and incoming fire, so bringing the ship into line with the target allowed for the most detailed view, at the cost of shifting that studied gaze from its actual path of travel.

Nikitovich looked up from her console. 'Debris is of a mixed composition.'

Additional details popped up on the screen, drawing her back momentarily. 'It looks like ... ablative armour and an extensive quantity of titanium. I'm also seeing quantities of copper, tungsten, rare earth materials, and significant amounts of ... sodium? No partial pattern matches in the database.'

'Can you confirm that the debris isn't from the *Terminal*?'

'They could have been elements of a ship, but not the *Terminal*,' responded Nikitovich. 'I've still got a few fractions of that on my scope; that debris is travelling away from us, with the emissions. I've got no prior flag on this, and it's just moving slowly away from the station's ... tunnel.'

'Gut reaction?'

'Whatever it was, I'd guess it was big, at least originally.'

Ships that simply wouldn't exist most of the time, Hubbard's mind uttered, hauntingly.

'Alright, I think we've got all that's of use right now,' he said, voice flat. 'Evans, put some space between us and the station again.

We don't know what it is, and it might have the same suspicions about us, if it is unmanned and damaged.'

He paused for a moment, the flash of the *Terminal* simply ceasing to be playing back in his mind.

'Nikitovich, dump all of this to RCOM and see if you can raise any kind of answer from them. Tell them we're on site, the station's acting inert, and that there is debris here. Maybe there was another ship at this station. Send them the plots of those unidentifieds, too and anything associated with them. Let's see if we can get more help with this.'

'Shall I tell them about the *Terminal Velocity*?'

'Yes. But I think they have more pressing matters.'

The *Improbable* settled into a distant orbit, its sensors picking slowly through the scene, like a blackbird lifting leaves in a garden.

'Incoming packet from RCOM,' shouted Nikitovich. 'Over to you,' she added, waving her hand in the direction of Hubbard. 'Secured. We're working with a delay.'

Hubbard looked at his display and opened the file.

'I've got two transponder codes. WEPS, bounce back, two beacons for you,' he announced. '*Excursion*, one prefix *Critical*, the other *Prompt*. Looks like they were Sarks, redesignated VF, whatever that is, last reported as in decommissioning.'

'Added to the sweep,' said Nikitovich. 'At least we've something concrete to look for.'

Hubbard bit his bottom lip, restless. The sensors and scopes remained clear, unrevealing. Nothing was moving, broadcasting, doing anything.

Show's over, he thought, forlorn. *There's nothing here to see.*

'Alright, Engineering, ditch weapon power. Give the reactors a break and shunt everything we've still got to hand back to shields and drives. I think whatever happened has already played out.'

Another message popped up on Hubbard's screen, a short ship-to-ship burst:

VSF again? Already? Glad you're in one piece, though. Bimbling your way. R.J.

He laughed to himself, his fingers falling to the ke–

'Fresh contact!' yelled Nikitovich, transferring the information to Hubbard's display. 'It's got a power source, very weak, can't lock it up.'

'Pilot, slew 80 right, nose down five, put the array on that,' Hubbard barked.

'It's not big, it's not the *Prompt* or *Critical*,' said Nikitovich. 'Arrays are coming around!'

The *Improbable* banked, its weapons pylons blotting out the sun as it rotated, bringing its armament and cameras to bear.

'Locking it up,' responded Nikitovich briskly, concentric rings marching towards each other on her display. 'It's small, really small, could be a munition, maybe something from inside one of those emissions. I've got a few weak signals!'

The *Improbable*'s cameras clacked and whirred as they drew the tiny object into focus.

'It's a–'

'It's part of a suit,' said Hubbard, inspecting its tattered remains.

It was rotating slowly, its arms crossed as if it had been folded and placed into a drawer.

A small, dim indicator was flickering on the front of it: DATA.

ACKNOWLEDGMENTS

I would like to take a moment to acknowledge those who supported me on this journey. A hearty tip of the hat, and all my thanks, to:

Ted Kingston
Caroline Kingston
Adrian Kingston
Kerry Kingston
Amar Hussain
Gareth Evans
CJ Hubbard
Macy Lu
Matt Patterson
Danny DeCillis
Romana Stefaniak

I would also like to thank you, the reader, for taking the time to read this, my first book. I hope you enjoyed it and, if you have the time, a review of it on your chosen platform would be much appreciated.

ABOUT THE AUTHOR

Lewis Kingston was born in 1986. His early introduction to the world of science fiction came in the form of a taped version of the original radio broadcast of *The Hitchhiker's Guide to the Galaxy* and, before long, he had consumed all of the books, the BBC TV series, and the radio script itself.

By the age of eight, he had moved on to titles such as *The Player of Games* by Iain M. Banks, only later his parents remembering what they contained, but, despite a voracious appetite for reading and writing, the thought of working in the field never crossed his mind. He subsequently studied Motorsport Engineering at Coventry, and graduated with a good qualification, but deemed himself not much of an engineer and sought work in other fields.

A chance interaction online in 2010 then led to work experience at Parkers, the new and used car guide, which spiralled into a multi-award-winning career in automotive journalism. He still works in the industry but, in 2022, he realised that, having never thought it possible to get into automotive journalism and ending up in it anyway, he should think it never possible to write a novel and subsequently ended up writing one anyway.

He has since decided to think it never possible to write more and is now working on a direct sequel to *Prompt Excursion*.

Made in the USA
Monee, IL
24 November 2023

47167585R00187